To Tetra with love.

Brian Chapman trained as a scientist and continued with academic research in the UK and North America until his late twenties. He then enjoyed a varied business career with over thirty years' experience of international commerce across the private and public sectors. It began with the Dutch multinational Philips Electronics with responsibility for product marketing and laboratory management. His marketing skills then transferred to the UK's National Physical Laboratory promoting scientific services and management of a government advanced materials research programme. This is Brian's first novel; he lives in Dorking, Surrey, with his croquet mallet, fishing rod and dancing shoes.

Brian Chapman

A LOVE OF IONS

AUSTIN MACAULEY PUBLISHERS
LONDON * CAMBRIDGE * NEW YORK * SHARJAH

Copyright © Brian Chapman 2025

The right of Brian Chapman to be identified as the author of this work has been asserted by the author in accordance with sections 77 and 78 of the Copyright, Designs and Patents Act 1988.

All rights reserved. No part of this publication may be reproduced, stored in a retrieval system, or transmitted in any form or by any means, electronic, mechanical, photocopying, recording, or otherwise, without the prior permission of the publishers.

Any person who commits any unauthorised act in relation to this publication may be liable to criminal prosecution and civil claims for damages.

This is a work of fiction. Names, characters, businesses, places, events, locales, and incidents are either the products of the author's imagination or used in a fictitious manner. Any resemblance to actual persons, living or dead, or actual events is purely coincidental.

A CIP catalogue record for this title is available from the British Library.

ISBN 9781035878154 (Paperback)
ISBN 9781035878161 (ePub e-book)

www.austinmacauley.com

First Published 2025
Austin Macauley Publishers Ltd®
1 Canada Square
Canary Wharf
London
E14 5AA

I would like to offer my sincere thanks to the team at Austin Macauley for their encouragement, experience and assistance in the publication of my first novel.

Table of Contents

Part One: Anions	11
Part Two: Cations	63
Part Three: Chemistry	113
Part Four: Reactions	157
Part Five: Side Reactions	197
Part Six: Free Radicals	235

Part One
Anions

Chapter 1

Some people plan their careers from an early age. Others choose a path when the time is right. Then, there are others who have it chosen for them. And finally, there are those who are not sure what a career path is in the first place let alone know how to plan for one; I'm one of those. So, let's call it serendipity, a bit like how life pans out in general; that includes love, it really does. Such thoughts pass through my mind just after the final exam results are posted on the faculty noticeboard of my solid and mostly pleasant red-brick university in South Wales. They're even posted in the Welsh language, which extends my agony even longer.

But then the next day, after a squalid evening enjoying too many Black and Tans in the Student Union, I find a note in my pigeonhole from Dr Jensen asking if I'd pop over to his office for a chat sometime. Noel Jensen is a bit of an oddity. He has the air of an American academic with crew-cut hair and some rather plastic-looking chunky shoes you might find a cadet wearing during a bout of military square bashing. His grey loose-fitting shiny suit matches his inquisitive eyes. But he's pleasant enough and we have always got on. After all, he gave most of my final-year physical chemistry lectures, particularly those dealing with the magical subject of chemical reactions involving electricity.

As he often tells his students, "Life is all about cations and anions"; the positive and negative charged ions floating around in liquids that are the basis of his pet subject, a potent cocktail of electrodes, batteries, electrochemical cells, and a lot else besides. In one of his more whimsical moments, he went further by chanting the refrain, "Cations deliver the electricity and anions accept it, just like the sexes". Many of his students consider him rather cool and ahead of his time but he often brings about quizzical looks from some of the more militant students and the department's younger staff. Jensen is nothing but direct to the point.

'Come on in, Paul, take a seat. So, any ideas about what you are going to be doing next? You did well in your finals.'

In fact, I ended up with a good degree after four years slog. It's probably the best I could have achieved or hoped for so I'm well pleased. But in addressing Jensen's question, I'm completely at a loss on what I should do or say. For some reason, I'm not feeling ready to go into industry or the commercial world just yet. On the rare occasion, I bother to look back at my life, there's nothing that seems to offer any sense of direction. After all, I was born at the end of the Second World War into what most people regard as a lower-middle-class family that works hard but with no history of higher education or university life.

Dad is in local government, a senior administrator as my mum likes to tell everyone, and my two older sisters work in offices and were married in their early twenties. My family is naturally rather proud while certainly a little amazed that I ended up at university studying, what to them at least is, a foreign language called chemistry. Not once has any of them asked what I'm going to do next in my so-called career. *Good job they haven't*, I tell myself. *Careers are for other people, aren't they?*

'Well, Dr Jensen, just starting to think about it. I like university life and doing laboratory work.'

'Oh, that's good to hear,' he says. 'Ever thought about doing research?'

'Didn't think I'd ever get a good enough degree to have a chance.'

'Okay, Paul. Well, you have. Look here, there's an opportunity come up at the University of Greater Manchester; one of the big pharmaceutical multinationals is having problems with metal corrosion in their bioreactors and they're keen to get some studies started. Any interest?'

It takes a while for his message to sink in. First, there's surprise and then there's an unnatural feeling of confidence that swells inside me. *But why pick on me?* I ask myself. Anyway, after a suitable passage of time staring at the floor carpet and unable to attempt any rational thought process or complex logic analysis, I say yes. On reflection, there probably isn't any rationale behind my decision but either way, I'll now have to explain to my proud, but probably disbelieving, parents that some weird research grant from the government and a major pharmaceutical company is allowing me to vegetate at university for at least another three years to study for a PhD. They simply won't believe it. Not sure I do really.

Two months later, I pack my bags and a great big metal trunk, sort out a bank account, and end up in the great metropolis that is Manchester, staying at some upmarket student accommodation called Piccadilly House. It's just off the lively Oldham Street, north of the university and city centre. Well, at least, I'm guaranteed to get a decent breakfast every day in this clean, if rather spartan, temporary accommodation. Life seems quite straightforward now as my research grant is well topped up by the pharmaceutical company; I'll cope well enough being largely self-sufficient and used to living within my means.

My parents have lived most of their lives in Boston, Lincolnshire, "in the Wash" as some of their neighbours jokingly call it. They aren't rich by any means so I'm well pleased to have managed so far on a student grant. Never had to, or never will, go to dad for money. Their upbringing during the war has filtered down into my attitude and values towards money and a lot else. Whilst I appreciate these traits, fixating on studying and bettering myself has led to the point where my social life is barely one level up from that of a monk. Perhaps I should've been more adventurous as a teenager and undergraduate.

That is apart from one or two wild drinking sessions trying to understand the Appellation Contrôlée of a French Chablis, endless mindless disco dancing, or a brief flirtation and general fumbling around with the blouse of a Swedish girl that served at the high table. Life's been tedious, even boring, so I hope and expect that my three years in the big city with few demands to travel home and more money in my pocket will prove a lot more exciting, and so they do.

First, it's time to meet my internal supervisor, Dr Victor Rawlinson, a senior lecturer in one of the biggest departments in the School of Chemistry, located in a severe-looking red-brick building just south of the city centre. He's a bit weird and even more scary than Jensen. *What is it about physical chemists?* I think to myself.

'Good to meet you, Paul,' after succumbing to a bone-crunching handshake. 'Have you settled into your digs ok?' Not waiting for a reply, he continues, 'I'll show you around the department and then we'll try and sort out a visit to Bristol to meet the guys sponsoring your research.'

Dr Rawlinson is in his mid-forties I imagine. He has very long hair, is not very tall, and wears these exotic Cuban heel-type leather boots. His muscular body bursts out of his rather tight-fitting suit. He speaks with a strong Mancunian accent and is the polar opposite of any academic I've ever come across; he's certainly not your typical chemist. But he's helpful enough and introduces me to all the other staff. The department is huge with a Professor Emeritus, readers, and lecturers including several DSc and the rest. But I get the feeling his little group are more than a bit out on a limb.

His main laboratory is called the Annex and is at the top of the building in a remote area; it's so isolated and I wonder why. At the end of my tour, we have a brief chat with the department secretary.

'Let me introduce Audrey,' he chimes in a rather affected manner. 'Audrey, this is young Paul Wright, my new research student from Wales. Look after him, he's a rather shy retiring type.'

I grimace and say hello. The lady in question is in her mid-thirties with a powdered smile, and neatly permed hair, and wears, what even in this day and age my mother would call, a twin set. Without a doubt, mum would admire Audrey, and clearly as does Dr Rawlinson, or Vic as he likes to be called. His deep blue eyes always seem to sparkle just a little more brightly when they speak to each other. He's a bit of a flirt but as time passes, I notice there are these lingering glances between them, especially when we meet up for our morning coffee.

It's also the time when I manage to irritate Vic the most by sticking to my boring pot of tea. I grew up without any semblance of coffee in the house. But it comes as no surprise when a few weeks later, one of the research fellows tells me that Vic and Audrey are having a not-so-secret fling and he's been seen taking her to an old grassed over slagheap near his home to sunbathe together. My imagination is in turmoil even at the thought of it. Fortunately, I get over it and set to work, well sort of, as Vic points me decidedly in the right direction.

'Go to the Main Library and start looking through all the literature in Chem Abstracts on everything related to corrosion in biological fluids and bioreactors. You won't find a lot, mind you.'

So that's what I do. Day after day, I walk across the Quad into the library and speak to this elf-like dark-haired girl behind the desk and start to read, and read, and read these bland scientific articles going back many years. After a few weeks of this tedium, I find out the girl's name is Barbara; she's rather quiet and shy. We do share a few choice words some days. On one occasion, I find myself asking the penetrating question, 'Have you worked here long? Do you just look after scientific periodicals?'

In my mind, her intellectual strength is clearly in her ability to reply in monosyllables. Her most memorable reply is "quite a while" and "mostly". She is, however, quite pretty, although the thought of sex with her never really rears its ugly head. It just as well that not much else did rear up because my literature search needs to go well. Although thumbing through a small pile of less than absorbing Chem Abs articles on bioreactors leads me to dwell on the subject of sex while growing up in the late fifties and early sixties. After all, I always assumed it was *de rigueur* for most young men to have some level of experience. However, this seems to have largely passed me by.

Perhaps a rather too cosy home life never really encouraged any experimentation whilst my memory only confirms that the three-letter word was never ever talked about at home, nor in school or anywhere else to be honest. It's not that I wasn't interested but maybe I'm just a slow learner. Whatever the reason, some of my friends from university who also had sheltered upbringings tell me, in no uncertain terms, that it's more accurate to say my experience is subterranean. Nevertheless, to the immense satisfaction of what passes as my virile young body, casting my eyes over Barbara from the bowels of the library continues to tell me something quite different.

Looking back, however, it's very sad to realise how one of my most vivid memories should be such a negative, although temporary, influence on my formative years. Then, as a spotty seventeen-year-old attending this one and only end-of-term dance in the girl's grammar school; a mere one hundred yards of virginal grass away from my boy's school. What a scary event as I didn't have a clue what to do, or when and where to do it. Like a moth drawn to a light bulb, the music started and I felt drawn to attempt a dance. Unfortunately, or perhaps fortunately, it was a super slow number with this girl called Lynn.

I'd come across her before in term time as an underperforming prefect when I was obliged to somehow police the fourteen-year-old boys as the deputy headmaster judged there was a risk of what he termed uncontrollable mixing at break time. Lynn was quite shy I remember and modestly dressed in a simple navy-blue A-line dress. But what really struck home was her hair, long auburn tresses halfway down her back held in place by a matching blue band. For some reason around this time, I started to take an active interest in how girls dress, something that lives with me to this day.

I remember thinking this was my big chance, so I quickly got into some form of dance hold and to start with, things went quite well. Ok, I knew I didn't have the best dance technique in the waltz, foxtrot, or whatever it was but I was at least moving in time with the music. Then halfway through the song, she quite calmly and deliberately, with minimal fuss, lifted my right hand back up to her shoulder blade after it was slowly drifting down to her left buttock. Nothing was said, it didn't have to be, as I shuddered to the end of the tune inconsolable, and everything just fell apart after that.

As a callow teenager, it was so embarrassing and I thought myself a wimp. Well, judging chemistry far too important to be distracted by girls, I moved on, and never met Lynn again, although I may still dream of what might have been.

But a crude lesson was learnt with a year or two of alcohol-fuelled disco dancing at university to overcome if not quite bury, the trauma. Thank goodness, as experience demonstrates to my scientifically trained satisfaction just how much dancing, and dancing well, is linked to the opportunities for sex. As I place the Chem Abs back on their dusty shelf for yet another day, I remember how much of my second year in Wales adequately demonstrated that principle. Of course, my memory is by nature selective but I still wonder at my dancing for four to five hours even on weekdays, and fortunately, with less and less need for alcohol.

However, one lurid highlight still haunts me. The thought of having my head buried deeply in the substantial breasts of a six-foot blond from Preston for over an hour never being quite sure whether she was trying to keep my head warm or enacting the semblance of a funky new dance craze. Thought more about the girls, both intense and shy, some fun, some serious with one even speaking Welsh, but inevitably to my mind, none of them were a patch on Lynn. And then, there was the sex, or the severe lack of it, being the least memorable part of undergraduate life, mostly a result of exhaustion or a hangover or both.

I feel a little sad. *Thank god for the tolerant Swedes, lessons learnt,* I tell myself but not yet fully put into practice.

Concentrating on my academic work is clearly the right move for me at the moment as research for most non-theoretical scientists is ninety per cent perseverance with some clear-thinking time and a little luck. Luck determined my supervisors and the nature of their, and my own research, interests. In my specialism, nothing has happened for months. I try to understand what's in the published literature, try and find out where the gaps are in knowledge and go on to devise some experiments to explain what's actually happening. This seems straightforward at first but I soon enter the world of genuinely novel research and the unknown.

Perseverance comes into play when I try and get some weird and wonderful equipment to work properly. After, I'll have to face the big question, can I obtain a reliable set of measurements that are repeatable? If that works out, then low and behold, all I've got to do is interpret the results and explain them to several sceptical scientists, and in my case, some hardnosed industrialists who pay me quite a nice bursary for three years. That's where the luck is going to come in.

With that in mind, after just two months of work, I make my first visit to Bristol and the pharmaceutical company with some serious corrosion problems in one of their multimillion-pound bioreactors. Outside Temple Meads station, I meet this chap in a driver's uniform, who is apparently called Clive and drives a splendid-looking black Rolls Royce. Whilst being driven to the factory to meet senior directors of the company, I sit in the back of this cavernous Rolls on an exquisitely leather-bound seat and let my mind go into a tailspin. What on earth are they expecting me to achieve in three years?

More importantly, right now, do they want a presentation or a report when I've only just got going with a literature search? Well, things turn from the scary to the bizarre when after travelling serenely for half an hour on minor roads, the car suddenly decides to break down. Behind the glass screen, I can hear Clive phoning someone. Phones in cars are a novelty for me but I forget this indulgence as after twenty minutes, this slightly less grand Rover resplendent in a deep burgundy colour turns up to collect me. Everyone is embarrassed when I eventually walk into the work's boardroom.

Fortunately, the meeting is rather low-key as the main purpose is to introduce me to Doug Ansell, their head of support services, and to be my main contact over the next three years. Doug, a cheerful, direct-speaking Australian, offers me a firm handshake followed by an apt choice of phrase.

'Apologies, mate, for the cock up getting you here. Let's hope your research goes better.'

He shows me around the plant and after inspecting their enormous and clearly very expensive stainless steel pressure cooker of a bioreactor, hands over some strange-looking metal samples covered in corrosion for my experiments. The visit ends with some tea and biscuits back in the boardroom and an ominous parting message from Doug.

'Good luck, mate, it'll be a tough nut to crack.'

As I'm driven back to the station aware that there'll be at least two more visits to Bristol to come, I quite like the thought of being treated like royalty and being met by Clive, even though it's only in their burgundy-coloured Rover. *After all,* I tell myself, *who needs a Rolls Royce in this day and age?* Largely ignorant of the perils attached to any pharmaceutical business, I dare to wonder if their decline in the perk of a director's car may reflect on the company's future finances and my own research grant.

But my biggest fear comes from the experimental work that I'm about to start in earnest and how my life as a rather innocent and overwhelmed research student is going to get a whole lot harder. *Forget the fancy limousines,* I tell myself, *it's literally upward and onward in Vic's unique laboratory Annex.*

Piccadilly House is a revelation. Three large Victorian-style houses linked together and modernised to accommodate over forty students. To my surprise, most of its inmates are final-year undergraduates with a few postgraduates and visiting students from the continent. Breakfast is a winner, everything from a full English to ham and cheese on pumpernickel bread. The smell of fresh coffee and Citanes cigarettes is everywhere and I soon take an interest in fresh ground coffee. We share bathrooms and kitchens, which is a bit grim, so I'll look to find some other digs soon but for now, life at Piccadilly House does have its advantages.

There are plenty of pubs and takeaway restaurants close by and it's only a twenty-minute walk to the main chemistry laboratories; long enough to consider my experimental work for the day and my social life at night. Things do have to change in my social life as I feel too hemmed in for my own good. Strangely enough, the same message has come from my parents who know little of what I do here. But whenever we speak on the phone, Dad always asks whether I'm enjoying myself and how "they hope it's not all studies and experiments".

But it's only now after a panicky first nine months, that I begin to feel at ease with the routine of university research and so look to expand my social life. By chance, one evening, I get a knock on the door and three undergraduates appear with a worried look on their faces.

'Hello there, I'm Jack. Are you a chemist? Can you help us please as we're worried we may be poisoning ourselves, and others?'

Jack Brownlee, Rex O'Connor, and Eddie Windsor are final-year so-called Agric students. Agrics, I'm reliably told, study what is loosely called agricultural science; otherwise known by many of the other students in Piccadilly House as farming for the thinking man, apparently, it's rarely a woman. Most are sent to study the modern ways of agriculture by their ambitious and rich farming parents. In practice, they're having a cracking time with wild parties every weekend while being taught a little of everything from soil science, chemistry, engineering, statistics, and modern management practice.

It's all weak beer through my chemist's eyes as I'm soon to find out. Even though it's late in the evening, these Agrics lead me to a kitchen at the far end of the corridor where they've rigged up a Heath Robinson distillation apparatus with a simple Liebig's condenser bought via mail order and a large rice cooker full of what appears to be frothy beer. Rex suddenly comes to the point.

'We're making pink gin for our party at the weekend. Not sure what we're doing. We've brewed beer from kits over the past year, storing it in plastic buckets hidden in our wardrobes. But we want some pink gin for the ladies, they're not all beer drinkers.'

I try to explain that I'm a physical chemist and not an expert in alcohol distillation and fragmentation collection processes, but they aren't listening or don't understand.

'Will we poison the girls?' Jack splutters. 'I have my eyes on this gorgeous blonde English literature student and want to impress her. They think we're all loud dummies in wellies with rich parents and nothing up top except a cloth cap.'

Trying not to nod enthusiastically and using my own limited knowledge, I tell them that if you don't measure the temperature of the distillate accurately, they'll end up carrying over methanol rather than pure ethanol. This will destroy their brains, assuming they have any, and eventually make them blind. It worries me that Eddie who says he studies chemistry books a bit more than the others wants to add a drop of phenolphthalein indicator to the alcohol to turn it pink. When I ask the three where they've got hold of the indicator, they turn uncharacteristically shy.

After complimenting Eddie on his knowledge, I manage to persuade him that it's not a clever idea as the girls will suffer violent diarrhoea and will add little to the gin's flavour. The Agrics seem pleased with my serious-minded responsible advice and by way of thanks, hand over a huge chunk of one of their mum's homemade bread puddings and an invitation to their party on Saturday night at the union building. Lucky old me, I think and hope.

The Rolling Stones' *This Could Be the Last Time* blasts out of the union building; there's a smell of cheap beer and fags in the air. Snappily dressed in my super large, home-knitted rainbow sweater with seriously skin-tight jeans, I creep nervously into the bar and function room. It's some time since I entered the world of disco and wonder if I'll fit in. There's a small dance floor at one end of the room where most students are standing and wriggling around the fringes of the floor like tadpoles bouncing up against the lily pads on a warm spring day. One or two of my friendly Agrics see me and shout, 'Here comes the chemist.'

It's obvious I'm one of the few postgrads at the party, which makes me feel even more self-conscious, so I grab a pint of some frothy beer which tastes as it looks, weak and badly homemade. My Agric friends are busy chatting up a group of what I suspect are English literature students, although their shouty chat describing their acres of carrots and spring greens is making little impression. A petite blonde girl standing next to Jack Brownlee sips a light pink coloured drink containing a slice of lemon; it's surely the best time to circulate and avoid any collaborative damage from phenolphthalein poisoning.

The disco quietens for a few minutes and I start to feel a bit spare. I drift over to the bar area where some nurses from the local infirmary are determined to dance the night away. Suddenly, I'm on the outskirts of Paris, as three elegantly dressed girls chat two to the dozen in French; there's the occasional English phrase thrown in but it's all bathed in a charming French accent. One of the girls is from Piccadilly House so I walk up and say hello. She nods knowingly and says, 'Very surprised to see you here. Aren't you the chemist helping the farmers?'

Taken aback, I smile and reply, 'Well, I'm doing my best. Not sure they take much notice, so just hoping the beer and spirits are drinkable.'

Her gaze lingers, she has doleful sensuous eyes, and continues, 'I'm Chantelle. It's Paul, isn't it?'

'Oui,' I mumble half-heartedly.

'Don't worry, Paul, I'm here to speak English; doing my MA in Middle English. You're a postgrad scientist I'm told, working in the laboratory all the time, blowing yourself up I suppose. You know those noisy Agric boys are very chatty but only talk about their daddy's huge farms back home. They invite us along to their parties, drink all the time, and otherwise largely ignore us. Maybe we frighten them off. Anyway, please let me introduce some friends of mine; Isabelle is our engineer and her flatmate, Kay, is from the biochemistry department.'

To my eyes, the three girls have an air of maturity, or perhaps it's just an ability to communicate in sentences which seems to pass by the undergraduates writhing away on the dancefloor to yet another Rolling Stones number. Chantelle is smoking Citanes in the most refined way. She has delicate fingers, long auburn hair, and a narrow face with grey-green eyes. The word chic doesn't do her justice as she wears a long black tight-fitting skirt with an off-white wrap around a blouse which just about hides her lacey flesh-coloured bra. Not sure if it's the latest fashion from Paris or Dior's so-called New Look, although Chantelle obviously takes her French dress sense very seriously.

Her friend, Isabelle, fits elegantly into some smart tight jeans and a black top; her dark hair is plaited and held in a bun. She's quietly spoken with a serious thoughtful expression on her olive-toned face.

'Haven't seen you at the Piccadilly,' I ask.

Isabelle replies in a beautiful French accent, 'Non, non, I live in a flat further out of the city centre with my friend, Kay.' She turns and looks at her friend then back to me. 'I'm doing an MSc in hydrology.'

Without thinking, I stupidly reply, 'How does a French girl come to study hydrology in England?' Almost before I complete the sentence, I catch sight of Kay smiling at my remark. She's sitting nearby and appears a little detached from the rest of the party. She has long dark, almost black, hair, and wears a thin cream-coloured wool sweater over a short dark brown skirt; it seems a rather old-fashioned look or perhaps traditionally English compared to her friends. Kay appears reluctant to join in our conversation. Nevertheless, I can't help but notice her large dark brown eyes that undoubtedly penetrate and question without her ever having to say a word.

The DJ is obviously fixated on the Rolling Stones as *I Can't Get No Satisfaction* is on the turntable and the dancefloor heaves yet again with a mass of writhing bodies. This might be my one and only chance to get a dance, so I pluck up the courage and suggest, that's about the strength of it, Chantelle might like to take to the floor. She puts her drink down, and strides into the melee dragging me by the hand. Swallowing heavily, out of the blue, a brief memory of schoolgirl Lynn floods back. *For god's sake, keep your hand away from her backside*, I tell myself.

Fortunately, and most frustratingly for me, I do whilst continuing to dance and trying to perfect looking cool with a novel but unconvincing ape-like manoeuvre that exaggerates my abnormally large hands and long legs as I'm well over six feet tall. Whereas Chantelle looks effortlessly sexy and elegant by simply gliding her untouched backside from side to side in time to the music. It's not until near the end of the evening when Isabelle slowly sidles up and practically drags me onto the floor for a final dance; her soft sweet-smelling arms drape around my neck.

But I'm soon aware that it's not my dancing prowess that she longs for but a prop to stand up against after too many of those dubious pink gins. As the music fades away, I ask Isabelle if she ever visits Piccadilly House.

'Ooh yes,' she slurs. 'Sometimes when all the French students get together for cheese and wine in Chantelle's room. You never know, I may see you there one day, *a bientot* Paul.'

From the corner of my eye, I glimpse Kay leaving. She's wearing a long beige Macintosh and sporting a dark red beret. *Very French,* I say to myself. When I'm back at Piccadilly House, I head for my bookcase and check the pristine version of a French dictionary for the exact meaning of *a bientot.* Maybe even sewage treatment can be sexy as I dream of Isabelle in a boiler suit.

Chapter 2

It's early summer. I have a rush of blood and buy a motorbike as a way of escaping Manchester into the countryside during the long and often dreary weekends. To my surprise, when I mention this to my parents, they're keen to help by sending me some money. I'm immensely grateful as they never have that much spare cash and I know they help my sisters quite a bit. For some weirdly irrational reason, I'm the proud owner of a second-hand Husqvarna 250 cc off-road bike. It looks the part, although sadly nothing like the bike Steve McQueen rode in the film *The Great Escape*.

But I like the rugged look and raw noise of a road bike, so I go the extra mile and buy some old leathers and a cranky helmet. My first ride out of Manchester on a bright Saturday morning makes me feel ten feet tall and ready to tackle any old barbed wire. Heading north, in a few hours, I reach the Forest of Bowland where after a pub meal and a pint, I check out the bike on some wooded dirt tracks. 'Freedom is here at last!' I shout and I just love it, and one of many weekends to come.

It's around this time I get to know a fellow student, George McCready, a biochemistry postgrad staying at Piccadilly House. Like me, he's just starting his research, apparently studying the role of aryl amidases and related enzymes in human muscle. This means next to nothing to me as organic chemistry in any form is a black art and should be avoided at all costs. Fortunately, we never really talk much about our research; George is a music buff and plays flute to grade seven, so we spend much of our time as regular concertgoers to the Halle Orchestra in the Free Trade Hall under the baton of John Barbirolli.

Our student cards get us into some cracking concerts and we're just stunned equally by the orchestral playing and how close we can get to the maestro himself. Last night, we heard Barbirolli playing Brahms' *First Symphony* and *Bachianas Brasileiras No 5* by Hector Villa Lobos for the first time. George and I get on so well. He's from Paisley near Glasgow and like me, he's always quick to escape the city. Every other weekend, we load up the Husqvarna, take to the road, and head for the Forest of Bowland. We go on ten-mile hikes along the surrounding valleys and through woods ending up in one of the local pubs to refuel on beer and pies.

It's during one of these beer-fuelled lunches, that I mention how I've met these gorgeous French girls at the Agric party.

'You must know them?' I ask.

'Chantelle and Isabelle, lucky old laddie you are.' George grins. 'Bet you had a good time.'

'Grand time,' I reply. 'Chantelle and Isabelle are cracking dancers, though Isabelle was a bit the worse for wear. Didn't speak much with Kay, a bit quiet and standoffish, didn't dance much either; she shares a flat with Isabelle.'

George frowns, looking puzzled. 'You don't mean Kay Levine? She's not French, and a bit older too. Very serious, long dark hair, pretty and quite tall. Must be her, who works with Professor Mikkelsen on enzymic pathways. She keeps to herself in the department. Very surprised to hear she was at a party at all as she hardly leaves the laboratory, either that or is on one of her so-called field trips to the back and beyond. Are you going to see the French girls again, Paul? Do I get an invite?'

'Who knows,' I reply, as we turn our minds to two bowls of spotted dick with steaming custard heading our way.

My second year at Manchester is dominated by a pattern of intense experimental work in the department's remote Annex; what a lonely thought it is. Vic and I set about devising a series of test experiments that will try and answer some of the basic scientific questions surrounding the project as well as feed some quick data back to the pharma company in Bristol. It doesn't take long to realise that my experimental work is very tedious to set up and the measurement runs are hugely time-consuming while each time their success rests on a knife edge. Barely halfway through my second year and I'm already thinking of a plan for one final set of critical experiments.

And sooner rather than later, I keep telling myself with the thought that my money will run out in less than two years. Worryingly, Vic rams home the point at one of our morning coffee breaks.

'Paul, you need to produce some of your pretty scans on the bioreactor's steel soon so we can make a stab at characterising a possible corrosion mechanism. That's the least our pharma company is expecting. You'll have to build a miniature bioreactor from scratch as soon as possible so you can test it out with your current measurement rig. Not so easy, my lad.'

It all sounds straightforward enough on paper but there's an awful lot of unknowns. Making or buying the bioreactor components and specialist test electrodes is a priority. Mind you, research at this level is always novel, untried, and risky but it needs to be for publication in peer-reviewed journals. If not, I'll end up with an MSc, either examined or through the dissertation, or worse still with no degree at all. I'm learning that the work is rarely glamorous or exciting; it demands perseverance, a strong will, and a large dash of luck. Nothing's guaranteed, it's mostly trial and a lot of error; patience is at a premium. And then, Vic adds another factor.

'You'll have to think about possible theoretical mechanisms involved in the corrosion process. Have a chat with Bill Townbee if you get a chance, he'll point you in the right direction.'

Over the next nine months, I spend ten hours a day building this exotic miniature bioreactor in Vic's remote laboratory. He leaves me to my own devices for much of the time which is unnerving. Then one day, he turns up at the laboratory sporting a stunning suntan in the depths of winter. Not surprisingly, Audrey is equally well-tanned, so although the slag heaps of Lancashire have their charms, they clearly have certain limitations. However, Vic's direction has really helped as I get to know Dr Bill Townbee over the past months. Bill is about fifteen years older than Vic, very much old school with a keen eye for detail and the practicalities of experimental work.

Late one afternoon, I spot him in his office so I knock on the door. He's in the middle of reviewing some draft papers; there's a mug of half-drunk freezing coffee with a skin on it sitting on his desk. We start to chat. Without my knowing, in a few short weeks, Bill is set to become a father figure and a wise confidante in so many ways. It's soon down to him that I make real progress with my research and he gives me the confidence to get out and ensure I enjoy myself too, well at least for a while.

Spring soon arrives in Manchester and the tulips, narcissus, and primula sunbathe in their smartly tendered borders alongside Piccadilly House. Walking around the city centre is now a familiar pleasure. While George and I continue to venture to the Forest of Bowland, I also develop a taste for black pudding and a variety of disgusting-looking grey offal served up for lunch at the University Graduate Centre. The restaurant is a mixture of light oak and plenty of brass fittings; it's a haven for us during the week. Unfortunately, I can't tempt any of my fellow students or even staff to follow the smells and my passion for its menu. George almost gags as I tuck into some lightly braised kidneys.

But it's one evening at Piccadilly House while on my way back from offering the Agrics some sensible advice on improving their distillation process from homemade brown ale that a pungent smell of Citanes cigarettes catches my attention. It comes from a partly open door, and as I pass by, Isabelle Hulot rushes out into a nearby kitchen to grab a tray of croissants, French sticks, and cheese. To my surprise, she recognises me.

'Oh hello, it's Paul, isn't it? Still blowing up things in the laboratory?'

'I'm just about in one piece. Good to see you again.'

She glances at the open door. 'Some of the French students meet up from time to time to celebrate our Frenchness as they call it. Do you want to join us? We don't bite, well not too much.'

I hesitate for a moment; there's a gruff male voice pouring his heart out from a tape deck. Isabelle smiles and adds, 'It's Jacques Brel, he's Belgian you know. The French love him. Come on, grab some cheese and wine.'

Before long, I'm sitting on a small sofa alongside her friend, Chantelle Lacroix, as two chaps called Pierre Germain and Jean Luc Bastian look on. Chantelle's memorable dreamy eyes flutter gently as she hands me a glass of burgundy. Her delicious French accent purrs as she tries to break the ice. 'Pierre and Jean Luc are on my MA course; we all love Middle English. Don't we, boys?'

Pierre and Jean Luc are keen to let me know that they're really Corsican and promptly apologise for their lack of finesse with the English language. However, I can only sit back and admire their swarthy good looks and easy charm. Obviously, Chantelle, and most likely Isabelle, admire their charm too, so much so I start to feel uncomfortable and out of place. Isabelle stifles a laugh, smiles, and kindly interrupts.

'They only tolerate me because my mamma sends over the best cheese. Isn't that right, Pierre? Try this Munster, Paul, it's wonderful. How are your experiments going? Is that the right term to use?'

My reply is suitably brief as I'm told that a certain Serge Reggiani track is about to play and everyone in the room is struck dumb by the prospect of his voice with all its heavy pathos. As a lad from the leek and carrot fields of Boston, this music is a revelation. These girls, intense romantic music and French food are now on my doorstep. Thinking I could do with more of this Isabelle appears to be on my wavelength and wants to make it happen as she quickly interrupts.

'Do you play pétanque, Paul? Some of us play at weekends in one of the local parks. Are you interested in having a go? It's good fun.'

Well, it is good fun, eventually, that is. Our first game is a disaster. The weather is chilly and blustery, the gravelly stretch of park set aside for the game is heavily pockmarked with puddles from a typical Manchester rain shower the day before. The rules seem simple enough, a bit like bowls on gravel with a French flourish when you throw a funny little heavy metal boule. I team up with a Welsh chap from Isabelle's hydrology department. He has an air of confidence and spends most of his time telling me what to do. Isabelle is sharing the spotlight with Monique Parot from Paris, a diminutive figure cloaked in a brightly coloured anorak and leggings, all topped with a bright blue cloche hat.

All are very stylish. Isabelle and Monique destroy our Anglo-Welsh partnership throughout the afternoon. Every time I get in a good position with a boule close to the jack, Monique hurls the last boule down to scatter them in all directions to claim a win. I vow never to take up any sort of bowls, grass, crown, or whatever in the future. Stupidly, after the game, I witter on to those in earshot that pétanque is a futile game with a flawed set of rules but wisely decide to only hint at that to Isabelle. Hypocrisy is about to play a part in my love life because I agree to meet up again for another go, just to see if I can improve, but I don't.

But I do like Isabelle, and a lot. She's very French and an engineer who wears very tight jeans and an even tighter blouse with a certain panache. She understands sewage treatment processes to the point where we spent the first sort of date having coffee in her flat talking enthusiastically about her dissertation on sewage. Her father is a professor of engineering at a university near Toulouse, who encouraged her to go on and study the science of water, as she calls it, at the University of Strasbourg.

She's always wanted to travel and her English is so good that she took the first opportunity after graduating to come to England and examine how the sewers of southern France may be improved by studying the latest developments in anaerobic digestion. Sometimes I think sewage dominates her life a bit too much, particularly as she lets me know one morning, 'Sometimes I wash my jeans three times a week to remove the smell from the digestion process.'

I nod thoughtfully. Isabelle always smells fragrant to me so I think it must be love. Throughout our long summer, Isabelle and I enjoy each other's company more and more. As I walk back from another humiliating loss at pétanque, Isabelle suddenly grasps my hand, turns round to look at me, and smiles. It's a strange and slightly disconcerting feeling to know that someone actually finds me attractive when I'm sober. Particularly for a rather reticent, long-limbed, and often awkward chemist in what is supposed to be the Swinging Sixties. It did seem to be passing me by but maybe not anymore.

I squeeze her hand and start to walk even more briskly back to her flat. Engineers characteristically take a no-nonsense approach to their work and to life in general. Maybe that's what I like about Isabelle as we start to kiss on the battered old sofa listening to the latest Johnny Hallyday album.

'Do you like Johnny?' She whispers after stroking the back of my neck for what seems ages.

I'm tempted to giggle for all the wrong reasons but instead, move my head gently up and down in rhythm to her stroking, I'd even say Maurice Chevalier if she keeps stroking any other part of my body. To my surprise, life in Manchester is changing fast and never more so than tonight.

George and I decide to move out of Piccadilly House and share a house which matches our current chaotic experimentation lifestyle. We're spending hour after hour in the laboratory and missing many pre-ordained evening meals during the week. Sometimes I'm not back at Piccadilly until well after eleven o'clock at night, exhausted and increasingly fed up with the noise from the Agrics. They party like there's no tomorrow despite the onset of their final exams. I'm told it takes about six months in my third year to write up a thesis, so peace and quiet is going to be at a premium.

I also like the idea of some extra privacy when Isabelle visits as I'm seeing more and more of her. Although Kay, her flatmate, is rarely around, Isabelle's sensitive to her feelings and says she worries about upsetting her.

'Sometimes Kay looks so tired. She's either out on a field trip or stuck in her laboratory, even at the weekends. I think her professor pushes her too hard or maybe it's just because she's so driven.'

A few weeks later, George and I are tucking into several pints of Old Peculiar alongside a heavy-weight cheese and black pudding lunch at our favourite "Hark to Bounty Inn" near Clitheroe when he mentions a possible house that's come up for rent. Apparently, there's this postdoc called Ping Chen from Hong Kong who's looking for two postgrads to share his flat. It's part of a large Victorian terrace house about twenty minutes' walk from Piccadilly House, and George is keen.

'Are you interested, Paul, because we need to act fast?'

'What do you know about Ping Chen? Have you seen the place?'

'He's a mathematician, quite inscrutable and works all hours, doing research in the economics department on some computer-based forecasting tool on financial growth patterns in the Far East. Sounds mind-bogglingly dull but don't know much else. His English is good mind you; he has an English mother. The house is clean and spacious and the rent's a bit cheaper than what we pay now but without the food of course.'

By the time we reach Ramsbottom on the A56 back to Manchester, we've decided to move in. All I can hear from George shouting at the back of my rather fruity-sounding Husqvarna is, 'Let's hope Dr Chen likes the look of us.' He does, and within the month, we're making ourselves at home in his modern three-bedroom flat. Ping Chen is very matter-of-fact in his approach to accepting new housemates. He's incredibly ordered and tends to keep to himself. Whenever I ask him a question about his research or sport, or whatever, he mostly answers in monosyllables except for two topics, cooking and Kung Fu movies.

Ping eats his meals of rice or noodles with a variety of vegetables gained from the local Chinese corner shop; he eats alone at exactly the same time each evening. Unsurprisingly, it takes quite a while for me to get used to Ping particularly his habit of sprinkling freshly grated red chillies on his toast in the morning. After a few weeks of settling in, I find this rather sad run-down old cinema just around the corner from the flat. It shows the latest Indian and Chinese films alongside some classic American movies for a ticket price that clearly isn't enough to pay for a cleaner or a repairman to sort out any of its moth-eaten seats.

But more worryingly, Ping comes back from viewing the latest Shaw Brothers movies so animated that I fear he might start chopping up the kitchen table in front of our eyes. He doesn't, thank goodness, and over the next year and a half, our friendship steadily grows to the point where he starts to share his evening meal with Isabelle, but fortunately, not his chillies on toast in the morning.

Looking back on our summer and early autumn, it's difficult to appreciate how intense my research work has become alongside my growing love for Isabelle. Both have grown and completely dominate my day-to-day life, it's an exciting time all around for both of us. My experimental test runs proving the reliability of vital components within the bioreactor come to a head. Every experiment is touch and go with hours of intricate assembly work and setting up the kit. Then, there's the nerve-racking collection of data over many hours in my lonely laboratory Annex.

Anything can go wrong at any time; a seal can literally blow a gasket or the elderly electronic recording equipment recovered from a wartime military research establishment can suddenly break down and having to wait many weeks for spares. Worst of all, if one of the delicate connecting cables buried inside the steel bioreactor suddenly breaks under extreme environmental conditions, all my data is suddenly lost or corrupted. However, after several weeks of repeated experimental runs, I'm ready to show the results to Vic. What's more, I've even used a novel electrode inside the bioreactor where the conditions are close to those found at the Bristol plant. He takes a close look, sits back in his chair, and smiles.

'Good job, lad. Why don't you write up the results into a paper and I'll send it off to one of the top journals and see if we can't get it published? What do you think? Does no harm to have a paper under your belt when you sit down at your viva. Have a go, lad.'

Still in shock from Vic's comments, I spend a few evenings looking at similar papers produced over the years. Then it takes a couple of weeks to produce a rough draft, which I nervously place in front of Vic at coffee time.

'Not bad, lad. Ok, I'm off for a short break now but go and have a word with Bill, he'll sort out the finer details and help with the discussion section.' Quite obviously, I can only assume that Vic's perma-tan is fading fast.

As I soon learn, proofreading is bread and butter to Bill and well before Christmas, my first paper is published. My face glows with pride as I wave it in front of Isabelle. We celebrate with a vegetable curry at our local Indian and a long stay in bed the next morning. I've about six months to complete all the bioreactor experiments and obtain a set of reliable and reproducible scans on real-life steel samples from the Bristol plant.

Doug Ansell decides to visit the Annex for a couple of days so he can visually inspect the bioreactor bomb and hand over more steel samples. He takes a good look at all the pressure gauges, electronic test equipment, and electrode cabling glued in place with the latest cyanoacrylate glue. He's poker-faced as he exits the laboratory, then mutters in his strong Aussie accent.

'Seriously, Paul, is this bomb actually going to hold together long enough to carry out any more measurements that'll be useful?'

'It had better,' I reply. 'Otherwise, the last two years will have been a total waste of time for all of us.'

Doug tells me he'll run some electron micrographs on the samples after I've had my way with them; after dropping him off at Manchester Piccadilly station, he leaves me with a typical cryptic one-liner.

'Let's hope they show some corrosion after you've done with them.'

As I return to work, an endless array of semi-permanent glowering skies hover over central Manchester, so there's nothing to tempt me away from the laboratory. I expect Isabelle will keep me on the straight and narrow too. Well, that's what I'm thinking as Isabelle spends most weekends at our flat; that is until one gloomy Saturday evening after sharing a Chinese meal with Ping, she suddenly blurts out one chilling sentence, 'Paul, you do realise I'll finish my dissertation in the New Year and will have to go back home straight after?'

Without too much thought, I quickly reply, 'Of course, I realise, darling. We've always known that, haven't we? Let's not talk about it now, there's plenty of time to think about such things when I've finished my experiments and you've submitted your dissertation.'

'But there isn't, Paul. I've had a letter from my sponsor, INSA. You know it's this new Institute National des Sciences Appliqués in Toulouse that I was telling you about. They're offering me a research post provided I qualify *cum laude*. They want to know my decision by the end of January one way or another so they can sort out their budgets. It's the job I've always wanted but now I don't know what to do. My mind and my feelings are all in a mess now, and what's worse, I don't know how you feel about the future and what you will do. Paul, I'm just thinking out loud here but would you come and live with me in France?'

Isabelle, as always, is direct and practical, very much the engineer. Sometimes she makes me feel superficial, selfish and uncaring. She doesn't mean to I know but sometimes I'm at a loss in what to say. I don't have an answer as I've never really given much thought to that possibility. Stumbling over some words, I say, 'I suppose we can always figure out something; after all, you'll be just across the Channel and we can meet up easily enough, can't we?' But as soon as the words come out of my mouth, I realise they sound all too glib. Isabelle jumps up from the small red settee in my room and glowers at me.

'That's not a relationship, Paul. Don't you care for me? How much do you care for me?'

Standing there, I'm unable to avoid her eyes, which well up more and more every second as I continue to trip over my words.

'Of course, I do, you know I do, but these bloody experiments are taking over my life. Sometimes it's been damn hard for me to think about anything else, about our future, seriously. And you know I will never do anything to interfere with your future career, knowing how much your work means to you. So sorry, Isabelle, don't know what else to say.'

'You've said enough, quite enough, Paul.'

There's a cruel silence before she grabs her coat and walks out of the front door in tears with a startled Ping open-mouthed staring at me. There's nothing from Isabelle for several days. I try and call her flat but Kay says she's either in the library completing her dissertation or too tired to talk, while adding sympathetically, 'She seems quite upset, there's clearly something weighing on her mind.'

'That's my fault,' I reply.

Kay continues, 'Perhaps you can meet her in the senior common room restaurant on Friday. As you know, she likes to go there and have her English fish and chips each week.'

Friday comes along and I order some fish and chips too as the black pudding and my favourite offal are not on the menu. Looking around, I see Isabelle sitting alone in the far corner of the restaurant. There's a gentle hum of chatter in the room as I walk across to her table. Her face is stern, she looks up and tries to smile but it's clearly a struggle. She points to the seat opposite and begins to say something in a hushed voice.

'I was sort of expecting you, Kay mentioned something. Look, Paul, do you really want to talk about things now or shall we just get on with our lunch?' After a few minutes of forced silence, she continues, 'This is difficult, Paul, but I've spoken to my parents and thought things through. It's time to concentrate on my degree and my career, so I've written back to INSA and agreed to join their staff when I get back home. My parents are incredibly happy. I think it's best, for both of us.'

Taking a deep breath, I lean across the table and take her hand; it's shaking like mine. Suddenly, there's a feeling of desperate loneliness that pours over me for the first time since I moved to Manchester. After what seems like an endless silence, I whisper, 'You deserve better than this, Isabelle. I'm only just realising how much you mean to me and now it's too late. I'll try and sort things out after I've finished my stint here, but honestly, I don't know what I'll end up doing. Everything's just a mess right now and I'm the cause of it.'

'No, Paul,' replies Isabelle as she squeezes my hand. 'It's no one's fault; we're young and our lives are ahead of us. I know you care for me but sometimes you forget to tell me how much. Sadly, people are not always in charge of their own destiny. Many people will have similar stories to tell but I'm sure we are the lucky ones as we can at least have some say in what we do next.'

'Events, dear boy, events,' I mumble in a pompous voice. Isabelle looks at me disbelievingly. 'Harold Macmillan after the Suez crisis,' I add.

'You're so English, Paul,' she replies as we laugh in tandem.

We agree to see each other as much as possible as good friends but by now, our time together is overshadowed by Isabelle desperately trying to finish her dissertation and the looming deadline from INSA. In truth, we often struggle to raise much of a smile in the weeks ahead but manage to face up to the reality of our situation and support each other as best we can. Feelings of guilt and sorrow follow my actions, or lack of actions, most days. Isabelle mentions something similar but she seems to deal with it better than me, day-to-day. But whatever our good intentions, I have this terrible suspicion that these feelings will stay with me for years to come.

There are very few days in early January where the dank overcast Manchester weather shows any signs of relenting. The only brightness during this time is that Isabelle submits her dissertation and I buckle down to finishing off my bioreactor research by running two experiments a week, each lasting twelve hours in the splendid isolation of the remote Annex. I somehow live in this endless twilight world where my spirits are only lifted when we take a farewell ride out to the Forest of Bowland to celebrate Isabelle's achievement.

She's always nervous about travelling on my bike but this time, she relents and hasn't a care in the world as we steam up the A56 holding as she holds on for dear life from the back of my rather husky Husqvarna. A vigorous walk follows over the muddy green meadows edging the banks of fast-running streams. We then settle down for a pub lunch at my old favourite, the *Hark to Bounty Inn.* A pint or two later, Isabelle whispers that her supervisor thinks she's certain to get her degree and, as they say on the continent, cum laude. We hug and kiss, but all too quickly reflect on the consequences. My whole body is shaking as I try to say a few words.

'You're amazing, Isabelle. Your parents must be immensely proud. I know I am.'

Her smile is electric but tinged with sadness. Within three weeks, I'm waving goodbye to her from the Port of Dover after promising to write and visit her as soon as I can. Those promises are soon to ring hollow as my final six months at Manchester just fly past.

Chapter 3

Vic is fussing over my latest bioreactor bomb experimental results. He asks me to repeat them but change the operating conditions. Then, he keeps banging on about the shape of the current-voltage scan printouts on our incredibly old Honeywell chart recorder and whether they are repeatable or not. He gets me thoroughly wound up at times. Eventually, he shows them to Bill who's reassuringly relaxed and encouraging. But I'm not and I tell them so with a real sense of gloom and doom.

'I'm not sure how much longer the cyanoacrylate glue will hold together the cable seals into the bioreactor. And I'm running out of the custom-made electrode material, it's so expensive and takes months to arrive and machine.'

Bill sighs ever so quietly and sips from what's left of some cold coffee languishing in his disgustingly stained mug. He then spends two hours alone with me on this dismal rain-sodden afternoon looking through all my printouts and lab books. Finally, he sits back in his chair and declares, 'Seems clear to me that the results so far can support any number of possible corrosion processes in theory. So what's your favourite, Paul?'

Feeling a little more relaxed, I tell him that I've checked with one of Bill's colleagues about possible theories published in the literature and how I consider one of the more unusual three-stage degradation pathways as the most likely.

'Have the electron micrographs come in from Bristol?' He asks.

'Yes, they show some pitting corrosion in three of the four samples.'

Bill is looking increasingly happy and then adds some final comments.

'Look, Paul, we don't need to run this work into the ground. As my old professor would say—if you look for perfection, you'll always be disappointed. I think you've got enough here to complete your writing up. Spell out the likely theoretical process and draw some conclusions; it's always good to point to some new train of work for others to follow in the future. Flag up what needs to be done if you can, that's how research operates after all. I'm sure these results will satisfy the Bristol crowd. Go away and check more broadly on any other published papers with this likely corrosion mechanism.

'Perhaps Lawrence Ostermann's group at the University of the Great Lakes may have something to offer. Then do the usual compare and contrast exercise for each theory against your data. As I said, if you have any ideas on future specific experiments that will likely back up your theory, then include those in the final discussion section. I'll have a word with Vic. How much of your thesis have you written up?'

'I've written the introduction, experimental and initial literature search, the electrode component characterisation work is mostly done.'

Bill continues to sip the dregs of his coffee, then finally looks up and adds, 'Okay, get on with writing up the rest of your results and we'll sort out an external examiner for your viva before the end of the year. Well done, Paul. It's not been an easy project, has it? But then again, it shouldn't be. A PhD has got to be novel, untried, and probing into the unknown, otherwise, it's not worth doing.'

I leave Bill's office relieved, very relieved. I hope Vic is on the same page as the Americans would say when I look at any of their television shows nowadays. Fortunately, Vic is in a positive mood when I see him the next day. He's just come back from a long coffee break with the permanently bronzed Audrey after hearing he's won another research contract from the government. After clearly hearing from Bill, he goes on to surprise me.

'Have you sorted out your typist yet, young man? You'd better hurry up, matey, because they'll be in short supply in the run-up to Christmas.'

My face gives it away. 'Not yet,' I mumble.

'Go and see Audrey, she'll point you in the right direction.'

She certainly does by introducing me to the ever-cheerful Barbara Rondell who, I'm assured, is one of the most experienced typists around. Audrey says she's very sound and I can only agree when I find her swathed in a wool outfit from top to just below the knee, supported by the most sensible shoes money can buy. Perhaps the horned rim bifocals add the final touch to her personality. However, she's a straight-talking Mancunian and immediately throws me a stack of questions I'm at a loss to answer.

'How many carbons, luv? Can you pay me by the page, each week? What've you got for me now? I can probably get going this evening.' And then, the most penetrating of all. 'What's your handwriting like, darling?'

But Barbara is also most reassuring, so much so that when I see George in the evening, I suggest she's the one when he eventually gets around to publishing his own thesis. But I plea with him, 'But not right now, George, please.'

As the nights get longer in the months running up to Christmas, I again inhabit this twilight world of writing and re-writing my thesis, alone in my room, mostly early evening through to the early hours. There's an occasional visit to the laboratory to show my efforts to Vic and Bill. My diet descends to custard creams, black pudding, homemade chips, and mushy peas. By Christmas, I'm addicted to Dextro energy glucose tablets, multi-packs of which I buy from the local Co-op. I rationalise this indulgence by the belief that I'll sacrifice my teeth for science. George and Ping are very understanding but insist I tag along to the local fleapit to break the monotony of it all.

Every week I succumb to the latest Bollywood romantic blockbuster or, if Ping comes along, the feeling of déjà vu at seeing another sequel to a Bruce Lee bloodbath. Sometimes the dismissive heavy petting of couples perched on the back row offers a pleasant distraction from the jaw-dropping carnage on screen or the barrage of high-pitched screeching from a myriad of violins and sitars accompanying the frenetic dancing of insanely beautiful sari-clad Indian girls. But there's another distraction I'm less happy with and that's writing to Isabelle.

At the start, it's every week, she replies with a detailed description of her new flat on the outskirts of Toulouse and how well she's getting on with most of the institute's staff. Jarringly, she tells me how much she misses me. But soon, inevitably, the flow of letters slows for both of us. I struggle to find anything new to say and I gradually push Isabelle to the back of my mind and succumb to the demands of the intense sprint to the finish line as my research grant and energy levels start to run out in January.

Then to make me feel even more guilty, I get a phone call from her this Sunday evening. She sounds guarded at first but asks how I'm getting on. I struggle to get any words out, and my heart sinks further when she gets directly to the point.

'Will you be coming to Toulouse after you've finished writing up, Paul? When's your viva? Do you know where you'll be working? Will you be staying on at the university?'

Instinct directs me to put the phone down on the desk as I take a deep breath. My mind is racing but going nowhere fast. Panic sets in as I can't decide whether to tell her the truth or what she probably wants to hear. In the end, I pick up the phone and hear my pathetic voice mumbling into the mouthpiece.

'I don't know, Isabelle. My supervisors want to see me in a few weeks to talk about the future. We'll have to wait and see.'

Her disappointment is palpable even from the end of the phone. There's a deep sigh followed by a trembling voice.

'I miss you so much, Paul. You're leaving me in some kind of limbo and I don't like it. I can't live like this any longer. I need to believe there's a future with you. Do you understand?'

'Of course, I do, Isabelle, but please just calm down. I'm so sorry but that's all I can say right now and I'll let you know as soon as I know any more. You'll be fine, I'm sure.' There's a long silence on the line before we recite our hollow goodbyes. I slam the phone down and shout out loud, 'Bloody hell! Oh bloody hell! What's happening here?'

But there's no one in earshot to answer. What have I said and done, or not done? I feel empty inside. Perhaps it's the guilt or a nagging doubt about what kind of future we'd ever have together. Why can't I decide, what's so bloody difficult about deciding? I love her, don't I? Then, the weeks float by and to my disgust, I'm consumed by the outcome of a meeting with Bill and Vic. From then on, our letters dry up and the bond is broken.

The meeting is tense to start as Bill and Vic check on the progress of the first draft of my thesis. They then seem happy enough as Vic confirms a provisional date for my viva examination in the New Year. He seems excited that my external examiner is Professor Charles Kaplan, a leading light in the world of physical chemistry who has just been made a Fellow of the Royal Society and Vice Chancellor of Southampton University. This doesn't pass unnoticed by Bill or Vic as Southampton is on a par with Manchester and a rival for the best research talent. Bill looks to be reassuring as my face must display visible signs of fear.

'Don't worry, Paul, he's very friendly and fair. We wouldn't submit your work unless we're confident about success.' Bill takes a sip from yet another ancient mug of cold coffee. 'Get us the draft as soon as you can; you should have plenty of time now as the experimental data and corrosion theory stand up well together. By the way, what are your plans, Paul? Any ideas?'

'I'm really not too sure. I like this type of research but of course, I need to earn a living.' Bill glances smartly at Vic before replying.

'Might have an opportunity for you to work in the States. Of course, you're familiar with the work of Lawrence and Susan Ostermann; they have a large well-funded laboratory at the University of the Great Lakes in the Midwest. They're on the lookout for some postdocs from Europe. Some of their research is on similar lines to your own corrosion studies but they've also got some impressive federal funding for their pioneering work on novel battery systems. Any interest?'

I say yes almost without thinking. Travelling sounds so exciting and adventurous, but then I typically hesitate for a minute or two. Perhaps I should give it some more thought. How will it affect my prospects? But nothing goes on to change my mind as I never really understand or care too much about what my so-called career goals are. This opportunity sounds as good as anything right now, that's if I'm thinking just about myself. Who knows, maybe it's exactly what I need right now, although some transient doubts over my future career and everything else continue to swirl around in an agony of uncertainty for a while at least. But what an experience, what an opportunity. Bill looks at me with his steely searching eyes.

'You sure, Paul?'

I nod several times. Bill smiles broadly. 'Ok, then I'll drop Lawrence and Susan a line and include your details; will keep you posted. You might find it a bit chilly at this time of year living close to the Great Lakes but it'll be a good experience for you, Paul, good experience indeed.'

Have no idea what to expect today but I end up staring at hundreds of passengers from the back of one of BOAC's first flights from Manchester to New York, and it's quite exciting. However, it's not long before my first experience of flying is rudely interrupted by the sound of a screaming child two rows forward being bribed with some so-called candy by its anxious red-faced and voluble Italian-American parents. Let's hope the chatter will calm down once we're at cruising height. In a way, it's a nice distraction as my mind is still buzzing and I need time to take stock of what's happened over the past two months.

Leaning back, I take some deep breaths as the seatbelt sign beeps and I start to relax. My thoughts turn to the copy of my thesis in the holdall under the seat ahead. Alarmingly, it's probably the only complete record of my last three years of work, so I'll stay close to it for some time. A pretty stewardess offers me a soft drink and my mind starts to run over past events in quick time. Well, Audrey was right, Barbara was predictably sound in delivering a draft of my thesis in plenty of time for Vic and Bill to scrutinise. To my surprise, they only had a few corrections and they even seemed to like my prose. So, it was all bound up and duly submitted ready for my viva.

Bill and Vic kept reassuring me that my viva was going to be very straightforward but never held back from reminding me that you can never be sure what theoretical questions the professor might ask to test your academic knowledge. I remember not being at the least reassured when my fateful day came and I surrendered myself to a cold and frosty morning at the Royal Institute of Chemistry building in Russell Square. This grand Victorian edifice was an unexpected location and even Vic, greeting me with a very firm handshake, seemed unusually tense.

Most of the day is now a blur but I still remember his only comment just before entering the oak-panelled room bedecked with grand paintings of the good and the great. *It was less than helpful as he took a close look at my recently cropped hair, a form of crew-cut suitable for the States,* I thought. Combing his fingers through his greying mane, he exclaimed in typical Mancunian vernacular.

'Hairs a bit dramatic, son, particularly for the Great Lakes at this time of year. You know if you cut your hair that short lad you'll lose all your body strength.' Staring back in blank amazement, I just wondered what's the point of making such a remark at this time.

After two and half hours, I exited the oak-panelled room for Vic to have a brief chat with Professor Kaplan. When they came out, Kaplan was all smiles as he shook my hand and said quite deliberately, 'Where are you off to now, Doctor Wright?' I proudly mentioned Lawrence Ostermann; he nodded knowingly and he was gone. Vic relaxed his shoulders, he looked and sounded relieved while adding a few typical remarks.

'Well done, Paul. All went smoothly, no changes or corrections were required. But you made rather heavy weather of one question. It was simpler than you thought but otherwise, the prof's only comment was how your selection of electron micrographs appear like surface craters on the moon. Not sure Kaplan's a big fan of microscopy.'

The plane's address system suddenly interrupts such thoughts and the pretty stewardess announces that dinner is about to be served. It's time to put the past month's memories behind me, although it still takes a while for my mind to settle. Aided by an almost edible meal and two small bottles of wine, one white and one red, my thoughts dwell on the friends and family I've left behind. I tried calling Isabelle several times with my news but without success, so in the end, I'm happy I wrote a long letter trying to explain how I felt, about not visiting her as I'm flying out to the States after my viva.

Deep down, I know my words are never going to be adequate; just saying how much I miss her and how I'll write often, and maybe visit Toulouse once I've settled in at Great Lakes. Thinking back even after this short a time, and in all innocence, I know I'm fooling myself. Maybe I never understood her feelings well enough or wanted to accept the reality of our lives moving inexorably in different directions, not just physically but socially, even emotionally. One of her French friends said just before I left, 'You can't maintain a loving relationship at long distance; it just doesn't work.'

She's right, of course, and my guilt flows from having no proper answers to the current situation that in any way satisfies my feelings towards Isabelle or hers towards me. Somewhere amongst all this turmoil, George and Ping gave me a good send-off at the local pub and we all hoped that one day we would get together. To my surprise, Ping pronounced that George and I were his ideal flatmates and that he had enjoyed our company. Poignantly, he remembered the pleasure of sharing his Chinese meals with Isabelle and how he began to enjoy Indian films for the first time.

Before leaving, I sold my beloved Husqvarna to George at a knockdown price as he had no transport of his own; he even wanted to take my leathers off me; *typical George,* I thought, while sentimentally asking him to have a pint and some black pudding in my honour the next time he's in the Hark to Bounty at the Forest of Bowland. George and Ping sent me off with the assertion that the USA doesn't know what they're in for. I hope that isn't going to be prophetic.

The Italian-American family have quietened down at last and I manage to get an hour or two's sleep. Between dozing on and off, I came to admire these doting parents and remember the two days I spent with my parents in Boston immediately after my viva.

Despite trying to explain my research work and showing them my thesis, dad kept asking me how I could earn a living wage from now on. He obviously felt it difficult to understand, even though I told him that the university in the States was going to pay me rather well for what I did. I added, 'It's what I want to do, Dad, it'll be an exciting experience; there's a different world out there.'

All he could say to this was, 'I've had enough exciting times during the war to last me a lifetime, but the world's getting smaller and changing so fast, so you'd better go where the jobs are, son.' My mum just wanted to know how long I'd be away and when I said two years with an option for two more, her face just dropped.

Holding back the tears, she mumbled, 'Well, just look after yourself, son. It's such a long way away. Won't you be lonely?' I did my best to reassure her and how I'd coped well enough in Manchester, but however much she tried to raise a smile, my lasting memory was of her very sad and crumpled face. Marion and Elspeth phoned while I was home and wished me luck. They were keen to find out where I'm staying to arrange a trip sometime in the future with their young families. Sadly, the costs involved make their hopes a pipe dream, so my memory of this brief time leaves me with an empty feeling in the pit of my stomach.

That feeling is still buried inside as the plane descends towards a snowy runway at New York's newly named JFK International Airport.

There's over a foot of snow everywhere to be seen from the back of my noisy Greyhound bus heading north on Route 75 from Detroit to Saginawbay, Michigan. Lawrence and Susan Ostermann let me know before I left Manchester that it takes about two hours from the bus terminal outside the Arrivals building at Detroit-Wayne Airport and that they'll meet me at Saginawbay's bus station. I feel anxious as my transfer flight from New York was held up for well over an hour for de-icing and clearing the runway after a snowstorm that came in from the Midwest earlier in the day.

The sun is setting when I reach Saginawbay and the temperature is well below zero with my breath transforming the air in front of me. It's with a real sense of relief that I finally meet the Ostermanns who go out of their way to offer me a friendly welcome.

'Good to meet you, Paul,' says Susan in a slow, relaxed, and in what I assume is a Midwestern accent, which I start to cherish from that day on. 'Hope you like snow.'

Her husband follows up with, 'How's the journey?'

'More used to the rain in Manchester, I'm afraid, but it was such an amazing ride, so I guess I'll get used to it, Dr Ostermann,' I reply, desperately trying to adopt a similar laidback quasi-American accent without much success.

'We'll get you settled in your apartment on campus as soon as we can. We can catch up tomorrow sometime. Please call me Larry, we're very informal here.'

The University of Great Lakes is just a twenty-minute drive from Saginawbay town. Larry explains how originally it was a late 50s purpose-built liberal arts college that expanded, like many American universities, into a spacious campus with greater emphasis given to science and technology courses, with lots of research funding to match. Saginawbay town lies close to the banks of the Bay which runs into Lake Huron. Before long, I'm settled into a modern and spacious staff flat with every convenience, including a well-stocked just about a walk-in fridge with some Molson Canadian beer and a stack of enormous beef and mustard sandwiches prepared by Susan.

The contrast to my gloomy room in the Victorian surroundings of north Manchester is so obvious. I tuck into the food and beer but it's not long before a feeling of overwhelming tiredness drives me to bed. Lying motionless, I re-live the memory of Larry driving down the town's main street blanketed in snow with the sound of country music echoing from brightly lit bars and restaurants. Several monstrous Chevy pickup trucks with jacked-up rear axles patrol menacingly up and down and there's the sound of a black and white police car siren blaring away into the distance.

Larry nonchalantly lets me know, 'Young guns letting off steam, Paul, a typical Friday night.' My last memory before falling asleep is of Bill Townbee telling me a few months earlier, "It'll be an experience, Paul". And so, it will prove to be in so many ways.

Six months pass and I'm lazing on the veranda of a log cabin on the shores of Lake Huron with two friends from the university. It's over eighty-five degrees and the onshore breeze is just about making the late afternoon bearable. Josie Mallander is a bright and young technical assistant from Canada and Michael Womack, is a fresh graduate student working alongside me in one of Larry's new laboratories. We've been out on the lake in a canoe for about two hours while Josie's mum, Ella, prepares some mountain-sized burgers and fresh salad for supper this evening.

We're all very hungry and tired while being serenaded by some well-camouflaged crickets and the occasional eerie whimpering of Canadian black-headed Loons on the lake. Michael mumbles to himself, 'That Loony sound gives me the creeps, especially after dark.'

'They're almost our national bird,' says Josie, who grew up across Lake Erie in Ontario Province and always makes a point of emphasising her Canadian heritage to anyone who would listen.

We've all got to know each other very well over the past months. Our research is centred around this large purpose-built laboratory that's separate from Larry and Susan's main departmental facilities. We work closely with Larry but most day-to-day contact is with Susan. She has access to a newly installed IBM System 360 main frame computer and some state-of-the-art inter-connected chart plotting kit. This kit is driven by some specially purchased bespoke voltage scanning equipment for our electrode and sample performance testing. We all realise this kit probably sets us apart from other research centres around the world, even though I'm familiar with it in a basic form during my Manchester days.

In the first few months, I spent my time learning to program the IBM computer well enough to automate the test rig and run hundreds of routine experiments quickly and reliably. Desk-bound computer programming is never going to be my forte but I stick to the task and in recent weeks the voltage scanning results have come in thick and fast. Sipping my Molson beer, I can't resist passing a comment to Josie.

'We're incredibly lucky you know, running our experiments on this automated scanning test rig. It would take me nearly a year to collect the same amount of data on those boiler plant samples using the old gear in Manchester. It was so time-consuming and boring at times; now we just press a few buttons and away we go.'

'Yep,' chips in Michael. 'So lucky too that Professor Ostermann has some great contacts with the local corporates, particularly the nuclear power plants around here and across the border. Susan knows many of the top engineers working on the new Chalk River reactor in Ontario.'

Ella pops her head around the door and asks Josie to start up the barbecue, and soon we're sinking our teeth into ground beef burgers drenched in dill pickle and mustard sauce. After finishing off another beer, I let everyone in on some news.

'You know Larry and Susan want to see us all first thing Monday morning, they've a new project starting up and plan to make our special test rig a big part of it.' With a glance at Ella beavering away at the barbecue, I laughingly suggest we best build up our strength over the weekend. Thrusting my empty plate forward, I say what everyone is thinking, 'What do you think about another round of salad and burger?'

Soon enough, we all gather in the Ostermanns' office on a Monday morning eager to hear what they have to say. Larry kicks off.

'Paul, I've had a look at your corrosion data from the last batch of nuclear boiler samples and I think we should publish as soon as we can. The way you varied the scanning conditions means we can have confidence in identifying the specific corrosion mechanism. Many people have been trying to establish just this type of mechanism for a long time. And it's your extra programme software for semi-automating the system that's made all the difference. What do you think?'

Raising my eyebrows, I grin self-consciously. He knows I'm keen to publish more peer-reviewed papers as I've only three to my name. 'Keen to write it up, Larry, but I'd like to include Josie and Michael as co-authors.'

'Ok with me,' Larry replies. 'This is exciting stuff with wide application, Paul. It's also good science and there'll be plenty more papers to follow. Not sure how much you know about our boring US politics but the government introduced the Atomic Energy Act of 1954 to try and get some commercial peace dividend from our wartime nuclear programme in Los Alamos. Over the past few years, Susan has been talking to the Chalk River engineers and she thinks your work can help them and possibly some of our new build pressurised water reactors in Michigan and Virginia.'

'They're interested in the corrosion resistance of the steels and nickel alloys they're using under some very harsh conditions, mostly it's the high temperatures. Your work might identify the corrosion processes alongside some lifetime testing using your automated scanning kit, although it means checking out the electrode components first to see if they'll survive the temperatures. Do you think that's a runner, Paul?'

My heart is racing but I suddenly feel quite brave. 'You know, Larry, we can run so many corrosion scans now that I reckon identifying a likely mechanism can be done quickly enough. Maybe the next step is to use the ambient temperature data to interpolate the corrosion rates to the higher working temperatures. We can easily cross-check the rates against classic weight losses in such cases.'

Larry removes his half-moon glasses and looks through the office window to the scanning kit in the corner of the laboratory. Returning his gaze, he challenges me again.

'Do you really think that's possible, Paul?'

'Fifty-fifty chance I'd say but worth a try.'

Larry turns to his wife. 'Well, in that case, Susan will introduce you to the engineers involved and they'll retrieve some suitable real-life samples from the affected areas. Josie and Michael, are you happy with this? If so, keep me posted.'

There's no need for them to answer as they're smiling already from ear to ear. Michael confronts us as we leave the office.

'Paul and Josie, we should go and celebrate this evening. I know just the place. Are you up for it?'

Chapter 4

As Michael said, he knew just the place to celebrate winning our major new project. We arrive at the Four-Square Bar and Restaurant on Saginawbay Main Street around nine o'clock in the evening. The neon sign outside boldly states it's the number one spot for "Country Music Every Night with Dancing". The place is packed with local townspeople and a few of the more affluent students I recognise from around the university. Everyone is sitting around tables with attractive so-called ranch girls serving huge steaks, burgers, and tall glasses of cold Molson. It's a warm evening and the aircon is blasting out around my ears.

The well-practised country band with a girl singer are decked out in matching brightly coloured check shirts, Texan hats, and the tightest of blue jeans. Their set is a series of homespun ballads and some slick finger-picking guitar country tunes that seem to get the audience up and dancing. I don't shy away from dancing nowadays but this is a whole new experience. Josie calls it country line dancing but whatever it's called, it involves some set moves repeated ad nauseum to the point where the dancers enter a mesmeric state, or maybe it's because they're just overcome by the alcohol. Josie bullies us to get up and dance.

'Come on, Paul, Michael, let's get up there and shake a few moves.'

Thirty minutes of hypnotic action follow where two local girls in big hats show this English guy a mean sequence of moves. So I'm hooked, as it knocks spots off any of the contortions I'm used to writhing around the French girls in Manchester's student union bar. Soon, there are some heart-wrenching ballads and everything starts to quieten down until there's a torrent of loud shrieks coming from two girls with a guy in an enormous Texan hat sitting just in front of our table. In an instant, the taller of the two girls jumps up grabs the other's shirt and tries to throttle her. She yells, 'Don't you lay your dopey cowgirl eyes on my Brad! Do you hear me, do you?'

She obviously doesn't because the next second, they are stretched out on the dance floor swearing and wrestling with each other, shirts and long blond hair flying in all directions. As if by magic, everyone around them starts to gently move their chairs and tables back. Nobody stops drinking or talking and one or two couples continue to smooch around the dance floor carefully picking their way between these very bad-tempered girls and their frightened would-be innocent standing in the middle.

After what seems like a lifetime with the band continuing to serenade the opposing factions, I hear a police car's siren and can see its flashing blue lights shining through the windows on either side of the bar area. Three burly armed cops suddenly enter, and march up to the guy who is now hatless and under a further torrent of verbal abuse from both girls. The cops pull him away from the melee towards an exit to one side of the bar. They then studiously watch the girls knock chunks out of each other for a good ten minutes until they are ceremoniously frogmarched out to the waiting black and white patrol car. With the band seemingly not missing a beat, a new line dance starts up amidst the cop car speeding off with all sirens blazing.

This is one of my highlights from the first six months in downtown Saginawbay, although I get the impression it's just too regular an occurrence as Michael and Josie say very little about it. Maybe I'm also getting to feel what it's like to live in this part of the US. Perhaps I'm even starting to think of it as my home, however, just need to make sure I steer clear of the locals in oversized cowboy hats or even worse, the oversized local policeman. By the end of the evening, the seemingly coy Josie asks if I'd like to learn a bit more line dancing, adding, 'Not all our bars are like this, Paul. There are regular groups practising in the town hall if you want to try sometime.'

Little do I realise that country line dancing is to prove my main source of exercise and enjoyment over the years ahead, although not sure it will be quite as dramatic as my first visit to the Four-Square Bar and Restaurant on that warm Friday night in downtown Saginawbay.

The next eighteen months are the most rewarding and intense for the three of us. We make progress across the board as Michael and Josie add further automation to the scanning test rig and establish a procedure to assess electrode performance. My priority is to analyse the huge quantity of data from Susan's steel and nickel alloy samples. After a few months of number crunching, I start to see patterns in the data which lets me fingerprint and characterise several corrosion mechanisms well enough to extrapolate their corrosion rates to much higher temperatures, close to those found in power plants. I also find a way to easily measure electrode lifetimes that are so important to the performance of the test rig.

Larry is in a bullish mood throughout our long and freezing winter. He pushes me to publish three papers in the leading chemistry and materials journals. As a result, I've been invited to present a keynote lecture at the annual American Association for the Advancement of Science meeting in Seattle while Michael and Josie visit the Chalk River site to give a poster presentation at a conference run by a company that sponsors innovative nuclear power plant technology. Work is firing on all four cylinders but my mood is often gloomy, which I largely put down to some loneliness and many long hours in the laboratory.

I'm not finding it easy to really get to know the other science faculty staff; they are so intense and even more work-driven than Larry and Susan. There's an occasional social evening and a youthful theatre group that insists on performing some hard-edged plays about the angst of young men and women fighting either the government or themselves, or both, which only depresses my mood even more. I'm reading the classics and top novels more than I ever did at school or university and fortunately, there's always some magical jazz of all genres on the radio but few operas or classical concerts to get my teeth into.

The Beatles are everywhere on TV even though they've finished touring. My life seems constrained; local music concerts are something I took for granted in Manchester or maybe I was just spoilt for choice. It's becoming increasingly obvious that even though our language is basically the same, our cultures couldn't be further apart in many respects and it matters to me. I'm taken aback by the eating orgy that's Thanksgiving and Christmas; it is literally too much to stomach. Larry and Susan are very hospitable and understand how I struggle at times. They invite me to a home-cooked meal every month with Susan's range of apparently special English dishes that I barely recognise.

My loneliness must also stem from a lack of letters from Isabelle. Mistakenly, I even try to revive our relationship by working hard at writing long indulgent letters during the winter months. Sadly, in the end, I stop. Her occasional letter tells me she's getting on well with her research and colleagues, and in her final one, she goes on at length about a particular senior lecturer in hydrology. Reading between the lines, it's obvious Isabelle is moving on with her life in Toulouse and our connection has now drifted totally apart. Perversely, this helps me come to terms with my own life here, although at times, I continue to feel guilty for not having done enough to try and understand Isabelle.

Sometimes I lie in bed and wonder what might have become of our relationship. There's more guilt to follow when I let my parents know I'm staying in Saginawbay for at least another year. Calling them long distance is so difficult and the silences from Dad and the sad voice of Mum holding back their emotions make things even harder to bear. My only comfort is in mum's letters saying how much Dad is proud I've found a proper career at last and doing so well. In the end, neither the letters nor phone calls provide much comfort as I ignore their claims to return home, I'm determined to stay.

Josie, our young athletic Canadian, is in her early twenties and a godsend. She takes me to my first-line dance class at the local town hall. Before long, I'm totally absorbed or even slightly obsessed with this so-called performance art form as an enthusiastic bunch of thirty and forty-year-olds turn up every Friday evening through fierce Midwest snowstorms. Josie is a tall rangy girl and clearly very proud of her Canadian heritage and upbringing in a small town midway between Toronto and Ottawa. I'm attracted to her but any thoughts of romance are quickly dispelled after she introduces me to her American boyfriend. In fact, she'd say "Such thoughts will never get off the ice".

She's an avid ice hockey fan and religiously follows the Montreal Canadiens in the Stanley Cup every year. It may have something to do with her broad-shouldered hunk of a boyfriend called Bruce who is a semi-professional minor league player from Detroit and knows some of the top players. Fortunately for me, Bruce is not cut out for line dancing. As my attempts to dance gather pace, I'm taken under the wing of David and Mirabelle Woolgar who seem to like my English accent. They think they can make a line dancer out of me, although my first attempts are a disaster.

I can't keep up with the speed of the steps and the music. After a couple of chaotic sessions, they take me aside and walk me through the most popular dances such as the Madison, the Stroll, and the Hully Gully. Soon, I'm mastering the Double Cross and the Cleveland Box. Within a few months, it's getting quite exciting as I skip lightly back and forth in time with the music and the calls from the master of ceremonies for two hours or more. Josie reckons it keeps me sane through the dark Michigan winters and I think she may be right. Word soon gets around about my dancing prowess, leading to some action with the local girls which amuses everyone in the laboratory.

Many locals come dressed as cowgirls for a special social dance on the last Friday of the month. One Joy Landau is difficult to ignore; a striking girl in her early thirties with blond hair tied back by a pink ribbon. After one dance, she literally strides up and whispers in my ear, 'Why don't you get some genuine cowboy boots, honey, and join our little group? We'd love to dance with you.'

So Josie is more than surprised the following Friday when I walk into the laboratory in a bright red and blue check shirt, tight blue jeans, some long brown leather cowboy boots, and a hat to match.

'Hey, partner.' She chuckles. 'Going to round up the horses?'

I feel so self-conscious and embarrassed as I try to explain. 'You know that some of the dancers like to dress up a bit each month, so I thought I'd get into the spirit of things. What do you think?'

'I like your style, boy, I like your style,' as Josie blurts out to everyone in reach of hearing. 'Watch out for those cowgirls.'

And I do, particularly Joy who asks after every class if I'd like to snowshoe in the woods by her lakeshore cabin sometime. Rightly or wrongly, I make some pathetic excuse and she looks disappointed, and I feel a real wimp. Maybe it's the confusion and disappointment over Isabelle which stupidly still plays on my mind even after all this time. Anyway, I tell myself, *Work comes first and I don't need any distractions.* But I keep going to the classes and Mirabelle loves my new gear and wants her husband to man up with some new gear of his own. I seem to have started a trend.

Slowly, the snows surrounding Saginawbay start to melt, the sound of sea birds returning to Lake Huron and life at Great Lakes University becomes even more hectic, well at least for me, Michael, and Josie. So much so that our test work and theoretical studies on the numerous nuclear power samples are delayed. It's no surprise then that by May, Larry introduces a new scientist to the team from the Chalk River Laboratories. James, or Jim McAndrew, is a second-generation Canadian whose original Scottish family emigrated to Ottawa in the 1920s for the fur trade. He graduated from the University of Ottawa and moved to Toronto to further his interest in materials science.

Chalk River Laboratories recruited him for their important new materials research projects. He fits in easily enough, Josie and Michael like him a lot, and he soon joins the social life of the university as a keen basketball player and a talented viola player in a burgeoning local chamber group. His talents speed up both our research and testing; our corrosion mechanistic studies on Susan's samples get an extra pair of hands which helps refine my initial modelling work. He also makes a big contribution to the lifetime assessment of new electrode materials for what is now a fully automated scanning test rig.

By late fall, two more papers are in print and I've been invited to conferences in Detroit, Virginia, and Upstate New York to lecture on our latest findings and theories. Shortly after my visit to Detroit in early October, I get a call from the research director at one of the largest automobile manufacturers in the city. He wants to visit the Great Lakes, look around our laboratory and talk to Larry and Susan about some new research work. After nearly two years at Saginawbay, I'm learning that top-quality scientific research in the States, particularly if it's important to the industry, is not only well-funded but that things happen fast, really fast. So, while I share a beer with Larry and Susan at one of our regular supper evenings at their lakeside cabin, Larry asks me a question.

'How do you think the meeting went today with that guy from Detroit?'

'I thought it went very well. It could bring some new work and applications for our test rig, they seem to have plenty of money.'

'You bet they do,' chortles Larry. Susan leans over and offers me another slice of her special pecan pie dessert. This is after a not-so-English barbecued chicken with southern-style grits. I'm stuffed already but I never refuse. Susan suddenly chips in.

'Paul, we've been meaning to talk to you about your work in the faculty, your future plans, career and all that. You've made a big impression over the past two years. We're delighted it's gone so well, although we realise you've found it lonely and quite difficult at times, especially during our winters. They take a bit of getting used to, I know. You've created such a great team with Michael, Josie, and now Jim. So how do you feel about staying on for another two years?'

I was sort of expecting this conversation to come up before Christmas as my postdoc funding is about to run out but, as usual, I haven't given it much thought.

'Well, Larry, Susan,' I say trying to be as casual and relaxed as I can. 'Always nervous when people start talking about my so-called career, I seem to have an in-built aversion to the idea. It's a sort of rebellion against my dad's idea of work I guess, not sure why really. Silly I know, but hey, no matter; it would be great to stay. I enjoy the research and it's going in a good direction and maybe one day my resume, is that what you call it, might be good enough to get a chance at a faculty post or something.'

Larry looks across to Susan with a worrying expression before replying.

'Look, Paul, I'll be straight with you. This is a small one-time liberal arts college. No doubt the science faculty is gaining a reputation but the university budgets are still geared to the social sciences, arts, humanities, and so forth, so the chance of a tenured assistant professorship in chemistry is very unlikely. Sorry to be so blunt but that's where we are. But what we can offer is a research post for two years with a significant increase in your salary and an exciting change in direction. If that's what you want?'

I hesitate for a moment. 'Is this all connected to that automotive guy's visit from Detroit? If so, then I'm interested.'

'It sure is,' chimes Susan. 'He's one of their research vice presidents and as you know, he heard your lecture last month. He went on to brief his board immediately. They're working on a first-generation lightweight secondary battery system to replace the lead accumulator in their vehicles. They figure if they can reduce the weight of the battery by even twenty per cent, it might help improve the fuel economy of their new generation of smaller compact cars. They've also got some other applications for the battery but they're not telling. I guess you've heard all about the decline in US oil production figures over recent years and how we're getting dependent on Middle East oil.'

'Well, years ago, old President Eisenhower used to say we wouldn't be able to do too much about this trend, and he's been proven right. Anyway, some of the automotive manufacturers want to mitigate against this risk and build a new generation of automobiles that have better fuel economy than our giant chrome-laden sedans coming out of Detroit right now. These new battery systems are just part of the picture, you never know what else they may be planning. Maybe they'll replace the whole powertrain one day, who knows?'

'Initially, they will fund a two-year project to evaluate electrode materials for the novel battery system they have in mind and hopefully, we can come up with a simple technique that calculates its so-called energy retention. The vice president says this is a crucial parameter for a go-no-go decision on any further investment in development and manufacture. They're very impressed with your published ideas on the theory of modelling electrode processes and estimating performance at higher temperatures. They wonder if it could be adapted or developed to establish the battery's overall energy retention.'

'They've set a budget and want us to start immediately after Christmas. They're keen to fund their own dedicated scanning test rig and have identified one of their brightest graduates to come and work here as part of our graduate programme. His name is Jacob Bronstein. He graduated in chemistry from Princeton and has been working on the materials side of battery development for the past three years. He's keen to do a PhD with us. You know that Michael is due to complete his doctorate in the New Year.'

Larry takes a gentle swig of beer and pointedly stares at me for what seems an eternity.

'There's only one catch, Paul. They insist that you head up the research team for the first two years. They might then consider handing over to a local guy; it could be Jacob or even Michael after that.'

'Blimey, but what about publications?' I quickly add. 'Are they going to stop us from submitting papers?'

'Good point, Paul, because they are not the only auto company working on new batteries and I know some of their favoured component materials are commercially sensitive. However, I've checked with our legal guys and they've inserted a clause in our research contract to make sure they cannot stop us from publishing your theories and the modelling of electrode performance based on some selected generic materials' test data. They may want us to hold back on some of the test data for their target materials or use some generic descriptions but they are genuinely interested in the concepts behind characterising battery performance so you'll be free to publish.

'I'm not going ahead with this project if we are restrained in any serious way. So, I must ask you once again, Paul, do you want to stay on and lead this project or not?'

I lean back in the chair; my stomach feels as if it's about to burst open after digesting two slices of Susan's pecan pie. But it isn't just the pie that's affecting me. My thoughts travel back once again to when Bill Townbee suggested I take on this trip to the US over two years ago. Yet again, I say yes, and even more quickly than last time. Larry and Susan smile broadly, look at each other, and visibly sigh with relief, after which Susan offers me some coffee. Over the following week, I try and call Mum and Dad to explain what's happening and how I will not be returning home for the upcoming Christmas holiday.

It's a strangely disjointed conversation as I hear the disappointment in their voices. Mum says she'll soon forget what I look like and asks if I've many friends. *Typical mum,* I thought, *so I try and reassure her that my work colleagues are also my best mates and that we spend time together in town and at a log cabin by the lake shore.*

'We enjoy ourselves, Mum, but there's no one special.' Dad asks lots of questions about the project which is difficult as I can't say too much over the phone, but I promise to write soon. As soon as I put the phone down, I feel very uneasy about not returning home for Christmas; a feeling that is only partly assuaged by writing two long letters before Christmas and in the New Year. I promise myself, and Mum and Dad, that I'll return to the UK for a short break in the summer; which I do.

The next eighteen months just fly past. Jacob joins us in late January and takes on one of Larry and Susan's physical chemistry classes by way of an introduction to the faculty. In early February, I get the team together one freezing Monday morning and formally introduce Jacob Bronstein while announcing that Michael has now completed his PhD viva and how he's now the new Dr Michael Womack. By tradition, we hand out doughnuts at coffee break and before long, Jacob is recounting his time at Princeton in one of the oldest chemistry departments in the country.

He's a bright, enthusiastic, personable twenty-four-year-old with a jutting jaw and a full dark beard. He's also very much a corporate man. I hope he'll fit in well with the team as Larry and Susan let me know privately that close collaboration with Jacob and the automotive company is vital for the project's success. By the middle of March, Jacob has assembled a new battery electrode scanning test rig in a small private area next to our corrosion laboratory and linked it to our upgraded IBM System 360 computer. He's full of confidence and asks if I'd like him to explain to everyone just how his company goes about assessing a new product or component like their novel battery.

As a result, one afternoon a few days later, Jacob sits us all down in the faculty's lecture theatre to go through the different development, evaluation, and testing processes that a big multinational company like theirs must go through before any product, let alone a novel battery device, is manufactured. He admits that the development team in Detroit is new to battery design. They've spent over a year defining the battery's performance characteristics which must be measured accurately before the company will agree on a release for sale to the outside world. It's particularly important as they plan to subcontract the manufacture to a small local jobbing company just outside Detroit.

He says it must be a truly rugged device; tough enough to survive the day-to-day use as a component imbedded in a complex, part electrically driven machine called an automobile. He's such a good speaker, so clear on the subject that most academics, including myself, know very little about. Everyone is impressed and even more so when he spells out what specific testing and theoretical studies are essential to support their prototype battery. I still recall his summary at the end of the talk.

'Guys, what will impress my bosses most with this prototype is getting some real data on the lifetimes of the candidate component materials under the typically harsh operating conditions. And second, what does the battery give you in terms of electrical performance? Yes, the usual data like the voltage, ampere hours, and all the usual published data that everyone reads about. But we need to drive this battery into the ground; and find out just how rugged it really is. And then, finally, show them some numbers for what the company defines as the battery's energy retention. In other words, how good is the battery in holding on to its energy levels or charge in real life?'

'This is a real problem for us in Detroit; we haven't really solved it, so we're looking for ideas and ways of measuring this factor accurately. It could be a showstopper in terms of signing off our prototype as fit for purpose and getting it installed in an automobile.' His eyes brighten as he ends with a nervous laugh. 'It's that simple, folks, so over to all of us.'

Jacob is a great asset to the team and his contribution continues to surprise me. Within a year, a legion of test rig data provides enough evidence to select the electrode materials for their first prototype battery. Then one day out of the blue, Jacob quietly informs us that one of the battery configurations they're keen on needs to operate at one hundred and fifty degrees. What a shock as we all thought most future car batteries must operate at ambient temperature. After a few days of panic, Michael and I decide to go back and look up our corrosion mechanistic work for steels and nickel alloys to see if that can help.

Would it be possible to fit Jacob's battery materials test data to our tried and tested theoretical work in some way and come up with a simple engineering model that we can put in the computer? And could this be used to predict the material's performance at higher temperatures? I'm not so sure but within a month, and to everyone's surprise, the results clearly show it can and we have a computer-generated model to prove it. The evidence is convincing enough for Larry and Susan, so we have another doughnut celebration day and I start to write up a comprehensive paper on the subject.

The next big question is how to measure the battery's so-called energy retention. This isn't going to be easy so ideas roll around in my head for several weeks. But last month's success spurs me on to think in a different way about problems; don't think in such straight lines but look at the overall picture, see what data and knowledge you have at hand and try to see how it's all connected. After a quiet week in the laboratory, I munch a huge waffle drowned in Canadian honey and dream of the weekend to come.

Without hardly realising it, I ask myself, 'What if we combine the mechanistic decay data from our corrosion work with the actual patterns of electrode decay found with Jacob's prototype over similar time periods?' It seems so obvious and although my approach seems a bit artificial, there's some intelligence in using the computer to do all the donkey work. So I let the team know and spend the next weeks at the computer keyboard setting up tedious, frustrating trial-and-error calculations using an iterative software programme to marry the two sources of data and calculate the battery's energy retention factor, as I decide to call it.

At first, the results are difficult to corroborate against our life testing on an early prototype but progress is sufficient to establish the principle and to my surprise, Larry is more than keen to submit an initial short communication paper to one of the leading journals. Jacob is ecstatic at the prospect and immediately wants more work done after reporting the findings to his development vice president in Detroit. He even treats us to a big burger night and line dancing in downtown Saginawbay. Without knowing, it's not long before this short communication paper is being noticed by more people than the automotive development engineers in Detroit or the typical handful of geeky specialist physical chemists and material scientists around the world.

Before I know it, the 1960s are coming to an end and the gaudy Christmas decorations on the main street glisten on the light covering of snow. I'm largely immured to the romanticised version of Christmas in this part of the US, although all their carolling, cookie making, and appearance of gingerbread houses in every coffee bar is of some comfort at a time I find particularly sad and lonely. It's past six o'clock and I've spent long enough all afternoon looking for Christmas presents for my parents, the Ostermanns, and Josie without much luck.

As I return to campus by town bus, I catch sight of two suited men getting into what looks like a large black sedan hire car parked right outside Larry's office. Walking past his office to my apartment block, Larry calls out through the window.

'What have you got on tomorrow morning, Paul?'

'Just finishing off the latest six-month progress report for our Detroit friends,' I shout. 'Latest results for energy retention factor are looking good.'

'Nice to hear. Can you join us at nine tomorrow in my office? It's important; there'll be bagels and coffee.'

'Sure. What's up, Larry? You look worried.'

'You'll find out tomorrow.' His voice dips at the end of the sentence as if his concentration is distracted by much graver thoughts.

When I arrive the next day, the office door is wide open and I can see Larry and Susan in deep conversation with the two men I saw yesterday. Susan is nibbling at a bagel but looks distinctly irritable with a scowl on her face. I've little time to think because as soon as I enter the room, the two men walk up and introduce themselves. Both have distinct British accents, are clearly well-educated, and are smartly dressed in dark suits that look from my limited knowledge to originate from Saville Row. The taller man with dark, carefully groomed, hair shakes my hand and is first to speak.

'Hello, Dr Wright. Very pleased to meet you at last. My name is Rupert Grenville, I'm the Science and Technology Commissioner at the British Embassy in Washington and this is my colleague, Michael DeLeon.'

Mr DeLeon smiles thinly and shakes my hand vigorously. 'I'm the first commercial attaché also based in Washington. Perhaps we could have a chat about your research work, Dr Wright.'

I turn to look at Larry who raises an eyebrow and suggests we sit down at the large table in the middle of the office. Susan pulls up her chair and joins us. Mr DeLeon clears his throat and starts to speak in a slow and deliberate manner, like a lawyer which confuses me from the start.

'We flew into Detroit yesterday and visited the automotive company that's funding your research and then drove up to Saginawbay to see the professors late yesterday afternoon. I'm pleased to say that everyone is being most agreeable and helpful with this turn of events. Most considerate all around, that's for sure.'

I continue staring at Larry and Susan in amazement, certain my face is reddening. 'What's all this about? Why are these two diplomats here and what the hell am I supposed to have done? I'm not a spy you know.'

Grenville laughs self-consciously and adds, 'I hear a slice of a Midwestern accent if I'm not mistaken after what I believe is nearly four years in Saginawbay? It's not only what you have done, Dr Wright, which is to be commended but what you are about to do that is more germane.'

'What I am about to do?' I fire back at Grenville.

'Well, let me come to the point. We, I mean the British Government, would like you to return to the UK at the earliest opportunity, certainly before New Year and preferably before Christmas. We'll arrange flights to suit you, of course. I'm sure you would like to meet up with your parents at some stage during the holiday period. However, we've taken the liberty of organising some accommodation for you in Cambridge, not too far from Boston in Lincolnshire I believe, which is at your disposal. We trust you'll find these arrangements in order and of course, any additional moving expenses will be covered by the embassy here or the British Government when you get back to Blighty.'

'Hold on, Mr Grenville, hold on just one minute.' With a quick glance at Larry and Susan, I blurt out, 'Do you know what this is all about?' But they both look too embarrassed to say anything.

DeLeon interrupts. 'You haven't briefed, Dr Wright, at all I presume?'

Susan appears about to explode desperately trying to keep her temper. In the end, she mutters, 'I thought we agreed to leave it to you to explain what's happening here. Paul, I'm so sorry but these Brits are keen to exploit your research in some way. They said it's a considerable opportunity for you and in the national interest, whatever that means.'

Larry butts in. 'Oh yes, I've spoken with the automobile company vice president first thing this morning to square things between us. They're happy for Michael to take over the academic studies but want us to keep Jacob in charge of their projects. They're only asking for you, Paul, to complete your six-monthly report before you leave. And to try and write up some draft papers for all to look at when you get the chance.'

I get up and walk around the office, eventually sitting down next to Susan. We look at each other and let out a collective sigh. She shrugs her shoulders in disbelief.

Grenville continues. 'I'm sure you have a million questions, Dr Wright, but at this stage, I'm not the best person to answer them. This is unusual I know but all I can say is that your work is of considerable importance to the UK and your return has been sanctioned at the highest level within government.'

Barely containing my anger, I reply, 'Do I have a choice, Mr Grenville?'

Mr Grenville smiles half-heartedly, stiffens, and adds, 'You always have a choice, Dr Wright, but I would not reflect on it too long.'

Larry grabs a cup of steaming hot coffee from his desk, gives me a knowing look, and replies in his most laconic and ironic tone.

'You'd better start packing, Paul. Bon voyage as they say, and well, happy Christmas.'

Susan can't restrain herself any longer and storms out of the office.

Part Two
Cations

Chapter 5

It's magical how a red sun can suddenly disappear behind an avenue of plane trees on the horizon with its glow bathing a shimmering field of wheat in the evening breeze. A kestrel flutters above eyeing a field mouse for its supper, and bees are humming their low notes near a hornbeam hedge that borders the field. A sea of golden wheat ears is ready for harvest and a faint murmur of a distant tractor with a combine finishes its work for the day. Luckily, I know all about this field and it'll have to wait its turn before succumbing to the tractor. But its time will come when the beauty of nature, the plough, the planting of seed, the sun, the rain, and the crude harvest will turn full circle.

So, I stand motionless and daydream as I do most evenings right here, right now. I've always loved these fields, amongst the peace and tranquillity of the crops. Can't fully explain why but they're a comfort to me. Even as a young girl just after the war, I'd spend most of the day collecting flowers from the hedgerows, trying to catch tadpoles in our local pond, and watching the seasons take charge of the cereal fields near my home in Leek. From an early age, I've always had a deep curiosity about living things whether it's plants, toads, birds, or even mice. It was second nature for me to explore and question the local farmers as I marched over their land.

That curiosity still burns bright. I want to examine everything and marvel at the complexity and variety of nature. My parents encourage me, particularly dad, and on this beautiful evening, I hear their voices so clearly. Dad asks, 'What have you been collecting today, Kay? Anything exciting?'

Mum responds with, 'Do you need any more jam jars? You haven't brought back any creepy crawlies into the house, have you?'

Dad stifles a laugh. 'Don't fuss, Rosie. Our Kay knows what she's doing, all those books she keeps reading.'

Mum would smile back. 'It's ok for you, Max, I don't know what I'm going to find under her bed from one day to another.' They then would look at each other, shrug their shoulders, and give me a gentle pat on the back. And I know they're only pulling my leg; that's what a mum and dad do. Because I know how much they adored their little girl, their Nature Girl, they would call me, and I know how much they loved me.

A series of high-pitched chirps from a brood of skylark chicks being fed grain and worms by their mother suddenly disturbs my daydream. The nest is in the margin of the field and I solemnly wish that this domestic scene will continue so the chicks can fledge before winter sets in. There's a stirring in the sky above as their mother sings blissfully on the way to ensuring her young family is spoilt with more grain and a juicy worm. Time presses against the darkening sky as I walk around the perimeter of the field carefully collecting sealed plastic tubs of wheat ears and stalks.

The six containers with blue coloured screw tops have been carefully labelled as to where and when, and by whom they have been collected. I quickly pack them away into my large blue rucksack. There's a small gap in the hedge and before long, I'm walking around the fringes of a small barley field filling up more plastic tubs, this time with red screw tops. This is my routine for the past three weeks and for another week to come. But these are no ordinary farmers' cereal fields, they're abnormally small fields sitting alongside each other growing wheat, barley, and corn.

To a farmer's eye, they're an oddity, planted with three different varieties for each crop ready for harvest in very few weeks. And stranger still, all these fields are under the watchful eye of the scientists and technicians stationed at the Grain and Cereal Crop Research Station, part of the government's Ministry of Agriculture and Fisheries, situated just north of the market town of Louth in the Lincolnshire Wolds.

Luckily, I have a strong relationship and fascination with the Station, as everyone calls it. There have been two visits a year collecting cereal samples for my research at Manchester University; they've been the happiest of times and after almost five years, most of the staff are now my friends. Some of the visiting students are undergraduates, and others completing their MSc courses in agricultural science. Most of them attend my lectures covering the basic theory of the Krebs cycle in mammals and, more importantly, the Calvin Cycle in plants. The students will then return to their farm conglomerates and countries to try and put theory into practice as everyone wants to improve their grain yields and nitrogen utilisation in wheat and rice crops.

The Station is my family and whenever I meet the students in the university's laboratories or senior common room, there's always a beaming smile as we chat about our time together. Everyone harks back to how much time is spent on tea breaks and the ten-mile hikes each weekend around the nearby villages, and of course, there's always the visits to the local pubs. To my mind, I'm at peace with myself during my visits to Lincolnshire, just relaxed and surprisingly more my natural self than amongst the hurly-burly of Manchester's hectic city life.

Sadly, I've come to realise that my inherent shyness leads to a rather too-introverted nature at times for my own good. It wasn't always like this, least of all as a very young girl but I became more aware of it and it was more noticeable to others during my teens. My appointment as a lecturer at the age of thirty by the Dean of the School of Biochemistry, Professor Andreas Mikkelsen, was a genuine surprise. I applied for the post at the insistence of Mikkelsen who said it would provide a good challenge for me but I never expected to get the job. Mikkelsen was my PhD supervisor and he has since told me I was by far the most qualified candidate and how my research into plant enzyme reactions is a significant contribution to undergraduate and postgraduate courses.

So, this is driving me to be more outgoing, responsive, and I hope communicative; Mikkelsen expects it from me and so do my students. Preparation of lectures is straightforward enough, after all, I got the top first-class biochemistry degree in the department in my year and my three research papers on the characterisation of enzymes affecting photosynthesis in cereals and grains have all been well received. I was even presented with the university's research medal and a two-year research grant. Nevertheless, running seminars and providing pastoral care to over twenty undergraduates and postgraduates does not come naturally.

I'm still learning and so my time at the Station helps to find my feet and I genuinely believe my confidence has grown over the years because of it. Fortunately, Professor Mikkelsen is also like a surrogate father to me even though this gentle giant of a man repeatedly asks me to call him Andreas. My respect for him as a man, now in his early fifties, is deep-seated. It comes in part from his redoubtable reputation as a member of Hans Krebs' research group at Sheffield University. He'd joined from his native Denmark shortly after the war as a bright and clearly ambitious young postdoc.

Surprisingly, he said it was the familiarity of our climate, the direct nature of Northern folk, and his love of the north that after ten years led him to move permanently to Manchester and become a British National. He's a kind thoughtful man and I admire him beyond measure.

The breeze starts to gain strength and even ruffles my recently cut short black hair. I tug at the zip of my anorak. It's nearly dark and I need to complete the final task of the day, collect six corn samples in a neighbouring field and store them in the giant refrigerators at the Station. I'm excited about the prospect of taking these fresh samples back to the laboratory for analysis. Over the past five years, I've undertaken laborious time-consuming investigations into the cereals using classical column liquid chromatography. As far as I know, it's still the most common technique capable of separating out the organic components from cereal and it goes back to my undergraduate days.

But it's terribly slow, repetitive work and only manageable with the help of some hardworking postgraduate students mostly from the developing nations across the world. Now with the aid of my grant and Mikkelsen's reputation, I've managed to purchase the latest high-pressure liquid chromatography equipment. It's taken over a year and a half to assemble the specially designed pumps, injection valves, and detectors but after the early trials, I'm ready to use the kit. With luck, I'll be able to fully identify and assay what is termed the photosynthetic enzymic activity of this latest batch of cereal samples. I still recall what Mikkelsen said just before I left for the Station at the end of July.

'Kay, I hope the harvest goes well because the next year or two will be exciting times with that new kit of yours. Have fun in the Wolds.'

We've always been optimistic about unearthing some far-reaching discoveries of the role that photosynthesis enzymes play in cereal crop development. I'm keen to get to grips with their structure and find out the part they play in the famous Calvin Cycle and development of wheat spikes. And after talking to the local farmers, I understand that wheat spikes are important to a crop's yield. Secretly, I'm also hoping to use some clever but expensive ion-exchange column technology that's just appeared on the market to try and prepare some derivative compounds of these enzymes.

In my imagination, I like to believe they can somehow supercharge photosynthesis and enhance the glycolysis of sugars such as glucose in the plant body. Perhaps one day, plants might be specifically bred to accelerate the overall cellular respiration process and improve grain yields. Who knows? This is my daydream and I going to share my ideas with Mikkelsen for the first time on my return to Manchester next week.

The sun finally disappears behind the row of mature plane trees as I pack away a final set of black-topped jars of corn, there's a faint rustle amidst the waving corn plants behind me. A hand gently touches my shoulder.

'Have you finished for the day, Dr Levine?'

I shudder and then freeze; my back is rigid and I let out a whimpering scream followed by an instinctive shout, 'Get away, get away, can't you? No, I don't want to, leave me alone. It's wrong, it's dirty.' My hands start to tremble and I shake uncontrollably.

'What's wrong, Dr Levine, what's wrong? It's only Mila. I've come to help you back with the samples, it's nearly time for supper.'

In an instant, I turn round and see the startled face of Mila Omondi, my MSc student. Mila is a charming, intelligent woman in her mid-twenties with a real authority about her, which I can only but admire. She's my most valuable assistant during these field trips as well as my laboratory in Manchester. We're staying at the same bed and breakfast in the village; I'm happy we do as I really like her and want to get to know her better. My heart thumps in my chest and my face reddens. Staring into Mila's dark brown eyes, I blurt out something not really knowing what I'm saying.

'Of course, Mila, I didn't hear you. You scared me for a moment. So sorry, so sorry! Don't know why I'm suddenly so jumpy. Not normally like this but sometimes bad memories flood back, too much daydreaming I expect. It hasn't happened for a while. It's not your fault, Mila, it's mine. Oh dear, it's time to stop being so silly and come to terms with things.'

Mila looks stunned and doesn't say anything for a while. Then she asks, 'What memories? What's upsetting you so much, Dr Levine? This is not the Kenyan bush, nothing bad is going to happen in these lovely Lincolnshire Wolds.' She smiles the kindest of smiles and takes my hand.

Time passes and I feel slightly calmer. 'I'm sure you're right. I know you're right but things happen to the old brain sometimes.' Sighing deeply, I add, 'Well, it goes back a long way to when I was a teenager, Mila.'

'Hope you don't think I'm being too pushy, Dr Levine, but do you want to talk about it? I'm part of a big family from a small village out in the bush and many strange things went on when I was growing up. So please, feel free to have a chat about it sometime, that's if you would like to. I won't be shocked, you know.'

'You're very kind, Mila. But it's not the best time right now, we need to get back and put these samples in the refrigerators as soon as possible.' For an instant, I feel embarrassed but add hesitantly, 'Perhaps we can have a chat about it one evening when we're back at the bed and breakfast. It's good to share things, I do know that. And oh, Mila, for heaven's sake, please call me Kay. After all this time, we don't need to stand on ceremony, do we?' At last, I begin to feel more in control of myself but wonder if I've done the wrong thing in offering to share my thoughts with Mila.

She smiles broadly, picks up the rucksack full to the brim, and starts to walk briskly back to the Station. Taking a deep breath, I exhale with a big sigh of relief and try to catch her up. On the way back, I go over what's just happened. It frightens me but deep down, I realise that however painful it is, I must try and be honest with myself and talk to somebody I trust about such memories that have lain dormant for far too long.

Mila and I spend the next two days painstakingly grinding the cereal samples into fine powders and apportioning them to glass vials ready for solvent extraction and injection into the high-pressure liquid chromatograph back in Manchester. The vials are meticulously labelled with individual codes and logged into a well-preserved laboratory record book. Mila is in the early stages of writing up her MSc dissertation in which these latest Station samples are a major part. She hopes the results might help her colleagues back in Nairobi decide what direction to take with their own research.

She tells me that after Kenya gained its independence from Britain six years ago, it set upon establishing its own nationwide agricultural research centre near Nairobi for Kenya and possibly for some of its neighbouring countries. Apparently, corn production in sub-Saharan Africa took off in the 1960s and her government is investing heavily in a national agricultural infrastructure. It's clear from the way she speaks that Mila is one of the local university's brightest students and is expected to play a key part in its development. She graduated with top honours in Nairobi and gained a scholarship to study at Manchester.

She breezed through her first-year examinations and I've guided her dissertation's research to improve the analytical techniques that help quantify the nutrient efficiency of their own cereal crops.

It's not a surprise that one evening, a couple of days later, I get a knock on my door at the bed and breakfast. I'm looking at a possible new dress pattern for some dark blue shot silk material that I've been given by one of my Thai students over a year ago. It's a beautiful material but quite stiff and I'm not sure what to make from it. There's easily enough for a simple sleeveless pinafore dress for say summer evening concerts at the Free Trade Hall but I'm still not sure, so will have to wait till I get back to Manchester. No way will I ever bring my dear Singer sewing machine away on a field trip, a precious eighteenth birthday present from Mum and Dad.

'Come in,' I call out, and Mila pops her head around the door.

'Hello, Doctor.' She hesitates, smiles broadly, and continues, 'Oh sorry, Kay, I forgot; it takes a bit of getting used to. Just to say that the other students have asked me to invite you to the Station's harvest party dance this Saturday at the Village Hall; it starts at seven-thirty. The Station is providing what they call a finger buffet. That's cold food, isn't it? There's going to be disco dancing too. Not sure if you ever go along to such dances but I thought you might like to go this time before we head back to Manchester. What do you think?'

This is the first time I've been invited to such a do for years. They're held once or twice a year depending on how much the Station can afford. I'm really pleased to be asked. 'Well, Mila, I'm not sure I'm a disco sort of dancer but you never know. It'll be lovely to see everyone before we go back, should be fun. Are you going?'

Mila nods vigorously. 'Oh yes, I want to wear my umbrella ball gown I bought in London. They're all the rage in Nairobi.'

'Please say yes to whoever is organising it. I'd love to come.'

'James Redpath, the chief technician, is in charge I believe. I'll let him know.' My face crumples at his name.

'What's wrong?' Mila prompts.

'Oh, nothing really. I think he's got a bit of a thing for me you know. Keeps popping into the preparation laboratory for no good reason. A bit creepy, not really my type. I'll have to be on my guard on Saturday. You'll keep an eye on him for me, won't you?'

Mila laughs. 'Don't you worry, Kay; he won't be a problem. I'll keep him dancing all night; he'll be worn out by the time I've finished with him. What will you wear?'

'Fortunately, I've brought a dress that might be suitable.' I go to the wardrobe and bring out a full-skirted scalloped neck cotton summer dress in a floral print that I made up in the spring. 'I'm afraid it's not one of those miniskirts that the girls like to wear nowadays. Seem to have missed the boat with regard to that fashion. Not sure I have the legs for them anyway.' But secretly, I'm pleased with the dress because it's a good fit and shows off my narrow twenty-three-inch waist pretty well. I've been lucky in inheriting the small waist from my mother.

Mila looks pleased. 'You'll look lovely, Kay, ideal for a harvest party. I wish I could wear a dress with such a slim waist but you always look lovely, very much the English rose.'

'Not sure about that,' I reply. 'But the party should be fun, something to look forward to after all the hard work we've put in. It's been an important trip for both of us you know.'

Mila grabs the wicker chair, sits down opposite the bed, and studies my face. 'Excuse me for saying something but why are you so worried about James Redpath? Is it because of what happened the other day in the fields, you know, the memories from when you were a teenager?'

Her question takes me aback at first and I'm even a little angry. It feels like an intrusion and by instinct, I avert my eyes and look at the floor and then at the dress on the bed. Mila gets up from the chair but I immediately seize her arm. 'Mila, please stay. You're very perceptive, maybe too perceptive at times. Maybe I do appear an English rose as you call it and bound by an English character at times that's not doing me any good. You come from such a different background, perhaps I can talk to you more easily. Well, I hope so as I would like to if that's ok I do need to talk to someone about some very personal things.'

Mila looks at me with a serious face but her eyes are tender and sympathetic. She whispers, 'You know I can keep a secret, so don't worry about that. If I can be of any help, then happy just to listen.'

I shrug my shoulders and get up from the bed. 'Ok, Mila, let's make a pot of tea and give it a try and see what happens.' After a couple of minutes, steam rises from one of those dreadful leaky steel teapots that all bed and breakfasts seem to have. We sip from cups that have that characteristic red glaze around their tops. Instinctively, I squeeze Mila's hand and start to slowly tell my story.

'As I may have told you, I grew up in Leek, near the Potteries, midway between Manchester and where we are now. I had a lovely childhood and spent much of my time in the fields near our home, out all day investigating the local wildlife in the woods and fields. Although an only child, it didn't seem to matter to me. My parents trusted me and let me roam the countryside as I wished even before I started at the local girls' grammar school. Mum and Dad were very proud of me for passing the eleven-plus as we call it and going to such a good school.

'Mum's a brilliant seamstress who worked from home and earned good money repairing neighbours' clothes, and curtains, and occasionally making up smart gowns for the wives of some of the local councillors that attend their posh dinner dances. This is the early 50s, Mila, Christian Dior's New Look fashions have just arrived from Paris and my mum was besotted with his latest designs. She would make replicas of his most famous dresses from British patterns sold in the big department stores at the time. She was a real expert and in many ways, it brought us together. I still have some of those dresses she made up for me.'

Grabbing hold of the dress on my bed, I continue. 'This dress is based on a pattern from Dior; it's his so-called Perou short evening dress, which goes back to 1954. Sorry, Mila, I'm getting away from the point. Oh yes, my dad was a soldier in the war. He was in fact a Sapper, part of the REME Corps, so he learnt his trade as a mechanical and electrical engineer in the army. He stayed in the army after the war serving mostly in England at the local barracks, although he did occasionally go abroad. He'd talk about his tours of duty in Germany and the Pacific Ocean.

'He was a wonderful and kind dad, always around for me and my mum, well as much as any serviceman can be. If I'm going on a bit about my family, it's because they're so important to me and I don't want to give the wrong impression or reflect badly on them in any way.'

Mila nods gently, edges closer, and puts her arm around my shoulder, adding calmly, 'Look, it's ok. I have all evening. There's no rush and it's important you say what you have to say, go on.'

'In some ways, I'd a rather sheltered upbringing. Mum told me about all the important things about growing up as a girl and my parents always warned me about hanging around with boys. But I had little experience of boys and certainly not from my grammar school. And not so much from the girls of my own age either who spent their spare time in coffee bars with boys listening to the latest skiffle music. In those days, skiffle groups were just starting up, you know Lonnie Donegan and all that?'

Mila looks puzzled and with some amazement, frowns.

'Well, I was never keen on him anyway, I preferred the ballet. Suppose I was a bit of an innocent and in some ways, probably still am.' Trying to stifle an embarrassing laugh, I add, 'Not sure why I'm telling you all this really. It must be so different to your life in the village when you were growing up.'

Mila laughs, nods and with some force, remarks, 'From my experience, boys will be boys, wherever you live or grow up, eh?'

'Ok, Mila, I'll get to the point. So, it was the day of the Queen's coronation, your queen too I suppose, a rather dismal day in June 1953. My dad was away and my mum had to work on some final adjustments to two evening gowns for the wives attending the local council's party the following day. One of my girlfriends from school was quite well-to-do and her parents had one of the few televisions in Leek at the time. She knew I was keen on the posh dresses, so she invited me over to watch the ceremony with her parents. It was a tiny black and white screen of course in a giant wooden cabinet I remember. So different from the smart new colour TVs that turn up in the Manchester shops nowadays.'

'It was an exciting time as I watched the ceremony from the eleven o'clock start to nearly teatime. Her parents laid on a special coronation tea of sandwiches, Battenburg cake, trifle, and Tizer, which was a real treat in those days. You probably don't know about Tizer, do you, Mila?' My memory of the day is so vivid, I giggle as I speak, but Mila just shakes her head and stares back in amazement. 'My friend's mum was going on and on about all these dresses and outfits on show from all the top English designers—Norman Hartnell, Cecil Beaton—but I remember telling her that Christian Dior was the first and by far the best of them.'

'Well, after teatime, I made my way back home across the fields and remember walking alongside a corn field not half a mile from home when I came across these couple of farm hands. They'd come through a gap in a tall hedge over a stile and were walking towards me. I didn't know them. One was a skinny chap in his mid-twenties, the other quite a bit older, thick-set, and looked quite powerful. They shouted at me, told me I shouldn't be in the field, that it was private property and that the farmer would make me pay for damaging his crops.

'But I knew all this was nonsense and said as much since I'd met the farmer many times in the past and he'd always chat away about his crops and what insects and bugs I'd found in his pond. They weren't listening though and before I knew it, the young one came up close, got hold of my arms and started to put his hands all over me, shouting at me that I should be more respectful or he would teach me a lesson.

'I could smell the beer on his breath but I managed to break free and run away. When I looked back, the older man was running after me and within minutes, he pulled me down to the ground.'

Mila sees I'm breathing heavily and my hands are shaking. My throat starts to close and I struggle to speak. She moves right beside me on the bed and holds my hand. 'Go on if you can.'

'You don't want to be hearing all this,' I say as my eyes start to well up.

Mila squeezes my hand tighter and says, 'Go on, Kay, some things have to be said.'

'Ok, ok, Mila. Well, this older man kept pushing me down hard onto the ground and started grabbing at my dress. I'm so frightened, Mila. He was so strong, I couldn't push him off. His big hands pushed up against my chest making it difficult to breathe. I started screaming. The older man started to shout too. "Come on young'un, here's your chance to be a man. I'll hold her down". The young man ran up and started pulling down his trousers, almost falling on top of me. I remember closing my eyes and nearly retching from the smell of him as he started to pull my legs apart, it was disgusting. That raw smell of sweat all over him was contaminating me, my whole body. Everything felt so horribly dirty and soiled; I screamed even louder, I couldn't stop screaming.'

My head falls into the outstretched arms of Mila as I close my eyes. 'I still remember almost every word that was said and everything that was done that day.'

'It's alright, Kay. No one's going to hurt you now, you're safe with me.'

I gulp in some air before continuing. 'I was screaming for my life and trying to push back these men for what seemed an age when I heard a familiar voice shouting at them. It was the local farmer. "What's going on here, Jackson, who's that lad with you, what's he doing? It's that half-wit Wordell, isn't it? What are you up to, my lad? Is that you, Miss Levine? Get off her at once, you heard me. What are you, animals? I'll have you horse-whipped if I see either of you near that girl again".'

'Mila, I can still hear the anger in that farmer's voice. He shouted, "Wordell, get to the farm office immediately, see the manager and get what's owed to you. I don't want to see your face around here again. If I do, I'll set my dogs on you. Do you understand? And you, Jackson, you should know better, man, you've got kids of your own".'

'The older man said they were just fooling around and there was no harm done but the farmer told him to go to the farmhouse and wait for him there. After that, the farmer helped me up and asked if I'd been hurt. He wanted to know if they'd done anything personal, as he called it. I knew what he meant and they hadn't, so I just told him I was alright and how I lived close by. He wanted to take me home but I refused. His last words were meant kindly I know. "Better tell your parents, lass. Deeply sorry about all this. Now get off home and try to forget all about it".'

'But I couldn't, Mila, not for a very long time. And for whatever reason, I didn't even cry that day, never once.'

Suddenly, floods of warm tears stream down my face over my burning cheeks and holding tightly onto Mila, I take another gulp of air.

Chapter 6

There's plenty to do before Mila and I return to Manchester this coming Sunday. I'll oversee the preparation of the cereal batches, seal them in glass vials, catalogue and pack them carefully away in wooden crates so they survive a trip in the university's old Land Rover. There are also my final reports to be finished off for the Head of Station, Dr Aden Jones, and Professor Mikkelsen. So, I spend most of today in my small office at the Station's main building while Mila is busy in the preparation laboratory. Next morning, I leave a note under Mila's door asking if she'd like to go out for lunch at the local pub, The Feathers. She pops her head around the office door first thing to say she'd love to and how it might be a good idea after what passed between us earlier in the week.

She asks how I am; we smile at each other and I let her know I've slept very well and there's no need to worry about me. Later, we meet up in the pub's Snug and order a ham and cheese ploughman's lunch with plenty of pickled onions. Mila has a peculiar fondness for pickled onions, apparently, they're a rarity in her native Nairobi and we agree a much better choice than the pickled eggs languishing on the bar counter every time we visit the pub. There's no one else nearby and we feel a little awkward about the silence between us at first. But Mila is such a no-nonsense open-hearted girl despite being some years younger, so she soon puts me at ease.

'Glad you were able to tell me your story last evening, Kay. It couldn't have been easy.'

'You're the first person I've ever really spoken to about what happened all those years ago. It seems so silly but I've never even told my mum or dad, I just kept it a secret.'

'But why?' Mila replies softly. 'Surely your family would understand and want to help?'

'I don't know why, although I regret not doing so now. Maybe I still feel partly to blame, even ashamed, about what I said to those men and the way I used to roam the fields and lanes every day without a care in the world. Maybe I felt too embarrassed to tell my parents, especially my dad. As I told you, he was a Sapper and a strong army man, so I wasn't sure what he'd go and do. But most of all, I didn't want my parents to think they were to blame in any way for what happened, letting me have such freedom at such an early age.'

I take a generous swig of my beer which feels unusual as I normally make a half pint last most of an evening. Our ploughmen arrive and we marvel at the size of the pickled onions and the fresh bread, wondering how on earth we're going to finish them. After a while, Mila looks up and puts her hand on top of mine. I know what she's going to say. 'You think I should tell my mum, don't you? You think I owe it to her?'

Mila sighs gently. 'Only you know what's best, Kay. Not sure what I would have done in your position. My experience growing up in our family's village is so different, particularly with my baba, my father. There was still a lot of violence against young girls in the neighbourhood back then. But I had five brothers and two sisters, and baba was extremely strict with us. He told his boys to treat girls with respect and if they didn't, he would make them pay. Once, one of my brothers and some other boys caused some trouble for a local girl. Baba lost his temper when he heard and, well, I won't say anymore but you can guess what happened.'

'Another time I remember my eldest sister, Imani, was attacked one night; she was just a few years older than me when it happened. The next day, baba came to me and said if any boy ever physically threatens me the way they did to Imani, then I should kick them as hard as I know how. "As hard as you can Mila, where it hurts", he said. "You understand, and then come and tell me".'

'So I did that just a few months later when I was fifteen. Let me tell you, Kay, I was a strong girl even at that age and when the word got around the village, I was never troubled again. But I didn't tell baba because I was so frightened, frightened of what his temper would lead to. Luckily, nothing else happened in the family as far as I know. Maybe things have changed back home, although I doubt it. It was rough justice, not your English justice, so that's why I'm the last person to tell you what to do.'

'Well, I'm glad I've told you my story, Mila. You've helped put things into perspective for me, thank you so much.'

'I think it did you good too,' says Mila.

'We shouldn't spend all our time talking about my problems. You've been so kind. Let's talk about the Harvest Party on Saturday as I'm getting quite excited about going.'

Mila quickly interrupts. 'We have one or two dances at the Nairobi Institute each year but they're very formal affairs with the expats dancing around as if in a straitjacket to some boring old-time music. It's not my idea of a dance, so I'm hoping this will be livelier, more Rolling Stones and Beatles.'

'I'm sure it will, Mila, a chance to let your hair down but I do hope they include at least one waltz. My mum and dad loved to dance whenever they got the chance, especially at the regiment's dances on camp. Dad would wear his smart dress uniform and Mum always looked so beautiful in one of her homemade creations.' My eye is suddenly drawn to the pub's old clock over the bar and I realise it's time to get back to the Station. We finish our drinks and squirrel away some of the remaining cheese and bread in our handbags for sandwiches the next day; the pickled onions were all gone.

As we leave, Mila holds on to my arm and whispers, 'Whatever you decide to do, don't leave it too late.'

Those thoughts stay with me most of the afternoon, although there's another I've yet to share with anyone, and that's my brief and rather sad experience with my first serious boyfriend, Simon Gardner. I still wonder if it was a reaction to the torrid incident as a teenager but maybe I'll never know. Thinking back, Simon was a nice enough chap, maybe a bit too nice on occasion, but I did quite like him. Joining the University Jewish Society was the best way to meet boys and we were both early on in our research careers. He seemed to like the same things as I did—music concerts, badminton and walking in the hills.

On the other hand, he'd go to inordinate lengths to explain what his theoretical physics research was all about. Sadly, I did struggle to keep awake at times. One evening in the Concert Hall bar after a Mahler concert, I remember laughing out loud and ended up saying to him rather pompously, 'I'll never understand why anyone doesn't think Mahler is just boring.'

I must have had a drink or two too many that night but shortly afterwards reflecting that perhaps Simon was the boring one, both in and out of bed if my memory is correct. Of course, there was passion at times, plenty of fumbling around and even a genuine release of emotions. But somehow his logical and thoroughly analytical brain made me feel as if he was preparing our sex for future peer review. Sometimes I feel bad about having such thoughts about Simon even now, although perversely, he could be so contrary, controlling even unthinking at times.

Maybe all men are like that I thought, mostly predictable, or perhaps I just attract men of that type. Who knows, perhaps my romantic illusions, or delusions, have died a death over the years, or my teenage memories colour my expectations of men altogether. Whatever the truth, I'll do well to try and put things into a better perspective. I put dear Simon, the love of my life for a few months at least, down to experience and make myself look glamorous for the Station's harvest party.

It's a chilly September evening and I'm glad of my long beige Aquascutum raincoat and dark red beret whilst strolling along to the village hall. There's the sound of a Beatles song blaring out from the disco and through the night air. For no reason, I feel a little anxious about fitting in with all the young Station students who'll be there. Then I think back to my time as a postgraduate, and my inseparable beret which reminds me of sharing my flat with a French postgraduate student called Isabelle and going along with her French friends to some ghastly so-called Agric parties at the student union.

Although totally absorbed in writing up my PhD thesis at the time, I couldn't help but be impressed by the French girls' sense of fashion and style, which I tried to copy as best I could. Sadly, looking back now, I realise what a poor flatmate I must have been and how I should've made a bigger effort. Apart from Simon early on, the truth was, that I hardly ever went out. Mind you, Isabelle also had this serious boyfriend called Paul and she'd often stay overnight at his place. In those days, as now, I'm engulfed in research and away on field trips to the Station. Nevertheless, I still have fond memories of the French students and I'm hoping to add a little French *je ne sais quoi* to the party with a little dancing.

To my dismay, it doesn't start well. As I step into the hall, I'm met by James Redpath, our senior technician. He seems to be hanging around the entrance inspecting every visitor with a rather supercilious attitude. He steps forward with his affected voice booming out for everyone to hear.

'Let me take your coat and charming beret, Dr Levine,' followed by a thin smile dragging wide across his face.

'Thank you, James. No need for such formalities, it's Kay.'

Mila is already enjoying the finger buffet, so I dash to her side and settle down to chat with some of our lively students and full-time research staff. One or two of the girls make some nice comments about my summer dress but it's clear current fashions dictate as the latest in revealing miniskirts and huge bell-bottom trousers are on show. The disco starts up again and from the corner of my eye, I catch sight of a larger-than-life pair of dark blue bell bottoms heading my way. Oh dear, it's James Redpath and he looks serious, very serious.

'It's time for some dancing, Kay. Will you join me?'

This doesn't sound like an invitation, more of a threat which I'm unable to just blankly refuse. So, for fifteen minutes I try to keep my distance from the continuously gyrating James who's clearly fuelled by some rather toxic scrumpy cider. Fortunately, I'm genuinely saved by the need to go to the loo, after which I make a beeline for the buffet tables now laden with desserts and tea from a huge silver-coated metal urn. It's not long before I get into conversation with the Head of the Station, Dr Aden Jones, a touch more soberly dressed in a sensible sports jacket over a rather loud check shirt with a huge pointy collar.

Strikingly though, his fashionable psychedelic pink tie does seem at odds with the rest of his outfit but overall, he's a good-looking man with a strong face and carefully trimmed, dark brown wavy hair. He also speaks in a lyrical Welsh brogue which I find rather intoxicating.

'So glad you could join us at our little celebration this year, Kay. Hope you're enjoying yourself. Some of our younger staff and students are getting a little excited at times, must be the scrumpy cider that seems to appear from nowhere every year.'

Trying to avoid staring at his tie, I reply, 'It's lovely, Aden. They're a fun bunch of people. I've had such an enjoyable field trip this time and got to know some of the students a lot better. Especially, Mila, she's been a great help in many ways and is a real character. So glad we've shared the time together, she'll do very well I'm sure, and I know Professor Mikkelsen thinks highly of her.'

Aden smiles. 'We all do, Kay. I hope your assay work goes well over the next few months. Andreas considers it to be particularly important as opening up a new strand of research in our field is rare nowadays. It must be quite exciting for you, particularly if some of your photosynthesis enzymes can be linked to the nutrient and production levels of some cereals.'

'Oh, that's a surprise, Aden. I didn't know he'd been in touch with you about it.'

'Just once or twice. He's keen to make sure you get all the cereal samples you need. Look, Kay, Andreas and I have known each other for many years and he wants to make sure that all of us at this little outpost of ours realise how critical the next phase of your work is going to be through to next summer. Well done, Kay. Carry on your excellent work and carry on with the support you give our students as well. I hear nothing but good reports from them, particularly the undergraduates who like to have you around to answer their questions. The youngsters obviously talk to you quite easily; it makes a big difference to their studies and the time spent away from their frenetic lives at university.'

My heart quickens and I redden on hearing such comments. This is news to me but I'm over the moon to have such compliments, but a little sad and confused as to why it has taken me so long to again attend one of these parties. The clock at the far end of the hall shows ten-thirty and the music starts to slow down. To my horror, there's the vision of a recognisable pair of dark blue bellbottoms coming ever closer. Before I've time to think of any suitable words of rejection, Mila swoops and grabs James' hand to lead him away to the dance floor with some prophetic words.

'Time to get down to some action, James. Shake a leg, my boy, it's dance time.' James looks in a state of shock.

A moment later, I hear the introduction to *Moon River* sung by Shirley Bassey. Aden, who's sitting next to me, suddenly stands and puts out a hand to ask in his strong Welsh brogue, 'Ah, at last, we have a proper Welsh singer. Would you join me in a slow waltz, my dear?'

Quite touched by his invitation, the evening ends with Aden guiding me around the floor in the arms of a stylish ballroom dancer, despite his tie. It's been a memorable night for many reasons. Mila and I never stop talking all the way back to our bed and breakfast, thanking Mila profusely.

'You saved my life by grabbing James,' I tell her.

Changing for bed, I can't help feeling a little pleased with myself by adding I hope a little of a French dash to the evening. *Things are looking up,* I tell myself while taking a while to reflect on such an eventful evening before drifting off to sleep.

Next day, we head west in our old dark green Land Rover on minor roads before reaching the A631 to Market Rasen and eventually, Manchester. It'll take about three and a half hours, so I'm happy that Mila is sharing the driving despite her coming up on the minibus with the other students. She's good company and I also want to talk to her again about what happened in the fields a week ago. Mila is one of the few students with a driving licence and who's not scared to drive the old Land Rover.

She says there's a similar vehicle at her Kenyan institute so she knows her way around its three-gear sticks, navigating the red-topped lever for two- and four-wheel drive and then the yellow-topped lever to override the four-wheel drive altogether. As she points out, there's no need to worry about the four-wheel drive today unless the heavy rain drives us into a ditch. She adds, 'It's strange as I'm so used to using the red and yellow levers around Nairobi with the poor state of the roads and endless flash floods in the rainy season.'

Surprisingly, we're seen off by Aden this morning and catch sight of him waving in our rear mirror. Mila can't wait to say something.

'That was kind of Dr Jones to see us off. He's such a nice man. I didn't realise he was such a good dancer. The students were most surprised to see you together at the end of the party waltzing around, quite the Fred and Ginger.'

The compliment is not lost on me but I reply modestly, 'Not quite, and it was a surprise for me too. A real treat, so glad my parents inflicted ballroom lessons on me in my early teens. You know, I'm usually a little sad leaving the Station after so many weeks but even more so this time; it's been special. By the way, we need to take it easy on the road, no speeding as we're fully laden with those precious glass vials in the back. If you'd like to take over after an hour or so, then I'll finish off as we get closer to Manchester; I know the easiest route to the laboratory. Are you ok with that?'

Mila just smiles. It's been raining continuously from the start, although the clouds are starting to break up on the horizon. Driving this old Land Rover is tiring and noisy but I notice, not for the first time, that it's somehow easier to chat to someone, even a stranger, on such a trip. I don't understand why but it feels quite easy for me to open a conversation.

'Oh, Mila, just thank you once again for coping so well with my outburst in the field the other day and taking the trouble to listen to what lies behind it. It was difficult for me. And yes, I'll speak to mum about what happened all those years ago but I won't do it straight away. Not at Christmas, at least, as I want that to be a nice holiday without any distractions. But I will next summer after we've finished all this assay work and written up some papers. You've been such a great help, Mila, more than you will ever know.'

'Pleased for you,' she says. 'It will bring you peace of mind, I'm sure.'

'Let's hope so. It's complicated as I need to explain to mum not only what happened that day but how it changed me, and not for the better. It made a big difference to my schooling and to everything for a while. Hard to explain properly but it made me less confident, less certain about things, and less happy-go-lucky. Not sure my parents would have fully understood. They probably put it down to a typical teenage girl growing up with all that entails.'

'Not everything can be explained by our hormones,' says Mila. 'Even my baba knew that. Are you still afraid of telling your dad? Surely, your mum will talk to him about it and he's not going to do anything rash now, is he? That time has passed.'

I hesitate for a moment while offering a deep sigh. 'My dad will never know; he died when I was twenty just before applying to university.'

'Oh, Kay. I'm so sorry to hear that, I didn't realise.'

'Yes, his health was gradually going downhill for some years. He was about to come out of the army and was only forty-eight. It affected mum and me a great deal of course. She had her army wife's pension and her seamstress work was quite a good earner at the time. But I had to delay taking up a university place for nearly a year to help look after her and see if she was alright. We were very close.'

Mila touched my hand on the steering wheel. 'May I ask what happened to your dad?'

There's a queue of traffic ahead so I concentrate hard and take some deep breaths while wondering what to say. 'I don't really know the full story. Mum never wanted to discuss it much, something to do with his blood she was told and I was too preoccupied studying or working at that time to ask many questions. It was so sad.' There's a tangible silence between us for a while but I continue. 'In fact, when the time's right, I should talk to mum about what happened. It's that I'm always so afraid of upsetting her feelings but I, we, should know the truth. The army can be quite secretive you know. He was based at the local barracks at the time and went to a military hospital nearby. That's all I know.'

Mila asks if she can take over the driving once we're a bit further along the A631. The rain starts to ease and I pull over in a layby to change over and have a snack of some tea and scones. As we start off, Mila suddenly asks, 'What do you mean the attempted rape having made such a big difference to your schooling?'

I'm shocked to hear the words attempted rape but Mila is right, that's what it was like in the cold light of day. I've always known that but somehow too afraid to recognise it or even say it out loud. Hesitating at first, I try to explain.

'Well, it's a convoluted story but basically, it put me back about three years in my education, but in many ways, it could have been a lot worse. The long and short of it is that I was doing very well with my "O" level studies at the grammar school. The "O" and "A" level exams had only just come out before there was the so-called school certificate. My teachers were telling my parents that my grades were excellent and fully expected me to go on to the sixth form and do well, particularly in the sciences. As you might expect, I particularly liked biology and other science subjects like chemistry and even physics.'

'Somehow, I even did well in maths and English. But after this attempted rape as you call it, everything changed. Not drastically at first but I started to keep to my room a lot more and began to feel uncomfortable around strangers, especially boys. Believe it or not, I stopped walking the fields, although thankfully over the years, I've forced myself to get back into the countryside which I love, but it was a struggle at first. That's why it was such a shock to my system the other day when all these memories came flooding back. You see, I thought I'd largely overcome these fears, Mila, where back then, I couldn't concentrate on anything for very long.

'My class work suffered and revision for exams was a real struggle. It got to the point where I only just got a pass in my end-of-year exams. As I was coming up to sixteen and exam time, the school spoke to my parents and suggested I might prefer to leave, find a job, and try and get what they called a technical education at the local Further Education College or one of the newly-formed Colleges of Advanced Technology. My parents were shocked and wanted to know what was wrong. But I couldn't talk about it; the school didn't know anything and couldn't offer an explanation.'

'It upset my parents greatly, particularly dad who loved to talk to me about engineering and science. He was so interested in the subjects himself and always had real faith in my ability. He would be so proud of what I've achieved now, I know he would. Oh, Mila, I'm so sorry to go on about all this again but you did ask.'

'It's such a surprise, Kay. I assumed you were on a fast track from school to university and research with top grades all the way.'

'Far from it but I had some luck too. My mother did some dressmaking for the wife of a local councillor who was on the board of a big local animal feed manufacturer. They were looking for a young laboratory technician in their quality assurance department at their Leek factory. Not sure how but I got the job, so at sixteen, with just a few "O" levels with average grades, I joined the company to work with their chief chemist, Trevor Aldridge. He was a lovely local man, married to a barmaid with two young children. We got on well from the off and he encouraged me to enrol on an Ordinary National Certificate, or ONC course as they called it.'

'It's an introduction to general science; these courses had only just been introduced to help under eighteen-year-olds, particularly girls, get a practical technical education out of school in a working environment. The company gave me a day off each week to attend the College of Advanced Technology at Loughborough as well as some evening classes. They were so-called sandwich courses. Have you ever heard of them in Nairobi?'

'They're new to me but carry on, it's most interesting and very forward looking I guess.'

'Well, I really took to the work and the course. Maybe it was the discipline of having to go to work, Trevor of course, or maybe the different surroundings. Not sure why but I found the routine work of measuring moisture, sugar and salt levels fairly easy, and after a year, the laboratory was running so smoothly that I started to take on more analyses. Trevor was pleased and so were his bosses. My interest in science came back and I raced through the ONC course with top grades in less than two years. My college tutor was so impressed, that he recommended I go straight into a three-year higher national diploma.'

'The company's business was doing well at the time so they agreed to hire a young student I could train up, allowing me more time to spend on my studies. The diploma course, a mixture of biology and chemistry, was so interesting that I knew then what I wanted to do as a career. It was to go to university and study biochemistry. My parents were over the moon and with help from my tutor, I won a scholarship to join the degree course at Manchester. By then, my father's illness was a lot worse, he was in and out of the military hospital. Mum was struggling to cope and I was taking on more of the chores at home.'

'Then one day, mum phoned to say we must get to the hospital immediately as dad was unlikely to survive the night. It was such a terrible time, mum needed me more than ever. Fortunately, we had enough money coming in to pay the bills and we got through that first year together. We became heavily dependent on each other; so much so, that it held me back from completing my diploma course. In the end, after a lot of hard work, I managed to pass with a distinction. By this time, I was nearly twenty-two and ready to enrol in the Manchester degree course in their second year. It was a roller coaster of a time but, Mila, I learnt two things; I'd made my parents proud with my studies and at last found my true vocation in life. Not everybody can say that, can they?'

The rest of the trip speeds by with Mila handing back the driving on the outskirts of Manchester with one final reflection on our chat.

'That's quite a story, Kay. You've not had things easy, have you?'

She then hugs me around the shoulders as I get ready to drive off in the direction of a large red sun setting against the stark skyline of Greater Manchester. In a half hour, we pull up at the back of the biochemistry department and drop off our cargo into the cold store. We look at each other and relax with a joint sigh of relief. But I'm very conscious of having chatted away for most of the trip.

'Look, Mila, again, very sorry you've had to put up with me rabbiting on for so long, it's really not like me.'

'Oh, don't be silly, Kay. I enjoyed the trip, all of it. Much better than being stuck in a coach with all those first-year students.'

Mila's such a no-nonsense girl; I just laugh and ask, 'Do you know what you'll be doing once you've got your MSc and return home?'

She grins and raises her eyebrows. 'Well, I'll have to get my MSc first.'

'Oh, I think you'll be alright, Mila. Your first-year exams are remarkably good and you've some useful results from the column liquid chromatography work. They're only going to get better if you use the high-pressure rig on this latest batch of cereals. Then it's just a question of writing up and away you go.'

This time, Mila sighs knowingly. 'You make it sound so simple, Kay. This is my first real dissertation.'

'It'll be good practice for when you go back to your department.'

'Oh yes, that's true. I'll have plenty of reports to write but as you know, I want my dissertation's conclusions to go further and hopefully, help define the future direction of our cereal research. The institute has some extra money now and we're a so-called centre of excellence within Kenya's National Agricultural Research System. And I'm still quite a junior in the department. Sometimes it's difficult to get my bosses let alone our neighbouring countries to ever consider funding novel methods for yield improvement in such staple cereals as wheat or, more importantly, corn, but I'll try.'

'I'm certain you'll make a big difference but let me know if I can be of any help. I'm serious. It means a lot to you and the future livelihood of your local villages, isn't that right?'

Mila nods vigorously. 'Yes, it does. We need to feed our growing population and not just rely on charity from abroad.'

After a long day, I finally drop off Mila at her digs and my thoughts turn from her work to my own research plans, which I've been secretly hatching at the Station. What will Professor Mikkelsen have to say when I catch up with him in two days' time?

Chapter 7

'Come in, Kay. I've almost forgotten what you look like, it's been such a while since we last chatted.' Professor Mikkelsen is resplendent in his familiar open-necked shirt, sitting behind the large oak desk decked with two large, framed photos. One is of him in a white laboratory coat standing next to Professor Krebs and another with his family on a beach somewhere near his hometown of Aarhus in Denmark. 'So, how did you get on in the Wolds this time?' With a smile on his face, he continues. 'That place so much reminds me of Denmark you know. Anyhow, you seem to have made quite an impression this time according to Aden, he called me yesterday.'

I blush before I have a chance to open my mouth. 'Oh dear,' I mutter. 'Word gets around I suppose.'

'Don't worry, Kay, your secret is safe with me. You needn't worry on Aden's account either,' he says as the professor succumbs to another obvious chuckle. 'He's got a stunning Welsh beauty of a wife and four little Adens at home to keep him busy. Well, he's not only impressed by your dancing skills but wanted to say how much he appreciates your work at the Station, particularly your help with some of the students and discussions with staff. He's also quite excited about your line of research and wants to do all he can to help. So well done, Kay, take a bow. Is that the right expression to use after you've danced?'

'It was a particularly good trip, Professor,' I say quickly trying to change the subject. 'We obtained lots of good samples from the three cereal crops and Aden hopes the enzyme assays will show up changes in enzyme activity for some of their semi-dwarf Chinese and Japanese varieties they're experimenting with.'

'Ok, spot on. Our dear Ministry of Agriculture and Fisheries will be pleased. So, what have you got planned from now on? Do you want to take me through it?'

'Of course,' I said. 'We'll start with the enzyme measurements on all the latest batches of wheat, corn, and barley as the top priority. This will complete our current phase of work on characterising the enzymes in leaf cellular photosynthesis and hopefully, the results will confirm our current ideas about how they link into the Calvin Cycle. Then, I'll go on and check their activity levels for Aden using our usual preparation techniques. The new high-pressure chromatography rig will surely do the job with either radiochemical detection or a continuous method using an organic ligand with optical detection.'

'That seems sound, Kay. Let's have a look at the final data when they come through and see if it changes our view on the possible mechanisms in play. Still not sure how important these different enzymes are in driving the Calvin Cycle, don't expect any significant divergence but you never know. Have you had any more thoughts on this aspect of the project?'

'Not really. I still view it as a starting point for understanding the role of enzymes in the processes involved with leaf cellular photosynthesis. Looks like the Calvin Cycle will need to be developed further over time and that probably requires some more theoretical work. Not sure we are at that stage quite yet but it's a good start.'

'Yes, I agree, Kay, but there's still enough in this assay work for two papers so we should try and publish in one of the top biochemistry journals as soon as we can.'

My heart is pounding away in my chest. Should I say something about my research ideas now? It may be the best time to chance it. The professor seems in a listening mood so I take the plunge.

'Professor, I've something else that might be of interest. It comes from talking to Mandeep Singh, the hydroponics expert at the Station, I think you know him.'

'Oh yes, nice chap. He keeps reminding me how he never gets his hands dirty.' He grins and laughs out loud, enough to encourage me to continue and bite the bullet.

'Mandeep showed me how he's managing to exchange ions in the plant leaf with ions from the hydroponic nutrient medium he uses to grow the new Asian corn and wheat varieties. He's analysed the leaf material and the exchange is confirmed, it even includes some metal ions. The measurements are repeatable and he's about to publish the results. It makes me think about how we might be able to change the nature of enzymes that catalyse leaf photosynthesis. For example, is it possible to use modified enzymes or their derivatives to accelerate the initial cellular respiration step, or even the later glycolysis stage to generate more metabolic energy? If so, can this process be scaled up and possibly used to accelerate a range of crop metabolic processes?'

Mikkelsen sits back in his chair and stares at the photo of himself in the Krebs laboratory. He closes his eyes for a moment and then opens them to face me. 'Aren't the current enzymes specific to the cellular type and nutrient mix, surely they are? So will the plant leaf tolerate such a major shift in its enzyme balance?'

'I know these are unknowns, Professor, but what if we can prepare derivatives of the current enzymes which not only mimic their catalytic effect but are more efficient or even perhaps act in some streamlined way as part of the Calvin Cycle? Didn't one of your ex-colleagues, Denis Snodin I think, from the Krebs laboratory leave Sheffield a few years ago to work in industry? Well, he's just published some work showing how a small change in enzyme structure, say adding an alkyl or carboxyl group, or even a metal ion, can be tolerated by leaf enzymes. And we know such structural group changes can affect the metabolic pathways of cereals.'

'Oh yes, I remember Snodin; a bit of a loner I believe. Glad he's found his niche. If I remember correctly, these enzyme derivatives require very long-winded chemical preparative procedures so I'm not sure how they will offer many opportunities for scaling up in the real world of agriculture even if they are effective.'

Hesitating and taking a sharp intake of breath, I continue.

'I know but well, here's a long shot. You may not know but over the past year, I've been in regular contact with our high-pressure chromatography equipment manufacturer. It's a temperamental bit of kit and I need regular help keeping it going. Well, their marketing product manager has introduced me to their supplier of specialist resin-based columns. We use some of them in our assays and to purify the enzymes. Their column manufacturer is based in Leeds and their marketing chap is quite chatty and always ready to help. He's invited me to their manufacturing site for lunch sometime.'

Mikkelsen raises an eyebrow. 'I see, another one of your conquests.'

'Purely business,' I retort, trying not to smile too much. 'Well, he's mentioned how they've some prototype resin-based ion-exchange columns for beta testing that appear capable of exchanging functional groups in compounds that aren't too far away from our photosynthesis enzymes. Luckily, these prototype columns are designed to fit into our existing column chromatography detection kit. I'd like to have a go at creating some enzyme derivatives like

Snodin's. But more importantly, go on and use them in Mandeep's hydroponic medium to switch the enzyme balance in the cereal leaf and see what effect it has on plant enzyme activity and metabolism. What do you think?'

'Let me get this right, Kay. We'll use our classic column liquid chromatography kit to create some derivatives of our well-characterised leaf enzymes. Introduce them into cereal plants via hydroponic feedstock, then go on to quantify the new enzyme mix and their activities. Then what, go on and see what the growth rates are against a control set of plants? Is that right, Kay?'

'Exactly, Professor.'

'Do you know which derivatives you want to produce first using these beta test columns?'

'I have a good idea from Snodin's work and talking to Mandeep. Mandeep says he's willing to set up a hydroponic controlled comparison experiment for me at the Station if I get your go-ahead. He's already spoken to Aden who's happy to go with it.'

'Will it depend on the enzyme derivatives working in fully anaerobic or aerobic conditions?'

'I don't know; no one knows so we will have to trial both environments to start with. But if these derivatives work more efficiently and Mandeep's relatively simple hydroponic process can be scaled up, then the available energy generated for metabolism from cell respiration and glycolysis of sugars may be magnified. It might just provide for a step change in nutrient utilisation and grain yields in the future. And we know how much that's needed to meet the huge demand for corn production in the UK but also across Africa. Mila, our own MSc student from the Nairobi Institute, will give testament to that as her own country's corn production has struggled to keep up with demand over the past ten years.'

Mikkelsen gets up from his chair and starts to pace around the office, then suddenly turns to face me.

'You really did have a productive time at the Station, didn't you, Kay? So what do I think? Well, from what I've just heard, it's one of the most exciting and innovative research proposals to come through my door for over ten years. It seems to be a major step up from the basic theoretical and analytical work of yours. But it's also a logical progression with a much wider application in the long term. I think you'll face a lot of technical unknowns and barriers; some of you haven't even thought of yet but that shouldn't stop you trying. Very well done, Kay. It's very much your project so I say run with it. I'll let Aden know but for now, what do you want from me?'

Almost speechless, I stare at Mikkelsen not quite believing what he's saying and with my mouth wide open. 'Oh, Professor, that's wonderful. I wasn't expecting that. So let me think. I might need a bit of money for the specialist columns. The company is likely to let me have one or two on beta test but I can't be sure. Not convinced my apparent charm extends our collaboration much further.'

'Don't be too sure about that, Kay, but anyway use the ministry's budget with a ceiling of three thousand pounds. Come back if you need more. What else?'

'My lecture and MSc supervisory work is well in hand but perhaps some extra hands for the preparation work on the current assays and the new derivative enzymes will not go amiss. The early experimental stages are bound to be very time-consuming.'

'Co-opt one of the first-year MSc students.' Hesitating for an instant, he continues. 'Hold on, I have an exceptional undergraduate who will appreciate some work in the holidays, I'll send him to you.'

Standing up, I give the professor my heartfelt thanks several times.

'Ok now, that's fine. Now I'll tell you what you can do for me. Just produce a basic project plan for this new work. I don't want a tomb, just segment the work into clear deliverables and set some dates so I can follow progress easily. Keep me posted on any interaction you have with the Station, particularly Mandeep and Aden. As I've said, I'll have a quiet word with them so they know I'm on board with funding and timescales.' After a short pause, he adds, 'A few words of advice from someone who's run fast with a risky project before and got themselves into a right pickle. Is that the expression?'

'Yes,' I say nodding enthusiastically.

'Look, it can happen to anyone. So first, finish that cereal assay work before getting too engrossed in the new project. Second, watch yourself with that column manufacturer's marketing man. The company will want something in return for their assistance. Most often, it's some free publicity and a mention in the published papers, which is fine but sometimes they might want to sign us up for some endorsement or whatever, even a non-disclosure agreement. Speak to me if there's any mention of this or any commercial contracts. Got it?'

Then, he follows up with a polite but rueful smile and a devilish glint in his eye. 'If this product manager wants something else from you, then that's none of my business and assume you can look after yourself when it comes to smart and pushy commercial types.'

Smiling broadly, I stop myself from replying. As I'm on my way out the door, he calls me back.

'One more thing, Kay. For heaven's sake, take a holiday sometime. You work ridiculously hard and take little holidays as far as I can tell. It will catch up with you sometime, so don't let it. It nearly cost me my marriage so be warned.'

'Oh, I will, Professor. I plan to take a long break this Christmas and later in the summer after the bulk of the work is complete.'

'Excellent, make sure it happens. As I say, it's your project but you have a life outside the laboratory too. Oh, and one final thing, which is starting to annoy me and is very English. Can we please cut out this professor nonsense once and for all? It's Andreas, got it?'

Unable to stop myself from laughing, I stare at him and end this endearing conversation by adding quite forcibly, 'Yes, Andreas, I've got it.' Then, I leave his office feeling quite numb and at least two feet off the ground. As soon as I'm back at my office, I call mum and we talk for, what seems and probably is, hours.

Mum makes a fuss over Christmas and I'm glad she does. As I walk through the front door and after all our hugs, she can't wait to tell me of her plans for the holiday. She's even happier when I tell her I can stay for two whole weeks. It brings tears to her eyes and an overpowering feeling of joy for us both. The tears continue when I say how much I want to be with her and how I need a proper rest after working flat out since my return from the Station three months ago. She's soon sitting me down in the front living room of our modest semi-detached house in Leek.

There's an enormous red amaryllis on the folded-down walnut dining room table alongside a few seasonal decorations dutifully hung around the house. The long narrow back garden is quite bare apart from a few mature evergreen shrubs in the borders; the privet hedge at the front is however immaculately pruned. During the summer months, the garden is her pride and joy, and even in the winter, mum takes time to cultivate cuttings in a small greenhouse which I bought for her fiftieth birthday. She had baked a Victorian sponge and puts out her best china service to welcome me home. It's obvious just how much she loves sitting down to chat away with her one and only daughter.

We've come to realise we're close friends as well as mother and daughter and this tradition really matters to both of us. Even though I'm away in Manchester for most of the year, we still feel close; she makes me feel safe and secure. I so much want to make this Christmas an extra happy time for her. She can't wait to ask so many questions.

'Have another slice of cake, love. Have you lost some weight? I know you've been busy working but I hope you're finding time to eat properly. How's your lecturing going and what's this new project you're always on about?'

I grab another slice of cake and top up my teacup. 'Don't fuss, Mum. I'm fine, no need to worry. Yes, I've lost a few pounds but started playing badminton regularly with one of my postgraduate students, Mila, the Kenyan girl I told you about, so I'm fitter than ever. My lectures are going well and I really enjoy looking after the undergraduates and postgraduates after a sticky start. They're a lively bunch; it's most rewarding and they seem to like me. And I've got this new project; Andreas says it's all mine and I should "run with it". It's very exciting but I won't be getting going properly until we've published all the results from the cereal crops that I've been working on for the past two years.

'After all, it's the main reason I visit the Station in the Wolds every six months. Andreas is reviewing a couple of papers I've drafted right now, so hopefully, they'll be in print soon and I can get on. I'll show you the papers when they come out.'

'I won't understand a word of them, lass. It's all mumbo jumbo to me but I'll have a quick look. Dad would've understood, I'm sure. Will your name be on them?'

'Oh yes, with Andreas' of course.'

'Who's this Andreas chap, Kay?'

'Oh, it's Professor Mikkelsen. You know, my head of department and faculty, my supervisor, and my boss really.'

'And you call him Andreas. Well, you're moving up in the world, my girl. Daddy would have been so proud of you.'

I grasp her hand and smile. 'I know he would, Mum. Andreas is such a nice man and amazingly, he thinks this new project of mine is really important to the development of the world's agriculture. Because of that, I wonder if you'd do me a big favour?'

'Of course, I will, love, what is it?'

'I'm pretty sure I'll have to travel a bit more in connection with this project; some lectures, visits to companies, maybe even a government ministry, who knows. But I'll need to look smart, extra smart.'

In an instant, I pop up to my bedroom and collect a brown paper parcel that's tied up in string. As I unwrap it in front of mum, I continue, 'One of my Thai students gave me this beautiful dark blue shot silk as a present and I've been meaning to make up something for ages but never get the time. Would you make a suit for me? I've got a pattern for a two-piece with a mid-length skirt and a three-button top. The pattern comes from one of Dior's early 1950s collections, I'm sure you know it. It's been copied so many times and I've found the pattern in one of Manchester's big department stores. It's quite slim fitting and originally designed for wool but I think it will suit me. It's a heavy-duty thick silk, good for the winter months too. Will you have a look at it?'

'It's beautiful, darling. Of course, I'll make it up for you. When do you want it by?'

'Oh, there's no big rush. What about sometime in late January or even later? Is that possible? I'll come home for a short break then as I won't risk the post.'

Mum has a closer look at the pattern and hesitates. 'Dior is very traditional, Kay, classic design of course, but nowadays girls seem to want to wear those short miniskirts and show their legs and everything; some are wearing what they call hot pants, I suppose you've seen them.'

'Mum, I'm in my early thirties and this outfit is for business when I'm surrounded by men in suits.'

'It'll look wonderful on you, darling, and as you know, anything from the New Look is a style that never goes out of fashion. Dior's the best, but I just thought I'd ask. Let me measure you up tomorrow morning and I'll have a look at the pattern and see if there's enough material. I would think so. You'll be needing some new court shoes to match of course.'

'Oh dear, I haven't thought of that. Well, perhaps we can go shopping after Christmas in the Sales.'

'That'll be lovely, dear. Ok, so now you can come and have a look at what I've been up to in my greenhouse. Not sure what to do with my dahlias. You're the expert on plants, aren't you?'

I laugh and give my regrets but despite her disappointment, she continues, 'After that, it'll be time to get the dinner on. There's a gentle hum of chatter and a tinkle of bone china in the background and it's obvious that mum is in her element. She carefully surveys everyone enjoying their afternoon tea and cakes. I've wanted to treat her to afternoon tea ever since Christmas and New Year were over. The Sales were as busy as ever so we pop into Harrisons, Stoke-on-Trent's premier tea shop, and it's so nice just to have some time to ourselves. Especially as mum has been busy entertaining two of dad's distant cousins who've kept in touch after his death. They've had interesting lives as they fled to Britain in the early 1900s as young boys with their father to escape the anti-Jewish riots during Russian Pogroms in Odessa and the Crimea.

My mum, Rosalind, or Rosie as they call her, enjoys cooking for them and she's clearly pleased her so-called famous daughter is getting to know them. My thoughts are still wrapped up in their history when out of the blue, a young girl in a black dress and pinafore comes to lay out a silver service. There's tea and a selection of refined sandwiches and dainty cakes on porcelain plates each carefully positioned on lace doilies. Mum sits upright and turns to face me.

'There's no need to go to all this expense, love, really.'

'It's my special treat, Mum. And it's been lovely to go around the Sales with you. We haven't done too badly, have we?'

'Well, you've managed to find a very smart pair of court shoes for that new suit of yours. You'll look so smart, my girl, when you give all those important talks. And I found that nice silk blouse to go with it too; a scallop neck suits you best.'

'Yes, it's lovely but you needn't have bought it for me. It's too much money.'

'Not to worry, Pet, I'm managing quite well on dad's pension and adding quite a bit extra with all these special gowns I'm making for all the rich and famous around Leek.' We laugh at the thought.

'Do you like your new winter coat, Mum? You'll wear it, won't you? There're still some cold months ahead.'

'Of course, I will. It's very posh, looks lovely and warm. Don't worry, girl, I'll wear it all the time. It gets chilly around Leek and I'm starting to feel the cold a lot more these days. It's a grand Christmas present but where do you get all your money from?'

'That's good, it should last you years. You know I've got quite a good job and my day-to-day expenses are really quite low. Would you like me to add a little more money to my monthly payments? I can afford it.'

'No, certainly not, Kay; you are generous enough.'

Mum starts to look a bit awkward, so I change the subject. 'And what do you think of my new beret? It's pretty, isn't it? Very nice and warm and the deep blue colour goes with most things, ideal for any time of the year. I've been looking for an extra hat for some time as I end up wearing my dark red one most of the time. Going to get my hair cut short to a half bob when I get back to Manchester, so the new beret will suit me very well; very Parisienne.'

Mum frowns and says, 'I don't know; you and your French look, Kay. Girls these days wear rather loud, brightly coloured outfits from Carnaby Street, not haute couture.'

'I know but it's what I feel comfortable in and it suits me. You know what they say, fashion is for today but style is forever.'

Mum and I laugh. 'So, Kay, are you going to find a boyfriend that appreciates your French style?'

I've been expecting a comment on the boyfriend front for some time, so I reply quite firmly, 'Look, Mum, I'm happy so don't worry, there's plenty of time, although it's not so easy to meet many nice men when I'm so busy at work. You'll know as soon as a good one comes along, promise.' I take her hand in mine and squeeze gently. 'Let's have some of that high tea, shall we?'

Mum smiles lovingly but then seems distant for a minute or so. She takes a handkerchief from her coat pocket and gently dabs her eyes. 'Dad would love to see you now, so grown up and doing well in your career, and I can see him tucking into those dainty little cakes.' She half laughs and then her eyes become a little more tearful. 'He'd be pleased as punch. Did you know he always brought me here the first chance he had after getting back from one of his travels abroad?'

'Don't get upset, Mum. I know dad would have been happy too. He used to love telling me all about his engineering days in the army and his friends from around the world.'

'It's alright, love. I'm ok, just miss him sometimes. He died so young, not even fifty.'

I hesitate for a minute but then ask, 'What happened to dad?'

'What do you mean, darling?'

'Well, why did he have to die so young? He was always such a strong fit man. Couldn't the doctors do something?'

'The military doctor said no, it was a serious blood disease. To be honest, love, I was in such a state. Well, you were at the barracks hospital with me so you know the medics seemed a bit puzzled themselves. Their top doctor, a Major

Kendrick I think he was called, was sympathetic but kept saying he couldn't say much more, so I just let it drop. Dad was so poorly and on loads of drugs to stop the pain. He just kept talking about some trip to the Pacific Ocean and some letters he'd received from a few of his engineering mates based in New Zealand. Don't know much more than that.'

'Do you have his death certificate and those letters, Mum?'

'They hung on to the death certificate for some reason, but it didn't say much as I remember. Just a long name for a blood disease. But the letters are probably in the back room with all Dad's old stuff, so we can try and find them if you are interested. He once mentioned some university report about some young Sappers he'd worked with over there. They'd been building an airfield and what have you on this island in the Pacific? Funnily enough, I remember it now because I think it was called Christmas Island.'

My mind races ahead but it's time to change the conversation so as not to spoil what's been a memorable day out. 'Ok, Mum, I'm thirsty. Let's ask for some more tea and we'll talk all about this when we get home.' To my relief, our outing ended as it began by chatting away arm in arm on the local bus back to Leek.

It's late February and the heavy snow in the north of England has been disrupting people's lives for at least a week. I'm pleased to be back home in my flat and go straight over to the window to look out on a slushy scene in north Manchester with the streetlights glinting off a layer of dirty sleet collecting on the pavement. Luckily, the department's Land Rover was available for me to visit Leeds and meet this chatty chromatography column marketing manager. But on the way back, some of the roads began to narrow from falling snow, enough for me to use the four-wheel drive.

As for my meeting, I thought it went better than expected with a traditional pub lunch in the city centre thrown in. I never needed any so-called charm offensive as the marketing chap was happy enough to give me two beta test ion-exchange columns and the promise of two more in a few weeks' time. The company seemed keen to provide the columns and technical support after I'd explained a little of what we're planning to do over the summer months. He just asked for the company to be mentioned in any academic publications, to which I readily agreed.

He said the company's research team came up with these new resin-based columns for traditional high-pressure liquid chromatography suppliers. But they also thought the resin chemistry behind them might find application in some new kit coming onto the market under the banner of ion chromatography. They genuinely seem to believe my work in modifying photosynthesis enzymes might prove useful in promoting their columns for analysis of real-world agricultural compounds. He labels it as a new and exciting growth market, although that sounds a bit too good to be true; nevertheless, I'm pleased to hear it.

There are three letters waiting for me on the doormat. One has a Ministry of Defence stamp, and the other two are from Elsevier Press. I quickly change out of my new blue silk two-piece suit I picked up from mum two weeks earlier. She has done a beautiful job of tailoring and fits me so well, that I hardly know I have it on.

It was only a brief visit but I let her know that I'd written to that senior army doctor, Major Kendrick, who treated dad in the army hospital. I used my official doctor title in the hope I'm mistaken for a clinician and get more information. I'd stressed in the letter that over the recent months, mum had wanted to learn more about what happened even though it was over ten years ago. I requested dad's death certificate and details of the cause of death. Mum was happy for me to do this, even though she's doubtful anything will come of it. Eventually, mum found three letters amongst all Dad's things that were from his friends in New Zealand's Engineer and Observer Corps.

One of the letters spelt out how they'd served on combined operations alongside British Sappers on Christmas Island during the mid-50s. They built an airfield and accommodation as well as acted as observers for tests on a new British superweapon. The letters didn't make clear what the tests were about but certainly, they refer to the reported atmospheric detonations of the British hydrogen bomb in 1957. Although short on detail, dad's friends were telling him to be aware that several of the New Zealanders were going down sick and that he should seek urgent medical help as soon as possible if he had any lasting symptoms.

One of his friends mentioned that Massey University on North Island was carrying out some checks on their blood and asking whether it rained much during their time on the island. After reading the letters, I decided not to say too much about the bomb tests to mum. After all, dad had obviously kept the contents secret from mum, so I would say nothing more until there was some definite news. With these thoughts, my heart begins to race as I open the letter with the ministry stamp. It reads:

Letter: Office of the Deputy Surgeon-General, Ministry of Defence.
pp: Surgeon-Colonel, Army Medical Department.

Dear Dr Levine,
Re: Medical Records Sgt Max H Levine

Further to your letter to our Lieutenant-Colonel Dr Kendrick requesting the death certificate of your father, Sgt Levine, and information on his cause of death, Colonel Kendrick has asked me to respond to you and your mother, Mrs Rosalind Levine. As was communicated at the time of Sgt Levine's sad death, he was being treated for a severe blood disorder, symptomatic of a form of leukaemia. In this instance, army regulations do not allow me to provide a copy of a death certificate. I have been advised that his medical condition was in no way related to his tour of operations in the Pacific during the 1950s.
Yours etc.

I'm uneasy after reading the letter, lying in bed for hours wondering what to say to mum and what her reaction might be. In the end, I call just after breakfast. She says straight away that she isn't surprised by the letter as she knows how the army works and how it keeps things close to its chest. I'm relieved and glad it's a bit of an anti-climax for her, although it makes me even more determined to do more. Mum goes on to say, 'Kay, I still don't understand why the nurses, or this Major Kendrick chap, didn't tell me straight at the time that it was blood cancer, what else? Instead, they show me this long medical name on the death certificate which I'm not going to get even now, am I?'

'Mum, I'm not going to let this drop. If I get the chance, I'll chase them again, don't you worry. There are too many unanswered questions for my liking and I won't be fobbed off by some surgeon-colonel in Whitehall. Why are they withholding the death certificate and how can they be so sure and quick to say the cause of death has nothing to do with Daddy's tour of the Pacific? That's not what we're hearing from New Zealand, is it?'

'Darling, you're too busy to be spending time on this. You've got your new project to get on with, that's far more important.'

'At the moment, maybe, and it may take a while but I'll get some answers one day. I won't forget this, Mum. I'll say goodbye now. All my love and thanks again for the lovely outfit, it's perfect.'

Putting down the receiver, I repeat the promise to mum and I'll damn well keep it. But for now, I need to push on with my work. So I'm relieved to open the other two letters from Elsevier Press with draft copies of the papers I submitted with Andreas. They'll complete a big chunk of my work on cereal chromatographic analyses characterising a good number of the key photosynthesis enzymes. Looks like both papers have been accepted for publication with the minimum of the referee's comments. Even though there's a bitter wind blowing and sleet's collecting on my heavy coat and beret, I march off to the university with a spring in my step and the belief there's nothing to hold me back now. Let's hope Andreas agrees.

It's nearly August and to everyone's amazement, Manchester has been bathed in sunshine for over two weeks. Professor Mikkelsen is also in a good frame of mind after returning from his annual holiday with his elderly parents in their summer home on the outskirts of Aarhus. He has set aside a whole day for me to bring him up to speed on the progress of my special project. He jokes that it's preferable to one of his routine dean of school meetings or completing some hideous paperwork for further government funding. His holiday spirit makes the meeting a bit awkward at times as he lets slip he'd never had any doubts about its success nine months ago when he said, "Run with it".

But he's honestly taken aback when he's able to evaluate my results so quickly, even though I've kept him up-to-date with progress on my experimental work and the Station trials throughout. However, this is the first time we've had a chance to sit down and assess all the results properly. As I run through the experimental work and the raw data in some detail, Andreas becomes increasingly animated. He listens intently for two hours as I explain how the special resin-based ion-exchange columns from the Leeds company are used to prepare three photosynthesis enzyme derivatives with our classic column chromatography kit.

Then I explain how I selected the prevalent enzymes found in cereals from our published high-pressure liquid chromatography assays from the past two years. The results show how both alkyl and metal group ion-exchange work for each enzyme, making it clear I am guided by Denis Snodin's full paper that Andreas obtained after a quick chat on the phone. We smile when I mention a few enjoyable weeks spent at a sun-drenched Station in March with the charming Mandeep, who ran one-off hydroponic trials under lights with selected wheat and corn plants. According to Mandeep, the derivative enzymes are clearly absorbed by the plants using their tried and tested nutrient-growing media.

He used control plants during the trial to compare any changes in the plant's overall growth rate patterns. I made the point that Mandeep and Aden were very keen to run these trials and arranged for their most experienced technician to eventually transfer the finished plant samples into vials. They were couriered to me before the end of July with Mandeep's statistical report on the evaluation of growth rate patterns. With a knowing grin, I couldn't help but remark that Aden's only disappointment was that none of his staff had thought of organising a dance party while I was there. Aden said he'd been badly let down, which I couldn't help but agree.

Andreas chuckles. 'Glad you're concentrating on the work in hand but I'm sure there'll be other opportunities for you to improve your quick step. Please continue, Kay.'

'Well, over the past two weeks, I and your very enthusiastic student have assayed all the plant samples to try and characterise the photosynthesis enzyme balances. It was also necessary to contract one of the department's analytical laboratories to run some extra glucose measurements.' Glancing at Andreas with a little trepidation, I add, 'Andreas, I've booked the costs to the MAFF budget as you directed. Hope that's ok?'

'I think Her Majesty's Government can afford it. Apparently, we've a new set of leaders after the general election and I'm made to believe that money will be sprinkled around quite liberally for future scientific research.' His voice rises gently as he asks, 'So where are we with the final results, Kay?'

Andreas has mentioned many times that in his experience it's quite rare that a series of quite innovative experiments are planned and carried out successfully. Even more to go on and deliver repeatable results that lead to what he calls demonstrable breakthroughs. My eyes fix on his, I can tell he's excited.

'Okay, Andreas, this is what we've found. As I hinted earlier, plant assays before and after the hydroponic trial show the enzyme balance is shifted significantly to include the derivatives. This is true for all the enzyme derivatives and plant types. Post-trial glucose measurements confirm at least a fifty per cent increase in the leaf glucose levels for plants containing the enzyme derivative when compared to their controls. Mandeep's analysis clearly shows a statistically significant enhancement in plant growth yield for the derivative enzyme-treated plants when compared to their controls. There's no clear indication as to whether this enhancement benefits from aerobic or anaerobic photosynthesis.'

'Overall, I believe the results demonstrate that photosynthesis enzyme exchange is possible in cereals. The technique improves plant metabolism through amplification of either cellular respiration or the glycolysis stages within photosynthesis, or possibly with both these stages simultaneously. Therefore, this enzyme amplification technique increases leaf glucose levels and subsequent cereal growth yields.'

'Impressive, Kay, very impressive. Are these results repeatable? That's the key question.'

'I think they are. Mandeep used the exact same procedure and cereal samples for this trial as for any of those trials he's published in the past. Confidence limits are the same at ninety-five per cent. The repeated glucose measurements on our normalised plant sample population varied by just two per cent, way less than the typical differences we found of fifty per cent. Finally, enzyme characterisation and assays follow the identical techniques and procedures we describe in our two most recent papers.' Taking a deep breath, I finish with a flourish but also a word of caution.

'I hope we're not running before we can walk, Andreas, but I've also drafted a paper, or rather a short communication, using these results because it seems clear to me that there's a significant story to tell here. Particularly, if it leads to some new work and funding opportunities.' I hand over my draft of the short communication to what looks like a bemused or even astonished professor. Andreas briefly scans my text and looks up.

'Quite honestly, Kay, I wasn't expecting this but perhaps, I should have. Look, it's getting near lunchtime. Why don't you go and have some lunch and leave me to my crispbread and yoghurt so I can read through this draft thoroughly? I suggest we meet back here at two-thirty. Happy with that?'

'Very,' I reply. 'Just one final thing. If this technique could be scaled up, it might offer real benefits to cereal farmers around the world. I had a brief word with Mila, you know my star student, before she left for Nairobi this week. She said her institute would be extremely interested in such research. But I'm not sure if I've done enough justice to the scope and impact of the techniques' application in the real world. It needs your overview of current and future work in the discussion section if you think that's justified.'

'Okay, I'll have a close look at those aspects too. Time for lunch.'

Eating alone in the senior common room is a blessed relief as I'm totally absorbed with thoughts from this morning's meeting. Believing a hearty meal is essential before going back to Andreas, I choose the Spanish omelette with an indulgent rhubarb crumble and custard to follow. Overall, I'm confident with the results and conclusions but unsure how Andreas will feel about rushing ahead with drafting the short communication, but I'll soon find out. When I return to Andreas' office, I notice he's behind his large dark oak desk, bespectacled, busy writing some notes on a large sheet of paper. Feeling nervous, I sit down on the other side of the desk and wait for him to finish. He looks up and is direct and to the point.

'Kay, as requested, I've drafted two paragraphs on the potential impact of this work and the need for new research and development to scale up the technique so it can be of genuine economic value to cereal producers and farmers around the world. This particularly includes parts of East Africa, Japan, and the Far East. Hope you don't mind but I've also added a short paragraph on how new seed types might be developed from the plants enhanced with these derivative enzymes; it's a further novel and exciting strand of research that may flow from your work. Otherwise, no need to labour the point, the results speak for themselves. Sometimes less is more, particularly in short communications—just think of Crick and Watson's paper on the double helix in Nature.'

'We need to get this information out there and quickly; well, I say we but I mean you. It's a brilliant example of superb innovative research, joined up thinking with wide application to the real world. If you're happy, make the minor changes I've marked up, add these paragraphs, and submit them for peer review. Copy me into your letter to the Elsevier Editor. Your name is as lead author, including Mandeep of course, and please refer to the Station and the Leeds company for the loan of the resin-based ion-exchange columns. Have I made myself clear?'

'Stunning work, Kay. You should be proud of yourself. Such intuitive research is rare nowadays and impressive. But let me finish on a personal note, Kay, if you don't mind. I'll ask again, are you planning to take a holiday any time soon?'

Catching my breath, I try to compose myself and look steadily into Andreas' blue-grey eyes. 'That's wonderful, Andreas, thank you so much. I didn't expect that. I'll let Mandeep see the draft of course and keep him and Aden up-to-date.

And, oh yes, I'm taking mum to York and then to Scarborough for two weeks to try and get away from everything. It'll be a nice treat for both of us.'

'Very good, just leave me a contact number just in case the editor wants to quiz me. Otherwise, get that paper submitted pronto, then go and enjoy yourself; you deserve it.' Andreas smiles broadly, and comes around from the other side of the desk to escort me to the door, but not before he gently pats me on the shoulder a few times as he might to one of his children. Thinking how honoured to be considered as such, I leave the office shaking my head in disbelief. A distant York Minster is bathed in sunlight on this balmy August afternoon; it's teatime on the terrace of the old Principal York Hotel next to the city's main station. We see a train departing for the north while waiting for a large pot of Assam Bop tea, some slices of fruit cake, scones and cream. Mum admires the historic terrace with its view over to the Minster and city walls before glancing down at a table laid with a beautifully ironed white tablecloth and silver cutlery. She takes a deep breath and looks lovingly over towards me ready to say something.

'Really not sure why you want to spend all your hard-earned money on this lovely tea and expensive hotel, my love. It's becoming a habit; must have cost you a fortune for just a couple of nights. Lovely treat though, it has been years since I was last in York. Dad used to drive me over here sometimes for the day so I could pick up my dress material from a little haberdashery close to the Minster. It's probably not there anymore.'

'You never know,' I reply. 'We can walk around the minster and along the river tomorrow if you like.'

'Oh yes, Kay. But why did you choose York to start our holiday?'

'Well, that's easy, because it's on the way to Scarborough.'

'Scarborough! Oh, darling, what a lovely thought. Why didn't you tell me earlier?'

'I wanted to keep it as a surprise, Mum. I've booked us into a nice bed and breakfast near Peasholm Park for ten days. It's close to South Bay and if the weather stays fine, we'll have a proper holiday together; might even take a dip in the sea.'

'Have you come into some money or something?'

'No, Mum, it's not so expensive and I've told you before, my lecturing job pays well enough. I even put a bit aside nowadays. Just really want to share this holiday with you, it's long overdue. I've neglected you.'

'No, no, you haven't, my love. That's nonsense. You've got your own life to lead but it's lovely you want to spend this time with me; it means a lot. Did you know dad and I went on our honeymoon to Scarborough in 1936? It was the same time as the Duke of York visited, you know Prince George, our future king. We had a lovely time. Mind you, you should've seen the crowds on the beaches in those days.'

The young waitress dressed in a too-short, tight-fitting black skirt with an even shorter white pinafore places the teapot and cake stand delicately onto the tablecloth and pours the tea. After a few minutes, I help myself to a scone, cutting it in half with some precision while mum takes a slice of the fruit cake. My thoughts race ahead as I've never properly decided on when is the best time to talk to mum about the attempted rape, as Mila calls it. This seems as good a time as any as we're together for the holiday to talk it through if she wants to. But I keep asking myself if I'm doing the right thing.

My heart is in my mouth at the prospect. Almost biting my lip, I slowly start to describe what happened in an as calm, matter-of-fact way as possible. She says little as I go along but I can see the shock in her eyes as she listens intently, her mouth slightly open. Coming to the end of my story, she suddenly grabs my hand from across the table. She's shaking as she squeezes it tight and doesn't let go. Staring down at her lap as if ashamed, she speaks slowly in a low faltering voice.

'Oh my god, oh my dear. I'm so sorry, I'm so sorry. If only I'd known. Why didn't you say something at the time? Did that man hurt you? Did he do anything to you, tell me?'

'No, Mum, really, he didn't. He pushed me to the ground and was going to. I could tell he was getting all excited but he didn't do anything because I screamed and the farmer came along just in time. But it scared me a lot. It opened my eyes to the ways of men in a bad way I suppose.'

'Oh, why didn't you tell us? Why? If your dad was at home, he'd have done something, you know that.'

'Because I felt and still feel a little guilty, Mum. I thought I was to blame walking across the fields and answering back to those men. And I didn't want dad to get into trouble by doing something silly. Who knows what he would have done? So I stayed in my room and became more and more nervous around boys and found it difficult to concentrate on my books or anything for a while.'

'Is that why you changed so much in your teens? We couldn't understand what was happening. We thought it was all hormones at the time. You used to be such a sunny girl, you loved the countryside, the animals and the flowers. And we always thought it best to let you enjoy your freedom and you were such a sensible girl getting on so well at school. You loved your books; the teachers thought you were set for some top exam results.'

'That's why I'm explaining what happened to you now. I've kept putting it off and still don't know if this is the best time, but let's hope so. We're together now so we can chat about it more if you want. It would have been my wish to explain what happened to dad too but that time has gone. You see, I loved that freedom you gave me; wouldn't have missed it for the world. It led me to what I do now, it's who I am, Mum. Yes, I had to go out to work and study for exams in a different way, but in the end, it hasn't held me back. In a funny way, I think it helped me be clear all those years ago about what I wanted to do with my life, working in the laboratory and in the fields.

'You helped me get that first job at that animal feed place, remember? So, thank you, Mum, from the bottom of my heart.' I lean forward, put my arm around her shoulder and kiss her cheek. 'But it's time to say something. I've thought about it long and hard and I need to be honest about it all, hoping you'll understand.'

'Well, you continue to surprise me, my girl, but I'm glad you've said something now. It's true, I dread to think what your father would've done.' She hesitates and stares at me with eyes that glisten with emotion. 'Did, err, does this what shall we call it assault, still make it difficult to meet boys, well men now, of course?'

'Yes, it did for quite some time, Mum, but not now. In fact, I had a boyfriend when I first started my research at Manchester, a chap called Simon Gardner. He was doing some very weird physics research which I could hardly understand.' Mum's looks surprised as I try to restrain a laugh.

'Why didn't you bring this chap home or something?'

'I know, Mum, maybe I should've, but it didn't last long, afraid I found him rather boring.'

'Boring, blimey, girl, you've got high standards. Most men can be boring in my experience. All they're interested in is football and drinking pints down the pub.'

'Not all men are like that. He wasn't all that bad but just too much theoretical physics for me; a bit too detached and intense in his head, away in the clouds at times. Maybe I'm over fussy but you never know, one day.'

'Well, don't leave it too long, my girl.'

We smile as the tension lessens. It's a real relief to see how her mood is settling down, however, I need to change the subject and thank goodness, she's happy too.

'Mum, I'm doing what I want to, and this is an important time in my career. You know that special project I told you about; well, it's gone amazingly well and Andreas, Professor Mikkelsen, asked me to submit a paper for publication because the results are so exciting. They may be a real scientific breakthrough and even help to develop the way modern agriculture works around the world, so there's no need to worry about me. I'm very happy.'

There's a happy silence as we tuck into some more tea and cake. Mum looks a little weary so I suggest we take a quick nap before an evening stroll and a meal in the hotel restaurant. She agrees but not before she insists on hearing more about my new research and what it might lead to. As we leave the tea table, she turns and gives me a huge hug. We can barely hold back such tears of relief and love. It's a comforting omen for the holiday ahead with the result that our stay in Scarborough goes just as I'd hoped. Over the ten days, we continue to chat about my latest project as well as try to understand more about dad's illness.

Only once or twice does mum reflect on the details of my teenage attack. Otherwise, she increasingly relaxes as we enjoy fish suppers and I'm shown where they visited as newlyweds. We climb Oliver's Mount, go swimming off South Bay beach, and even compare our tans for the first time in many years. Mum is always adorable and I love her as any daughter would but she's also a best friend, a feeling I know we share. We return home in good spirits, except just hours after I get back, there's a phone call from Andreas. He's been trying to contact me for at least two days, so I ask what's wrong.

'Nothing wrong, Kay. Only I showed your draft short communication to one of my tame MAFF officials attending our latest project review meeting. He called me back the next day to ask if you'd go to London next week and present your findings at some inter-departmental meeting. Kay, something's going on with this new government but I'm not sure what. Can you prepare something?'

A week later at the start of September, I find myself in the bowels of a grey modernist government building just off Victoria Street in the city of Westminster. In front of me is a group of mostly middle-aged men in very grey rather poorly fitting suits listening intently to me going through my research project. I've entitled the presentation "Cereal Metabolism Amplification using

Modified Photosynthesis Enzyme Technology". No one has interrupted me yet, although I spot one or two of them taking notes and whispering to one another.

Their chairman, Dr Malcolm Edgerton, is a thin, bespectacled balding man wearing a bright yellow kipper tie that's a little at odds with the rest of his persona. Edgerton met me on arrival and I recognised him from one of his rare visits to see Andreas. He introduced himself as the deputy chief scientist for the ministry, but he didn't say which. He thanks me at the end of my talk and asks for questions. A profound silence follows as I nervously collect my papers together. A small group at the far end of the room start to chatter amongst themselves, it's rather disconcerting.

Have I pitched the talk at the right level, did they understand it, do they care? Who knows, I ask myself. Then, this youngish chap in a sharp-cut navy-blue suit perched right at the back of the room stands up and asks if I've any thoughts about scaling up the enzyme amplification process via either the production of derivative enzymes or the hydroponic exchange process itself. This throws me off for a moment, so I end up telling him I've no concrete ideas for either but think it's important at this stage to widen the scope of my research to include other cereals and some of the other photosynthesis enzymes.

He nods knowingly and adds, 'Quite so, and would you be investigating the raised sugar level effects on plant growth in any of this new work too?'

'Absolutely,' I reply. 'It's one of the most surprising results from the research so far.'

He nods again. Edgerton interrupts and asks whom I know at the Station and if they've been helpful in supporting my work. I smile while mentioning Aden and Mandeep.

Edgerton says he's very pleased to hear that, looking knowingly at the group of faces in the room and adding quite forcibly, 'Sometimes, Dr Levine, their work is quite forgotten and underrated just because it's out of sight in the Wolds.' He closes the meeting, again thanks me profusely, and asks if I'll forward twenty reprints of my short communication to him personally once published. He invites me to join him for what in his words, 'Are a surprisingly tasty finger buffet with a good selection of red and white wines.' I'm hungry after an early start, so I make a dash for the food.

Everyone at the meeting seemed friendly enough and came up to me for a quick chat during lunch. They recite their names and departments, but unfortunately, they're soon lost on me. But as I'm about to leave, the questioning younger chap walks up and gently shakes my hand.

'Splendid talk, Dr Levine, spot on. Hope you weren't too intimidated by all those serious-looking men.' He follows with a slight grin above his very closely shaved chin.

Taken aback, I reply, 'It's not the first time I happen to be the only woman in the room and it probably won't be the last, but I'm glad you found it useful.'

'Quite so, quite so. By the way, my name is Jeremy Winstanley. I'm a member of the Science and Technology Group within the cabinet office and I've a role in trying to get lots of different government departments to talk and hopefully work together. Not always that simple you know.'

'I didn't know,' I reply rather bluntly.

'What are your duties at Manchester, Dr Levine?'

It seems rather trite to explain what I do but I reply anyway. 'As a lecturer, I teach undergraduates the core elements of biochemistry in plants, supervise postgraduate research students as well as run my own research projects under the direction of Andreas Mikkelsen,' while adding how it's a pleasure to work with him.

'Top man, Dr Levine, top man.'

As I turn to leave, he raises his voice slightly and comes to face me directly. 'What plans do you have for your future at Manchester, Dr Levine?'

'To carry on with my research, of course. This latest project raises more questions than answers so there's plenty to do.'

He has a glint in his eye while his mouth attempts a smile. 'Absolutely, Dr Levine, glad to hear it and well, cheerio, I'm sure we'll meet again sometime soon and thank you for coming. It's been most enlightening.'

Sitting back in a shabby colourless seat on the train back to Manchester, I look fondly over the burgeoning green fields through a dirty window that's magnified by the glare of the late autumn sun. My thoughts are muddled as I reflect on the substance of the meeting. It wasn't a typical academic research lecture; the audience was an odd mixture of individuals, some scientists for sure but others were government officials with strange titles. What do they want from me and why does this rather enigmatic distinctly suave Jeremy Winstanley, with the posh public-school accent and smart suit, seem so confident we'll meet again, and soon?

Part Three
Chemistry

Chapter 8

Jeremy Winstanley is not a jazz fan and certainly not a disciple of any strand of chaotic modern jazz fusion that I'm familiar with. He's clearly dismayed when I suggest we meet at Ian Carr's Nucleus concert one evening in late September 1970. Winstanley knows Cambridge from his student days but insists he's not aware of its modern jazz club that has sprung to life on the edge of Cambridge's ageing Kite district. It's close to Midsummer Common just off Fitzroy Street and the evening air vibrates with the sounds rising from the club's rather dingy and smoke-filled basement. Jeremy looks a bit overdressed as he picks his way through the standing audience spellbound by an exotic mix of Indo-jazz music emanating from a rather basic small stage.

Everyone listens intently, transfixed apart from an occasional bout of sedate applause following a solo that finds its way through to the surface of a hypnotic jazz rhythm. He grimaces as he heads for a scarce wooden seat at the rear, carefully studying my face to identify the start of a dark beard that needs some attention. No doubt he's feeling worried that this quite valuable scientist is going native and in what his friends in the foreign office might think. 'It just won't do,' I mutter to myself in mock indignation and a state of mild intoxication. He attempts to sit down trying not to interrupt a major riff in the music; unsuccessful, he forces a smile as I mumble some words in his ear.

'Hi, Jerry. Glad you found the place ok? Sorry if it's a bit noisy but the first session is coming to a close. I'll be with you in a while.'

Jeremy looks puzzled and offers a sardonic grin. 'Glad you can tell. We'll speak soon. Can I get you a drink?'

'Yes, please. A pint of Abbott would go down well.'

Jeremy immediately sneaks away heading for a small bar at the back of the room to wait. After a raucous round of applause, I arrive at the bar and he gesticulates upstairs and shouts a half command.

'Can we please go upstairs to the main bar? It might be more discreet and certainly quieter.'

Avoiding the urge to laugh, I nod knowingly. 'Good with me, let's go.'

Sitting directly opposite, he delicately sips some light shade of red wine and opens the conversation.

'Glad you've fitted into Cambridge life so well over the past nine months, Paul. You obviously like the place. On your own tonight?'

'Afraid so,' I reply. 'The engineers are undertaking a pub crawl down the Mill Road as we speak, followed, I suspect, by a late-night curry. And our chemists are attending a stag night at the brutalist architectural delight that is the university centre. They may even meet up at some point, god help us.'

'The university centre. Is that off Mill Lane near Scudamore's punts?'

'Yes, it is. I thought you knew Cambridge pretty well, Jerry.'

'Must be after my time, thank goodness. Are you still happy with your accommodation, it's nearby I believe?'

'Yes, very close, just around the corner, in fact. I like the Kite area, plenty of good curry houses and takeaways nearby if I get desperate, and the flat's very spacious and affordable. Mind you, I don't know how you found it, digs are in short supply in this town.'

'Many students live in college of course, as I did. Father's Provost of Gonville and Caius and it's his sister who owns your flat. She's living in New Zealand with her husband, a professor of pharmacology at Massey University. That's how the flat became available.'

'What did you study, Jerry?'

'Natural Science Tripos, but struggled rather too many May Balls.'

'Sorry to drag you to the club tonight but you said it was very urgent. The band is quite famous and I didn't want to miss out on their only gig in Cambridge, but it's probably not your cup of tea.'

'No, not quite. More of a Monteverdi fan myself.'

'Vespers 1610, clever piece, polyphonic psalm settings moving away from the contrapuntal. Heard it at St John's College chapel just a few weeks ago. The trouble is, I got switched on to this modern jazz stuff by listening to all those local radio stations around Saginawbay. They don't have the Third Programme over there, you know.'

Jeremy looks slightly wide-eyed at me. 'It's called BBC Radio Three nowadays, of course, Paul.'

'Oh, seems to have been a lot of changes while I've been away. Not all of them good I suspect.'

'Yes, quite right.' There's a real sense of urgency in his voice as he shifts in his seat. 'Well, anyhow, first of all, very glad to catch up with you face to face at last after what seems a very long nine months. Thank you for all those telephone chats and your timely monthly reports. You've done a superb job in difficult circumstances. The department is well pleased. Professor Kaplan at Southampton is also delighted with your contribution and very much looks forward to the collaboration going forward and from what I've heard so does the team you've built up.'

'That's a relief, I must say it was a bit of an odd meeting with Kaplan in the New Year and especially for him to allow me to butt in and help some of his own research team. Not sure what to expect, after all, he was my PhD external examiner.'

Jeremy's face takes on an intense character. Speaking softly, he continues. 'Look, Paul, I wanted to meet now to brief you on certain decisions that have been taken and what's about to come your way with regard to the project.' He takes a small notebook from his jacket pocket and writes something down before handing it to me. It reads "PANDORA".

I wince and grin all at the same time. 'Is this what the project's going to be called?'

Jeremy nods determinedly while placing the notebook back in his pocket.

'Does it imply that the powers in charge don't really know what's about to come out of the box?'

Jeremy smiles thinly and pompously announces, 'Let me say I hope, correction, I'm sure the planning and the quality of your staff will provide a high level of predictability. Although research is always research, our ministers are fully aware of the risks. Just for your information, Paul, it's got that name because it starts with the letter P. The previous project was called Odyssey, you know the poem by Homer. The cabinet office likes classical references even if they might shed some doubt on their outcome.' He laughs affectedly while continuing with his rather stern manner.

'The project's full go-ahead has been signed off by the Secretary of State. The budget comes from a newly created government department called Trade and Industry or the DTI. It has responsibility for energy production and science but also includes the old Ministry of Technology. Initial funding is for two years with an option for yearly extensions depending on progress. Most importantly, the project is being run by the science group to which I belong. As you know by now, it's part of the cabinet office linking to all Whitehall departments. The office also includes the chief and deputy chief scientists who report directly to the PM.'

'The deputy is taking a particular interest in this project and is fully aware of all our partners. I can't say much more than that at present. All of this is confidential, at least for the present. That's why we've asked you to become a casual civil servant and sign the Official Secrets Act. I'm sure you'll respect that.'

'Christ, Jerry, this is getting serious. What's next? Maybe I should get a smart suit like yours.'

He laughs. 'No need, you're the scientist, not me. I steer well clear of any laboratory. Just two more things you ought to know before I leave you to your musical chaos. The project will be launched officially at a DTI Press Conference at the RAF Heddington site in mid-November, I'll confirm the date next week. Science editors from the broadsheets and specialist energy periodicals will be invited along. Secondly, you'll be expected to attend and be on the podium to answer questions from the media. Hope you find that acceptable. My press office will help you prepare.'

'You may also be approached by the media for comment beforehand as events like this always get leaked. If approached by any journalist, contact the press office immediately. Don't be tempted to answer what may seem quite innocent questions at this stage. Hope I've made myself clear. Any questions, Paul?'

I try to absorb what Jeremy is saying but fail. My only question sounds a bit panicky. 'Who else will be at the press conference from the project team? Am I going to be left alone? I'm only one cog in the wheel you know.'

'Of course, you're not, Paul; apart from the minister and government officials, the full project management team will be there. But let me make one point clear. Like it or not, you'll be one of the main faces of the project to the government, the press and the public. As I made plain months ago, this project is about the delivery of a viable local energy supply network via an army of innovative portable energy units across the UK, and perhaps a lot more besides. In the end, it means these people will expect to see some professional-looking equipment that is rugged, fully tested, and scaled up ready for manufacture, and not some amateurish laboratory prototypes.'

'Is that fully understood by you and your team? There's big money going into this project, taxpayer's money, and in many ways, the scaling up of the engineering and performance testing for manufacture is key to its, sorry, our success. Paul, you're the beating heart of this project and everyone who works on it. Rightly or wrongly, people will expect you to know something about almost everything. You don't need to be the leading expert, but you'll need to give the impression you are on top of all aspects of the science, engineering and delivery. It means keeping an ever-watchful eye on the overall prize for UK Ltd, and especially for our current government. Sorry to spell it out so bluntly.'

I feel my jaw dropping and struggle to say anything useful. Jerry has the last word.

'Don't look so worried, Paul, you'll be fine. We wouldn't have selected you for the role unless we had good evidence you'd cope. We checked out most if not all of your academic contacts over recent months and you pass muster. Otherwise, if that's all, I'll say goodbye and see you on press day. Good luck.'

I order another pint of Abbotts and return to the gig; the band are well into their opening piece. Everyone is listening to another complex melodic strain of Indo-Fusion music but I'm totally distracted by what Jerry has said. My mind is in flux, so I leave to wander through the narrow poorly lit streets of the Kite and head for Midsummer Common. As I walk along the bank of the Cam towards Jesus Green, I look back and try to make sense of what's happening in my world. My thoughts stretch far and wide.

They go back to my arrival at London Heathrow just before Christmas. How I'm met by this well-spoken and smartly dressed official called Jeremy from some Whitehall department that I've never heard of but who seems to know Rupert Grenville, this embassy chap I'd met in Saginawbay. He's considerate and anticipates me spending Christmas with my family in Boston but wants to let me know he's arranged some accommodation in Cambridge. Everything moves quickly after the holidays and my two weeks with the family certainly prove difficult.

Although happy to see me, I'm forced to explain why I've suddenly come back to England to an increasingly sceptical and bewildered father. Fortunately, mum is the opposite and naturally pleased despite a struggle to recognise her only son sporting Midwestern cowboy clothes and a quasi-American accent that's too weird to be true. They wonder why I'm moving to Cambridge, which is tricky as I know so little myself. In the end, I tell them it's an important government job and pleased to go along with it.

But the real struggle is adapting to arriving back in Boston and dear old Blighty after so many years in Michigan. It was such a strange experience and made me realise how cut-off I'd been from a large part of the world, and a world I thought I knew. In truth, I'd lost track of the news from England; so much so, that I'm still surprised how much things have changed and how I still need to catch up. Such as the so-called Swinging Sixties that seem to have passed me and my parents by. On the other hand, shop prices have gone through the roof while some European countries struggle to get oil supplies from the Middle East; the TV shows a war in the region, which seems to be making matters worse.

All this seems so strange as the price of gas and hamburgers on Saginawbay's main street never seemed to change from one year to the next. Perhaps I just didn't notice as I rarely travelled outside of Michigan State and after all, the US is such a big country. Then there's British politics which I take a greater interest in after my first few months back. It's amazing how people's attitudes towards the government of the day have changed. Everyone seems angrier with authority in all its forms. They aren't sure what the next government will do next, and there's this general election on the horizon too.

Dad seems so angry too, he told me there's a shortage of coal for the power stations after the coal miner's strike the previous October. He showed me some old newspaper cuttings hinting at bombs about to go off in England during the summer months because of riots in Northern Ireland's Derry and Belfast. Lots of people have been killed and buildings blown up, it looks like it's only a matter of time before the bombs cross to the mainland. Apparently, dad's neighbours with sons in the army are posted to Belfast to construct some kind of Peace Wall and their families are fearful as they don't know when the violence will stop.

Dad has always been down on today's young people by complaining bitterly about how young students spend all their time rebelling and not buckling down. He's fed up with the street protests against the Vietnam War and how a couple of years earlier, the French Government nearly got thrown out by students rioting with workers in Paris. Whereas, mum just keeps quiet as she's always been more understanding of the younger generation.

My thoughts hark back to those first two weeks of gloom and doom. They affected me to the point that even now I get a hopeless sinking feeling in the pit of my stomach as I walk by the Cam on this chilly late September evening. And sad too, realising how relieved I was in leaving my parent's house and moving to Cambridge. To a new flat, a new job as a casual senior scientific officer, and a first-class train ticket to go and visit the friendly Professor Kaplan at Southampton University.

It's nearly midnight and I've been walking for nearly an hour. My thoughts are disturbed yet again. This time by the rhythmical sound of water running up against wooden punts. I hear girls giggling and men egging each other on in the distance. The partygoers are close to Jesus Green Lido and College Boathouse, my guess is they're the remnants of my chemists' stag party as their best man is a graduate and oarsman from Jesus College. If so, then how little do they realise what lies ahead and what I will come to expect from these bright young scientists working on Project Pandora? There's a shiver down my spine as I brace myself in the cold damp night air.

There's a sudden fear from Jeremy's words, the fact I'll be facing journalists who assume I'm some sort of world authority on the first generation of battery networks helping to solve the UK's or even the world's energy supply problems. *But I'm no such expert*, I tell myself, *only a minor cog in the wheel of a project that's yet to get seriously off the ground in any practical sense*. And there's my ignorance of the story behind Pandora; how its success depends on a small research group at Southampton University and these young inexperienced Cambridge chemists and engineers parachuted in over a matter of months that I barely know.

My body is in a cold sweat as I walk briskly to my flat. My heart's thumping and my head's racing as I find refuge in my front living room. I tell myself, *To prepare, and get ready, but how? How did I get myself into this position?* This wasn't meant to be any part of my career. Why didn't I just say no to those smooth-talking Washington diplomats nine months ago? *Serendipity, not again*, I tell myself, while sitting in front of a fierce gas fire spluttering into life. All my senses tell me to get a grip, and quickly. Sleep is impossible, so I pour myself a large glass of bourbon, which I gained a taste for from all those balmy nights in my favourite Saginawbay bars.

How can I cast the story of Pandora in the round so that it's not too buried in the minutiae of day-to-day research? I turn to some notes from my first of many visits to Southampton University. But I struggle to concentrate as my memory drifts towards a curious first encounter with my illustrious external examiner and, originally, rather a scary vice chancellor, Professor Charles Kaplan.

Closing my eyes, I recall it was the middle of February and how there's sleet on the pavement as I marched into the impressive building housing the vice chancellor's office. It's a large office but its grand occupant is strangely smaller in stature than I remember, quite unassuming. He makes every effort to be friendly calling me by my first name. He asks if I'd enjoyed working with the Ostermanns over the past four years. To my surprise, he seems to know a lot about me as he goes on to relate how he was once a postdoc at Princeton for some years just after the war.

Making the point that US universities seem to have a lot more cash for basic research compared to the impoverished Brits. A good part of our conversation that day quickly returned as it was not what I expected from Kaplan.

'Probably a bit surprised to be dragged back to Blighty and meet up with me again, eh, Paul? To tell you the truth, so am I but the world turns in mysterious ways, doesn't it? Anyway, let me get to the point. I've been asked to brief you on a project that you've been seconded to work on. Knowing Mr Winstanley from the cabinet office, he's probably said extraordinarily little about it so far. However, I know he's asked you to sign the Official Secrets Act, although I'm still not quite sure why.'

I shared his surprise, nodded, and made a similar point. Kaplan just shook his head and continued.

'Well, ok, it's done, let's move on.' He then explained how he and a group of other vice chancellors from the larger research universities meet regularly with the deputy chief scientist to share information on their latest research. 'It's usually quite a tedious affair, often a chance to grumble about the state of research funding in this country, but with a government official they hope has some influence on policy. However, the previous month I'd mind to mentioning Miriam's work; that's Miriam Handley, I'll introduce you later. She's one of our senior research fellows. Never quite sure what to call them nowadays, eh? Bright girl, very lively and fun to be around. A bit militant if you know what I mean, Women's Lib and all that. You'll like her.

'Anyway, for some years, she's been looking into new types of battery systems called enzymatic bio-batteries. To be honest, she has a group of three, a postdoc and two postgrads. It's not strategic work for our school but we like to speculate on occasion with some genuine blue skies research. It's got some research council money behind it. Sorry, Paul, let me get on with this story. Well, I casually mention how her work has been going very well when both the deputy chief scientist and this chap, Jeremy Winstanley, who attends these meetings, eyes suddenly light up; they get quite excited.'

'There follows a lot of questions and before I know it, they're down here again quizzing Miriam and looking at her prototype devices. They're so impressed with her research as it apparently chimes with some target list held by their office that addresses the key science priorities within Whitehall, whatever stripe the government happens to be.'

Half asleep, I hear the bells of Great Saint Mary's Church chime at two o'clock. Charles Kaplan's voice still rolls around in my head. He's saying how he'll hand me over into the capable hands of Miriam and how he offers all the help he can to get the project going. Then remembering his final words that felt like a compliment at the time and still do now at this unearthly hour with bourbon burning the back of my throat.

'Paul, have a word with Miriam's postdoc, James Alonso. He's quite excited about your short paper on automated test rigs for assessing battery performance, particularly your attempts to calculate a battery's so-called energy retention levels. Seems to think they're an important factor with their prototype devices; says they could be a real "showstopper", as he calls them.'

Sometimes doing nothing is a good decision. Sometimes letting nothing happen is the right move. And sometimes falling asleep and waking up at ten o'clock the next morning in your armchair overheating from a glowing gas fire is just the ticket. The shock galvanises me into action. I shower, eat a good breakfast for once, and even try to dress smartly before mounting my newly minted Husqvarna Sportsman road bike to travel to ex-RAF Battle of Britain station at Heddington. This large historic site just south of Cambridge is where I've my office and laboratory.

Riding out of Cambridge in the cold light of day, it's blatantly obvious that I'm no form of an expert on enzymatic bio-batteries and kick myself for not probing the experts more once they'd moved on-site. Miriam certainly is an expert and will bamboozle any journalist who wants to listen on the subject. But I need to talk with some authority on the topic; hardnosed science journalists, chief scientists, and even ministers of the Crown will expect me to know the basics of how things work. So I'll speak with Miriam this morning and ask her to go over what she told me at our first meeting and try to understand what, if anything, has changed over the past nine months.

Just for once, she isn't at her laboratory bench tinkering with the prototype, so I poke my head around her office door and offer to take her to lunch; she accepts with a smile. As Kaplan repeatedly delights in telling me, Miriam is a larger-than-life individual with a cheerful personality who loves what she does. She's not difficult to like and it's great fun working alongside her. A tiny lady in her mid-thirties, I've rarely seen her without her old-fashioned voluminous white laboratory coat. She's an intense figure, so it's easy to accept that some people may find her more than a bit intimidating.

Like many a dedicated scientist, she expects everyone to have the same enthusiasm as her; sadly, some people don't and she'll not suffer fools gladly. Often opinionated, Miriam has little time for government or its officials and prefers working at the laboratory bench rather than attending what she calls pointless badly run meetings. It's an opinion I empathise with. Her husband disappeared after a few years, so she enjoys the time spent with her so-called lads at the bench. Miriam is a fun lady but very direct when help is called for. Not surprisingly, we end up going to the local pub for lunch and sit down with a couple of shandies and some homemade game pie. She's not slow in coming forward.

'What's up, Paul? You look worried. Can't you keep that bunch of young chemists and engineers in some sort of order?' She laughs boisterously.

'Well, yes, but for your information, Miriam, the chemists were out on the piss last night at a stag do, heard them trying to punt along the Cam to Jesus College at God knows what time. Don't expect to see much of them today. And not sure I'd want to get too close to the engineers either since they were on a pub crawl with a late-night Indian along Mill Road.'

'They're only young graduates, Paul. They need to let off steam after all, they've been working hard you know.'

'I know, Miriam, and by the way, I'm not so old.'

'Well, you look it today. Did you get any sleep?'

'Not much and that's why I need your help today. Can you spare an hour or two this afternoon?'

'Of course, anything for you, sweetheart.' She giggles.

'Enough,' raising my voice for effect. 'Look, I've been so absorbed in building and commissioning the performance test rig that I've lost sight of the fundamentals of how this bio-battery of yours works. And more importantly, what's going right and maybe what's not going so well. For instance, I'm still running into loads of problems trying to marry the basic performance computer simulations for your latest prototype with the data sets using our wonderful new state-of-the-art IBM 360 mainframe computer.'

'That should be sorted soon enough, you know that. We've finished collecting data for most of the likely configurations. Not sure we can change much else at this stage, although scaling up may bring us some opportunities. Come on, Paul, what's the real problem?'

'Ok, I had a visit from Jeremy Winstanley last night telling me I'll be one of the faces of our imaginatively called Project Pandora at the launch event in a month's time. I'll need to answer questions and speak with authority on all its aspects. So, I've started to panic, Miriam, and wonder if you could guide me through the principles of operation of your bio-battery once again and the latest changes from your time here.'

'Is that all? Of course, love to. Glad the suits are putting you in front of the firing squad rather than me. Not my thing, darling. Too impatient and I'll end up being rude to those grey men in even greyer suits and that wouldn't do, would it? After all, they're funding my research team right now.' She smiles broadly, takes a large swig of shandy, and then insists, 'I'm hungry, let's eat.'

Miriam and James Alonso are waiting in the laboratory with the latest manifestation of their prototype laid out on the bench behind them. Over the past months, they've provided me with loads of valuable electrical output data for the device and tried to scale up the design to increase its power output with some success. The device is of a more elaborate construction than their original in Southampton but it's based on the same principle. About the size of a large oven, it's a stack of three pairs of electrode plates fixed on top of each other; there's some sort of liquid feed into the top pair.

The electrode pairs are the colour of graphite and there's some thin plastic material between each pair. Liquid reservoirs are attached to the top and bottom with the bottom reservoir half-full of something that looks uncannily like water. The whole device is open to the air.

'Still looks a bit Heath Robinson, doesn't it?' Miriam says. 'But we'll tidy it up a bit if you want before we put it on show.'

'Erm, it's at least a two-year project, Miriam, so it's what anyone would expect from a blue-sky project at this stage.'

'I know, but first impressions matter, don't they? And particularly to those well-suited people. So right now, James and I thought it best to bring you up-to-date in front of the beast. He'll take you through the different component configurations a bit later but first just a reminder of the basic principles to help you in your new role.' Miriam clears her throat; James tries not to smirk.

'First, a bit of history. By chance in the early 60s, I came across this US reference to an enzymatic bio-battery whilst reviewing some theoretical publications from two of their so-called Ivy League colleges. They like to have these Big Science jamborees every year and I was invited to attend several years running; quite an honour I believe. The more I looked at those papers, the more I wanted to get stuck into developing some actual kit. Don't know why because I'm a biologist at heart not a chemist. However, I got distracted by the physical chemistry for some reason that I'd rather forget, too long and complicated a story to go into here.' She chuckles to herself and carries on.

'So, James and I start to produce a prototype not too different from what you see here. And to our great surprise, it actually worked. Let's have a look at what we've got. The top electrodes are covered in a substrate that's fed with a particular glucose fuel in the presence of oxygen. We've deposited some clever enzymes on the substrate to generate electrical energy from the glucose. We're still tinkering with the enzymes and the plastic separator that carries the old hydrogen ions to the other electrode to produce, guess what, lovely water. Yes, that's what's in the bottom reservoir.'

'Not sure if you want me to go into the aerobic enzyme processes involved but most biochemists, or even lowly biologists like me, would know all about them; exciting stuff, eh? The plastic separator keeps the electrodes electrically apart, so the current can flow around the external circuit to end up with a working bio-battery. Our original single-stack version kept going for over two years. It just needs a top-up of the glucose fuel now and again. As you know, most of our time at Heddington has been trying to make sure this scaled-up version is reliable and generates a steady current and voltage. That's where your clever test rig comes in.'

'It'll allow us to automatically assess its overall lifetime performance and the critical energy retention factor as we go big time in scaling up the device ever further. Only generating a few hundred watts at present but seems our men from the ministry want us to enter the kilo or even megawatt range. We've our doubts about that but it's up to your clever young engineers and chemists to sort that out; so it's over to you, Paul.' Her eyes glisten as they focus on me and I suddenly realise why some people find her intimidating. James interrupts and is obviously keen to add to the lesson.

'Can't tell you how exciting it was to read your paper on the estimation of an energy retention factor for the first time? Never thought it was possible. We realised early on how important the factor will be to the commercial success of the bio-battery. By their nature, using enzymes on a substrate must affect overall design and make it less likely to retain much of its energy, say compared to a classical fuel cell or nickel-based battery. There's a need to overcome this limitation as soon as possible. We then read how you dealt with simple metal electrode type batteries and feel sure you can provide the same type of computer-simulated performance data model for our baby and predict which component to change and by how much.'

'Thanks for your vote of confidence, everyone. From what I see so far, it looks like the device's empirical decay characteristics suggest any loss in energy retention is much more complex than I've come across before. But that's why we're here I suppose. Miriam, what's gone well and what hasn't?'

Miriam's back visibly stiffens and she speaks in clipped tones. 'Scaling up to three tiers is fine. Electrical output is good, ampere hours have increased and the energy density is still high. Fortunately for us, even this three-tier beasty is clean and safe compared to some of the so-called gas-based fuel cells being produced right now. However, our biggest problem is trying to maintain its enzyme coverage and glucose supply to the substrate. We treat it as a rechargeable secondary battery; it's very responsive to charging but for how long under full load conditions is still an unknown as it seems to gobble up glucose fuel at a rapid rate.'

'Can't it be treated like a regular fuel cell, Miriam? You know, keep feeding the top electrodes with glucose so the power will keep flowing. Why recharge?' I ask.

James looks puzzled. 'We've never really treated it like that. Couldn't figure out where to get a continuous stream of low-cost high-purity enzyme-compatible glucose feedstock in the first place. I suppose it's a thought, Miriam?'

Miriam casts her eyes sharply at James and back to me. 'It's a thought alright; just wonder if our bosses have had exactly that same thought.'

Chapter 9

Early November and mum is on the phone telling me how she's been invited to this Charity Fireworks Night Party with a nice gentleman, the brother of one of the ladies she makes dresses for and who sits on Leek Town Council. She's not sure if she should go and equally unsure what to wear if she did. Mum has clearly lost some of her self-confidence and needs a bit of moral support. Normally, I phone her every Monday evening as she likes to hear all my news but this call is turning out to be a bit of a surprise as she starts asking for my advice.

'What shall I do, Kay? He's very insistent.'

'Do you like him, Mum? Maybe he's a bit too pushy?'

'No, no, he's fine and very polite actually.'

'Then go, it will do you good but for heaven's sake, wear something warm. That new coat I bought you for a start. We usually get our first frost on bonfire night and you don't want to be walking around shivering.'

'Are you alright, my girl? You sound a bit agitated. You don't think it's wrong for me to go out with him, do you?'

'Of course not, Mum, very happy for you. Dad would want you to have some fun, you know he would.'

'Well, what's wrong then? You're not normally this short with me on the phone.'

'Sorry, Mum, didn't realise. Nothing's really wrong but Professor Mikkelsen has asked me to see him early tomorrow morning, for an important meeting he says. Sounds rather edgy himself, a bit formal, not really like him, so it's making me nervous too. Not sure what it's all about, says he wants me to meet some people. It's probably nothing but I'll call you tomorrow evening and let you know.'

'That's fine, as you say it's probably nothing and your work is going so well, isn't it?'

'Yes, very well, Mum. My new paper has just been published. It's only short but looks impressive; all my postgrad students are complimenting me, so that makes me feel extra special. Don't worry, Mum. Speak soon, lots of love.'

As I put down the handset, I let out a big sigh. It isn't like Andreas to be so mysterious and I'll have to wait a few hours more to find out what's going on. My irritability stretches to wondering what to wear. White blouse, black trousers, and my knee-high black boots. Must wear my boots in case I need to kick somebody. My boots are ready to go into action as I enter Andreas' office and hear a familiar posh-sounding voice.

'Lovely to see you, Dr Levine, I hoped we'd meet again soon. You know Dr Edgerton from MAFF of course. You met during your visit and he's a regular visitor to Manchester.'

Both sit around Andreas' desk with cups of tea and biscuits on a tray in front of them. My shoulders drop instinctively as Andreas catches my eye. He appears uncomfortable, and fidgety even sitting behind his desk. He smiles thinly before remarking, 'Take a seat, Kay. Would you like some tea?'

'No, thanks, Andreas. Nice to meet you again, Mr Winstanley, and you, Dr Edgerton. I'm a bit surprised. Hope there's nothing wrong. Did you get my paper reprints?'

'Yes, indeed, that's why we're here. Excellent paper, quite ground-breaking I would say. What do you think, Andreas?'

'Totally agree, Malcolm. Will open up a completely new line of research which I'm looking forward to your department funding.' Andreas grunts quietly to himself as if it's a regular part of their repartee expected at such meetings.

'May I pick up on that, Professor Mikkelsen, and put Dr Levine out of her misery as to why I'm here?'

'A good idea, Jeremy, please do.'

'So, Dr Levine, now we're all aware from your discovery that it's possible to modify plant photosynthesis enzymes to stimulate the production of glucose in cereal leaf, and how this may, indeed, have a direct bearing on the cultivation of cereal crops. In fact, as Professor Mikkelsen has pointed out, many poor countries in say Africa would greatly benefit from such research to help improve their staple food production levels. I'm also to understand that this is a strong motivation for your research which is to be commended. But I must tell you that your work extends well beyond agriculture.

As such I want to explore how you may help maximise its impact on the different research strands being undertaken across government. That sounds rather grand I know, doesn't it? But that's sort of what I do in the cabinet office. I report to the deputy chief scientist and our recommendations mostly end up in cabinet.'

I look to Andreas and Dr Edgerton for some comment but there's none as Winstanley continues.

'Let me get to the point. As you know, your presentation was attended by several academics and government officials. Amongst them was a Professor John Arrowsmith, who heads up the Department for Alternative Energy Sources at Imperial College and is an adviser to the government. You may remember him?'

I don't and feel unsure how to reply, so I give a faint nod of acknowledgement. Winstanley ignores this and carries on. *Those black knee-high boots are becoming more and more useful*, I think to myself.

'Well, Professor Arrowsmith has been tasked to run a multimillion-pound, multidisciplined research project to deliver a UK-wide so-called Alternative Energy Supply capability for the first time that's based on local networks of a novel enzymatic bio-battery. This start-up project is initially for two years but may well be more; it's funded through numerous budgets within MAFF as well as the Science and Energy Production budgets of a newly-formed government department called Trade and Industry. Manchester's MAFF research budget is now part of that pot of money as is the work of the hydroponics group run by Dr Mandeep Singh at the MAFF Station in the Wolds. He's already a valuable colleague of yours, I understand.'

'You know his name is on my paper and his laboratory trials are vital to the success of our research,' I reply with some tetchiness.

'Yes, of course. Of course, Dr Levine,' he says quickly repeating himself.

'Sorry to be so blunt but how does my work fit into this bio-battery project? I know nothing about batteries.'

'Well, as I understand it, this enzymatic bio-battery uses plant-based glucose as a fuel. The proposal is for you to provide this enzyme-compatible fuel by optimising the enzymatic modification of cereal photosynthesis. Your expertise is needed to generate a fuel stream that ensures this fuel cell can run continuously and is economically viable. You'll have the help of some of our brightest young chemists and engineers to scale up the hydroponic production process for commercial manufacture of a battery being developed solely in the UK.'

'You'll also be able to recruit additional postgraduate staff from Manchester. To sum up, we, I mean this new department, would like to co-opt you to work on this prestige project. It's a significant opportunity for you as it's destined to have high visibility within government circles and eventually, if successful, amongst the general public.'

I quickly interrupt. 'Mr Winstanley, surely there are other biochemists around in the UK or even abroad who could take on my research and apply it to this project and do a good job. Why me?'

'Dr Levine, because anyone who heard you speak the other day, including Professor Arrowsmith, will realise that you're the obvious person, probably the only person, to take on this role. It's that clear, believe me. One other point which I'm detecting from your response so far. This project is not meant to divert you away from your current research involvement in the agriculture sector. Far from it, the extra money and staff that come with it will give your enzyme modification work a real boost. So, what do you think?'

Everyone is looking at me. I stare down at my knee-high boots spattered with mud from a passing car as I enter the department this morning. They provide no answer, so I start to feel defensive and try to stall long enough to give myself time to think. 'Where is this project being run?'

Winstanley is eager to reply. 'From Cambridge; new facilities have been commissioned. Professor Arrowsmith is looking to bring the senior scientific teams together in the next two weeks. There's a government press conference scheduled for the last week of November with a minister present.'

'Heavens, but I can't just drop everything, nobody can.' Catching Andreas' eye, I plead, 'What about my lecturing duties and postgraduate research projects? They'll all need supervising.'

Andreas stares straight back at me. I've not seen him so intense and serious before. He's hesitant but slowly starts to speak.

'Kay, this is as big a surprise for me as it is for you. As Jeremy hinted and will testify as such, this new government of ours, elected only this summer, wants to do things differently with its allocation of scientific research funding.' With a quick glance towards Jeremy, he continues. 'They want to create what they call Big Science that has a real and immediate impact on the public at large and uses the economy of scale only found by working across government departments. That's the message coming out of Whitehall. Am I right, Jeremy?'

'Couldn't have phrased it better myself.' Smiling broadly, he adds, 'You should be a politician.'

Mikkelsen grimaces and quickly continues. Kay, this is a real opportunity for you and I must say quite a coup for Manchester. The vice chancellor is aware and very supportive but the final decision is entirely yours. Just to say that if you decide to go with it, your time away would be considered as a sabbatical, which is not unusual, although you're quite young to be given the honour.' Andreas covets an embarrassed smile. 'I understand you will be part of the civil service in some way but any of your colleagues will still be attached to the university.'

'Your lectureship on return to Manchester is guaranteed; your salary will be unaffected, although I gather there are some extra benefits as you'll be working away from home. Jeremy has also promised to look at the pension superannuation side of things. Another member of my staff will fulfil your lecture duties, you can continue to supervise your research students at a long distance so to speak. Of course, you'll be popping back to Manchester as and when you like.'

Quickly catching my breath, I reply with an abrupt thank you. 'So, Andreas, when do I have to decide?'

'Jeremy would like an answer by tomorrow morning. Apparently, there are lots of things that have to be put in place from his end. Isn't that right?'

'True enough. This approach to government research is new to many of us I can assure you, so there are lots of officials, even the odd minister or two, asking questions and running around as we speak. However, it's been signed off by cabinet.'

'Not much time to lose,' I add wistfully. 'I would like to sleep on it, Mr Winstanley. I'm sure you'll understand and I'd also like a private chat with Andreas sometime soon.'

'Fully understand, Doctor. Until tomorrow morning then. I've decided to stay on overnight, Professor Mikkelsen. I'll get my office to sort out a hotel. Perhaps we could have dinner tonight?'

Andreas nods and thanks Winstanley.

'I know Dr Edgerton wants to have a further chat with you, Andreas, before getting back to London.'

Getting up to leave, I've a compulsion to ask a blindingly obvious question. 'Does this enzymatic bio-battery thing actually work?'

'Dr Levine, I've seen a prototype and it works. Whether it can be scaled up and manufactured to provide a significant contribution to our future energy needs is anyone's guess. It's what we call in government circles "taking blue skies research to market"; it's essentially a sign of a market failure. There are no guarantees, it's a complex and novel design but unless we try, we'll never know. Everyone involved in academia and government recognises this is top-end risky research funded by the British taxpayer. Nevertheless, everyone in the know is optimistic and wants it to happen. I know no more than you in that regard. Until tomorrow morning, Dr Levine.'

This unknown bureaucrat is turning my world upside down. I feel resentful and I don't like him much. But after some thought, I ask myself, is it just me? Stuck in my comfortable and predictable academic world with some sort of control over my day-to-day life? Or have I forgotten how my research over past years is paid for by people up and down the country who have no idea or will not even care what I do? Take mum, for example, even though I do my best to explain to her. But I so much want my work to lead to something good and useful in the world. Don't know why but improving food production for the poorer nations of the world is very important to me.

However, Winstanley's offer makes me realise I'm just a small cog in a very big wheel. Perhaps, I'm just too precious about my work and only want what's best for my career. Most people don't have anywhere near the same opportunities as I do. After a restless evening and interrupted sleep, I see no rational alternative to reluctantly agree and join the project. Next day, Winstanley can't wait to tell me how delighted he is and how I should be assured that my work will continue in its current vein and be of wider benefit to the community with many more publications to follow. He asks if I'm happy to move into some Cambridge Don's accommodation in the next two weeks.

Apparently, he's already arranged for some self-contained rooms that overlook the beautiful Tree Court of Gonville and Caius College. He understands that Don is away on some very long-term sabbatical in Paraguay digging up some old fossils. 'It's just five minutes' walk from Kings Parade and Kings College Chapel, Doctor.' He asks if I've any interest in music as he can arrange for tickets to attend some of their concerts. He keeps talking about his father being rather important in the life of the college. This begins to annoy me but what aggravates me the most is his insistence that I sign the Official Secrets Act.

'Why the hell do I need to do that?' I cry. 'It's ridiculous. We're researching batteries for the public's energy supply, for heaven's sake. What's the secret about that? You're encouraging me to publish in the scientific press so all the results will be made public anyway.'

'Dr Levine, you are quite right of course but this is just routine practice. You're acting in part as a civil servant, so it is expected. You'll be privy to certain restricted information. After all, I've already made you aware of changes in government practice that are still restricted or press embargoed. So please, just treat it as part of your terms and conditions of employment, thank you.'

I glower at him for what seems ages but, in the end, relent and sign. Deep down, everything's happening too fast for me; it all feels too slick and I really don't like Winstanley let alone trust him. Sometimes he's just too many answers for everything. Maybe he's been around politicians for too long, but my mind is made up as a chat with Andreas earlier that morning is quite sobering. He says he understands my reluctance and is very sad to lose me for some years but the budgets for my enzyme characterisation work and the trials at the Station have been commandeered, so I'd have to move in a different direction anyway if I refuse and stay on in Manchester. But he wanted to tell me one thing.

'I've always tried to protect my staff from these budgetary issues but as is normally the case with a new government; it comes in with a new broom and we must all realise that they want to be seen to be making a difference. They are by and large our paymasters. Yes, the university has a certain autonomy but money is always in short supply, no more so than now.'

Andreas says he's confident I'll make a success of the project and should steer the research as much as possible in the direction of agriculture and food supply. He's spoken with Mandeep and Aden Jones; they will support me in every way. Andreas reassures me yet again that there'll always be a lectureship back in Manchester but makes clear his feelings before I leave.

'Don't worry, Kay, keep in touch. Embrace the change and be part of a big project. Enjoy Cambridge, it has a lot to offer.'

My evening call to mum is a big surprise for both of us. I break the news that I'm leaving Manchester for Cambridge. She asks if it's a promotion and thinks it's wonderful that I've got the opportunity. She's excited for me, telling me how lucky I am to go and live in such lovely surroundings. She even promises to visit once I've settled in, adding, 'I might like to bring along this gentleman I'm going to the fireworks with, if that's ok with you, Kay?'

'Gosh, Mum, is this getting serious? What's his name?'

'No, no, my girl. Don't get carried away. It's just nice to have someone to do things with. He's called Eric.' There's a long silence, after which mum suddenly proclaims, 'This move of yours will do you good, my girl. After all, Cambridge is only an hour or so further away than Manchester, so we can still have our teas together, can't we? There must be some nice places to go for a proper high tea in Cambridge.' Within weeks, I can only but agree as I peer out of the window onto the manicured grass and a tight bundle of trees in the centre of Tree Court.

Soon after arriving in Cambridge, Winstanley hands over a dossier of research papers and notes from Dr Miriam Handley of Southampton University. There's a bout of intensive reading as I want to try and get my head around enzymatic bio-battery technology. On the positive side, my temporary home is stunning and I start to feel more at home in the Don's quaint rooms surrounded by my bits and pieces of furniture with plenty of well-stocked bookshelves that share a home for my record collection. Although the Don found a home for most things, he's woefully short of wardrobes, and especially from a woman's point of view.

My first impression from seeing undergraduates and academics cross the Court to High Table each evening is that I'm going to need a lot more formal evening clothes. It's not a total surprise before I'm invited to attend one of their regular college dinners. Next day, I phone mum asking her to look out for some of my old cocktail dresses and scarlet doctorate gown; I plan to pop back home at the weekend, letting her know "it's time to ditch all those mothballs".

Jeremy Winstanley is keen to brief me on Professor John Arrowsmith soon after he finds out Pandora has got the go-ahead.

'You need to know about John Arrowsmith, Paul, it's important.'

This begins to worry me as he goes on to paint a disturbing picture of the man I'm due to report to over the months ahead. Apparently, he's a gaunt man in his mid to late fifties; many see him as an archetypal academic. Quietly spoken but with a sharp mind, and an equally sharp turn of phrase that leaves people in no doubt who's in charge of a meeting or project. He's spent almost his entire academic career at Imperial College. Over the past ten years, he has shown a growing interest in energy policy around the production and distribution of oil and gas from the North Sea and the growth in commercial nuclear power.

Arrowsmith is a regular contributor to top-level international conferences as well as the UK's broadsheet press. He's gathered some top-flight engineers and economists who spend their time leading an unpredictable debate on the benefits of alternative energy sources. Apparently, when the professor speaks, people generally listen, and that includes the government of the day. Jeremy let me know that the professor was on hand to advise the cabinet office a few weeks after the new government was formed this summer. He's a sort of guru according to Jeremy, who continues painting his personality portrait to great effect.

'He's outwardly patient and well-mannered but his fierce intellect makes everyone around him feel intimidated and more than a little anxious. It's as if he can read your mind and as such expects you to do more and think more all the time. He's not comfortable to be around and doesn't like delays or excuses. After just a few weeks in post, he has managed to irritate most of the government officials involved with Pandora. So, Paul, be aware, that he treats lame administrative excuses on managing budgets or staff secondments with utter contempt, so you know what to expect. Such disputes, apparently, came to a head at a fiery but brief Whitehall meeting with the deputy chief scientist.'

With the outcome that within days, Arrowsmith is sitting in our newly decorated conference room at RAF Heddington waiting for the arrival of his specially selected research teams. It's just after nine o'clock on a Tuesday morning; a thunderstorm is shouting at everybody from outside. In fact, it's so dark, I can easily see the lights from the old airfield and the main hangar glows in the rain as a stream of the car's headlights pass through the main gates. I roll up to the gates on my Husqvarna. There's a sole policeman on duty directing visitors to the offices. On reflection, perhaps, I should've shared a car with one of the chemists in my team as I stand up my Husqvarna and remove some of my damp waterproofs.

They've largely protected me from the storm but my shoes are soaked through and my new olive-green corduroy jacket feels damp and crumpled. *Not a good start*, I mumble to myself whilst walking towards the main door where several of my young scientists are collecting. There are some unfamiliar faces too. Amongst them, with her back towards me, a tallish woman wearing a long beige Macintosh, black court shoes, and what looks like a deep blue beret perched on top of closely cropped shiny black hair. There's something strange about her and I look again; I have a sense that her silhouette is familiar.

I follow everyone into the large conference room where Professor Arrowsmith and another austere-looking man are shaking hands and introducing themselves. Arrowsmith is adjusting his dull-looking woollen tie and asks his secretary to ensure there are enough glasses and jugs of water on the conference table. There's a tea and coffee trolley against the wall with plates of bourbon and custard cream biscuits. He walks across and takes one of the bourbons; it's obviously been an early start for him from his north London home, and clearly, he's partial to the occasional bourbon. I can hear Arrowsmith muttering quietly under his breath, 'At last, we can make a start.' Raising his voice, he continues.

'Please, sit where you like, we'll get started at nine-thirty.'

I'm just about to sit down when a familiar voice echoes around the room.

'Paul, what the devil are you doing here?'

'Ping, Ping Chen. I could say the same about you. It must be over three years,' I retort.

'Nearer four, I think, Paul. Great to see you. How are you? How's the US of A? Did you manage to survive the Midwest?'

'Got a bit chilly at times but it was a great experience, lots of fun, and the research worked out well. But the world's a different place now. Where are you based? Still in Manchester crunching those numbers?'

'No, left a couple of years ago. In Whitehall for my sins.'

Arrowsmith taps a glass with his pencil. It's a dull sound as the glass is half-full of water, and sadly, so are the words that follow.

'Ladies and gentlemen, perhaps you can reminisce a bit later. It's time to get started, I think. Paul, will you sit here please?'

My neck and shoulders tense up before I can reply. 'Yes, of course.' I realise that I'm getting increasingly bound to this austere character. He's my boss and it's making me more than a little uneasy. We've never met, with only the odd phone call in the past weeks to discuss the organisation and the commissioning of laboratories. *He singles me out and with that recent warning from Winstanley, my future reality starts to set in; heart pounding,* I tell myself to sharpen up. In front of me, ten people surround the table including the professor's secretary taking shorthand notes.

At the far end, the woman I think I recognised has been hanging up her Macintosh and blue beret. Her back is towards me; she'd turned slightly after Ping's greeting but now quickly grabs a seat and I finally catch sight of her face for the first time. Her large, deeply intense dark brown eyes stare back at me.

There's a millisecond of recognition. Her dark brown bordering on black hair is cut back to a bob. She's wearing more make-up than I remember. Our eyes meet again. She takes a long careful look and smiles. I smile back. Her name echoes around my brain, Kay Levine, Isabelle's flatmate.

Such thoughts cascade through me like a river as I can't quite believe my eyes after all this time. A series of painful and difficult memories start to return. A chimaera that quickly falls away to the stunning presence of Kay wearing a simple white tailored shirt, a string of large black beads and neatly creased black trousers pinching at her narrow waist. There's a flashback to an Agrics party when I first saw her and Isabelle's comment on what defines a French woman. Style is universal and timeless. French style represents its most elegant of forms; if it's black and white, then that style must be Coco Chanel.

I guess Kay must have absorbed so much of that style around Isabelle and her French friends. She's so elegant and sophisticated now, but just as I rise to say hello, Arrowsmith clears his throat, looks down at his notes, and starts speaking in his most deadpan of voices.

He welcomes us all and introduces himself and his colleague, Dr Malcolm Edgerton from MAFF. After surveying the scene, he literally directs us all to give our names and say a few words about our backgrounds. He explains how he's been asked by the government to lead this innovative interdisciplinary research project called Pandora and how it's this new government's first attempt to combine resources across Whitehall and tackle the strategic long-term needs of the UK's energy sector. He confirms that the goal is to produce a scaled-up pre-production model of an enzymatic bio-battery here in the main hangar at Heddington.

The design is to be suitable for commercial manufacture and capable of local installation at key locations across the UK's power grid. And then, to everyone's obvious annoyance, he spends a tedious amount of time on what seems to be an arcane description of his so-called four pillars of research which will combine to successfully achieve our primary deliverable, as he calls it. This project management jargon is going to irritate us all, I'm sure. The first pillar is with Miriam's group who'll continue to develop the bio-battery prototype to maximise energy output and reliability.

Second, my team will attempt to scale up its construction, build on and test the bio-battery's electrical performance and energy retention capability ready for commercialisation. Third is Kay's research which will look to optimise her novel glucose fuel production technique using derivative enzyme photosynthesis of common cereal crops. Finally, after looking up from his notes and quickly glancing over to Ping, he describes a fourth pillar providing mathematical and computer analysis to all groups and developing what Arrowsmith terms as a project critical economic impact assessment tool for the pre-production model.

Alas, as Arrowsmith makes clear, Ping's expertise is urgently needed across Whitehall, so he'll only be on-site for a couple of days a month. The professor ends his diatribe by encouraging us to make good use of Ping's time and expertise. He then somewhat reluctantly directs his attention to a figure in a smartly cut grey suit sitting next to Kay. Maybe I'm not totally surprised to meet Michael DeLeon again after almost a year. After all, as commercial attaché at our Washington Embassy, his job was to initially tempt or even push me to leave Saginawbay. Arrowsmith makes clear that all commercial issues and relations with our international partners, whoever they may be, will be handled by Michael who's on secondment from the omnipresent cabinet office.

The professor's voice gradually fades into the background; perhaps he realises he's addressing a group of experienced research scientists as he offers some half-hearted words on how he's full confidence in the management team around the table, and that he's personally optimistic we'll deliver the project in a timely fashion. Without waiting for questions, he turns to me and declares that I'll take on the day-to-day coordination role across the four groups. He'll review progress every three months with those present but stresses how I'll report directly to him monthly with any major issues.

There'll be a formal review by the cabinet office after eighteen months with a strong prospect of continued funding for another year at least. There's a press conference to launch Pandora in two weeks' time at the DTI's Victoria Road site in town; most of those around the table today will be expected to attend with one or two sitting alongside the Minister of State and deputy chief scientist to answer questions. He ends by asking me to show any new members present around the Heddington site and after rising from his chair, quietly leaves the room followed by Dr Edgerton and the secretary, while on the way grabbing a custard cream and a bourbon biscuit for good measure. *It must have been a very early start*, I muse.

Following this procession, I stand and look around the table. There's complete silence; everyone's looking at me. I'm lost for words but smile manfully and finally blurt, 'Help yourselves to tea and coffee, and biscuits if there's any left.' There are a few stifled laughs as I walk over to the window and catch sight of our two austere scientists being driven away in the back of a chauffeured car just as the heavens open up again. My gut instinct tells me that what happened is a very bad and totally inappropriate way to motivate a talented group of people who collectively hardly know each other.

Someone needs to shift the atmosphere that's been left hanging in the room. But what should I do? I detest Arrowsmith's formality; it never works for me and it won't work here, as I recall my time at Great Lakes and the way the Ostermanns, Jim, Michael, Josie, and myself all worked so easily together. My thoughts continue to drift in that direction until they're interrupted by the sound of a spoon tinkling in a cup and saucer close by. For a start, I wasn't sure it was Paul Wright even when he raised his voice and called out the name Ping. He looks and sounds quite different from how I remember him. We only met a few times at a party or when he occasionally popped around to my flat to spend time with Isabelle. At least, he's smiling back so he must remember me and I'm pleased to know someone amongst all these new faces sitting around the table listening to that severe-looking professor. Paul looks, well, older I suppose, more grown up. Perhaps, it's his dark bushy beard and he's broadened out a bit too. I rather like the natty corduroy jacket which suits his easy, relaxed manner and, yes, he's got a touch of a laconic American accent too.

To my surprise, I'm equally impressed by the background of our so-called management team. Although probably lucky to miss out on having a serious chat with Arrowsmith during my MAFF presentation; his acerbic manner is in sharp contrast to how Andreas might handle things. And then, there's Miriam Handley who seems a real bundle of energy and will be fun to get to know. Dr Edgerton is another familiar face and, in many ways, a reassuring presence amongst the young Cambridge chemist and mechanical engineer, Elizabeth Saxby and Marcus Cochrane. Good job they sat next to one another as they looked a bit fearful of what they were hearing.

Ping, I know slightly through Isabelle; she thought him a kind soul and a super Chinese cook for a mathematician that is; he clearly gets on well with Paul. Looks like he's going to be busy with some sophisticated computer-driven economic forecast models for different government departments including the treasury. Then finally, there's this new face, Michael DeLeon, who was at the Washington Embassy when Paul lived in the States. Paul seems a bit suspicious of him or is it my imagination? He's also gained a slight American lilt to his voice and is quite tight-lipped about his role, which is unsettling. Not sure why but I expected to see Winstanley today, but I'm not disappointed.

Paul's looking out of the window; he appears serious and distracted. Maybe I'll go over and say hello, and find out what's expected of me and what happens next. This old ex-RAF base is a maze of corridors so I wouldn't mind a tour round by our new leader. I grab some tea and wander across.

'Hello, Paul. It's been a long time since we last met in Manchester.'

Paul turns slowly, looks directly at me for what seems an age, and replies, 'Oh, hello, Kay, what a surprise to see you here. How are you?'

He still seems distracted so I carry on with some small talk. 'I'm fine, good to see you too.'

'I had no idea you're involved with Pandora. Should've known I suppose but it's been a bit chaotic these past few weeks. What made you get involved?'

With an ironic laugh and a shrug of my shoulders, I add, 'Didn't know anything about it until barely a month ago. Still quite a shock. I gave a talk at MAFF to all these government types and then a visit from Jeremy Winstanley inviting me to join this secret project. Guess you know Jeremy?'

'Oh yes, I know Jeremy.'

'Well, to be honest, Paul, I wasn't that keen to take up his offer as it takes me away from my research and lectures.'

'So, what or who changed your mind?'

'Well, my department head, Professor Mikkelsen, was told in no uncertain fashion that he's about to lose his agricultural research grant that funds my work. My glucose amplification technique is aimed at improving crop production levels but now it's been drawn into battery development, which I know nothing about. But a change of scenery may not be such a bad thing for me. Anyway, in the end, not much of a choice really, so I'm on an open-ended sabbatical. It's all a bit weird.'

Paul smiles and appears genuinely sympathetic about my predicament as he continues, 'You don't sound too enthusiastic, Kay. Sorry to hear that.'

'That's ok. I'll buckle down, don't worry. It's just disappointing.'

'I'm sure you will, Kay. Please forgive me, I need to get up to speed with your research and will do so I promise. Look, I've been so absorbed over the past nine months with commissioning my test rig and recruiting young Cambridge scientists that I've failed to get to grips with the glucose fuel delivery side of things. From what's been said today, it looks like your part of the project is closely aligned with your agricultural research, so I wouldn't worry too much. I'm sure there'll be every opportunity to publish your findings when they're relevant to agriculture; just make sure you do, eh.'

'I hope you're right,' I reply. 'Will you be able to show me around today? Do you know where my laboratory and office are in this maze?'

'Yes, of course, Kay. First, will you excuse me? I need to speak to everyone before they wander off.'

Paul turns to face the group collected in the room and raises his voice to announce that he'll take any newcomers around the site in fifteen minutes but be sure to grab that last biscuit and meet him in the main hangar. Paul and I then wander along a narrow corridor which eventually opens out into an enormous hangar filled with lifting gear, work benches and some heavily insulated power cables hanging from a gantry. He points to his elaborate battery performance test rig standing in one corner and connected by cable ducts to an air-conditioned computer room.

I'm impressed; this is not small-scale research and his tour makes it clear how busy he's been over recent months. There's a row of furnished offices along one of the corridors leading from the hangar. A suite of well-stocked laboratories snakes off down another corridor. My special chromatography equipment is expected from Manchester in a week or so but apart from that, everything else is in place. There's even a small laboratory for Mandeep to prepare his crop samples. Miriam and I managed to have a quick chat during the tour as she showed me her three-stack bio-battery prototype on a bench close to my own laboratory. I'm starting to feel a bit more comfortable about things.

Paul, however, still appears anxious as he looks to provide some carefully chosen words to the whole research team that I hope will further allay my fears. He stands in front of the prototype bio-battery with a self-conscious grin on his face before he starts to speak.

'Look, everyone, you've all had the formal introductions from Professor Arrowsmith. I must admit, this wouldn't have been my approach today but let's just see what comes out of our Pandora's box.' Everyone gives a collective sigh; Paul just laughs and continues.

'Ok, it can, it will only get better. But the prof is right about one thing, this project will only succeed if our four so-called pillars work closely together. We all come to the project with different science backgrounds, from different angles and with different experiences. I'm here to ensure the project doesn't go off track. You'll soon find out I'm no Professor Arrowsmith.' Paul grimaces.

'So let me lay down one ground rule which I've learnt from my days freezing to death in the Midwest. I'll be moving a large table into this hangar close to where our pre-production bio-battery will be built. Then I'll buy the best coffee machine money can buy and every Friday morning, go down to Fitzbillies in Trumpington Street and buy the stickiest Chelsea buns they've got. At eleven o'clock every week, without fail, we'll meet and put the world to rights. No topic is off limits, even our research.' He smiles broadly and ends with a heartfelt, 'Are you happy with that?'

I see plenty of nodding heads and some relief in people's faces, including mine.

'By the way,' he quickly adds. 'If I'm laid low or overslept, or troubled by tedious civil servant's meetings, then Elizabeth here has agreed to take on the Fitzbillies' duties. If you can't make our Friday morning meetings, then you'd better come up with a damn good excuse for everyone to try and believe when the next time we meet. Ok, that's it for now. Make yourselves at home, our little on-site restaurant is open for business. We need to get our heads together this afternoon for those attending the press conference; my office is next to the computer room so you know where I am.'

Paul has made a good start, I think to myself. *Time to get down to work.*

Chapter 10

Minister of State, Department of Trade and Industry, November 1970...

Ladies and gentlemen, members of the press, I am delighted to welcome you here today at the government's new Department of Trade and Industry for the launch of an exciting, ground-breaking scientific project called Pandora. Just over eighteen months ago, we marvelled at Neil Armstrong stepping onto the moon's surface for the first time. We are in an era of scientific discovery. Technological achievement is coming to the fore and affecting all our lives at pace. And we look forward to decades of invention in computing and portable electronics that will change the world we live in beyond our wildest dreams. But we are also in a world of uncertainty, and no more so than in the security of our energy supply that powers these inventions and is fundamental to our way of life.

In recent years, we have seen energy shortages across the globe with high oil prices and wars in the Middle East. We have also seen serious threats to local energy supplies from civil disruption such as the student riots in Paris, anti-Vietnam War unrest on the streets in many countries including our own, and sadly, the prospect of sectarian violence in Northern Ireland spreading to the mainland. We cannot ignore these threats; the government has a duty to protect and enhance the energy supply mix and infrastructure of this country.

Your new government wants to face these challenges head-on, spearheaded by a strategy of energy diversification that is driven by the UK's world-leading scientists and engineers. There are inviting opportunities ahead with a new natural gas supply from our oil fields in the North Sea and a burgeoning nuclear power industry that offers a substantive clean energy source. But this is not enough to rightfully maintain this country in the top tier of high-growth industrialised nations.

Therefore, I am pleased to announce today that Professor John Arrowsmith, Head of Alternative Energy Sources at Imperial College, will lead a multidisciplined team of seasoned scientists and engineers in Project Pandora.

This government-wide, fully-funded project is tasked to deliver a robustly tested enzymatic bio-battery power supply for local installation across the UK grid as part of an ambitious diversified energy network. This new power source is based on novel fuel cell battery technology developed at the University of Southampton.

The prototype will be developed for large-scale manufacture encompassing the broadest level of commercial involvement and exploitation. It will provide for substantial economic impact on the country's energy supply portfolio. Research will be centred at the government's new multimillion-pound incubator facility at Heddington, near Cambridge. Pandora will initially run for two years with the strong prospect of further funding. Members of the press will be invited to Heddington to see how the project is progressing in the near future.

Project Pandora is the first tangible example of a new way forward in how this government funds collaborative research and drives innovation across the country. It will address the big questions of the day as we face a rapidly changing world. Our experienced research scientists and engineers will forge the way. Other projects will be announced in due course. I am sure you will want to join me in wishing Professor Arrowsmith and his team, some of whom are here today, every success with Project Pandora. I will now hand over to Professor Arrowsmith to answer your many questions. Thank you and good day.

There's a spattering of applause from some civil servants sitting at the front of the audience as the minister leaves the auditorium.

Miriam looks up after reading the government's press release.

'Is that all the minister had to say, Paul?'

Elizabeth and Marcus quickly follow. 'Sounds more like a political exercise than the launch of an exciting new science project. Was the minister up to speed with the brief? Weren't there any questions from the press, Paul?'

It's the first Friday morning get-together after the press conference and I've left copies of the press release on the large table before everyone appears and starts to eat their Chelsea buns. I see Ping and Michael are getting hot under the collar with such comments and look to just about to say something while Kay appears subdued. I must say something about the press conference to those who didn't attend—that's Miriam, Elizabeth, Marcus, and the younger Cambridge scientists, who in the end weren't invited along in the first place. This will be a difficult exercise, so best get on with it.

'Look, everyone, of course it's political. A new government wants to impress in any way it can. That's what you'd expect. And yes, the minister's speech is very much motherhood and apple pie, as my American friends would say. There were a few questions for us on the platform and it must be said that the science correspondents seemed very excited by Pandora. I'm hopeful there'll be some intelligent articles written in journals such as the *New Scientist*, so let's wait and see.'

'Paul's right,' says Kay, greatly to my surprise. 'One question was about our work on enzymes and how glucose is a critical part of the bio-battery. Professor Kaplan answered it very thoroughly, Miriam, as you'd expect. He spent some time describing the role of the enzyme-coated mediator, and how it switches on the electrical energy in tandem with my derivative enzymes that amplify glucose production in the cereal leaf for use as battery fuel. He was very clear on what further research needs to be done and the importance of our joint work in characterising enzymes.

'Ok, there were some obvious questions about when we might expect to see the first scaled-up prototype and its commercial exploitation, but I must say Paul was very careful with any predictions on that score, which is a good thing.'

Michael DeLeon chips in to say how his colleague, Jerry Winstanley, stood in for him on the platform. 'He has a broader knowledge of Pandora and made the point to everyone present, including the minister, that it's very early days to identify any commercial partners, although it's the government's intention to maximise any spin-offs or benefits from the research across what we call our wider government stakeholders using third parties where possible.'

Everyone looks a bit flummoxed by Michael's jargon but I'm more than a little relieved that Kay and Michael have backed me up. I make a point to thank them later, and anyway, their comments allow me to end the meeting on a positive note.

'Just to say, folks, that Kay, Professor Kaplan, Michael, and I had some very good chats with the press after the speeches. They genuinely think Pandora's worthwhile despite the less-than-subtle hype from the government. They told us they'll report our research as factually and as often as their editors will allow.'

This goes down well with the young graduates. There are a couple more questions for me but as best as I can judge, everyone appears fully behind the project, for now at least, despite the obvious scepticism about the political games being played out. However, it's Kay's response that surprises me the most. Over the past weeks, she has been rather quiet, thoughtful, and very serious whenever we bump into each other. Even enigmatic and a little aloof at times but I'm beginning to warm to her as the days go by. Not sure why as we're so different in character but there's a definite presence about her which I find quite attractive.

Maybe it's because she thinks a lot about the values surrounding her research or its importance to the wider world. Who knows, but whatever it is, I'm finding myself drawn to her and wanting to get to know her better. So, I decide to take advantage of Jerry's surprisingly generous nature for once by remembering how Jerry sidled up to me after the conference to say how well it had gone.

'Paul, just to thank you personally for sticking with it over the past nine months. I know it hasn't been easy, being dragged away from that delightfully chilly Great Lakes and parachuted into this unknown project.' He goes on to hand me two tickets for the Festival of Nine Lessons and Carols from Kings College this Christmas Eve.

'I thought you had to queue for them,' I ask.

He just smiled saying his dad, yet again, had had some influence on their allocation and finishing with a characteristic barbed comment. 'I know you love good music, even chaotic modern jazz, so make good use of them; you deserve it.'

As I wander down the corridor to Kay's office, I'm unsure if this is such a good idea as I pop my head around the door. Kay is sitting behind her desk engrossed, as far as I can see, in some analysis of a chromatographic chart with lots of sharp peaks and troughs. Still unclear what I'm doing, I level my shoulders, straighten my back, and stride through the door with an air of indifferent confidence.

'Have you got a minute, Kay?'

'Of course. Come in, Paul, take a seat.'

'Just want to thank you for supporting me at the press conference and our meeting, it was a great help. These events are new to me and I'm not quite sure what our younger scientists make of it.'

Her warm dark eyes linger; her face is relaxed and content. 'They're certainly new for me too, Paul, although I'm starting to learn how securing pots of research funding works in government circles. My old boss, Andreas, has always kept me away from these black arts until now.'

I laugh and note the softness in her eyes, which increases my confidence. 'You probably know a lot more about it than me in the UK. Things move a lot faster and aggressively in the States; well, thanks again.' Hesitating, my hands start to shake but I decide to press on. 'We need to talk sometime about the design of the automatic glucose extraction system for your cereal crops. There needs to be a scaled-up fuel supply for the demonstration prototype at some stage. Marcus and Elizabeth already have some ideas, so it would be good to get our heads together in the New Year. What do you think?'

'Yes, good idea. Sooner rather than later as it's something I haven't given much attention to so far.' She gets up and takes a few paces from around her desk. 'May I make a suggestion?'

I nod eagerly.

'Should we invite my colleague, Mandeep Singh, from the Wolds Research Station to join us for one of these meetings? Perhaps, he could stay for a few days. He has lots of experience in handling crops and his knowledge of hydroponic cultivation and harvesting is vital.'

'Oh yes, please invite him down. No need to ask my permission, do what you need to do. I'd like to visit this Wolds Station myself some time.'

'Righto, he'd like that; he's a very nice man. In fact, Mandeep and the Station staff are important to my work in so many ways. They're the ones who can make sure our so-called cereal metabolic amplification using derivative enzymes is truly viable and of real value to agriculture around the world. It's dear to my heart, but you know that, so I'd very much like you to visit the Station, perhaps when we start our next round of hydroponic trials in early spring.'

'That's a date then, Kay.' I suddenly feel a little awkward as I realise what I've said. Gripping the sides of my chair, I continue. 'May I ask you something? It's not work-related.' Not waiting for a reply fearing the answer, I add, 'I believe you're keen on music, erm, good music I mean.' Clearing my throat, I say, 'Isabelle once mentioned that you liked to go to concerts at the Free Trade Hall.' Her eyes open wide and I worry I've said too much, after all, we've not spoken a word about Isabelle before.

'Yes, I like classical music a lot.'

'Well, in that case, are you staying on till Christmas Eve or leaving for home earlier?'

'Planning to leave Christmas Eve, mum expects me then. Why?'

With just a little irony in my voice, I take the ultimate risk. 'Our mutual friend, Jeremy Winstanley, has given me two tickets for the Festival of Nine Lessons and Carols at three o'clock on Christmas Eve. I'm sure you know all about it as Gonville and Caius is just around the corner from Kings Chapel. I wonder if you would like to go; tickets are like gold dust.'

'Ah well, you do have all the right connections. I thought you had to queue for tickets on the day.' There's a stifled laugh followed by a nail-biting hesitation, and to my huge relief, a "yes".

'I've only ever heard it on the radio like everyone else, so it would be a real treat, thank you. Not what I was expecting,' she says as she smiles broadly and her eyes brighten.

'Well, surprises can be a good thing sometimes, can't they? So, I'll see you at about two-thirty outside Kings College Chapel.'

She conjures a slight nod as I turn to leave and allow myself to breathe again. It's not till I close my office door that I hear myself muttering, *What was all that about? What just happened there and what the hell does Kay think of me now.* The glorious example of late perpendicular Gothic architecture that is the roof of Kings College Chapel is being dusted with a covering of snow as I wait for Paul. I'm early and feeling the cold despite wearing my heavy winter tweed coat and favourite dark red beret. My thoughts run in all directions as I tell myself to relax and try not to show my nerves.

Paul surprised me. His invitation came out of the blue. Although thinking about Isabelle, I'm starting to understand why she liked him so much. Back then, I thought she could do much better for herself. He seemed rather young and immature, perhaps because I was a few years older and he seemed so full of himself. But Isabelle always said he was kind and thoughtful, although a bit boyish at times. She liked his energy and enjoyed her time with him, such as going to the Yorkshire Moors on what she called his Husky motorbike. Isabelle told me she'd grown very fond of Paul and wanted the relationship to continue but didn't know how it could with the demands of their academic studies going in such different directions.

And she's right; timing is so important when it comes to building relationships. Everyone knows that, don't they? The clouds tighten above and I fiddle with my gloves as the temperature drops and snow whitens the manicured lawn outside the chapel. Stamping my feet seems to make a difference as I think back over the past month in Cambridge, mainly getting to know Paul better and realising how his time abroad has changed him. He goes overboard in making time for everyone on the project and how he desperately wants to weld this disparate group together and make them feel an important part of a team.

It must be difficult as he's still quite young and his own research is very demanding; it's so time-consuming but I can see how his personality is very well suited to the task. In fact, I rather envy him despite first having doubts about his so-called US style of doing things. It was a bit brash at first but things have settled down and I now find Paul's increasingly laidback laconic ways along with his rather rugged exterior, long hair and beard to match a real breath of fresh air. Even, although I dare not admit it to myself, his selection of bright check work shirts and blue jeans are rather attractive, and such a contrast to those boring old corduroys worn by the Cambridge set.

As one of my American Master's students used to tell me, "He's real cute". I must admit that one day, I hope he'll give me a lift on the back of his beloved motorbike, that'll be a thrill. Just now I'm wondering if I should invite him back to my room after the concert for a coffee. Will that be giving the wrong message? What message do I want to give? Thinking of messages, what do I tell him about Isabelle since she's written to me on and off from France in recent years and mentioned her move-in with her boyfriend, a senior lecturer at the institute?

Of course, it's none of my business, I tell myself and maybe he knows anyway. What should I do and say? Suddenly, the cold wind grazes my face and I confront my daydream that's run riot. Maybe this isn't a date after all but Paul just doing what he needs to do to make me feel part of the team. My name echoes across the snow as Paul rushes to the chapel entrance and apologises for being late. I tell myself, *Don't overthink things, Kay, as I'm prone to do. Just enjoy the music.*

Indeed, we do. The music is joyous and still ringing in my ears as we look out over a picture postcard snow scene in front of my rooms at Tree Court. I'm not leaving Cambridge till seven o'clock, so there's time for a coffee and I'm pleased Paul said yes. We talk about the concert and I soon realise how knowledgeable he is about music and his love of modern jazz. I can't avoid pulling a face, saying it's just a noise to me but he doesn't seem to mind. He says I'd think differently if I'd been lucky enough to hear all those wonderful jazz radio stations broadcasting across the Midwest and how there's a homegrown modern jazz club right on our doorstep in the Kite.

'Do you know the Kite?' He asks.

I confess I don't, so he explains it's a rather run-down area with rows of terraced houses and some sorry-looking shops. 'Plenty of atmosphere but not much money,' as he puts it, 'unlike the rest of Cambridge.' He lives near the Kite saying how 'The Kite suits me, it's away from the city centre and I feel at home there.' I ask Paul about his time living in the USA and how he had coped.

'It was wonderful,' he replies. 'Best decision, although there are regrets. Saginawbay was a real eye-opener and difficult at first. The folks may speak the same language, of sorts, but their way of life and attitudes are so different.'

Our eyes meet for a moment as I think back to Isabelle. He's hesitant and gulps at his coffee before continuing.

'Look, Kay, like all big decisions in life, they do have consequences. Research opportunities were great, working at the university, spending time around the town and lakeshore were exciting, and I made some good friends.' He turns to look out the window, then slowly turns back to catch my gaze once again. 'But I also lost a special one as you know, Isabelle.'

'I'm so sorry, Paul. I know you were close.'

'Have you heard from her?'

Oh hell, my mind is all at sea as I'd hoped he wasn't going to ask that question, but it was inevitable I suppose. Holding back for a moment, I eventually admit she's written on and off over recent years.

'Don't look so worried, Kay, you can say what you like. That chapter is over for me, although I still feel guilty and sad about what and how it all happened. I'm sure she's given her point of view and I must take a large share of the blame. In truth, it was the wrong time for both of us to settle down in any way. I was young and, well, obsessed with my PhD work at the time to the detriment of almost everything and everybody around me. Has she said anything about her lecturer friend? Be frank, Kay.'

'Oh dear. Well, just to say they've moved in together.'

His eyes drop. 'I see,' he whispers. 'Time moves on for everyone, doesn't it? It did for me big time as I was planning to stay at Great Lakes for quite a bit longer. Then one day just before Christmas, I get kidnapped by these two chaps from the UK Embassy in Washington. They wanted me back home pronto to join some mysterious project. Still not quite sure why I said yes, mind you. It happened so quickly but a year later, here I am. They said it was of national importance, whatever that means, so it's a bit difficult to refuse, isn't it?' Paul starts to laugh. 'So much for my career going up in smoke but I see your career has moved on leaps and bounds in Manchester.'

There's a palpable but tacit silence between us. I take a quick look at my watch; we've been talking for nearly an hour. Paul starts to get up from his chair.

'No need to rush off just yet, Paul.'

I'm still thinking about what he said about my career and how he sees it. Maybe it has moved on, but has it really? Feeling confused, I look to change the subject and end up giggling for some silly reason. Paul eyes me and smiles back waiting for my reply.

'Well, Christmas beckons I suppose, must drive back to Leek tonight and meet mum's new boyfriend, Eric, and get into the holiday spirit.'

A deep furrow travels across Paul's brow as he dons his coat.

'Time to go, I think. Interesting times ahead. So Eric is a new boyfriend eh, that's quite a big deal. Well, you'll want to be on your way soon, I'm sure, as the weather's not great. May snow some more and you've got a few hours' drive.' As he departs, he looks back, smiles broadly, and adds, 'Have fun, take care.'

Paul's last words trickle through my mind as I sit around the table in our sitting room with mum and Eric enjoying a cup of tea on Christmas morning. It's funny or maybe just a coincidence that Eric's first question is straight to the point.

'I bet you've met plenty of eligible intelligent young Cambridge chaps by now?'

All I can do is concoct some enigmatic, although factually correct reply. 'Well, Eric, some are homegrown and some from far and wide.' I wonder what in god's name I've just said whilst trying not to show any emotion.

Mum and Eric look at each other, then at me, with equally blank expressions. Mum offers around more buttered teacakes grinning as I try and restrain a laugh. Awkward, yes, but it's the happiest I've seen her for some time, or maybe it's just me. Early May and Cambridgeshire's large skies and its black-ploughed Fenland fields lie ahead. Kay is driving north in her department's old Land Rover through the towns and villages of March and Chatteris. She's keeping her part of our non-date by introducing me to friends and colleagues at the Wolds Research Station. The sun shines brightly over early crops in full blossom on either side of the road whilst mature spring flowers glisten in the hedgerows. There's the unmistakable sound of a whining kestrel overhead as Kay slows almost to a stop behind a large prehistoric muddy tractor. She's delivering the latest batch of derivative enzymes for trial by Mandeep in his beefed-up hydroponic facility.

Optimistic as ever, she's telling me how this batch of enzymes will help optimise growth yields from three different cereal crops. After a busy three months, it's good to see her so relaxed and she clearly loves being back in the country. While I'm the opposite and feel distinctly uneasy. Not with Kay who's now a good friend and more than just a colleague; in truth, I'm only too aware of being attracted to her more and more each day. No, it's not her but that a vital important aspect of my research is becoming a real struggle. So much so, that when she asks why I'm so deep in thought on such a lovely day, I take the chance to share my burden.

'Sometimes there's too many things going on, Kay, it's difficult to keep any sense of perspective you know. Overall, we've made good progress and Arrowsmith seems happy enough following our last review meeting. And I must say, it's a real bonus that you and Miriam are working so closely together. Miriam told me she was hoping that would be the case as she thinks you might hold the key to finding a cheaper, specially tailored, and more readily available mediator enzyme for the pre-production prototype.'

Kay smiles broadly and says Miriam is a scream to work with and that they have some promising candidate enzymes already.

'Must say, you also seem quite confident about this next round of cereal trials.'

Kay nods vigorously as she slickly runs through the gears at a level crossing.

'If that's so, can we use this batch of crops to evaluate the design of the automated glucose extraction system?'

'I can't see why not,' she replies.

'And are Marcus and Elizabeth involving you fully in their design work?'

'Oh yes, fully, no need to worry there. They're very bright and the design is coming along quite quickly. Their initial assessment of the basic US design concept was very thorough. Using mechanical pulping in a circulatory organic acid system looks like a winner, although they may want to improve the acid recycling step and wash cycle. We need to extract the maximum amount of glucose component from each leaf and fibrous material.'

'Excellent. I wish my work was going so well.'

She turns around and glances at me with a look of concern. Should I confide in her? It doesn't take me long to decide.

'Maybe I'm looking too far ahead, Kay, as my test rig is recording some good performance data for the three-stack prototype. Energy density, component lifetimes, and electrical characteristics are by and large what we were hoping for. Even the computer simulations from the data extrapolated to a low megawatt pre-production bio-battery look good. Our engineers are making good progress in building a fifty-stack pre-production prototype, although it's a pain that Arrowsmith keeps pushing for a hundred-stack unit for some reason. Anyway, all the components are on order, so we'll soon have something to show our masters.'

'So, what's the big problem, Paul?'

'It's the Ping factor. Proving the economic viability of the pre-production prototype without any accurate knowledge of one of the bio-battery's fundamentals, its so-called energy retention factor.'

Kay jerks back her head. 'What's that, may I ask?'

'It's how well batteries retain their electrical energy; depends on the chemical processes involved and their decay rates, a characteristic of the basic design and key components. You know, the electrodes and separators that give the battery life in the first place. The trouble is we need to measure an accurate energy retention factor for the prototype so Ping can check the viability and long-term use of the bio-battery in the real world. At Great Lakes, we got some good results for a more traditional battery design while working with this automobile company from Detroit. We had a fair idea of what it might be from earlier theoretical decay rate mechanistic studies, and our computer programme iterations did the rest.'

'Miriam and James got very excited when they read my paper on the subject last year because they know energy retention is critical to the success of their bio-battery. You see, theoretically, fuel cells and especially biological-type batteries are known to have poorer energy retention. Now I'm no battery expert, so I don't have much of a clue as to what the decay rate mechanism is for a three-stack prototype so the computer is literally just hunting around and turning up rubbish. It's very frustrating and more than a little worrying I can tell you.'

'How do you know it's rubbish?'

'Yep, good question, Kay. Mainly because when we enter the prototype's functional data with a traditional decay mechanism into the computer's iteration programme, it doesn't give the same result twice. It's as if it can't deal with using normal whole numbers or integers to process the data using our current programme. Sounds weird, doesn't it?'

'I'm not really a mathematician.'

'Nor am I but that's what's happening. I've even tried entering a fraction rather than an integer into the programme, strangely enough, the results appear better. Explain that. So it may be that establishing a likely decay mechanism will depend on what's called, wait for it, fractional calculus. A weird world of semi-differentiation and semi-integration that's difficult to get our heads around and even more difficult to know how to treat these functions in the first place. If that's the case, our usual computer programming is going to struggle to deliver an accurate retention factor for our prototype design even though we've got one of the best and most expensive IBM mainframes around.'

'Sounds beyond me. By the way, who is we at Great Lakes?'

'Oh yes. Michael Womack, an excellent graduate student in my team.'

'Can't he help with this problem? Two heads are better than one surely and you can't be responsible for everything, Paul. After all, you're leading the team, in charge of building the prototype, and having your own test rig measurements to do as well.'

'I know, sometimes everything's a bit much, but let's not worry about that now. Looks like we're entering the Wolds.'

'Paul, why don't you get Michael over here for a while to see if he can help with the maths? Surely, Arrowsmith would allow that.'

'Spot on, Ma'am,' I say jokingly. 'Sure am glad you invited me to join you in this old Land Rover. Great idea. Wish I'd thought of it. Seriously, I'll speak with Michael and Arrowsmith as soon as I get back to Heddington. Let's just hope Michael is free to visit. Right, let's head for the Station, chin up.'

Kay blinks for an instant, turns, and looks sublimely happy as she puts her foot down hard on the accelerator.

Part Four
Reactions

Chapter 11

Six months on, I'm meeting Michael Womack at Cambridge Station after his flight from Detroit. It's easy to pick out his Midwest drawl amongst the received pronunciation of the student hoards lining the platform.

'Hi, Paul. So this is the famous Cambridge, England. Quaint little old station; trains are kind of neat too.'

It's good to see him again. He hasn't changed much and he seems happy to see me. It's his first visit to England and he wants to make the most of it, so I promise to show him around London, the university, and the Cambridgeshire countryside. Fortunately, he already knows it's very flat here. Lucky for me too Larry Ostermann was very enthusiastic about the visit when we spoke in May. He thought Michael might be able to help after working on many more different battery types and with their success in fine-tuning the calculation of energy retention factors.

Larry let me know it'll be a terrific experience for Michael away from Great Lakes, so we went ahead and arranged a six-month sabbatical. It's a welcome relief to shake hands with him at last.

'Great to see you, Michael. We'll sort out your digs today and then introduce you to the team tomorrow.'

'Wasn't expecting to hear from you again, Paul. Heard you'd been grabbed by the authorities to work on some secret project but not much more. Then had this strait-laced English guy called DeLeon from your Washington Embassy come over and check me out. What does he know that I don't know already?'

Stifling a laugh, I tell him not to worry about that too much and how I'm pleased to hear an American with some sense of irony, such a fine British trait. 'Have you had a chance to look at the bio-battery stuff I sent you?'

'Yep, looks a bit weird compared to what we've done in the past but I think you're right about the fractional integer nature of the decay mechanism. If so, our computer programming skills will be tested. Should be fun; at least we can test it out against some real-life performance data you've gained from well over a year now.'

'That's true, Michael. We've plenty of performance data, so glad you're an optimist.'

After a quick tour of Cambridge, I drop off his luggage at his digs and we go for a curry at my favourite Indian restaurant on Mill Road. As I imagined, Michael falls in love with our Indian curries straight away, adding a few laconic comments.

'We don't get this good a curry in Saginawbay if at all I tell you. Mind you, the beer is a bit warm, isn't it?'

At least, I don't need to worry about Michael's nutrition over the next months. Next day, we tour the Heddington site and make a few introductions.

'Michael, let me introduce you to the lady that suggested I get you over here, Dr Kay Levine.'

'Happy to meet you, Ma'am.'

I catch Kay smiling at his address. 'Same to you. I hope you enjoy your stay and that some of your good manners rub off onto Paul whilst you're here.'

My mind goes into spasm. Kay is flirting with me, she is. We're getting on well I know, but that well. My feelings are in a sort of no man's land for an instant; I stay silent. Kay notices my change but continues to smile. For no good reason, my memory goes back to our visit to the Station during the spring and it isn't our review meetings with Mandeep and Aden Jones that come flooding back. No, it's nothing like that. What I remember is Kay being treated like royalty when we arrived, the warmth shown by Mandeep and Aden as friends, not just colleagues and how I was envious and wanted so much to make an impression.

A view reinforced by Aden who went out of his way to say how lucky I am to have Kay working on Pandora and how one day her research will open the prospect of a sea change in cereal yields and food supply across the poorer nations of the world. It was an even greater shock to hear how Aden had gone to the trouble to organise a special Station Spring Dance for her in the village hall. I recall walking beside her to the hall with the calls of summer migrating birds such as flycatchers, swifts, and doves flitting over the fields punctuating the warm spring evening air. How Kay looked stunning in her summer dress with its large turquoise belt that matched her hair band.

Kay was a revelation that visit. I remember complimenting her silky dance skills after Aden led her around the dance floor to the latest romantic hits from John Denver and Rod Stewart. Then wanting to impress Kay so much by rashly asking the country band if they'd play a popular American tune for country line dancing. To my surprise, they did and somehow everyone followed my lead to a popular Madison dance. It was the first time I'd danced in nearly two years and luckily, most seemed to enjoy the experience. Kay was clearly taken aback by my dance skills when she suggested I organise some line dancing sessions in the main hangar at Heddington. My mind seems in free fall when suddenly Kay breaks my trance.

'Michael, you should join Paul's weekly line dance evenings while you're here, they're great fun. I guess you can dance.'

I'm now aware she's staring at me. 'Now don't embarrass me, Kay, I'm supposed to be the team leader here.'

'Don't take any notice of him, Michael. You must know he's very good, we all enjoy it.' The beginning of November in Cambridgeshire almost always introduces the first severe frost of the winter, and 1971 is no exception. An east wind snakes through the narrow streets of Cambridge city centre. Students and shoppers alike bustle along wrapped up against the cold in their woolly hats and scarves as I sit patiently near the bay window of my favourite old-fashioned tearoom just off Green Street. Miriam strides along the narrow pavement. I tap the windowpane to beckon her in. She greets me with her usual enthusiastic beaming smile.

'Sorry, I'm late, Kay. Normally have a bit of a lie-in on a Saturday morning, although not today.'

'Glad you could make it. Would you like tea or coffee, perhaps a pastry?'

'Black coffee for me and a couple of slices of buttered toast wouldn't go amiss. Breakfast seems to have escaped me.'

Stifling a nervous laugh, my eyes drift down to her tiny leather mini skirt and tight-fitting rainbow-coloured Angora sweater. She looks amazing when she's out of her laboratory white coat. To the point, she makes me feel quite old-fashioned and dreary at times. She's so much fun but also a bit of a handful to deal with at times. 'Isn't it a bit cold for a miniskirt?' I ask. It's rhetorical, of course, as we both know the choice of any outfit is not at all rational for Miriam.

'Would you believe it; my darling ex-husband called me first thing this morning to interrupt my beauty sleep for what reason I do not know. He seems to want some company, my company for heaven's sake, but I told him to sod off. He's just feeling sorry for himself after his latest bright young thing walked out on him. Men, who'd be doing with them, eh.'

'That's a bit damning, Miriam,' I reply.

Smiling serenely, Miriam continues without waiting for breath. 'You clearly rate them, or at least one of them.' Her coffee and toast arrived. She follows up with an urgent request for the waitress. 'Got any marmalade, love?'

Trying to catch my breath as well, I nervously respond with just a little tongue in cheek. 'Eh there, so what are you insinuating by that?'

'Come on, my lovely, it's pretty clear you've got a thing for Paul.'

'No, I haven't got a thing as you say. What makes you say that?'

'It's obvious when you're together. It's all in your chemistry; some of his physical and some of your bio.' She's giggling before even ending the sentence.

'Well, it's true, I do like him. In fact, I like him a lot. Mind you, I didn't at first but he sort of grows on you. As you know very well, I wasn't that happy when I arrived at Heddington. Didn't want my work at Manchester to be hung out to dry. Even now, I'm still trying to figure out what the project's goals really are but I'm not alone there. But Paul has done a wonderful job in getting us to work together as a team and I feel at home in Cambridge now. My digs are amazing and I'm happy with how my own work's going along. It's true, I wouldn't have thought that possible a year ago but Paul has made me look at things differently I suppose.'

'Paul's done that. Wow, it must be love.'

'Don't talk such nonsense, Miriam. I'm getting a bit long in the tooth for all that stuff.'

'Well, you don't look like a Women's Liberation activist for sure. You're never going to go along and scare poor old Bob Hope half to death by throwing flour all over him at the Miss World competition at the Albert Hall, are you?'

My jaw drops as I look at this tiny lady taking another bite out of her toast. 'You did that, Miriam?'

'No, I didn't, but something inside me would have liked to. Some of my friends from university college did and said it was a real scream. Look, men can be a real pain but like you, I certainly won't stop trying to love them if the right one comes along.' There's a sudden shiver across her shoulders. 'Ouch, it's a bit chilly this morning. Perhaps the miniskirt wasn't such a good idea, eh, Kay?'

'Perhaps not,' I say trying to show some sympathy. 'Well, I suppose it's the same for me but we all go about trying to reach out to love in our own different ways.'

'Does he know how you feel?'

'Of course not,' I riposte.

'So, what are you going to do about it?'

'Don't know. No idea how he feels about things. He's had this serious relationship with my French flatmate in Manchester but that went pear-shaped, so maybe it's once bitten twice shy.'

'You're not going to know unless you get out of that laboratory of yours once in a while. I know I'm the last one to talk but if you take off that virginal white coat of yours, you can look quite beautiful. Hope you don't mind me saying, but it's this traditional classic style of yours with some French thrown in. Not the latest fashion of course but if it works for you.' Miriam glances down and adjusts her miniskirt. She tries to clear her throat and adds, 'Mind you, Paul might actually like that sort of thing.'

'I do get out and about now and then, Miriam, not exactly a nun you know. Well, I've thought about asking him to the cinema one evening, there's a Claude Chabrol season at the Arts Cinema and I'd like to go. Not sure if he's a fan of foreign language films but I know he likes French girls.'

'Kay, my dear, what have you got to lose? He's not an ogre, seems a very lively, kind and thoughtful man. Has quite a rugged look, like he's just come off the prairie. A bit Americanised but so what, and quite a mean dancer too. Boy, his line dancing is fun, isn't it? Keeps my body in trim, otherwise, I'll be struggling even more with these skirts.'

I sit back and sip my tea. Miriam is just wonderful, very much a woman of the times. So brave in many ways. Just wish I had her confidence. The cold is making me hungry, so I call out, 'Waitress, do you have any of those delicious Dutch apple tarts, you know the ones with the cinnamon?'

'Dutch courage, Kay?'

'Why not,' I reply.

Kay is running through the latest results from the Station's hydroponic cereal trial in my office. Yet again, Mandeep's analysis shows statistically significant enhanced plant growth yields from the recent batch of derivative enzymes when compared to his controls. She's yet to complete glucose analyses but seems very confident in gaining further improvements in leaf glucose levels. As a joke, I suggest she goes and celebrates her success, maybe spend some time on her Christmas shopping. She finds my comments amusing for some reason. There's a glimmer of a smile as she turns to leave. I'm anxious to get on and meet with Michael to go through his ideas on establishing the best decay mechanism for the bio-battery.

He's starting to use data sets from Miriam's three-stack battery prototype, so I'm keen to learn his early thoughts. The young engineers also want me to pop into the main hangar and check on progress with a critical stage of the fifty-stack low megawatt pre-production unit. Despite all this, I see Kay hovering nearer the door.

'What's up?' I ask. 'Thought we'd finished. Did I miss something? Is there something wrong?'

She looks unsettled. There's a muffled sort of laugh followed by some agitated quickfire words. 'No, nothing wrong, I'm fine. By the way, do you like foreign language films? French ones, for example.'

Quite taken aback, I hesitate for a moment not knowing what to say. 'Well, not sure if I've seen that many, if any.' Open-mouthed, I try not to be too serious but end up being boringly ironic. 'Not too popular in the Midwest, I'm afraid. Why?'

'Oh well, it's just there's a Claude Chabrol season on at the Arts Cinema and they're showing his latest *Juste Avant La Nuit* tomorrow evening.'

'Just before Nightfall,' I translate triumphantly. 'Who's this Claude Chabrol?'

Kay's eyes suddenly fix on me. 'Oh, I'm impressed. He's France's Alfred Hitchcock. Would you like to come? You're keen on everything French, aren't you?'

She reddens with a worried look on her face and adds, 'So sorry, I shouldn't have said that.'

Amazingly, Kay is asking me out for a date. What do I say? It isn't like her; she's always so direct on anything scientific but quite reserved with anything of a personal nature. She still comes over a bit shy at times. I've no clue about French films; Isabelle kept me away from them for some reason. *But then*, I think, *what the hell*. If Kay's bold enough to ask me, then she must like me a fair bit, so why not? Catching her eye, trying to appear relaxed and casual with my reply.

'That was a lucky guess with the title and no worries, it's fine. I've said most of what I want to say about Isabelle. As you say, I do have a little history with the French nation.' Trying to smile, I continue, 'Isabelle never properly introduced me to her beloved French cinema. What's it about? Do you think I'll like it?'

'Um, hope you might. It's about how a man who handles guilt within his family after a tragic accident with his lover.'

'Blimey, Kay, that sounds profound. Guilt, I certainly know a bit about that. Ok, let's go for it. I assume it's subtitled, otherwise I really will struggle.'

'Yes, of course.' Kay pauses briefly as she leaves the room. 'Good. Then, shall I see you outside the cinema in Market Passage, say seven-thirty?'

'It's a date,' I mouth, and immediately catch my breath after thinking I've said the wrong words yet again. We look at each other, she fidgets with the doorknob and I with a pen in my hand; I hear Michael striding up the corridor as Kay rushes through my door. Michael eyes Kay, then greets me with my mouth wide open, and we're all left speechless. It's a quarter to ten when we walk out of the cinema foyer. The night has a cold chill about it and there's a hint of sleet in the air. So glad I've got my dark blue beret on as it always makes me feel warm and cosy. Paul is impossibly silent and I wonder if it's been a big mistake inviting along; he probably thinks it's a total waste of time. I'm on edge and don't know why. Perhaps because I still don't know Paul that well outside of work and I don't want to be disappointed, either with him or myself. The silence is unbearable, so I jump in.

'Do you want to come back for a coffee or something stronger? Not too late for you, is it? Or would you prefer the pub? They should still be open, shouldn't they?' I hold my breath as Paul avoids my gaze.

'Oh, yes, that'll be great, Kay. I could do it with a drink. A hot drink will be spot on; it's extra cold tonight, should've worn my heavy coat.'

'Was it that bad a film, Paul?' To my surprise, I catch sight of his eyes glistening in the yellow light from a solitary streetlamp.

'No, not at all; just trying to make sense of it all. Give me a few minutes, I don't see that sort of film very often you know.'

We start walking to my rooms hardly saying a word, although I'm quite exhilarated and my heart's racing. It's taken me a while to appreciate how surprising and unpredictable Paul can be at times. He's the polar opposite of my old flame, Simon Gardner. I shudder at the thought of Simon and walk ever faster before muttering, 'Oh good. Let's wait and have a chat about it over a hot drink.' To my amazement, Paul asks for hot chocolate and quickly grabs a large slice of my mum's homemade fruit cake. Maybe he doesn't get much home cooking. After a studied silence, Paul gradually starts to open up.

'Ok, that film, it makes me feel submerged by guilt. I'd feel bad treading on a fly right now. Sounds silly, doesn't it?'

'Really? I noticed you were a bit tearful afterwards.'

'Yes, bit of a shock, eh,' he replies. 'Maybe the film exaggerates everything a bit too much. You know how the husband waits too long to tell his wife and explain just how his lover died; that it was an accident, during what, some sadomasochistic game? And when he does explain, she forgives him totally and keeps forgiving him. But he doesn't want that, does he? He wants to be punished, so it ends up making his guilt even worse; it grows inside him like cancer. Horrific, the film shakes you, but slowly and deliberately. It's very clever, it eats away at you. Guess we all carry some guilt inside us from living our lives as we do, about certain things, don't we?'

I ease back in my chair and try to relax as Paul carries on talking, slowly drawing breath.

'Well, I suppose it's best not to go on any more about Isabelle but you know her so well. You see, I still want to explain to her why or how I let her down, ending everything in the way we did. Never really had that chance and now it's too late. How I just let things drift between us; maybe the film is a stark reminder of what I did or didn't do. Also, why I must try and not to let the same thing happen again? Sorry, Kay, this must all sound rather ridiculous.'

My heart is pounding as Paul puts into words exactly what the film says to me too. I can't believe his reaction to it. Was I hearing him correctly? My thoughts swirl around as I suddenly hear myself saying, 'Paul, I'm so sorry. I didn't think seeing that film would upset you so much, about Isabelle I mean after all this time; really, I didn't. But pleased you sort of liked it; it's the best Chabrol film I've seen so far, although was a bit surprised by the opening scene.'

'Yes, I wondered what you were taking me to see. For a while there, I thought it might be one of those clinical split-screen Swedish sex movies that are doing the rounds nowadays.'

I try and change the subject. 'What did you make of Stephanie Audran?'

'You mean the wife?'

'Yes, she's a lovely actress, very mysterious,' I reply.

'Oh, gorgeous auburn hair and green eyes, very French. What else can I say?'

'Well, you've said enough, I think. That's put me in my place. She's the wife of Chabrol you know and in most of his films.'

Paul falls silent for a while, then suddenly adds, 'Guilt, it's so overpowering at times, isn't it?'

My thoughts miraculously go back to the time when I was attacked as a young girl. Stupidly, I still believe I was partly responsible in some way but quickly chastise myself for being so silly to think that way after so long. But I still do wonder and now slowly express my thoughts.

'Yes, it can be.'

Paul's forehead wrinkles. 'What's the matter, Kay? You look sad. Nothing wrong, I hope. I'm sure you've nothing to feel that guilty about.'

I so much want to let my feelings go and say something; somehow, I know he would understand. 'Everyone owns some guilt. I certainly do.'

He looks surprised and frowns again as his eyes turn directly towards mine. He speaks quietly at first.

'Do you, er…can you…? Do you want to talk about such things, Kay?' Hesitating for a moment longer, he starts to get up from his chair. 'Perhaps, it's getting late, I should go. We have some busy days ahead before the Christmas break.'

'No, no, it's alright, Paul. Stay, I don't go to bed that early. Erm…look, what I'm going to tell you is just between us, you understand? I've only ever told one other person apart from my mum. It's going to sound silly, even irrational I know, but bear with me. It would be nice to say something, particularly after what you've said about you and Isabelle, and guilt.'

'Oh, Kay. I'm sorry, shouldn't have said anything. I'm sure it's going to be none of my business, so please, don't say a word if you feel uncomfortable. Mind you, I can keep a secret.'

'It's fine, Paul, I trust you.' Feeling awkward and embarrassed by having to say as such, I take a deep breath and as calmly as possible, describe my story of what happened all those years ago in a farmer's field. How I still feel partly responsible and guilty for what happened, and how I'd let my family down. As in the film, I should have acted more responsibly and at least told my parents sooner, they would have understood. Without warning, I start to shake deep inside as I come to the end. My cheeks burn but strangely, there's this feeling of welcome relief growing inside.

Relief that I've told someone with such ease, and how glad it's Paul. The shaking ebbs away and I'm left with an overwhelming feeling of peace and calm. Paul gently interrupts after listening so intently.

'That Chabrol chappie has a lot to answer for.' We spontaneously laugh out loud. 'Thank you for trusting me and telling me your story, Kay. It can't be easy and I'm not going to offer any glib replies either. What happened, happened. I'm sure you realise it could have been so much worse, although frightening enough, and you were so young. But you, guilty? No, no way were you responsible for what happened that day. Look, it's getting late but if you can bear it, let me add some light relief from my early days in the Midwest that, well, might or might not add some perspective. It sums up how we are often a hostage to events that are out of our control; after all, police deal with these incidents all the time.'

Smiling at Paul, I nod knowingly. 'That would be nice, good to change the subject and stop me from rattling on.'

'So, it's the first time I visited downtown Saginawbay, trying to soak up the local atmosphere by visiting this large bar on the main street. The bar is smart enough, crowded, and the place to go if you want to get to grips with their homespun country music. I'm just sitting calmly with a beer when these two women start bashing the daylights out of each other on the dance floor in front of me while this hunk of a boyfriend in a smart-looking cowboy hat stands by powerless. After the dust settles, all three are shown the door by the burly local cops.

'I ask one particularly scary-looking cop who separated the ladies what the hell was the fight all about. He turns around very slowly, looks me in the eye as if I'm from another planet, and says, "Stuff happens, son, stuff happens and life moves on. We're here to listen, make some sense of it all, act and then try to pick up the pieces". And he's right, Kay. All you can do is talk it through and try to pick up the pieces, see if it helps but finally move on. I think it's time for both of us to move on, don't you? And it's also time for me to go, it's well past midnight. Where's the time gone? We have a busy day ahead.'

Paul heads for the door, he stands motionless for an instant, then turns to face me. 'Have we been on a date, Kay? In the States, this is a big thing you know. Used to hear the girls at line dancing class talk about dating all the time as if it's a rite of passage. Never sure why.'

'I suppose we have,' I reply sheepishly.

'In that case, may I return the compliment? One of my chemists has two spare tickets for the University Christmas Dinner Dance at the Grad Pad off Mill Lane. Would you like to come? It's a black-tie affair. Some of my group will be there, Miriam and Michael, not as a pair you understand.'

Walking up to him and looking into his eyes, I can only but smile, nod, and give him a gentle kiss on the cheek. A bit prickly and rather a strange sensation; that's something I'll have to get used to.

He whispers, 'It's a date then,' as he enters the stairwell.

'For certain this time,' I reply.

He walks down the narrow set of steps out into Tree Court. Through the window next to my bed, I see his footprints reflecting off a bed of snow bathed in a yellowish sodium light on his way home to the Kite. I pull the curtains, undress quickly, and lie down with a thousand thoughts but instantly fall asleep.

Next day brings anxiety and irritation in equal measure on a typical cold and frosty morning in rural Cambridgeshire. Professor Arrowsmith and Malcolm Edgerton are holding their final review meeting of the year. Apparently, the message emanating from the government is that their officials are overall pleased with the research and the development of a fifty-stack pre-production prototype while Arrowsmith keeps pressing to have something to show the press by late summer of next year. For some pedantic reason, he insists on proceeding step by step through every aspect of my glucose optimisation work and design of the automated glucose extractor unit.

He seems relatively happy with the other groups, especially Paul's latest test rig performance data from the three-stack prototype. Everyone agrees that the evidence so far suggests a low megawatt prototype is still deliverable. Ping is present for the first time in weeks and reports on some good progress in developing his economic impact assessment model. He glances over to Paul before pointing out that the government is keen to invest in the bio-battery but must be sure that future megawatt production units can deliver a sustainable contribution to the UK grid network.

There's a lengthy pause from Ping before he focuses on the priority for Paul and Michael; to derive an accurate energy retention factor for the scaled-up battery, otherwise, his economic forecast model will be less than useless. Arrowsmith raises an eyebrow and looks sternly in Paul's direction without saying a word. There's a cursory glance around the table before he briefly thanks everyone for their efforts. His final utterance is a less than enthusiastic "happy

Christmas" peppered with the mild threat that we should expect an even busier New Year.

There's this audible intake of breath from most of us present as we stare at some vague spot in the centre of the tabletop and fall silent. It's with some relief that Dr Edgerton provides a lighter touch by chatting with some of us and offering a friendly handshake. Whilst Edgerton's stays on for some time, I notice Arrowsmith quickly draws Paul to one side, subsequently leaving the room together.

Later in the week, Paul organises a special Christmas line dancing party; he wants everyone to let their hair down. The hangar is decorated like a barn with box loads of tinsel and he insists everyone comes in their homemade country music outfits and be prepared to follow his calling of dances to the strains of some authentic Midwest rock and roll. It's a good job Miriam bullies me to attend his regular line dance sessions as we're now quite proficient. Secretly, I'm really looking forward to the evening as we've made a real effort to dress up as cowgirls by finding some obligatory knee-high leather boots. It doesn't take long for the party to take off as the younger scientists are no strangers to having a good time.

As the evening progresses, I notice Paul is taking a special interest in my cowgirl outfit, so much so that Miriam takes me to one side to point out how he hasn't taken his eyes off my tight denim jeans and blue silk shirt all night. My cheeks glow like beacons as he dances alongside us for most of the time. And how amazing is everyone's enthusiasm for following Paul's calling out the routines and demonstrating the steps? He's obviously proud of his authentic line dancing skills and outrageous cowboy gear from his time at Great Lakes.

What's more surprising is how everyone managed to find such garish outfits from around Cambridge. Later in the evening, I stand back and take a close look at Paul's dancing. He's clearly in his element, uninhibited and having so much fun. I rather envy him and certainly come to admire him. As I look at the young faces around the hangar, it's obvious that where he leads, others follow. Around midnight, Paul is quick to offer me a lift back to my rooms on his Husqvarna. It's my long-anticipated and exciting ride at the end of a thrilling evening, which stays long in my memory.

I decide to travel home for Christmas a few days earlier than most of the team. Mum is keen I get to know Eric Smithson a lot more. Her chap, as she calls him, is fast becoming important to her and I'm happy about that. However, before leaving, I set about Cambridge's rather quirky gift shops for a last chance at some Christmas shopping for the family. It's where I stumble across a genuine silver Texan Star bootlace tie which is an ideal gift for Paul. At Heddington, I take the plunge to pop into his office and let him know of my travel plans, sort out arrangements for the Grad Pad Dinner Dance, and hand over his Christmas present. As I close the door, he's just coming off the phone. His face is deeply lined, so I guess he's just been speaking with Arrowsmith.

That guy never lets up, he mumbles to himself.

'You look worried,' I reply to a clearly irritated Paul.

'Oh, it's nothing I don't know about already. He keeps going over what he said to me privately after our last review meeting.'

'Was it when Edgerton was chatting to everyone and you suddenly sneaked out of the meeting?'

Paul smiles. 'Yes, Kay, it was. Can't keep many secrets from you, can I?'

'You can if you want to,' I say.

'Think I can trust you by now, Kay.' He grins but still has that anxious expression in his eyes.

'But I don't want to say too much to everyone until after Christmas, after all, it's holiday time, isn't it?'

I nod reassuringly but secretly hope he'll say more. Paul takes a deep breath before continuing.

'Overall, Arrowsmith was complimentary in some ways after the meeting. In fact, he took me aside to thank me for generating such a good team spirit within the group and to say my efforts have been recognised by the department. Mind you, not sure how much good that'll do me. However, he wanted to warn me that there's growing pressure from the deputy chief scientist and his junior minister to have something solid on show for the public to justify their expenditure. A bit of a flag-waving exercise he calls it. To be fair, Arrowsmith understands full well the nature of research but still urges us, or rather me, to move on with constructing, wait for it, a hundred-stack pre-production unit in the New Year.'

'In his estimation, it's the best chance of delivering a truly megawatt output unit. But, Kay, it was at this point his usual dour demeanour became most agitated by acknowledging how he was under severe pressure to deliver just like the rest of us. He made it clear that Pandora is largely seen as his pet project in current government circles. I told him how I understood but my doubts over deriving an accurate energy retention factor have not gone away for even the three-stack prototype. And stressing how those uncertainties will almost certainly be magnified when applied to a much scaled-up unit.'

'It was time to be blunt I said. If we skate over this issue now, then we won't know what changes to make to the basic bio-battery design further down the line. It's one of the biggest risks we face, I said, and Ping agrees with me one hundred per cent on this. After all, I brought over Michael Womack for just this reason and he's already made a difference. But research of this kind takes time and results are never guaranteed. By the end, Arrowsmith just gritted his teeth, shook my hand, and wished me a happy Christmas. I tell you, Kay, a cold chill ran down my spine that day and it wasn't from the inclement weather.'

Paul puffs out his cheeks which migrate into a deep sigh as I struggle to say something meaningful.

'Don't know why I'm telling you all this right now, Kay, except to let you know that the next few months are going to be pretty hectic, like being under the cosh big time. I have to come up with some answers for Ping's model very soon. Sorry to burden you but you'll find out soon enough in the New Year. Hope you understand.'

Stepping close, I place my hand gently on his shoulder and give it a squeeze. 'Thought something has been troubling you over the past few days, glad you can at least talk about it. After all, I've told you plenty, haven't I? Please try not to worry too much over Christmas, you deserve a break; hope I can be of some help when you get back.' We go on to talk about our travel arrangements and I hand over my present. Visibly embarrassed, Paul also struggles to say the right thing.

'I've no idea what to get you, Kay. So sorry, all I can come up with are those tickets for the Grad Pad Dinner Dance. Got no excuse, just don't know what else to say.'

'Please, don't open my tiny little present until Christmas Day. I can assure you the dinner dance is a real treat for me, an opportunity to dress up in my new evening gown. Mum has gone to town and mostly hand-sewn my strapless emerald green full-length taffeta ball gown.'

Paul seems taken aback by my description of the gown but soon brightens up, edging a little closer before whispering, 'Don't worry, I've already done something about a tuxedo for the evening. By the way, if we don't get a chance to talk much after the dance, then have a wonderful holiday with your mum and her new man.' He looks me straight in the eye and says, 'By the way, you're already helping me, Kay, believe me.'

Driving past the American Cemetery west of Cambridge on my way home, I look back over the past weeks and peer into the future. Christmas is going to be quite a new experience. It'll be so different as I'm more content with myself and happier than I'd ever imagined even a year ago. Pandora is a challenge, yes, but my research is still going well with some top-quality papers on their way. Despite Paul's doubts about the project's future, everyone else at Heddington is full of optimism. Our close-knit team of young scientists, indeed friends, are doing their level best with a project that places many different demands on all of us. We're enjoying ourselves and learning new things with Paul making that possible.

As I glance through the windscreen over the furrowed fields of dark earth, my thoughts wander and eventually return to one lasting memory. When Miriam and Michael, a few days earlier, look around and smile a million smiles as Paul and I stride onto the Grad Pad dance floor. There's my beautiful ball gown and the joy of dancing a never-ending slow waltz to *Moon River* sung by Audrey Hepburn from *Breakfast at Tiffany's*. How our gentle kiss and hug at the end of the evening seems to tie us together for a fleeting moment. What heaven it is as my journey home just speeds by.

Chapter 12

Everywhere is grey. There's a thunderous leaden sky as I crawl down Jesus Lane on my Husqvarna past the splendour of St Johns College and head for Fitzbillies bakery shop. Predictably, it was equally grey yesterday as I stared out of a train window on my way back from London after an urgent summons from Winstanley. Arrowsmith and Edgerton wanted to talk about future planning. Maybe it was just the inevitability of such a meeting that made me so gloomy as the train sped past the barren fields around Cambridge with furrows still tinged from an early morning frost. Gloomier still was the stark outline of trees shorn of life, branches bending against the cruel east wind.

Worse still, today, the people are grey. Busy people on their way to work or their studies dressed in heavy duffle coats, and serious-minded postgraduates proudly covering their faces with their precious college scarves. But my mood begins to lift as I turn into Bridge Street and catch sight of Kay in a heavy tweed coat and blue beret standing outside the bakery with three boxes of what I hope is their finest Chelsea buns. It's well past eight o'clock on a Friday morning and I called her earlier to see if she'd collect the buns in exchange for a lift to Heddington.

Thank goodness, she said yes and how well she seals the deal with the most delicate of kisses on my cheek as I draw up beside her. Her nose is cold, her cheeks glow pink as I mutter under my breath, 'There's a welcome dash of colour amongst all this damned grey. And thanks for collecting our goodies,' as she places the cakes at the bottom of my cavernous rucksack for safekeeping. 'How was your Christmas and New Year with your mum and new man?' I ask desperately trying to restrain a smile.

'It was lovely, Paul. Eric was very jolly and they clearly got on very well. It's the happiest I've seen mum for some time. She's been a long time on her own so I'm happy for her. What about you? How long have you been back?'

'Oh, I came back immediately after New Year. Glad I did as Winstanley called me to an urgent meeting yesterday in Whitehall to talk about future plans. Bit grim really, very much back to earth with a bump. You'll hear all about it at this morning's meeting but it's not much different from what I told you before Christmas. Oh yes, nearly forgot. Talking about Christmas, thank you so much for my impressive Texan bootlace tie.'

'Did you like it?' She asks.

'Oh, it's really cool as they say in the Midwest. Don't know where you found it but I'll treasure it. Can't promise I'll wear it around the laboratory though, but definitely during line dancing.'

'That's good, it was only a little something. It seems to match your persona.'

I laugh. 'Blimey, Kay, my persona, that's a bit much. Didn't know I had one of those. We'd better get off. I'm afraid you'll have to swap that lovely beret of yours with this battered old helmet, sorry.' Kay squeezes her beautiful black hair into my shabby spare helmet and grabs me around the waist before we speed off towards Trumpington.

'Paul, talking of Winstanley, I have a favour to ask that your Mr Winstanley might be able to help with. It's a personal matter but important for my family, although not urgent. Perhaps we can chat about it another time.'

At some light, I turn briefly to face Kay. 'Interesting. Are you his secret admirer?'

Kay squeezes my ribs and shouts as the engine noise starts up again.

'Another time, Paul, another time. But I think he may be able to help. He's very well-connected across government, isn't he?'

'Very well-connected, believe me!' I shout back. Time flies by as we chat about our holidays until I drop Kay off near the main entrance. On cue, her exquisite beret is perched over the hair at an elegant angle before she strides up to the main door raising her arm as she enters with a "see you later". I park the Husqvarna and start to think about what exactly I'm going to say at our Friday bun meeting. A couple of hours tick by and everyone is seated around the large table with hands and fingers glued together from daring to eat a Chelsea bun. Ping is still wiping his hands free of treacle as I open the meeting.

'Glad to see everyone back from their holidays in one piece. Pleased you can be with us too, Ping.' He splutters something unintelligible but gives up with any further attempts as he tries to finish off a mouthful of the bun. 'Sorry, Ping, bad timing; anyway, let's have some fun, folks. We'll go around the table so everyone can tell us what you've not missed while away on holiday. That's right, what you've not missed. That's apart from the dreadful coffee, the line dancing, and of course, writing tedious reports to satisfy government officials. Come on, let's hear from you. There must be something else.'

Everyone bursts out laughing but wisely keeps their counsel, so I continue. 'Right, I'll start. Well, you lot for a start.' The group breaks out with more laughter. 'Ok, that's not true. I miss the lot of you, even you, Ping.' Ping grimaces as I glance furtively towards Kay at the far end of the table. With some relief, the young chemists share some banter and the atmosphere lightens further. It's essential for us all to start this year relaxed, optimistic and in good spirits. There are a few more minutes of banter before I deliver the news.

'Look, everyone, some of you attended the review meeting before Christmas where it was made perfectly clear that it's going to be a busy year ahead. And it will be as I was down in London yesterday to see Professor Arrowsmith, Mr Winstanley, and Dr Edgerton for a planning meeting.' A po-faced Michael DeLeon throws me a quick glance as I mention Winstanley's name. I smile back serenely. 'Let me say at one stage during this planning meeting, a junior science minister popped his head around the door. He wanted to stress the importance of Ping's economic assessment model to the success of the project and to wish me luck.'

Raising my eyebrows, I continue. 'I wasn't sure what to make of that remark at the time but I'm guessing this software model will affect all of us at some stage and not just those directly involved in the research. We all need to understand that I guess.' I steal another glance towards DeLeon. 'Apart from that, the main bone of contention from yesterday is that the government wants us to construct a hundred-stack battery prototype as soon as possible, preferably before the end of the year so they can show the press something substantial. A press conference will be held this coming September come what may and the junior minister will be there.'

Michael DeLeon is eager to interrupt. 'A date has not yet been set but we expect it to be early September as it coincides with raising the public profile of similar initiatives from the government.'

'Ok, thanks, Michael. However, it needs to be said that in the end, I negotiated with Arrowsmith and he agreed that we'll initially build a fifty-stack prototype with an integrated glucose extractor unit ready for the press conference. You've all been working on this prototype, so it's well-advanced.

Be aware, that I pointed out that its electrical performance will need to be fully characterised using our test rig by then and that we expect it to generate a few megawatts. As a result, I'm now handing over all my test rig work and the team to Elizabeth who I know will do a thorough job.

'Some of you will be aware that Professor Arrowsmith has been pushing for a hundred-stack prototype for some time. It can sound more impressive to politicians and the press, and it may offer a better chance of generating up to a gigawatt. But I made the practical argument that there's physically very little to choose between these prototypes at this stage once the glucose extractor unit is attached and how our research time must be spent on other more critical areas. So, Kay is now running a further hydroponic growth cycle on selected cereals with her friends at the Wolds Station. After all, we need sufficient fuel stock to demonstrate the effectiveness of the current prototype at the press conference.'

'It's also crystal clear to all that more effort is needed to confirm an accurate and reliable energy retention factor for economic impact modelling. All our available computer resources will be applied and Ping, Michael Womack and I will now be freed up to work more closely together in what some in the department like to call a mini task force. Wish us all luck. We'll continue using the three-stack prototype data at first but quickly move to the fifty-stack design and, with luck, look to obtain its decay data next month. I'm banking on the fact that the energy retention data doesn't force us into making serious design changes to the enzyme-coated mediator or the base electrode materials.

'Miriam and James will monitor our results closely so they can suggest any immediate low-level design modifications. But make no mistake, I made it clear at yesterday's meeting that there are no guarantees at this critical stage of the project.' Repeating what I said at yesterday's meeting, I glibly remark, 'No one can ever be sure what will pop out of Pandora's box from now on.' But I quickly own up with, 'That didn't get many laughs yesterday and I'm afraid it looks like it's falling on deaf ears today.'

DeLeon raises more than one eyebrow and visibly sighs, but Ping and Michael Womack nod vigorously to back me up.

'So, there we are, everyone. That's the plan for the next nine months or so. There's a lot hanging on the line but we can do this. So, what do you think?' I ask for questions but there are none. Kay catches my eye and nods approvingly. Surprisingly, everyone stays upbeat during the rest of the meeting. With a real sense of achievement, I close the meeting and grab a sticky bun. Michael

Womack and Ping join me to hammer out a week-by-week action plan on how we'll go about calculating accurate energy retention factors. They commandeer the remaining Fitzbillie's Chelsea buns on the way to my office; a good decision as those discussions drag on for the rest of the day. As winter turns to spring, Pandora gradually evolves along the lines Paul set out in the New Year, and so does my relationship with Paul. Not passionately, which is a relief in a way, but thoughtfully, cautiously, and like any serious endeavour, not always smoothly. For me, our time together feels comfortable and suitable for the situation. Nowadays, I'm far too cautious in expressing my feelings for someone but that's how I feel right now and fortunately, it looks like it suits Paul too. Everyone knows we're dating; they take it for granted. Miriam often asks what's holding me back but her experiences of love, romance and relationships are coloured by her own disastrous marriage.

For her, it's more a battle; an exciting battle of the sexes where you play out a game that in the end no one can ever win. She likes the drama and the passion, she's happy just to exist together whatever happens. Trying to explain to Miriam that I'm not like that falls on deaf ears. For me, passion is fine, more than fine, but commitment should be the goal and that takes time and hard work. But that commitment is something I'm not sure about or even ready for just now as I look towards so many hectic months ahead. It's lovely being with Paul; he's a breath of fresh air. He's never dull or boring, well except when he goes on about fractional calculus, but I so much admire the way he runs our team.

He has real charisma; I can tell the young scientists adore him, they even come and tell me so. He hates me pulling his leg about his persona but I've surprised myself for coming to admire his mid-Atlantic ways. He cleverly combines the best of a can-do way of thinking from his beloved Midwest with a natural English-laden street credibility that's full of understatement and realism. Not one person in the team has a bad word to say about him apart from Michael DeLeon, who makes it obvious that Paul plays fast and loose with his comments on this government and its officials.

So, we're comfortable together, not comfortable as in taking one another for granted but just easy with each other and I love him dearly for that. However, I become increasingly aware of these feelings in early March while immersed in setting up a final hydroponic growth trial at the Station and helping Marcus and the engineers test the glucose extraction unit. I've also had a self-inflicted deadline to complete some final edits on two research papers. Time races by, although we still find time to go to some wonderful concerts in the college chapels, and then one evening, I invite him along to a high table at Gonville and Caius Hall and readily admit how eating quail and drinking thirty-year-old Tawny port from their cellars is an unreal experience.

Perhaps, the port has a calming effect on him since he readily forgives me for creating a mad panic to find his old scarlet academic gown from Manchester. What a surreal evening it is as we laugh about it over one final glass of port. My growing attachment to Paul is made more intense a few weeks later when he invites me to his favourite modern jazz club in the Kite. I don't like jazz so have resisted his invitations so far but now it's too churlish to refuse. As we near the club sounds from this evocative music saturate the air and grow louder still when we creep through a small door at the back of the club. A timid-looking bouncer insists we're lucky to hear such a stellar saxophonist as Barbara Thompson and her husband, John Hiseman, play a set.

The place is packed out, cigarette smoke overshadows its tables, making it difficult to breathe or even see the band at times. I hate cigarette smoke and tell Paul as much; at least we're near the exit so there's a fresh draught of night air every now and again. Unsurprisingly, it takes time for me to unscramble the tune from the improvisation and giddy virtuosity of the soloists, but boy can they play. Their intricate wall of sound overpowers some in the audience; it's almost hypnotic as I get caught up in the rhythmical musical patterns ebbing and flowing. Paul says he's over the moon I've found jazz at last; he's not even upset when I irritatingly ask him to look out for a healthier venue next time.

He stifles a laugh as he thinks it doubtful any such venue exists, so we happily let the subject drop. On my way back to his flat, I begin to wonder if he expects me to stay the night. My mind is muddled in what to say or do. It's not the sex thing as I'd like to stay. I've no doubt it'll be enjoyable as he's kind, and attractive, and I'm even getting used to his beard. No, it's what follows that intimacy. The intensity of my, our work, just now is such that deep down, I'm feeling it's probably the wrong time to go any further. My thoughts are all over the place. Does he think the same way?

We settle down on his battered old settee covered by an enormous burgundy-coloured throw. Paul offers a large whisky and a doorstop of a ham sandwich. He says he's always hungry after a jazz night from the adrenalin rush. We kiss and kiss again. He sits back and looks at me lovingly with those dark brown eyes.

After hesitating for what seems like an eternity, he speaks in his calm but authoritative way. My body tenses but he reacts immediately.

'Don't worry, Kay. I'm not going to insist you stay the night though I'd love you to, god knows I do; that must be obvious to you. But not sure that's right just now. Hope I can explain and you'll understand.' He edges ever closer and there are more hugs and kisses. I take his hand; my heart is racing as I'm fearful of what's to follow. Struggling to understand what he's saying, all I can do is reply irrationally.

'Oh dear, why not? Don't you find me attractive enough? I know I'm not exactly Miriam?'

'You're joking, Kay. You're gorgeous and stunning. You must know how I think about you; I've made my feelings perfectly obvious. It's been difficult to control myself at times. Can't get enough of your figure-hugging frocks and wild selection of berets.' He chuckles and starts to squeeze my hand. 'No, it's not that. I've thought about asking you many times. No…It's, well, I'm trying to think of you, of us I should say, and not just being selfish about just what my body is telling me. In my way of thinking, this isn't the right time for either of us to go further, but I think, I hope you realise that too.'

I'm not sure if I was disappointed or pleased at first. Paul is always truthful and very direct; I admire him for it. Many men would essentially say nothing and do everything. Another time, I may want that but I suddenly remember what Isabelle said late one night before she left for France. 'Paul finally understood he has to talk to me about his feelings, and he can do it, but it's all too late for us.'

Paul keeps hold of my hand and continues to explain how it's such an intense time for all of us. Ping and Michael are driving him, all of us, nuts trying to solve this energy retention factor problem and how he just couldn't cope with anything else right now. He's not sure how he'd cope with any major distractions but how he thinks badly saying this. And how I'd certainly be a very large distraction, which is nice to hear. He knows he's being selfish in one way, although damn stupid in another.

Apparently, Arrowsmith is pestering him for progress updates almost every week and how he'll be lousy company, irritable and, besides, he just hopes I understand. Paul is so serious, he's clearly prepared for this chat by carefully thinking through the situation despite his, and mine I suppose, healthy sex drive. I grip his hand tightly, kiss him again, and try to reassure him that everything's ok between us and that I mostly feel the same. He then tells me there's one thing he's curious about but afraid to ask. He knew Isabelle confided in me at some stage before they broke up. Isabelle was hurting and he felt sure she'd want to talk to someone. He says he wants to clear the air between us about Isabelle right now, so I quickly interrupt him.

'Yes, Paul, Isabelle did confide in me but only at one level; we were never that close.'

He understands but recounts how absorbed he was in finishing his PhD and how he'd started to shut Isabelle out. In the end, she made the decision to break up and go back to France. Paul says he didn't have the guts to confront such issues at the time and that he doesn't want the same to happen again between us. There's anxiety written all over his face when he says he's fearful that events are repeating themselves but how he's wiser now and cares too much to let things drift. That's why he's so unsure of what's best for us right now but wants to be straight and talk to me about it openly. I take my time in replying to such fears.

'Look, Paul, they're no guarantees in life. From my limited experience, there are no easy answers either and you may well be right, the same could happen again to us. All I know is that I share your concerns, they're real to me too but I want us to carry on and enjoy each other's company. Have fun but somehow keep our feelings in check as best we can until sometime soon the way ahead seems clearer. It's a risk of course but talking about it this evening makes it seem the obvious, maybe the best, although inevitably most frustrating way forward. Does that make any sense?'

We look at each other and wonder if we are fooling ourselves; how that sometime may never come or whether the time is ever going to be right. It's all so pathetic that two relatively young people allow their passion for science to dominate to a point where we let our lives drift by, to just wait and see. Paul has often said that taking no decision is, or can be, an effective decision by itself. But whatever the rights or wrongs, that's our collective feeling as the chapel bell strikes midnight and we kiss before Paul escorts me back to my rooms.

To my immense relief, the first thing next day Paul does is come up and put his arm around my shoulder and give me a big squeeze. Instinctively, I asked Paul if he'd like to go and see the latest Claude Chabrol film at the Arts Theatre. I'm so glad he says yes, albeit he wryly adds how he can't wait to start feeling guilty all over again. We both laugh as I elbow him in the ribs, after which he feigns pain and admits it really hurt.

'You don't know your own strength, Kay,' he complains.

'I think we both know our strengths and weaknesses by now,' I reply as we nod in agreement and in sympathy.

It's the middle of July and Paul is trying to steer a punt upriver to Grantchester Meadows for a picnic on a hot and humid Sunday afternoon. He's struggling in comparison to many practised undergraduates shooting past us. I try not to tease him but suggest he concentrate on the job at hand rather than eyeing some of the undergraduate girls sporting a wide selection of miniskirts, which I thought and hoped had gone out of fashion by now but had clearly not. Paul remains silent while getting frustrated as the punt swerves from one bank to another. Eventually, we get back to the middle of the river but he's irritated so I tease him further.

'Thought you'd have plenty of practice canoeing on your favourite Great Lakes, so should be able to steer straight along this tiny River Cam.'

Fortunately, he calms down enough to listen to the endless description of my day-to-day struggles at work. Glad he's so attentive as I'd be bored stiff by now. I'm so absorbed with the world around the laboratory that I'm giddy with excitement. Particularly today, I've been bragging about reprints of two new papers on cereal growth enhancement using my derivative enzyme substitution technique. Our punt slowly edges around the long bend towards Grantchester Meadows. Paul's gaze is suddenly distracted but not by a girl's miniskirt this time. I ask him what's wrong. He knows me well enough to realise I won't put up with some pathetic excuse or bland reply.

So much so, that it's not long before he tells me how over the past week his so-called mini taskforce has abandoned their time-consuming tried and tested iterative software programming to calculate the infamous energy retention factors. He says it's simply not giving reliable enough results or meaningful answers when plugged into Ping's economic model. More alarmingly, the powerful IBM computer is taking hideous amounts of time and memory shunting round and round in circles with Miriam's fifty-stack prototype decay data. As he feared, the results are worse than those from the three-stack prototype. He's doubting his decision to move on from the three-stack prototype but now things must change and change fast.

'What's next?' I ask.

He's quiet for a very long time while he tries to avoid two punts bound together and steered by some spotty-faced youth wishing to impress three girls in very small bikinis. Paul eventually turns my way and continues.

'We know that the bio-battery's mathematical decay function is so complex that we're using calculus to differentiate its electrical decay function to assess the energy retention factor. Unfortunately, as we guessed, the decay function has this partial integer in it. It could be a half, a third, whatever. We're still guessing. Our programme software is also guessing to try and get closer to a constant value that we can use. Well, it doesn't get that close, repetitive iterations don't work. We never get the same result twice and sometimes the figure just drifts off with time. It's a bit like those physicists working on the Manhattan Project developing the first atomic bomb.'

'Some thought it would ignite the atmosphere and the whole world would go up in smoke and radiation. They didn't trust the calculations or couldn't decide who was right, so in the end, they just took a punt.' He lets out an ironic laugh. 'Well, at least we're still here. Look, Ping is a brilliant mathematician but he tells me that trying to differentiate this type of function from normal calculus with a computer programme is a nightmare, it's beyond him and the machine. So, things are getting desperate. We need answers before the September press conference.'

'Oh heavens, Paul. What are you going to do?'

'Good question. Well, we might have a plan B. About two weeks ago, Ping casually mentioned that he had come across this obscure electronic or electrical technique that seems to give answers to solving complex functions like ours. He's perpetually curious by nature and a good job too. Well, we're having coffee with Marcus Cochrane at the time and he suddenly mentions that he's heard a similar story from his old chemistry professor at Downing College. He tells us that the professor has just died, which did not amuse us at the time, but how he'd dig out the professor's old papers from the library.

'It appears the professor was trying to measure and re-calculate some weird and wonderful, and apparently quite useless, metal ion diffusion coefficient with a fractional integer embedded in its decay function. Marcus described how he'd connected the electrical output to some simple resistor-capacitor parallel network and, lo and behold, it produced a time-independent straight line. More importantly, it was reproducible and a verifiable constant. We couldn't believe this story at first but Ping and Marcus quickly rigged up a similar parallel network in the laboratory with help from one of the younger engineers to see what happens using Miriam's three-stack decay data.

'Amazingly, it gave some of the best results so far for the energy retention factor. They look like credible figures, not sure how accurate yet, but more repeatable than anything we've had so far. The downside is that Ping thinks it might lead to a real problem if such a factor is put into his economic model. He's gone away to test the figures as we speak. We're all waiting for him to return and tell us what's happening. You can understand why my mind is a little distracted at present. Although, I must say, your lovely summer dress has much more to offer than those skimpy miniskirts or bikinis we've passed.'

Paul's words are accompanied by his annoying mocking laugh, so I splash some water over him to cool him down. Our day ends with a relaxing picnic in the meadow beside the bank. As the sun sets behind nearby trees, and with the talk of nuclear radiation, I take the chance to mention dad's death from a mystery illness just after the war.

'Paul, you remember I said something about a favour you could do for me one day, a personal favour.'

'Oh yes, sorry, I forgot to ask. What's it all about? Something to do with Winstanley, I remember.'

'Well, you seem to get on with him quite well. Not sure I trust him much but that doesn't matter. He's very well-connected in government circles, that's what matters.'

'Yes, he is; the cabinet office has fingers in many pies.'

I explain what happened to dad and how we haven't received a meaningful answer about his death from the Ministry of Defence; how I've received letters from his old army colleagues in New Zealand mentioning the nuclear bomb tests in the Pacific and how they think it may have something to do with the cause of dad's illness.

'That must be worrying and upsetting for you, especially your mum. What do you want me to do, Kay? Just say.'

'Well, I know it's ancient history for many but mum would like to know exactly what happened. Dad never said much to her, nor did the military doctor in charge, so I thought Winstanley might be able to get some up-to-date information from his Ministry of Defence contacts. Could you ask him a favour? I think it'll come better from you; he comes across as condescending with me.'

'Sure, no problem. Next time I see him, I'll ask. He talks regularly to MoD officials in Whitehall. Mind you, I'll be surprised if he finds out anything that's too new. Everybody seems pretty tight-lipped about anything to do with the nuclear test programme. Too many leaks. Oh dear…sorry about the pun, in the press already but I'll ask. Will that do?'

'Of course, I know it's a long shot but I promised mum I'd find out what happened and it's important to me too. Dad was a wonderful man and always believed in me. Just want to know who's to blame and why he died so young; people in government should be held to account.'

Paul puts his arm around my shoulders and squeezes gently. 'It's time to get back. I'm hoping Monday morning will bring some news from Ping.'

It's dark by the time I get back to Gonville and Caius. The porter tells me there's been some post waiting for me from Saturday morning and he wants to make sure I collect it. There are two letters hidden in my pigeonhole. One is from Manchester and the other has a Kenyan postmark and stamp. I settle down on my bed with some hot cocoa and start to read. The first is from Andreas confirming receipt of my reprints; he goes on at great length praising the quality of my Heddington work. He says he's received many requests for reprints already from around the world, as far afield as East Asia and Africa.

It's unlike him to go overboard with praise and even half-jokes that my reputation knows no bounds. Thank goodness for mum's wise words as she always warns me not to get too big-headed, although Andreas' letter won't help much with that sentiment. But when I read my second letter, things became quite surreal and I began to cry. It's from Mila at the Nairobi Agricultural Institute. She says she's been following my research very closely, how it's being discussed regularly by her colleagues, and how proud she is to tell them how she was a student of mine.

To my amazement, she believes some of my results will eventually give practical help to the people in her part of East Africa, even the people from her village. These letters help me acknowledge how my life has changed so much in the past years. I'm both happy and sad in equal measure. Happy because I have a chance to carry on with my research here with Paul, and sad because I miss the special warmth and humanity of Mila all those miles away. For some hours, I struggle to sleep but the next morning, whilst bleary-eyed during breakfast, I write a long rambling and very personal letter back to Mila as her true friend.

Chapter 13

After posting Mila's letter, I pop into Paul's office to see if he has received any news from Ping. He has but it's not clear cut. Ping thinks the economic model is hypersensitive to any minor changes in the value of the energy retention factor. First calculations for the three-stack prototype are inconclusive, although Ping thinks they just might provide a basis for using a bio-battery as part of the UK grid network. The worst-case scenario, however, is miles away from generating any useful economic return. It would only offer a marginal top-up to the energy supply that's currently available, or likely to become available, from the grid.

Paul thinks this is very bad news for the overall Pandora project but his mini task force has agreed to press ahead with using the resistor-capacitor network idea as they're getting closer to confirming a realistic electrical decay function. Engineers are making up sets of what they term electrical ladders with different lengths and combinations; they've opted for testing sets of twenty, sixty, and a hundred parallel linked resistor-capacitor pairs. Paul is hoping the different lengths will span the predicted electrical decay characteristics and allow the most accurate energy retention factor to be calculated for Ping's model.

As it is, everyone thinks it bizarre that no one really knows how or why the electrical ladders work, but they do a better job than any computer programme and deliver a result almost immediately. Paul is quite excited by the prospect.

'You just need to measure the output voltages from the electrical ladder's network, it's amazing,' he says.

If they can quickly home in on the right ladder network, then they'll go on and test it with data from the fifty-stack prototype. Paul is so reassuring and thinks there's just enough time to run the economic model before the forthcoming press conference. He has informed Winstanley who's going to brief the deputy chief scientist and eventually the junior minister. Ironically, Paul has already been congratulated on getting this far with his ideas but Winstanley has told him privately that some government officials are starting to get quite anxious.

The final days of summer hurry past as the evenings start to close in during my visit to the Station to help Mandeep complete his final hydroponic cereal trials. Returning to Heddington, I plunge headlong into the final testing of the glucose extraction unit. Everyone else is frantically trying to complete the construction of the fifty-stack demonstration unit and finish off all necessary electrical test rig measurements. Paul is working all the hours of the day and looks like it. We know it'll be a struggle to share any precious time together. He's very apologetic but as far as I'm concerned, this is exactly how science research proceeds.

At times, it's frantic and there are never enough hours in the day for what turns out to be a series of critical measurements. While this is followed by periods of tedious repetitive work where nothing much seems to happen. To his credit, and for his and my own sanity, Paul finds time to take me on the back of his Husqvarna up the A10 to Ely and the Wicken Fen Nature Reserve. Apart from that, we meet up for the occasional drink at the Mitre on Bridge Street or I go around to his flat in the Kite on a Saturday afternoon to cook him a meal. He often falls asleep on the sofa straight afterwards but at least I feel of some practical use to help boost his morale in some way at this critical time.

It's the second week of September and we're enjoying a brief Indian summer. Temperatures are in their mid-seventies and most mornings, I take a walk from Gonville and Caius to the banks of the Cam. Trees are still heavily laden but there are the first signs of them being on the turn. A quick glance at my watch tells me it's just after six o'clock and I'm wide awake, much earlier than usual, and feeling strangely nervous. I'm feeling even more nervous for Paul as yesterday everyone at Heddington was on edge, and now the day of the press conference is finally upon us. Somehow, an anxiety expressed by unknown officials in Whitehall seems to have permeated through to all of us.

Staff have been invited to the main event in the afternoon but Paul asked me and Miriam to attend a final briefing session at nine o'clock with Arrowsmith, Edgerton, and Winstanley as well as the deputy chief scientist. It's taking me some time to decide what to wear for the day. In the end, I choose my smart two-piece shot silk suit, knowing Paul will be pleased as it looks like I'm trying to impress the top brass. As I enter the hangar, Paul is showing someone, I assume to be the deputy chief scientist, around the fifty-stack prototype and integrated glucose extraction unit. As best I can judge, he seems impressed. Paul looks around and makes the introduction.

'Hello, Kay. Let me introduce the deputy chief scientist. I don't think you've met before. Dr Levine is overseeing the optimisation of our cereal glucose fuel stock and works closely with staff at the Station in the Wolds. She helped develop the hydroponic growth trials with Mandeep Singh and the glucose extraction unit you see here.'

Prompted by Paul, I take my time to describe my cereal derivative enzyme characterisation work and to his credit, the scientist shows a keen interest and wants to know what impact my work will have on cereal growth yields in the future. Miriam stands nearby but is uncharacteristically quiet and obviously wants to stay in the background. We nod and exchange glances but I feel more than a little sorry for her as she rarely gets proper credit for inventing our bio-battery. Sadly, her in-built cynicism holds her back from saying too much, particularly when civil servants are around.

As our chat comes to an end, I notice Winstanley approaches Paul to check if everyone has seen enough and to suggest we get going with our busy agenda in the meeting room. It doesn't take long before my early anxiety is reflected by everyone sitting around the table. Arrowsmith begins in his customary stilted fashion.

'First of all, Paul, I would like to thank you and your team for such a splendid job in getting the demonstrator unit ready for the minister and the press. I'm sure everyone will be highly impressed by what they see and what you've achieved in just under two years. It's an excellent example of collaborative multidisciplined research within a tight timeframe and will undoubtedly shine a light on the role of this exciting new incubator facility. Your latest report on the bio-battery fuel cell's performance is impressive. Miriam, your invention has proven to work remarkably well. The current demonstrator will surely deliver tens of megawatts from a relatively modest supply of cereal fuel stock.'

The deputy chief scientist offers his own congratulations and hints that the minister may well use Pandora as an exemplar, as he puts it, for further initiatives. Looking around the table, I couldn't help but notice that unusually for him, Winstanley looks edgy, even tense, as he scans several sheets of paper in front of him. I assume they contain a draft of the minister's speech. He looks up.

'Ladies and gentlemen, I can only endorse the deputy chief scientist's comments and particularly wish to thank the team around this table for the quality, enthusiasm, and dedication to their work, and so ably led by Paul.' He hesitates to clear his throat. 'However, I would just like to dot a few Is and cross a few Ts before the minister stands up. We're expecting a large contingent from the scientific press, some broadsheets, and most likely one or two radio and TV channels to join us this afternoon, so we need to get things right. After all, the minister will use this conference to announce further government initiatives on similar lines to Pandora. Naturally, we need to be absolutely certain about what is being stated in our press release and by the minister.'

Raising the papers in front of him, he continues. 'If I may, I'll summarise the relevant passages in this draft to make sure we're all happy and content that your research supports the substance of the words so to speak. I'm sure there'll not be a problem but it's just worth taking a few minutes to check, don't you think.' Winstanley turns to Paul. 'I notice Ping is not with us today to provide the latest data from the economic impact modelling for the demonstrator unit. As you know, the deputy chief scientist and indeed the minister have a particular interest in that aspect of the work.'

A tired-looking Paul raises his head and replies, 'We're expecting Ping to join us anytime. He's catching the earliest train out of London this morning. As you're aware, Jeremy, we've had some serious problems in getting an accurate and reliable energy retention factor for this bio-battery to use in Ping's economic model. Our computer's iterative software method wasn't working well enough owing to the complexity and unusual nature of the enzymatic bio-battery's electrical characteristics. This has troubled us over the past six months and we've only just got to grips with it.'

The deputy chief scientist coughs briefly and interrupts. 'I must say the mathematical manipulations involved with your work, Dr Wright, are stretching all our knowledge to the limit.' He smiles benignly and adds, 'But you realise how important this aspect of your work is to the eventual rollout and successful commercialisation of the fuel cell.'

'Indeed, I do. I'm pleased to say that in the past few weeks, we've adapted a novel technique using an electrical resistor-capacitor ladder to finally get an accurate energy retention factor that can be used with confidence. I won't go into its ins and outs just now; Ping and I have provided regular reports to Jeremy and Professor Arrowsmith.'

'And I've read them, Dr Wright,' interrupts the deputy chief scientist. 'Fascinating and ingenious it is too. Carry on please.'

'Well, last week, we rounded on the optimal ladder to generate a reliable factor for use with the fifty-stack demonstrator. Ping has run this factor through his model but wants to use a second set of the prototype's electrical decay data to see if the calculations are replicated or need refining. He'll report on that run as soon as he gets here; I know no more than you at this stage.'

Paul anxiously steers his eyes towards me but all I can do is smile to reassure him. Suddenly, I catch sight of a car drawing up outside the building and hear Ping striding on the gravel towards the main door. Winstanley narrows his eyes and stares at Paul before continuing.

'Ok, it sounds like we might be hearing from Ping soon, let's hope so. Now let me just outline what the minister in his statement will say. He'll confirm that the demonstrator unit on show is a proven stepping stone to achieving the first generation of commercially available potential gigawatt bio-fuel cells. It is the first example of an energy platform based on the sustainability concept…from Cereal to Power. The government is satisfied that proof of concept has been demonstrated and met all the stringent criteria necessary to provide a novel economically viable standalone source of green energy.'

'It will sit alongside a new generation power grid that looks to shift the UK's energy mix away from the extensive use of climate unfriendly labour-intensive coal and paves the way to secure the many benefits and advantages from the future adoption of natural gas and nuclear power. The government will continue to fund the Pandora project for as long as it needs to take this proof of concept forward to commercial manufacture via a competitive tendering process.'

I wince at the phrase…from Cereal to Power. It's trite and meaningless.

'You seem unhappy with something, Kay,' mutters Winstanley.

'The bio-fuel cell runs on a specific glucose composite mix that happens in this case to be extracted from cereal. But it could possibly come from another source of glucose,' I explain.

'Quite right, Kay, but our public relations team tend to like a popular catchphrase and reference to glucose composite mix or even just glucose is a bit too, um…techie for the general public.'

Although not surprised, my back and neck muscles tighten as I rile against Winstanley's condescending attitude. However, for everyone's sake, I ignore him; this isn't the time to quibble over the choice of a phrase, so I keep my mouth shut. It's clear Winstanley is operating in transmit mode only as he looks around the table and asks if there are any problems with the conclusions and proposals in the statement. Paul starts to ask something about whether there's sufficient evidence to support a future gigawatt bio-battery when Ping bursts into the room with a sheet of paper in his hand. He's red-faced, highly animated, and stares at Arrowsmith, who looks him in the eye and quietly asks him to sit down before continuing.

'Good of you to join us, Ping. Jeremy is just going over the minister's statement. I assume you've seen the latest draft.'

Slightly breathless, Ping replies, 'Yes, I was handed a copy late last night.' Taking a large gulp of air before he blurts out to everyone in earshot.

'And you can't run with it. Not as it is, the economic evidence is not there to fully justify introducing the bio-battery in its current form as an integral part of the UK grid.'

Paul interrupts. 'Ping, what are you saying?'

'I'm sorry, Paul, but as agreed yesterday, I ran our optimal energy retention factor through the economic model again last night. This time using the latest set of electrical decay data taken from the fifty-stack unit. The results are almost identical to the first set, they're rock solid with minimal standard error. The model's KPIs show it will have minimal impact on the overall grid power levels over the course of a twenty-year lifetime, even with the projected hundreds of units of a potential hundred-stack device.'

'KPIs?' Edgerton asks, who's remained studiously quiet so far.

'Key Performance Indicators,' replies Ping with an air of disdain. 'They all point to the battery not retaining sufficient power for long enough to be of any significant use under a heavy load. Not with the current construction at least.'

Colour drains from Paul's face as he quickly responds, 'What if we make further changes to the enzyme mediator and electrode structure of the battery, Miriam? Can anything be done there?'

Miriam starts to speak but is interrupted by the deputy chief scientist. 'Have you looked at modifying the design at all, Dr Handley?'

Miriam struggles to continue and keep her temper but adds forcibly, 'Yes, we have. I've used different combinations of enzyme mediators, changed the enzyme deposition process, and even switched to a different type of plastic separator without any significant effect. Kay and I have also tried to improve the bio-matching of my enzyme mediator to her novel derivative enzymes glucose product without effect. They all give the same electrical decay data that goes into the calculation of the energy retention factor. It will need much more work to see what else can be done.'

Arrowsmith jumps in. 'Ping, are you absolutely certain about these model calculations?'

'Absolutely certain, Professor, I wish they were otherwise.'

The deputy chief scientist scrutinises each of our faces in turn. He shuffles slightly in his seat, whispers some words to Winstanley, and pronounces in his measured way.

'Ladies and gentlemen, we need to deal with this issue before the minister arrives. Thank you, Dr Levine, Dr Handley, and Dr Edgerton. There's no need to detain you any longer. Dr Wright, I'd like you to stay, please. Could one of you please ask the ladies dealing with refreshments to send in some tea and sandwiches as we may need to stay here and work through lunch? Thank you all again, we will see you at two-thirty for the press conference. The minister arrives at two o'clock.'

On that instruction, Miriam and I leave the room. We struggle to know what to say as Dr Edgerton comes up and tries to reassure us.

'Things will turn out ok, try not to worry. This is when the top brass earns their corn.'

I look at Miriam and shake my head. My twisted memory is of Paul's grey face angrily distorted by shadows of anxiety, and being thoroughly excoriated by Winstanley and Arrowsmith as he faces the eye of a political storm that must still run its course.

There's a steady hum from radio and television equipment as I quickly straighten my skirt and top before entering the hangar. It's two o'clock and powerful television lights focus on a podium with a lectern in the middle and half a dozen chairs on either side. A spotlight shines on the fifty-stack prototype at the far side of the hangar. Marcus Cochrane and Elizabeth Saxby are nearby with several journalists deep in conversation; flash bulbs explode, and there's real excitement in the air. From where I stand, the prototype is alongside an experimental version of a domestic video player connected to the latest commercially available portable colour television.

It makes me wonder how much mum would like one instead of her tiny old black and white set. A government promotional video is running with several earnest academics in hard hats and yellow vests standing in front of a nuclear power station as they try to crystal gaze into a future UK energy supply industry.

From speaking to one or two of the journalists, their endless optimism seems misplaced, but perhaps journalists always worry about what academics and politicians say to them. Whereas, I'm increasingly anxious for Paul and my colleagues as the noisy clock over the main entrance ticks closer and closer to two-thirty.

Suddenly, two broadsheet science editors walk forward and ask how I've come to be part of Pandora and what's it like working here. They question why my enzyme work is so important to the development of the bio-battery. They seem genuinely interested in what I do, so it's a chance for me to explain in some detail and introduce Mandeep from the Station. Mandeep asks if they'll write a story about how derivative enzymes can improve cereal crop yields in the Third World. They say it's more than likely as it's a strong angle for the general public who like stories on how technology spin-off improves their day-to-day lives.

One even quotes an example of how Teflon-coated frying pans came out of NASA's space programme. A minute later, from the corner of my eye, I spot a young lady press officer dressed in a dark blue two-piece heading for the microphone. She asks everyone to take their seats as the conference is about to start. TV and radio crews get into position and I join Miriam, James Alonso, Mandeep Singh, and Michael Womack on a row of seats reserved at the back of the main audience. With the minimum of fanfare, a smiling science minster in a very expensive grey suit, Professor Arrowsmith, the deputy chief scientist, Winstanley, and Paul climb onto the podium.

Paul looks intensely serious and to my eyes, almost in shell shock. I'm guessing he hasn't had much time for any proper lunch and he hates sandwiches anyway. He blinks as he faces the audience and lights. He briefly catches my eye and I see he's shaking his head almost imperceptibly from side to side. No one else will have noticed but it's clear from his body language that he's deeply unhappy. The press officer makes the introductions and invites the minister to come forward. She says copies of his speech and press release will be made available immediately after the minister sits down. I look towards Miriam; we try to smile but visibly stiffen as the minister stands up.

The minister's opening remarks don't seem to connect to anything that is on show in the hangar. He's almost semi-detached in his manner as we look around and wonder why we're all here. Referring to his earlier speech so many months ago, he uses Pandora to promote the role of the government in funding science and technology innovation. He highlights how this Heddington incubator and others to follow are critical to securing new large-scale research funding following the UK's entry into the European Economic Community.

As forecast, he describes two more government-funded projects based on the current template and ominously the lessons learnt from Pandora. I look towards Paul and Miriam; they're open-mouthed, lost in thought. To my amazement, it's only now that our work is going to be mentioned in any detail as the minister says he would like to add some final remarks.

Minister of State, Department of Trade and Industry…

Ladies and gentlemen, let me conclude by offering my sincere congratulations to Professor Arrowsmith and his team here at Heddington on the fine multidisciplined research that has taken Pandora forward over the past two years. It shines a welcome light on the quality and depth of our UK research base in natural sciences and engineering of which we must all be proud. As we look around us today, their work on an enzymatic bio-battery is a stepping stone to the development of alternative energy sources. Their proof of concept in realising Cereal to Power provides for exciting new opportunities and applications.

My department will now undertake a wide-ranging feasibility study to actively exploit this innovative low-cost fuel cell technology across the government. Examples may be found in the realm of local government power supply contingency planning, in-theatre military applications, and many other exciting areas. We may look forward to its eventual rollout and commercial manufacture via a competitive tendering process in the not-too-distant future. My thanks go to all the staff at Heddington for such an enjoyable day and for showing me the fruits of their research. Thank you.

The minister walks back from the lectern, shakes hands with all those around him on the podium, and slowly looks ahead for the exit and the government Daimler. All the while, his words swirl around in my head; in-theatre military applications, no mention of the UK grid network. My whole body seems to tremble; first from the shock of his underwhelming dismissive words and then from anger, just raw anger. Miriam puts her hand on my arm and squeezes gently to calm me down, but instinctively, I pull away.

Wondering what's happening to my emotions, I glimpse Paul having a final chat with the minister. My torment is complete as this grey-suited official and his entourage slide past me towards his car. Time is suspended, anger isn't, and without further thought, I stand up and shout incoherently towards Paul.

'No. No. Is this what our research has come to? Is this it? In-theatre military applications. What have you done? What have we done to deserve this? Why? His words are cheap, but their meaning is dear, and they will cost us.'

Winstanley glares at me from the podium. Press correspondents, television and radio crews turn in my direction, eyes wide open. There's a prophetic silence; within seconds, there's the toxic sight of a collective shrug of the shoulders. Everyone is closing their notebooks and packing up their equipment ready to leave. And to my horror, I join them.

Part Five
Side Reactions

Chapter 14

The pilot's plummy voice floats over the speaker system to announce our BOAC VC 10 flight is preparing to land at Nairobi International Airport. It's late afternoon and he wants us to know that we'll soon be feeling the benefits of a hot Kenyan sun and beautiful blue sky. Ground temperature is in the seventies and a quick glance at my fellow passengers tells me they're eager to welcome the contrast between the leaden skies and the frozen ground of Manchester. It felt strange putting on a thin cotton dress in my flat during the middle of winter but Mila made sure I knew what to expect some weeks earlier.

Somehow, five months have passed since I walked out of the Pandora Press Conference and how my life has been turned upside down. Life's serendipity keeps such strange bedfellows. For how fortunate it was that Mila and I kept in touch after her heart-warming letter of last summer whilst trying to erase the memory of the horror from the Pandora project. I'm still unable to come to terms with how it was so ruthlessly abandoned and its scientists moved on. Except one hurtful dismal memory persists—a coy Winstanley announcing that Paul will stay on to finish any remaining prototype development work with a skeleton staff and the picture of a heartbroken Paul letting slip at one of our wash-up meetings that he'd been given little choice if he wanted any further government work.

Paul said he'd help finish the minister's feasibility study, a study he described as a facile paper exercise. As our conversations became more and more strained, I realised it was inevitable that I'd turn in on myself and look to self-analyse what happened. Stupidly, I started blaming myself and of course, Paul, although we were ably aided and abetted by Winstanley for allowing Pandora to degenerate into some pathetic pet project for the minister and presumably the military establishment in some bizarre way. I've never really come to terms with what happened, how the project's grand ambitions were highjacked without any serious consultation with those actually working on it.

Looking back, I was probably naïve in terms of the government's actual intentions or their subsequent behaviour. Nevertheless, I feel manipulated, knowing that the fruits of my research are so abused in such a shabby twisted way while understanding full well their potential for doing good in the world. I keep telling myself that's the real reason I'm flying to Nairobi and not running away.

Although my first time on an aeroplane, and a long-haul flight to boot, with all the excitement, I'd fallen soundly asleep soon after take-off. Perhaps I was over tired from the hectic packing or more likely BOAC's generous glass of complimentary red wine on an empty stomach. Who knows, but after an hour or so, I suddenly woke up with a start. That's when I began to think about all the people I'd left behind. Especially how much I owe Andreas Mikkelsen and my loving mum for getting me through such a low and difficult period. And then, there's Paul. At the time, I simply couldn't face him or even be around Cambridge any longer.

After such a wretched bout of anger with everything and everyone, rightly or wrongly, I hurried back to Manchester as soon as I could to my haven that was the department and Andreas without knowing what lay in front of me. Andreas made it clear early on that I could return to lecturing but with a shocking caveat, he insisted my research change tack because so much of his MAFF funding had been transferred to other projects. With my barely concealed scepticism, Andreas tried to explain that these funding changes might turn out to be a positive outcome of Pandora.

Fortunately, we could always speak frankly with one another. He's very direct, a trait I much admire, so a week later while having a coffee, he gently questioned if my perspective on academic life had changed. He said he wasn't pushing me in any particular direction but he's very perceptive where people are concerned. He somehow knew I was getting frustrated, particularly about how my research hasn't been translated into anything useful in the real world. In the end, we agreed that there was a need for change for several reasons, one being my feelings for Paul. Luckily for me, he never pushed further on that subject, which came as a relief because my emotions were still raw at the time.

But he said that his own path had changed at a similar stage in his career and that I should not be afraid to act or take a risk. By chance, I'd mentioned my continued friendship with Mila, so we agreed to write to Mila and explain my situation to see if we can foster a collaboration in some way. It was a refreshing idea and within weeks, Andreas popped into my laboratory with the news that the institute was offering me an initial six-month research fellowship working alongside Mila to help devise a long-term research programme based on the use of derivative enzyme technology.

Their goal was to improve the growth yields of the common strains of cereal cultivated in Kenya. Andreas went on to speak with the institute's director and sort out a generous stipend for me. I remember racing back to mum one weekend to seek reassurance after panicking over all the practical difficulties of living abroad for the first time and whether I could cope with the change. Mum, as only a mum can, gave me all the practical help she could muster but most valuable of all, she gave love and kindness to her only child, who despite her years was but a little frightened.

Such memories and feelings persisted throughout the flight, even while resisting the efforts of an over-eager air hostess trying to sell me some expensive duty-free perfume. Despite those feelings of uncertainty fading over the past months, I cannot escape the fact that I'm leaving the UK with some deep regrets. Regrets of unable to properly say goodbye to Paul and how I said never to contact me again, even though I still miss him. Sadly, regrets over losing contact with so many good friends from Heddington, Miriam, James, and Michael. Then there's the restlessness that bubbles to the surface some nights while I lay awake and reflect on my behaviour at a critical time.

The inability to control my emotions, even my anger, at that fateful press conference. How I embarrassed Paul, my friends, and myself in front of everyone. It's easy enough to rationalise why I reacted that way but I still find it hard to understand or accept the fact that I made little attempt to give Paul any benefit of the doubt. Perhaps, I should have realised what was happening on the day, or even earlier, with events that were well beyond anything we could control. But I didn't. Now it's too late as I take my first step onto the tarmac at Nairobi International Airport.

Hopefully, it's time to come to terms and live with my behaviour, with those regrets and the sadness, well, as much as anyone can. Without a doubt, though, these past five months have made me more determined to gain the most from this opportunity, to work hard at this fledgling agricultural research institute, and to take the chance to experience my deep longing for the countryside and its wildlife in such an exotic part of the world. To live with all that uncertainty and regret but with the growing ambition to make a success of my time here. These thoughts come to a timely end to be overtaken by the need to drag two large suitcases through the Arrivals hall.

Particularly, as one is carefully packed with a couple of the special ion-exchange columns from my favourite Leeds company. Their Customs and Immigration take forever to let me through despite kindly ignoring both the carefully wrapped columns. It's with some relief, that I catch sight of a smiling Mila, who's frantically waving from the other side of the building's main exit. Then, suddenly, I'm hugging her as if we've never been apart. She looks radiant in her brightly coloured shift dress, her eyes beaming with a smile that lights up her whole face. She grasps both my hands; our eyes meet and she's the first to say something.

'Oh, Dr Levine, it's so wonderful to have you visit my homeland and work with us. It's a great honour for the institute and my colleagues. A big welcome to Nairobi.'

'My dear Mila, I thought we'd sorted this out long ago. Let's start by not having any of these silly formalities. It's Kay, remember, and I'm so very happy and excited to be here. It means a lot to me, more than you'll ever know. It's going to be such a wonderful experience.'

Mila looks a little confused at first but quickly replies, 'Oh right, of course, so be it. I'm certain you'll enjoy your time here. Everyone is so looking forward to meeting you and we'll do everything possible to show you our wonderful country. And you'll never be cold, I can almost guarantee that.' We both laugh as Mila continues, 'Let's get your bags in the car and settle you into your new home.'

We set off for the institute in her vintage dark green Land Rover. It's just like being on one of our field trips at the Station all over again, except this time, we travel along the broad thoroughfares of historic Nairobi. The streets are bleached by sunlight and filled with noisy cars, horns blazing. Policemen in smart white uniforms and gloved hands perch on raised wooden platforms directing traffic at every major crossroad. Pavements are lined with date palms and crowds of people spill out from busy bars and restaurants. High-rise angular modern buildings glisten in the sun and I'm soon struck by the sheer vibrancy of this modern bustling city.

English signs are everywhere and it's not long before I catch sight of what Mila calls British Expats dressed in thin brightly coloured cotton dresses and lightweight safari suits walking languidly home at the end of a working day. This is a young dynamic city full of optimism and energy. Mila epitomises that optimism as she drives through the western outskirts of the city.

'You've had a very long flight, Kay, so I'm taking you straight to your new bungalow close to the grounds of the institute. It's to the northwest of the city centre and normally takes about an hour if the traffic lets us. But as you can see, we've lots and lots of cars on the roads. Mind you, it wasn't like this as a young girl growing up; things are changing fast and Nairobi is now a prosperous city. We've been independent for just ten years you know, and everything is expanding so fast. Our economy, the population, our academic community, and scientific research too.

'You may not be aware but the historic English-speaking countries of Kenya, Ghana, and Malawi have all received some very generous World Bank and Overseas Development Aid in recent years; it's given our cities a real boost. But as you can see, Kenya still has a close connection with the old British Empire. See, we're driving down Princess Elizabeth Way, past Coronation Avenue and King Steet. Victoria Street is over there to the north. Believe it or not, most of us still love your royal family, we like our queens.' Mila glances around to check on me and sympathetically remains silent for the rest of our drive.

Tiredness gives way to a yawn as Mila lets me know we're getting close to arriving at my new home. I've no idea what to expect except it's not going to be some bland concrete hotel in a dusty street. We drive past some small wheat and corn fields that remind me of the ones cultivated at the Station. There's a group of date palms and tall spiky bushes ahead that surround a large, grassed area containing three smallish wooden bungalows. Mila pulls up beside the middle one and shifts my heavy suitcases onto its raised covered veranda that's complete with a rocking chair, swing seat and a low table.

She enters the building and brings out a large jug of water, what looks like fresh mango juice and some neatly cut rounds of sandwiches. I sit on the rocking chair and take a long deep breath; it's heaven to stop travelling and bathe in the peace and quiet of the early evening. Mila offers a glass of chilled mango juice; the taste is a revelation. Looking out, I notice my bungalow is surrounded on three sides by an amazing array of trees and bushes. I recognise papyrus, avocado and mango. We sit quietly for some time before Mila breaks the silence.

'This is your new home, Kay. I hope you'll be comfortable. The bungalows on either side are rarely occupied, so you'll have plenty of privacy. You'll find most things you need inside but it's not a hotel so no waiter or air-conditioning.'

She smiles. 'In the rainy season, you might find the humidity too much but the slatted windows will help cool you down at night. Might take you a while to acclimatise though. The institute is close by and the fields we passed on the way belong to us and form an important part of our research programme.'

'One field of wheat is being used to experiment with your derivative enzymes; we're using the same ion-exchange column mentioned in your last paper from Project Pandora. Everyone is waiting for the trial results but sometimes our laboratory analyses take a bit longer here. Well, that's enough from me for now.' Mila gets up to leave and points to the sandwiches, saying she'll pop over tomorrow afternoon.

'Get some rest, Kay, it's been a long trip; call my home if there's anything urgent you need. My township is only half an hour's drive away. I've left you a few basic provisions in the fridge but don't worry, I'll show you around the shopping mall and market tomorrow.'

We grab each other's hands and hug. Mila's eyes start to well up.

'You don't know how happy I am to be here, Mila.' My throat tightens and my eyes mirror hers. Telling myself that my adventure has begun, I settle back in the rocking chair to the accompaniment of a host of noisy, angry cicadas. I make light work of the sandwiches and marvel again at the taste of fresh mango while anticipating a good night's sleep.

My first month at the institute passes like a whirlwind. I'm not sure what Mila has said to the staff but I'm treated with amazing kindness. Within days, I'm introduced to the director, Dr Usha Chadha, a charming Indian woman in her forties who studied in the US. I learn that over recent years, there's been real pressure placed on Kenyan Asians, including some of their top academics, to move on with many fleeing to the UK. Mila says it's no secret that their government is keen for local Kenyans to take on the senior roles in their institutions. But Usha, she's so well-qualified and respected that everyone believes nothing is going to change any time soon.

In fact, her US passport helps secure some much-needed research grants. My other main contact is their Head of Cereal Research, Professor Joseph Wasike. Joseph studied in London and happily for me, knows Aden and Mandeep from the Wolds Station quite well. He's keen to let me know confidentially that it didn't take them long to convince the institute to offer me the fellowship. As Joseph points out, 'We all live and work in a small and closely knit world of experimental agriculture research.'

Keen to make an impression, it doesn't take me long to plan a series of experiments and trials that not only mimic my own work at Manchester, Cambridge, and the Station but to take the research one stage further. There's clearly no need for small-scale laboratory-based hydroponic trials in Kenya as the rainy season spans April and May and earlier trials have shown that their much larger batches of lower-concentration derivative enzymes from the ion-exchange columns work well. But I soon came to realise that Joseph expects even more from me as he places me in charge of planning the future direction of their wheat growth development programme.

It's such a shock that he places so much trust in me so early on and I feel very aware of my responsibilities. All this comes as a welcome relief and a genuine distraction from any negative thoughts I harbour over Pandora. To my delight, Mila shows me around the cereal fields where batches of derivative enzymes are trialled. Rigorous hydroponic culture is replaced by the young plants lined up on either side of carefully sealed irrigation channels made from locally baked clay. The first crop is expected in early June.

Another priority is to improve the turn round time for samples in their analytical laboratory. As a first step, I purchase some up-to-date equipment from a well-established UK supplier. Everyone agrees there's an urgent need to quickly measure glucose and enzyme levels in young plants. Embarrassing as it is after the first few months, Joseph, Mila, and her hardworking laboratory technicians insist on telling me how exciting my work is and to my surprise, I already feel quite at home and a valued member of the institute.

So much so, that one day, I buy a car so I can drive into Nairobi and explore the local townships. Everyone insists that walking into the city centre in the heat of the day with the heavy rains to come is silly, particularly for a white-skinned expat. One of Mila's brothers sells cars at a local garage so in a rush of blood, I buy this battered old blue VW Beetle Convertible; it's noisy with a piercing whine from the engine in the back but fun to drive. At first, driving on crowded roads is scary but my panic soon subsides with the help of several polite and reassuring local policemen stationed at busy crossroads.

By now, my working week is taking on a regular pattern until one day when I make a new acquaintance. Sharing an afternoon coffee break with Mila and Joseph is one of my favourite times and I'm also addicted to their homemade mango sundae. Joseph has been meaning to introduce one of his colleagues from the University of Kenya in central Nairobi. Apparently, today is the day as this tall, good-looking man in a loose-fitting denim suit sits down at our table. He's introduced as Professor Richard Kinama from the Plant Science and Crop Protection Department; a young, energetic, and seriously ambitious scientist with a growing international reputation.

At first, he's rather too flattering for my taste saying how he's been closely following my work on derivative enzymes for some years. He believes my results might be of value to his line of research. The professor immediately invites me to visit his laboratories and he's very insistent. So, by the end of the week, I'm driving across the northeast outskirts of the city to the university's main campus surrounded by its own beautiful, landscaped grounds. He's very charming, perhaps too charming, as he takes the whole morning to show me his laboratories and introduce his teaching and research staff.

It almost feels like an interview and somehow, I'm not surprised when he suggests we meet again. Despite his attention, it's a relief to get back to the institute and seek out Mila so I can quiz her about Richard Kinama. Her reply is revealing.

'Well, Kay, I'm not surprised you ask about him. Professor Kinama is a very bright man and he's made a real name for himself in a short period of time. He's a man in a hurry and undoubtedly a true expert in developing new strains of wheat and maize seeds. He's also well-connected to some important government officials and our international funding agencies. Joseph tells me he's not the best teacher and often neglects his lecturing duties. Don't know if you realise but the university only got its independent charter in 1970. Before that, it was part of a group of East African colleges and institutes. Now it's got its own money and they're looking to make a name for themselves in the region.

'Our institute works closely with the university's agricultural departments; we're the practical real-world arm of their research with all the experience, outdoor facilities, and land to literally take their research into the field.' Mila starts to giggle after I ask her to continue with her story about Kinama. 'Look, the collaboration works well enough, most times, and it'll be a good thing for you to get to know him while you're here. Kinama and Joseph are friends and he's clearly taken a liking to you and your research.'

'Is it that obvious?' I ask.

'Oh yes,' says Mila letting out an embarrassed laugh. 'He's a very confident chap with lots of charm. They say he likes the ladies but has a little too much regard for himself at times.' She grins. 'But I'm sure you can look after yourself in that respect. If our latest trials are successful, the next step will be for him to use the plants with modified enzymes to develop new seed strains with enhanced glucose levels. Which is what we all want, isn't it?'

'Don't worry, Mila, I've had enough of personal relationships for the time being.'

'Oh no, don't say that, Kay. Scientists have plenty of emotions too, we all need them.'

I grimace. 'I'll try and remember that.'

Strangely enough, I think back to this conversation three weeks later while sitting on my veranda after narrowly avoiding a soaking from an early evening downpour. Everyone keeps telling me what to expect from the April rains, now I understand. It started raining heavily from four o'clock and it's only now beginning to dry up. I've invited Mila for supper and I nervously bring out my first attempt at a local Nairobi dish. One of her favourites is Nyama Choma and I've used vegetables instead of meat as Mila is vegetarian. She's genuinely surprised that I've even attempted such a dish, especially when it comes to my version of local dumplings called Ugali made from maize flour.

Ugali is so filling that I struggle to get through much of it, whereas Mila tucks in and is pleased to pronounce that they'll make a Nairobian of me yet. For once, the cicadas are quiet so only a repetitive drip, drip, drip from the surrounding trees on the wooden roof keeps us company. A content-looking Mila helps with me the dishes as I get straight to the point with my news and ask for help.

'Joseph came to see me this morning, Mila, and told me he's been asked by Professor Kinama if the institute would release me for a day or two a week to present some lectures at the university. Kinama wants me to talk to his MSc students about my research into derivative enzymes and glucose production in cereals. He also wants some basic lectures on photosynthesis and the Calvin Cycle in plants for his final-year students. Apparently, he's told Joseph that there's no one better qualified to do the job at present.' I raise my eyebrows and shrug my shoulders. 'What should I do, Mila?'

'Well, of course, Kinama is right, Kay. I say take it, it's a great opportunity for you. You gave me the best possible start in Manchester and I'll never forget your lectures and your help with my research project. You'll be a great asset to the university and Joseph may see it as a way of building better links between our departments even if it's only for a few months. Make sure you get properly paid, though, you deserve it.'

'Oh yes, Joseph says I would be made a visiting lecturer for my time and put on their payroll if it's allowed. Thanks, Mila. Right, it's a big decision so I'll sleep on it. Joseph seems to be happy enough.'

Mila casts her eyes towards me with some suspicion and adds, 'Kinama can be very charming as you know, so just make sure you send him the right signals early on.'

'Oh yes, I'll make sure I do that alright if I go ahead.'

We sit on the veranda and drink tea. Then just as Mila is leaving, she retrieves some letters from her bag saying the post had come after I'd left the laboratory for the day. I take a quick look and thank Mila. One is from mum; we've been writing regularly about once a month. I'll write again soon if I go ahead and accept this visiting lectureship. The second is in a large envelope and from Andreas as I recognise his handwriting. It's been nice to keep in touch as we're preparing some joint papers using my latest results here. Tearing open the envelope, I get a shock; it includes a letter with a Cambridge postmark. I fix my eyes on it for what seems ages. My hand starts to shake as I look up to Mila but only stare into nothingness.

'What heavens is the matter?' Mila asks. 'You look as if you've seen a ghost. Are you ill? Is it the Ugali? Sometimes it can sit a bit heavy on the tummy.'

'No, no, it's ok, Mila. Just a bit of a shock. One of the letters is from an old friend. I wasn't expecting it.'

'Looks like more than just a friend, Kay. Is this when you stopped being a one hundred per cent scientist?' She adds wryly.

'Perhaps, Mila, perhaps.'

'In that case, let me leave you. I'm sure you don't want me around any longer. Plenty to think about, I think. Perhaps a bit premature but many congratulations on becoming a visiting lecturer at the University of Kenya. No looking back now, eh?'

I keep busy tidying up for as long as I can but eventually go to my bedroom and change. That letter and Mila's comments set my brain racing; my thoughts travel far and they're hard to deal with. Such as when will I ever stop living in the past? I start to open the letter, then grab a glass and pour myself a large Changaa spirit, its Dutch courage, as I slowly read Paul's neat handwriting.

Paul Wright, Cambridge, April 1973

Dearest Kay,

I know we agreed not to contact each other after you left Cambridge and I fully accept and respect that decision. But I asked Andreas Mikkelsen to pass on this one and final letter to you, wherever you are. So sorry to do this to you but I explained the reason why and he relented in the end. Please, do not blame Andreas for agreeing and for any delay. He always had your best interest at heart. Let me say our time together in Cambridge was very special. Well, it was for me and I sincerely believe it was for you too. For that reason, I now wish to have one last try to explain my side of events leading up to that terrible press conference.

At the time, I was told not to pass on this information to anyone, but that is nonsense for someone who gave so much to the project. You deserve better, as I did, from our masters in Whitehall. It has been a bitter lesson to learn for both of us I am sure. I don't expect forgiveness or want your sympathy; you were angry and disappointed, and I know you expected better of me. Truly, I am disappointed in myself but time moves on, and all I can do now is to be totally honest with you.

I had no idea that Pandora was going to be effectively cancelled on the day of the press conference. As you know, my work with Ping was touch and go but I fully expected the project to continue. It was only when we heard Ping's news and views at that fateful morning meeting that the mood changed. After you left, it became clear that Winstanley and the deputy chief scientist already knew of Ping's results from the night before and had indeed been concocting an alternative speech for the minister for some time. Not sure why they were not upfront with us earlier at the meeting; being generous maybe they just wanted to test if we had some design improvements in the locker.

But I find their whole approach duplicitous in the extreme. Just to be clear, I was not consulted further in any serious way except being asked to go on the platform to show support on behalf of the project team. Ping and I tried to argue for more time to see what design changes could be made to improve the bio-battery's energy retention but they would not hear of it. Arrowsmith was silent throughout, he seemed very disappointed. They wanted to press on with other projects and not spend any more departmental money on Pandora; money that had already been earmarked for new projects announced that day.

Money and politics shout the most loudly, I think. Winstanley said Pandora had done its job and he had already discussed its wider application within the Ministry of Defence, which was keen and had much bigger budgets.

I will say no more on the matter. Pandora is the past and you will make your own judgement on what I should or should not have done. I can only say how sorry I am for the way things worked out. It hurt you deeply, I know. As a result, we will never see each other again. But our time in Cambridge was a joy that I will never forget. The line dancing, madrigals in the chapel, jazz in the Kite (perhaps?), Claude Chabrol, dancing to Moon River at the Mill; those memories live on. Your beautiful dresses, your stunning dark eyes and hair, and oh yes, your berets.

Wherever you are, I wish you well, that you find success with your amazing research and that it makes a real difference to hungry people around the world. After all, that is what you have always wanted. I will be leaving Cambridge soon for pastures anew, although I am still not sure where. Arrowsmith says he may have a project that makes better use of my skills but I am not so sure and need time to reflect on my future. Look after yourself; do not forget to put on that beautiful emerald green ball gown once in a while.

Yours ever, Paul

P.S.

As promised, I spoke with Winstanley about the death of your dad. I realise you never really liked the man but he did, however, speak with his contacts at the Ministry of Defence and at a particularly high level within their Medical Corps. In confidence, he confirms that there is increasing evidence and concern that many British and Allied troops on the ships patrolling the Pacific at the time of the nuclear tests on Christmas Island and elsewhere were affected by radiation levels held within rain clouds. This is almost certainly the cause of the high numbers of recorded deaths from blood and other cancers, including your dad. This information has not yet been made public in the UK.

The ministry and the local medics who treated your dad will deny it. However, he strongly suggests that you and your mum keep in touch with your dad's New Zealand army friends to help push the authorities for full disclosure and compensation. Winstanley told me privately that it may take many years to achieve this and that our past Allies are more advanced in wanting to uncover the truth and make a claim. He wishes your family well with your endeavours.

My body crumples as I return the letter to its envelope and place it carefully into the decorative-style Japanese jewellery box resting on the dressing table; a box mum gave me before I left for Nairobi. Without warning, tears streaming uncontrollably down my cheeks. I pour myself another Changaa and curl up under a sheet to try and sleep. But it's impossible and not because of the driving rain bouncing off the roof. I call Mila the next morning to say I'm not feeling well and go back to bed searching for a few hours' peace and sleep. At the end of the week, I drive over to the university to see Professor Kinama and accept his offer of a visiting lectureship.

On my return, Mila and Joseph show their delight at my news. Soon enough, Mila takes me to one side and asks how I'm feeling as she guesses I've been deeply troubled by the mystery letter.

'It's ok now, I'm fine, Mila,' I reply. 'I can honestly say that the letter made my decision easier; no need to worry about me.'

That same evening, I wrote to mum with my news and Winstanley's account of dad's illness and how she needs to keep in touch with his army friends. There's a letter from mum shortly after saying how happy she is about my new job but wondering if I'll be staying in Nairobi longer than six months. Little do I know then that the next time I put pen to paper, I'll mention how there's a rumour the university may even be thinking of appointing me as a part-time lecturer in biochemistry, hopefully with some research money. So I start to worry how mum will take to the news as it comes with tenure but just trust that she'll understand.

As I look back over the past months, I'm not totally surprised by this turn of events. Kinama and Joseph have reviewed all the results from our latest field trials. They're using the most popular local wheat crop variety for my derivative enzyme exchange. What's surprising is that Kinama's laboratory has gone on to cultivate a novel seed strain from the harvested mature plants. The improvement in growth yields is stunning and such success points to a significant programme of collaborative research ahead. Strangely enough, Joseph and the institute's director have said little so far about my fellowship coming to an end.

That's until the end of August when the Kenyan summer is almost over and everything starts to change after I'm suddenly called to a meeting with Professor Kinama in the vice chancellor's office. When I ask what it's all about, I get a set of blank faces. So, after a tense few days, I'm waiting nervously outside the VC's office wondering what's in store for me. Fortunately, I don't have to wait long and to my surprise, Usha pops out of the office and quickly ushers me in to introduce the vice chancellor. Kinama mouths a brief hello and there's some tea with a little small talk between us before the VC gets to the point. The memory of the meeting stays with me.

'Well, Dr Levine, firstly, thank you for coming over to see me at such short notice. We all realise how busy you are so I won't take too much of your time. Richard and Usha tell me your derivative enzyme research is starting to show real promise and that you're also managing to enthuse some of our brighter students in the Plant Science Department. Just to say…very well done. Just thought it might be useful to put you in the picture concerning the future broad direction of our agricultural research and academic studies across Kenya, well actually in a good part of East Africa too.'

'As you undoubtedly know, we're a newly independent country with a university sector that's developing fast. This hasn't always been the case, although we're now in receipt of some generous funding streams. Earlier this year, we learnt that we've been awarded a significant grant for a five-year research programme; the monies come from the World Bank, some extra Overseas Development Assistance, and our regular NGO partners. This research forms a central pillar of our government's strategy to increase the productivity of the land, improve our natural resource management, and achieve sustainable growth within the agricultural sector.'

'As you're aware from living in our country for some time now, the aim is to safeguard food security, alleviate poverty and diversify crop production to improve overall living standards for our rural people. Dr Levine, these are big ambitions. We have a strong infrastructure with several agricultural research institutes and stations across the country. But we know we can't achieve these ambitions alone. We need help from the best scientists in the field from around the world. Well, just to save you from too much embarrassment, your research expertise in the field of improving cereal growth is internationally recognised.'

I feel myself redden and quickly interrupt the vice chancellor. 'Oh, that's very kind of you but perhaps it's a little, erm…overstated.' I smile knowingly.

The vice chancellor beams back. 'What did I tell you, Richard? The British are so naturally understated, even too modest at times. Aren't they, Dr Levine? Perhaps, that's a lesson you can learn from them,' he says, laughing quite loudly as he continues. 'I understand your fellowship and sabbatical from Manchester University is coming to an end. Therefore, let me speak plainly, Dr Levine. The university would like to offer you a permanent post of lecturer in biochemistry in the Department of Plant Science and Crop Protection.'

'To be clear, your teaching work will carry on as it is with lectures and tutorials at the university. But of equal importance is your research. We will set a budget so you can continue with the work centred around the institute under Usha and Joseph Wasike's direction. One of your key roles is to ensure this research is fed into Richard's work here on developing new seed strains, so your findings can be energetically taken up in the field, so to speak.' The vice chancellor looks around to Richard and Usha who nod in almost perfect unison. 'Finally, this is an important role, Dr Levine, which I have no doubt you will fulfil admirably with what I understand is your innate intelligence, tact, and careful leadership with all those concerned.'

Richard and Usha weigh in with more complimentary words and even more vigorous nodding that makes me feel even more uncomfortable. The vice chancellor looks pleased with himself and finishes with a flourish.

'So, Dr Levine, what do you say? Oh, and by the way, I've called your Professor Mikkelsen at Manchester over the past week to explain our proposals and he's fully supportive. He said he was not the least surprised and sends his best wishes.'

Driving back through the noisy streets of north Nairobi in my battered old VW Beetle, canvas-top down and a gentle breeze through my hair tempering the heat of the late afternoon, my thoughts turn to what lies ahead. How I must write to mum as soon as possible confirming the vice chancellor's offer and promising to explain more on the phone very soon. Then to get on with my new life in Kenya, in this exciting vigorous city. Whatever regrets I feel for Paul, for not working with Andreas again, and most of all for mum and her happiness, they must all be set aside.

There'll be some tears shed over the few months ahead I know, but I understand that whatever regrets I do have about my previous life, my future now lies in Nairobi and East Africa.

Chapter 15

Professor Arrowsmith's face shows very little emotion as he struggles to negotiate our last Pandora review meeting at Heddington. It's the end of March 1973 and I detect an air of disappointment or even embarrassment as he tediously checks through all our reports that back up his feasibility study. It's a low-key affair anyway; Miriam, Malcolm Edgerton, Elizabeth Saxby, and Marcus Cochrane are with me but Michael DeLeon and Ping have moved on to one of those new research projects announced by the minister at the fateful press conference. Michael Womack has returned to Canada for another research fellowship with the Ostermanns. Kay left Cambridge well before Christmas after submitting a typically thorough account of her enzyme work.

Arrowsmith's sad demeanour reflects how his ambitions for Pandora drained away and it's quite clear to all those around the table today that he'd not been consulted in many of the critical decisions. They were all left at the door of the cabinet office. At the end of the meeting, he makes a sincere attempt to wish us well in our future careers. Elizabeth and Marcus look to the commercial world whereas Miriam returns to Southampton to press on with her love of enzymic reactions and bio-battery design. After six miserable and turbulent months, I'm eager to get away from Cambridge for all sorts of reasons. And that's what I tell Arrowsmith when he enters my office before setting off for London.

'What are your plans, Paul? Any ideas?'

I sigh and shrug my shoulders. 'Nothing definite yet; most probably go back to my parents for a short break and start looking I suppose,' I say as I crumple into my chair and take a large gulp of air. To my surprise, Arrowsmith makes himself at home by sitting on the other side of my desk. There's a pause for a few moments before he catches my eye and continues.

'Paul, you've been badly treated here, we all know this.' He hesitates and casts a quick look around the room to check if the door is closed. 'And you're not alone, I might add. You've done a splendid job pulling the team together and your own work with Ping and the test rig is first-class. It's not your fault the economics didn't add up and the fact this government has a particular public agenda to satisfy. In my opinion, this ingenious bio-fuel cell will eventually find wide application but unfortunately, this government wants quick winners. Politicians are an impatient species, short-sighted at times and the current political situation in the country is getting very testy indeed.'

'Short-sighted at times,' I retort. 'But thank you, Professor, my group had many good scientists working flat out on Pandora and they deserved to be treated so much better. Unfortunately, like my good friends and colleagues, I need to move on and look to my future, although it's going to be difficult.'

'Look, Paul, I wonder if I can help in some small way. In addition to my research at Imperial on alternative energy sources, I also provide research staff and strategic input to the government's TACT group at Leicester. Have you heard of them?'

'TACT, no, they're new to me. Maybe that's why it has that name?' I offer a faint smile while Arrowsmith steadily ignores my attempt at a witticism and continues without a glimmer of appreciation.

'Yes, we love acronyms. It's the UK's Technology Assessment Centre for Transport. It's housed in the new Engineering Building next to Leicester University. There's a team of about sixty government scientists working on assessing future transport technologies. One section is looking into the next generation of secondary and primary batteries. Principally for trains, of course, but it could also be for cars, buses, or even small planes. There's also a group of materials scientists developing some new components for the batteries. Not sure what the rest do, could be something to do with new suspensions or the drivetrains I suppose.'

'Anyway, quite frankly, Paul, there's not been a lot coming out of TACT over the past year and everyone I speak to in government circles agrees there's a need for a shakeup. Winstanley reminded me that you did some more traditional battery development work with an automobile company in Detroit a while back. With your project management skills, your electrical test bed, and that clever fractional calculus analysis software, I'm sure you'll be able to inject a sense of urgency and make a real difference up there in Leicester. What do you think, Paul?'

My heart sinks. *It's not more of the same,* I tell myself. Do I really want to go through the same exercise as Pandora only this time with a group of underperforming and frustrated government scientists? But at least they're not working on bio-batteries. I sit back in my chair and consider the alternatives and the immediate priorities. There's no doubt I need the work and certainly don't want to be an itinerant research fellow all my life. While for my own peace of mind, I need to get away from Cambridge as soon as possible. There are too many uncomfortable memories that need driving away. Arrowsmith quickly interrupts my train of thought.

'I'd like to show you around, Paul. No commitments at this stage but can we arrange to meet in Leicester, say, next week or the week after? But just to let you know, I've spoken to Edgerton about this. You may not be aware but he's moved from MAFF to the DTI as their Head of Science and Technology with overall responsibility for TACT. He's very keen that you take up the helm in Leicester in what he terms a casual civil servant role, at PSO grade. We both want this battery group to get a grip on the work, after all, it's public money we're talking about here. But it's entirely up to you, Paul.'

'Professor, after Pandora, I'm not sure I fit into the civil service culture, casual or not, and what's a PSO in real money?'

'Well, that's exactly why you will do a good job at TACT. Oh yes, a PSO is apparently a principal scientific officer; sort of group manager, in effect reporting to the director. Can you make it next Wednesday or the Wednesday after, say eleven o'clock? We can meet in their splendid restaurant. I'll send you the details; Edgerton will be there too.'

So, is this how careers are decided? By being in the right place at the right time and meeting someone who knows somebody, who knows somebody else. It's serendipity all over again. I can't seem to avoid it and reluctantly tell Arrowsmith that I'll sleep on it. Back in my safe little flat next to the Kite, a glass of the remnants from a fine bottle of bourbon that Michael Womack left behind is in my hand as I chew over the nature of my career path, as everyone calls it nowadays. Some scientists are naturally driven, of course. Driven by science, their goals, their egos, or just raw ambition.

Deep down, I know I'm not one of those scientists and TACT would never satisfy those ambitions if I were. But Leicester offers me a way out of my current stasis; it gives me time to think about what I really want to do with my life. A restless night follows aided and abetted by the remains of the bourbon. Eventually, I persuade myself that I should at least consider Arrowsmith's offer and see if my immediate future lies in Leicester, then hope I don't live to regret it.

Before letting Pandora go for good, there's one thing I must do before I get out of Cambridge. One thing I've been holding back from for months but continues to confront me. I must write to Kay promising myself it'll be my one and only letter. After another restless night, I make a brief phone call to Andreas Mikkelsen in Manchester to convince him, and me, that it should be written and to ask if he'll forward it. He's fully aware there's unfinished business between us and, not surprisingly, reluctant to interfere as he told me how Kay was very angry. He doesn't promise to do it but says he wants to help if he can.

So rightly or wrongly, and I hope for her sake as well as mine, I take time to write and tell her the truth about what happened during the last days of Pandora from my perspective. From posting off my letter, there's a deep sadness that haunts me to the core. A sadness that obscures a time of real joy; in many ways, the happiest time of my life that ended so abruptly. A time when memories of Cambridge are subverted by the actions of seemingly dispassionate individuals who appear to have little care for the personal lives of scientists or even a project they initially committed to so publicly.

That underlying sadness continues to the present, a year to the day after I moved to Leicester. Why do I suffer this recurring feeling? A sense that I'm treading water, passing the time, or even running away from something that I know not what. To outsiders, I have little to complain about, compared to so many of Leicester's residents who've lost their well-paid jobs from traditional industries. There's my spacious new flat in Birstall, an attractive village just three miles north of the city centre and close to the A6. Every day, I set off on my trusty Husqvarna along a road that skirts the River Soar to this bright new Engineering Building in the city centre.

I've been lucky in making some good friends in the time, two university staff who invited me to their family homes in nearby Highfields to share some of their family's amazing curry evenings. To top it all, I even volunteer at the Leicester Speedway and get the chance to try out my Husqvarna on their famous dirt track. It's also fortunate that Dr Edgerton is very welcoming and he bends over backwards to make sure I get a bit of cooperation from this ailing TACT battery group. Some of the staff are already seeing a difference by using my electrode performance test kit which followed me from Cambridge.

All these things are true I keep telling myself, but why do I still feel this emptiness inside? Or is it simply loneliness? Do I still miss Kay so very much? Will I ever get over her? As I've done for quite a while now, I sit down to my supper and sink into what I call my period of quiet reflection. Even if I don't want to admit it, I'm more alone now than ever I was on my first day in snowy Saginawbay on the shores of Lake Huron so many thousands of miles away.

It has taken time to get used to working in this 1960s-style Engineering Building. Some call it post-modernist; all glass and steel with plenty of open-plan offices, spacious laboratories, and well-designed engineering workshops. Maybe it's because of its fancy zigzag roof of glass and plastic that is such a feature of the Leicester skyline. One thing Arrowsmith did get right was his praise for its sumptuous restaurant. Every Thursday, I confront the same question from the matronly-looking Indian lady in an orange sari adorned with an enormous white pinafore.

'What are you having, me duck?' Her voice resounds from behind the steaming serving counter. But there's never any question really as I point to my usual dish.

'Chicken curry please and throw in naan bread.' I point to some curried vegetables. 'And what's that?'

'It's spicy okra, darling. You'll like it, good for you, plenty of roughage. What about your pudding?'

I stare at a large tray of steaming pineapple upside-down pudding. 'That looks good.'

'Custard or cream, me duck?'

'Custard please, that should keep me going for the rest of the day,' I add jokingly with a stifled laugh. Looking around for a spare table, I see my two university friends, Ramesh Kumar and Pooja Mahendra, sitting at the far end of the noisier-than-usual restaurant. As I particularly want to join them, I grab some cutlery, a copy of the Leicester Mercury, and with a brief hello, sit down between them. 'Curry days are so popular, aren't they? It's becoming a habit of mine, having my main meal at lunchtime; it saves me cooking in the evening. Are you doing the same?' They reply almost in tandem.

'Hello, Paul. Well, it's subsidised by the university, isn't it?'

Nodding knowingly, I dip my naan bread into the curry and glance at a stark headline on the front of the Mercury. Ramesh notices it too and is quick to comment.

'That IRA coach bombing on the M62, it's a bit too close for comfort; those soldiers never had a chance. Terrible, just terrible, and there'll be more.'

An animated Pooja follows with, 'Religious divisions never go away you know. We've had them in Tanzania for years; that's how we ended up here.'

Not fully appreciating Pooja's comments, I look to change the topic of conversation. 'It's not a good start to the year, is it? If it's not IRA bombs, then it's the oil crisis or a shifty-looking Richard Nixon coming unstuck in that Watergate scandal. Really riveting TV, mind you, a bit like a train crash in slow motion, don't you think? It looks like we're having a general election at the end of the month for good measure.'

Oddly enough, we often talk politics over lunch, which is a real eye-opener for me, but I'm glad I didn't say any more after realising religious conflicts are a big part of their recent history as Ramesh and Pooja told me they left their university in Dar es Salam a few years back in a great hurry clutching their British passports. So best I concentrate on picking their brains as experienced materials scientists because I've some real problems in TACT that need sorting. It has taken quite a while to grasp what is going wrong and what needs changing in my research group. As expected, overall progress has been slow with their work largely predictable and uneventful.

My ten well-qualified chemists and mathematicians are busy enough assessing four battery designs that might eventually be suitable for use as a subsidiary power source in trains and buses. After getting to know them, I unfairly judge that many joined TACT because they like messing about with trains, both toys and in real life. My predecessor has been moved sideways into a management role somewhere in the bowels of DTI's head office with the impression from Edgerton that he was out of his depth. However, I can't help thinking that many career scientific civil servants are generally very able and thoughtful people.

They seem personally well organised but sadly less driven by project outcomes than their need to keep publishing reports or papers that end up lying on shelves collecting dust. Instinctively, they realise that doing this for long enough in their own narrow technical field will get them recognised by their masters to earn their ritual promotion. Cynically, I think many are skilled at serving time in a pleasant largely undemanding environment. Some staff clearly look at me with some sort of misplaced envy. After all, as a PSO, I'm allocated an office with a table of a certain size and a carpet of a particular design.

But then, early on, I went and raised a few eyebrows when I moved out of my office into their open-plan area. Mind you, it has certainly helped with commissioning my electrode performance test rig and getting to know two capable mathematicians trying to modify our old fractional calculus software programmes. I'll need them to calculate energy retention factors for two of the shortlisted battery designs. Fortunately, this time around, the remaining designs are much simpler than the bio-fuel cell model and quite similar to the ones we studied from the Detroit motor company.

So, the good news is there's at least a clear pecking order in their test performance and specifications and a workable battery looks well on the cards. Edgerton and Arrowsmith seem happy enough and have let me know the government is talking to third parties to competitively tender an eventual optimal design for large-scale manufacture.

But despite all this, I still have an overriding feeling of déjà vu with the project over the past month. Their battery design concepts have been around for years. They use a highly reactive metal separated from an equally reactive second electrode by a solid and supposedly inert porous ceramic membrane, or alternatively, by a less tried and tested novel plastic membrane to transfer ions. Membranes fail, so my group is busy checking battery lifetimes with the different membranes, even though everyone keeps telling me that estimating membrane lifetimes is black art as no one knows for sure what causes them to break down in the first place.

Three weeks ago, at our director's progress meeting, I asked our head of materials what they measure to check if a batch of ceramics is going to pass muster. Suddenly, he becomes evasive. I then confront their lead researcher, Bob Fenton, who's equally evasive. Next day, amongst a stack of Bob's routine test data, I came across some pore size measurements for a candidate ceramic membrane batch. For whatever reason, this catches my attention and I decide to plot Bob's data against our current best assessment of battery lifetimes; amazingly, there's a direct correlation.

I show this to Bob and he appears surprised, and even more so when I point out that this might offer a quickfire check on whether a batch of expensive bespoke ceramics can ever deliver a reliable long-life battery. Bob says he'll show this to his boss and then, out of the blue, three days later, the director instructs me to stop discussing their material property data with Bob Fenton or anyone else at TACT.

Perhaps, I'm still suffering from post-Pandora paranoia but as I'm given no explanation, I decide to interrupt Ramesh and Pooja as they tuck into their curries and ask what the hell they think is going on. Neither works for TACT so ask them to be discrete; they're good friends and I trust them implicitly. It's no big secret what my group is working on since TACT and the government are always publicising their investment in developing the next generation of advanced materials technology. It's all part of their so-called UK transport system for the twenty-first century. So, I ask the question.

'Guys, please tell me why talking about ceramic pore size makes everybody above a certain pay grade in TACT clam up?' They look at each other and smile broadly. Ramesh speaks first.

'Paul, we know all about the ceramic membranes you're using and why. It's obvious, everybody wants to use the material and there's lots of mechanical and electrical testing going on around the world. Our guess is that pore size is critical to their long-term structural performance and the chemical stability of your battery. You see, too big a pore and it doesn't physically separate highly reactive components; you'll get an electrical short out or worse, an explosion. Too small a pore and you start getting into electrical resistance problems, weird chemical reactions and before long the whole ceramic structure breaks down. Again, you end up with an electrical short or even worse, it stops transferring ions and the battery's electrical performance just drops off.'

'We can give you a lot of names for what's happening but that's not the issue. The real issue is how to manufacture ceramics to give a consistent bulk pore size across the whole membrane; that is a black art, always has been. We know the guys in TACT's materials group and they've known all about this for some time. There are probably some patents on the sintering processes being filed as we speak; quite often there are some clever tricks to the black art not covered by their patent scope or being reported that significantly improves the quality of the manufacturing process. If so, well, that's like gold dust.'

'But if it becomes known that you can select ceramic stocks for reliable long-life battery manufacture by simply measuring its bulk pore size, well, this effectively undermines their black art and the patent; that's invaluable to any competitor. Probably, it's all tied up with their commercial negotiations and confidentiality agreements. Mind you, it may not be as simple as bulk pore size, it rarely is, but no one knows for sure do they? Maybe they already knew about your findings Paul and are keeping stum. Most ceramicists will see pore size as an obvious characteristic to test, we measure that all the time. Even so, this doesn't reflect well on the level of trust within TACT, does it, Paul? Perhaps, they're unsure you can keep a secret?'

I shake my head in disbelief but reply calmly. 'Well, I wasn't expecting that. If you're right and it sounds plausible, then I don't know why it should surprise me. But it does, and I'm deeply disappointed. These things happen too often for my liking. Bugger me, chaps, I'm a scientist, an inquisitive scientist, so what do they expect me to do if they just clam up all the time and stop discussing anything?'

Ramesh looks anxiously at Pooja and continues. 'Look, Paul, we haven't said anything about this to you, you understand. You can't mention our names to anyone; we're not civil servants but we've all done test work for Bob Fenton's group in recent years. It wouldn't look good for us if he found out, would it? Of course, we could be totally wrong about this.' They look at each other avoiding my eyes. Ramesh is hesitant but insists, 'We know the ceramics business, Paul; it's a small and specialised research world, and I think we're right.'

We finish our curries and I thank them with a tinge of guilt in my heart. 'So sorry to ruin your lunch. I owe you a big favour but for now, who's for coffee? My treat.'

A few days pass and I'm glad I've had time to mull things over. I decide to press on with this ceramics issue and asked to see the head of materials and TACT director again. Our meeting soon becomes awkward, almost embarrassing. Neither is willing to pass comment on the idea of linking bulk ceramic pore size to battery life prediction. They have a bare-faced cheek to suggest it's not relevant to my work and that I should concentrate on establishing the electrical performance and energy retention factors for the time being. This rankles me to the edge of frustration that I ask the director to explain why he won't discuss it. As expected, he says it's a commercial issue and refers me to Dr Edgerton.

With inordinate restraint, I tell him I'll take it up directly with Edgerton at his next visit. The director's own irritation becomes apparent when I point out that this shows a real lack of trust and poor communication between groups. I make the point directly.

'Trust and open communication are essential for success with any project of this type. My experience with government officials during Pandora is surely a lesson for us all. This project may well go the same way.'

The director retorts, 'Paul, please remember you're a casual civil servant, still quite young, so you must be mindful.'

Unable to take his patronising attitude any longer, I avoid reacting to this none-too-subtle threat and storm out of the meeting mired in frustration and anger. It's clear my so-called career as a casual, let alone permanent, scientific civil servant is coming to an end. A week later, I'm having a private chat with Dr Edgerton during one of his regular monthly visits. He's obviously been briefed by the director and makes a real effort to placate me. He tells me he's on my side in this dispute but cannot intervene in the day-to-day running of the laboratory. He readily admits that this arrogant treatment of senior staff and lack of communication holds back research and it's probably the case with other projects within his department.

However, he says it's extremely difficult to remove career scientists without a long drawn-out grievance procedure that's both expensive and divisive; not everyone can be moved sideways to head office. He concedes my observations on pore size are relevant and sensitive to the patent protection and commercial negotiations surrounding future ceramic component manufacture found in our battery designs. He'll make my information known to the lawyers and their commercial manager but insists I respect my duty of confidentiality before making one final point.

'Paul, we wanted you to join TACT for just the reasons you raise. To try and break down these stupid barriers created by scientists, and yes, government officials in defending their own positions and careers. It's probably held back advancing our battery development for years and we must do something about it. I can tell how frustrating it is for you and you're angry. Try not to be. Carry on the best way you can and we'll see what can be done with the structure and personnel here. Sometimes very clever people cannot see outside of their own little silo. TACT and Pandora are living proof of that. I wish it was different, Paul, I wish it was.'

We part on good terms. As Dr Edgerton leaves, I tell him I'll say no more about my concerns. Being selfish, my own research is progressing well enough and I'll need a good reference sometime in the future. Outwardly, my breezy disposition is in stark contrast to my gut reaction that nothing is about to change in TACT any time soon. My confidence in our civil service and its ability to change is rock bottom. Pandora let me down, TACT is no better, and now my enthusiasm for even this type of research is waning, and waning fast.

It's time to look elsewhere, not for some elusive career progression but for some edifying work that I believe in and be proud of. Little do I know that serendipity is just about to play a key hand once again.

Mrs Ramesh Kumar's curry evenings are famous amongst the Tanzanian community that settled in the Highfields district of Leicester during the early 1970s. Every month, Sanah, as she is known, shares a marvellous array of classic Gujarati dishes with her neighbours' families, friends, and just occasionally, some specially selected guests. Luckily, I'm one of those guests and I've been regularly gorging myself on her traditional vegetarian khichdi dishes with crispy rice balls, Maru Bhajia chilli potatoes, and sumptuous chutneys. It's mostly comfort food for her university friends who emigrated from Dar es Salaam and finding their feet in the local community.

Ramesh and Pooja are well-known in the area and well-respected. They like Leicester, and as ardent dirt bike riders back home, regularly visit Lions Speedway's race nights at their famous stadium on Blackbird Road. I've seen them a few times in the stands and happily offer them a ride on my Husqvarna at the end of most curry evenings. They're so enthusiastic that I suggest they come along to this evening's practice session for keen amateurs that's organised by the Lions. I'm also thinking it's time to repay the favour for all their ceramic expertise.

They grab at the chance and soon I'm riding alongside Ramesh, Pooja, and half a dozen other amateur riders under the searchlights, negotiating the treacherous dirt track bends with all the noise and dust that entails. They've brought one of their London friends along who's staying with them for a few weeks. He's introduced as Vikram Mehta and for the most part, stays in the safety of the stand because Sanah told her husband that he's too important a friend to get hurt riding dangerous bikes round and round for no good reason. Well, by the end of the evening, everyone, including me, is high on adrenaline and we need to calm down.

Walking through the stadium's run-down grubby-looking mock Tudor façade, I start up a conversation with Vikram. He says he's a consultant to the ODA, the UK's Overseas Development Administration that supports various charities in Tanzania. He lives in one of the large townships close to Dar es Salaam but spends half the year in London. He's quite chatty about his work.

'Things are changing at the ODA, it'll soon be a separate ministry with the new Labour Government, so we're pushing officials to give us more support for the charities operating out of our offices in Mombasa and Dar es Salaam. We've always had Oxfam and some religious groups working with us to improve the water supply in the villages but we want to do more. We're lobbying to get more money for extra wells, water pumps, and improvements in water quality through filtration, but it all takes time. It's a long-term issue for us but there's also pressure coming down from our own government's new villagisation programme.'

'What's that?' I ask, suddenly feeling very ignorant.

'Well, in its wisdom after independence, the Tanzanian Government decided to try and form our scattered rural populations into more manageable larger villages or units, a sort of compulsory collectivisation. I dare say it sounds a bit strange to you but there's big money available. It means we can put our charitable efforts, and hopefully some extra pounds sterling, into improving the lot of these larger villages and small towns with plentiful cleaner water. Our government hypes it up a bit as it's all part of their so-called Arusha Declaration signed in 1967.'

'So I guess that's quite a big deal for your country.'

'It's a very big deal indeed, Paul, although it depends on who you talk to as it's quite a contentious issue. My job is to work with your government to expand our Mombasa office, import the latest water services kit such as pumps and get everything up and running in those new collective villages. But we want to do so much more, pumps are just a starting point.'

'What do you mean, Vikram?'

'It's like this, Paul. We're looking at ways to harvest water from the surrounding areas into these new villages by pumping it through a network of small underground canals. Sadly, many of these villages still don't have any reliable power supply to run the pumps or any other kit along the route. Manual pumps are fine for small villages but not for these new small towns. With the prospect of future canal networks in place, then we'll have to upscale everything in the towns including their local power supplies. We can use generators, of course, but diesel or petrol are not always available and quite frankly, not that cheap anymore, so we're looking around for what else is available.'

'The trouble is, we get offered all these wonderful bits of new kit that don't last a minute in the field. Unfortunately, first, we must test this kit properly in our harsh environments to decide what we can use and if it'll be reliable enough. So, it's time to look ahead and decide what makes sense to import or whether we make things locally so the villages eventually become self-sufficient. No one in my part of the world wants to be dependent on charity or foreign government giveaways forever. Sorry, Paul, I can get a bit evangelical at times with such a big job ahead and our Mombasa site no more than a shipping office despite being the main entry port for most of East Africa.'

'You see our ambition is to one day broaden our charity work and expertise beyond Tanzania's borders, but of course, that depends on the local politics and probably some sizeable World Bank and UN grants.'

'I see now why Sanah insisted you are too valuable to get wiped out by a dirt track bike. Pity, you would have enjoyed the buzz from us bikers doing our stuff.'

Everyone at TACT is glad to break up for the Christmas holidays and I'm no exception. News of the campaign of IRA pub bombings this autumn is shaking many people's confidence in the government and the country. Everyone I know is hoping for a happier and more peaceful 1975. I hope it's happier for me too as my research continues to provide clear evidence for a preferred battery design, although the frosty relationship with our materials group manager and director continues to sour. My mood is also up and down; I look for any distraction from day-to-day work and still maintain this empty feeling when around my flat in the evenings and at the weekend.

Meeting with my Tanzanian friends at the Speedway track during weekday evenings is a godsend. Weeks and months pass by and my chat with Vikram fades into memory until past New Year when Sanah brings us together again at one of her special curry nights. Vikram is again eager to talk about his consultancy and charity work. He mentions how certain aspects of his work, I think he means the money and grants, are moving in the right direction. He takes a particular interest in my research and oddly enough, asks how I'd go about assessing new electrical power sources. Maybe Ramesh or Pooja have said something; perhaps too much.

Anyway, I tell him how it's all relatively routine by now and how my next project, if I ever have one, is still up in the air. With his connections in the government, I feel uncomfortable saying too much or offering too many opinions about the scientific civil service. But he goes overboard in congratulating me on what he regards as my valuable research and wonders how it can be applied more widely. He reminds me of one particular issue.

'You know, Paul, reliable backup power supplies in the townships and villages around my part of the world are very hard to find.'

To my surprise, he showed an interest in the results from Pandora and asked if I could send him some information and details of my scientific background. Perhaps, I should've questioned him at the time but everything falls into place when Vikram phones one morning to ask if I'd meet him in Whitehall sometime towards the end of January. He's reluctant to say any more over the phone but I can guess what might be happening and I readily agree. It's very intriguing and a day away from the laboratory is no bad thing at present.

What have I got to lose, I tell myself as we meet a few weeks later in a smart hotel lobby just around the corner from Victoria Station. Vikram ushers me into a function room and invites me to meet an old friend of his. My shoulders drop as I come face to face with Jeremy Winstanley as he strides up to shake my hand.

'What the hell are you doing here?' I ask.

Blinking slightly at the tone of my voice, he retorts, 'Now I know I'm the last person you want to see right now but Vikram has kindly invited me along. For my sins, I still have some responsibility for liaison between our new Ministry of Overseas Development and the cabinet office. Vikram tells me I may be able to oil a few wheels in some way.'

Less than impressed, I mutter, 'Good god, Jeremy, you do get around. Is there any pie you don't have a sticky finger in?' Jeremy and Vikram smile broadly. Vikram turns to me and jumps in quickly.

'Let me explain, Paul. Jeremy has been filling me in on your background and despite the problems with Pandora and the department, he has a very high regard for your talents.'

'That's a joke, Vikram. Those problems as he calls them, his or their departments pulled the rug from under me, all of us, working on Pandora.' I turn towards the door but Vikram continues to speak quite forcibly.

'Paul, don't storm out. Please, try not to be too harsh on Jeremy. He has regrets and was only following his master's wishes you know. He's been a great help to my organisation for quite some time now. Perhaps, you could just let me get my story out.'

I glare at Jeremy but out of respect for Vikram, sit opposite him trying to stay calm and courteous. 'My apologies, Vikram, no offence intended. I'll keep my counsel and listen. Go ahead.'

'As you know, Paul, I'm a consultant to the old ODA and now with this spanking new ministry. However, you may not know that I represent an organisation called the OEAC, the Organisation of East African Charities.

Governments love their acronyms, don't they? We're a particularly well-funded charity that pulls together all the different charities and projects in my country and that of Kenya, Uganda, and so on; in fact, most democracies of sorts in East Africa. As you're aware, it all started in the 1960s with some water supply projects but now it's much wider. Do you remember our conversation on how we're supporting Tanzania with its villagisation process?

'Strategically, while not trying to be too grandiose or pompous about it, we could say we're fast-tracking the development of post-colonial democratisation and infrastructure investment within the region. Well, I won't bore you with all the politics at play but just to say the UK's Ministry of Overseas Development is one of several countries and UN agencies that are willing to help. OEAC is expanding its remit and growing fast. We need good people to move it along in each country and a top priority is to introduce tried and tested robust new technology into the villages and townships wherever they may be. And your knowledge of state-of-the-art portable power supplies, including a possible cereal-fuelled bio-battery or fuel cell, is very attractive to the OEAC.'

'Blimey, so that's where Pandora fits in then?' I add, eyeing Winstanley who looks eager to speak.

'I briefed Vikram in detail a while back, Paul; both the good and the bad parts of the project as it seemed relevant to OEAC's goals.'

'Err…ok. Please go on, Vikram,' I say as I continue to mumble some gentle expletives under my breath.

'OEAC is at a point where we have a bunch of keen graduates from the University of Dar es Salaam wanting to assess new technologies in the field but have little or no experience and no one to lead them. So, we're looking for someone with the ability to take on this role and sort out which bit of kit actually works and take it forward. It could be a novel power supply, some filtration kit, semi-automated water pumps for towns, or even a small sewage treatment plant. Who knows what? In fact, whatever's potentially the most valuable to each individual township.'

'Let me get to the point, Paul. If you're looking for a change of direction, then there's a new post being created at the OEAC, the current job title is Director of Technology and Innovation. That person will be based in Dar es Salaam but we're looking to expand our current import office facility on the Kenyan coast in Mombasa. We're advertising the post next week and we, and that includes

Jeremy, would very much like you to seriously consider applying. I realise this may come as a bit of a shock but what do you say?'

I sip some icy cold water from a cheap-looking glass tumbler whilst looking around this dreary room with its bland mass-produced photographs on the wall and a set of uncomfortable-looking minimalist metal furniture. My eyes meet Jeremy's.

'Is this your doing?' I ask.

'Certainly not, Paul. I'm only here because Vikram asked for my opinion of you and for me to offer reassurance with regard to this important long-term initiative and our government's committed support for the OEAC. Our funding is relatively small but useful. However, the OEAC is surprisingly well-funded anyway and totally independent in what it does and how it goes about doing things. Let there be no misunderstanding, Paul. I've not spoken a word of this to your director at TACT or even Dr Edgerton. It's your decision entirely.

'Anyhow, I'm not sure you'll take any notice of my views nowadays, and I can hardly blame you. But good men are hard to find and you've a track record in taking risks with your career and tackling new challenges. You've no ties as far as I understand it…'

Winstanley stops mid-sentence; our eyes meet again for an instant before he continues.

'Perhaps, I've said enough. Only to add that I'd very much like you to consider the post. Details such as their terms and conditions of employment, etc., well, Vikram will spell those out for you. Not my business, you'd be an OEAC employee. They're not over-generous; after all, it's a charity but I'm certain it will be an exciting and wholly worthwhile adventure completely free from our government's and my interventions.' He grins and goes to order some tea for two, returning suddenly to firmly shake my hand and leave while wishing us both well. I sit back, exhale, and pour tea from a fancy teapot into two bulk standard white cups with those artificial gold rims that you find in most hotels nowadays.

I spent the next two hours with Vikram going over the job description, the practical day-to-day work that's going on in the field right now as well as the administrative and coordination duties surrounding their Tanzanian staff. Vikram is upfront with me in spelling out some of the tricky liaison duties with the governments, NGOs, and charities in the region starting with Tanzania and Kenya. He says the new director needs to be part diplomat but I'm assured there'll be experienced senior OEAC staff to hold my hand if necessary. The contract is initially for five years underwriting the OEAC's long-term commitment to its technology objectives.

He will let me know when the advert is published; it's to be circulated in the UK, Tanzania, and Kenya with an appointment expected before the end of the summer. As Vikram leaves, he puts a hand on my shoulder and wishes me good luck with whatever decision I make, allowing me to sit quietly and examine my future before returning to Leicester, excited and full of trepidation.

Weeks fly past. In many ways, research takes a backseat, although I doubt many will notice. There are times when I'm consumed with confusion over my future, particularly when working alongside people with long-established settled science careers. But I'm coming to terms with a deep-seated feeling that I don't really care for that kind of life anymore. Perhaps, the split from Kay is partly to blame but my search for answers goes nowhere; week after week, I'm lost in what to think. The only consolation is the many hours walking along pleasant lanes around Birstall and the River Soar having difficult conversations with myself.

This is starting to worry me as I've no close friend to confide in and my parents just wouldn't understand. They're always going on about how lucky I am with such a steady job in the civil service after having at last got over, what they call, my wanderlust. They so want me to settle down but I'm not even sure I know what that means anymore. But it's time to make some sort of decision and as I stroll along the riverbank, one beautiful spring evening chatting to one or two fishermen trying their hardest with worm and maggot, my gut instinct shouts…OEAC. Right now, it's the easiest decision to make but as a half-rational perfectionist, it takes two more evenings to justify it.

I tell myself, *There's a need for a change, a significant change, or why bother?* Research has plateaued, and I'm going through the motions with nothing of real substance emerging in recent times. There's little chance of publishing peer-reviewed papers any time soon, if ever. Worse still, a realisation that disenchantment with the British establishment, the state of politics in this country, is holding me back. Maybe I'm an idealist but scientific research in TACT and Pandora now appears semi-detached from the real world in the hands of their masters. My fear is that everything, including the bio-fuel cell, will end up as some report lodged on a dusty old shelf somewhere in Whitehall.

I'm probably overreacting to this continual drip, drip, drip of news on IRA bombings or deeply depressive endemic political stagnation and short-termism handed out by whatever government is in power. Perhaps, harking back to my time in the States, and their amusing Watergate scandal played out on TV that undermines faith in government, any government, and their politicians. Surely, I'm not alone in thinking this but as Winstanley so astutely observed, I've no ties and if I care to believe him, there's no UK government influence on OEAC's charitable activities. My current morose, never-ending feeling of treading water, is starting to sink my soul. It's time to act; I send my application to the OEAC the next morning.

From a time of doubt and stagnation, I suddenly find myself facing lots of stimulating conversations. An interview in London with OEAC's chief operating officer lasted a whole day. There's an animated discussion with a young-looking Kenyan researcher from the omnipresent Professor Arrowsmith's group at Imperial College. We discuss the potential use of a ruggedised bio-fuel cell as an alternative power supply in African villages. By the end of the day, I had the clear impression they wanted me for the job. Within two weeks, I'm OEAC's first-ever director of Technology and Innovation with a start date of September in Dar es Salaam.

With giddying speed and absolutely no regrets, I offer my resignation to the TACT director. He has expected it for some time, I'm sure, but he still takes it quite personally. Not sure I care either way but I do care what Edgerton thinks. He's more sanguine, more understanding, and appears genuinely pleased I've found such an exciting opportunity. He sees I'm at a crossroads and says he's rather envious of my decision with plenty of warm praise for my work over the years. He finishes our chat on a positive note.

'I hope we can adopt some of the attitudes and skills you naturally bring to collaborative research. You've shown us a new way and we need more people like you. But I fear it's going to take a generation or more to genuinely make a difference, so good luck.'

Other conversations leading up to my departure are more emotional and much sadder. I let Ramesh and Pooja know of my decision as soon as I can. As we sit down in the Engineering Building's restaurant for one last curry together, I can tell they know already. Their broad smiles and pats on the back follow a shake of hands.

'Looks like Vikram has spilt the beans already. Did you have something to do with getting me the job?' I ask.

'No, not at all; well above our pay grade,' says Ramesh. 'We may have had a little word with Vikram early on and invited him for a curry evening. But no, it was the OEAC who took the initiative, nothing to do with us. Apart from Pooja, our families all come from villages scattered far and wide; we want to bring our next generation into the twentieth century. It's so important, that's why we're over here now, earning good money too.'

Pooja can't restrain himself, blurting out, 'We're so pleased you've got the job, Paul. You won't regret it. All our colleagues, and especially those with families in the villages can't wait to see the difference you're going to make with all this new technology. It's exciting news. Many congratulations, you're the right man for the job and by the way, Sanah is organising a special curry evening before you go.'

It's humbling listening to Ramesh and Pooja. I struggle to say much over lunch except for some timid words about how it's an onerous task and it'll take many years to make any real difference. But they understand all of that; I don't need to manage their expectations thank goodness. My spirits rise further at Sanah's special curry evening when everyone tells of their best restaurants in Dar es Salaam, even though their local Maru Bhajia are not as good as Sanah's homemade spicy ones. Then a close neighbour insists on telling me where to live outside of the capital with the name of an uncle who owns several bungalows near the city's beautiful tropical gardens. My heart sinks as I leave Ramesh's house for the last time and wave vigorously before starting up the Husqvarna.

I travel home for a couple of days before catching my flight to Dar es Salaam. It's a chance to have what will be a difficult conversation with my parents and to say goodbye to Marion and Elspeth. Mum prepares a wonderful traditional lunch as only she can. We sit in the garden; dad sips a cold beer and my nephews and nieces play in a paddling pool on a scorching hot day at the end of August. Marion quizzes me about my new director's job and how I'm going to cope with the continuous boiling hot weather. Their questions are endless and I barely know how to answer them. Unsurprisingly, dad asks me bluntly why I'm giving up a good civil service job and deserting this country.

Mum hardly says a word except to know if they've got a National Health Service and if I'm afraid of getting malaria or something worse in what she calls Black Africa. I try and reassure her by saying I survived the United States well enough for many years. But sadly, in truth, there's nothing I can say, or want to say, to appease their views. When it's time to leave, everyone gives me a hug whilst reminding me, in concert, that "I've always been an independent Bolshie sod, very much my own person, even as a boy". I take it as a compliment.

As I walk down the front path, dad rushes up and hugs me for a second time. It's a powerful hug this time, he means it, and it's a new experience for me. He whispers with tears in his eyes, 'Paul, I'm not religious, son, but God be with you. The whole family are so proud of you, you know, and I'm proud of you. For heaven's sake, write to mum sometimes and come back and see us whenever you can. We know it won't be easy to keep in touch, it's a long way away. Marion and Elspeth are busy with their kids and thankfully, mum's busy helping them most days. But mum will miss you, she's always had a soft spot for you.'

I'm shocked by dad's words. Maybe I'm starting to understand him properly for the first time. I hug him back and he doesn't jump away. Struggling to get my words out, I reply, 'Will do, Dad. Look after mum and the girls, tell them not to worry.'

It's stifling and humid as I walk the short distance to Boston Railway Station. My thoughts slowly adjust to the idea that within hours, I'll be on a flight to Nairobi, then on to Dar es Salaam via East African Airways. After boarding the train, I enter an empty carriage and realise it isn't sweat that's slowly sliding down my face onto my open collar but tears.

Part Six
Free Radicals

Chapter 16

'Doctor Levine, you're soaked through, let me get you a towel to dry off. It was bright sunshine less than half an hour ago with hardly a cloud in the sky, the storm must have come in very quickly.'

After blinking several times, my eyes gradually focus on the vice chancellor's secretary. She's wearing a gorgeous loose-fitting dress in a traditional brightly coloured pattern resembling the leaves of a plant with purple flowers. I don't recognise the plant so I'll ask her. 'It surprised me too, Almasi, saw the clouds darken and rushed to pull the canvas top over my old Beetle before everything got soaked. Nearly left it too late; looks like Nairobi's rainy season has come early this year. Didn't think I needed an umbrella quite yet. Almasi, which plant is that printed on your dress? It's beautiful.'

'Not sure but it could be an unusual variety of jacaranda, not from around here though.'

She goes into the cloakroom next to the vice chancellor's office and brings out a large blue towel to dry my hair. I grab the towel and sit on the plush leather chair opposite her desk. We're both staring at some rotatable wooden blocks that serve as her calendar. There's a bowl of stunning red tropical flowers which again I don't recognise at the other end of the desk. The wooden blocks show 14 March 1976. Almasi turns to face me and releases a gentle sigh.

'It's well over two years since you joined us, Dr Levine, it seems to have gone by in a flash. Is that what you say?'

'Yes, it is, and it has. So I should be used to your rainy season by now, shouldn't I?' With a gentle laugh, I add, 'Better try and dry my hair, otherwise I'll look like a drowned rat in front of the vice chancellor.'

It doesn't take long to dry my hair as I've converted to having a full bob cut in this tropical climate. After moving towards the window that overlooks the campus gardens, I notice the rain is beating down on a line of cars next to the carefully manicured flower beds. The downpour is so heavy that large drops bounce off my Beetle's canvas top. With a sigh of relief, I wonder what damage such a soaking would have done to its electrics, so glad I made it just in time. A few minutes later, my arms and legs are just about dry, although there's a characteristic smell of damp clothes lingering in the air. Almasi collects the towel and I settle on a leather sofa in the far corner of the room.

Almasi appears from the office. 'The vice chancellor will be quite some time I'm afraid, Dr Levine. He's been in a meeting with the Head of the Agricultural Research Institute, Dr Chadha, for most of the afternoon; but he's particularly asked for you to stay on. He sends his apologies.'

'I'm in no rush. I had two lectures and a tutorial this afternoon with my MSc students, so I can do with a quiet sit-down. I won't disturb you, don't worry.'

'I'll get some tea and perhaps a few biscuits, Dr Levine.'

'That'll be lovely, thank you,' I reply.

About every six months, I meet the vice chancellor for an informal chat. He's keen to monitor how I'm getting on, I'm quite flattered. He takes a rather fatherly and protective attitude towards me, although I think he's also got an eye for the ladies in general. He's this polite, rather old-fashioned, larger-than-life man from Nairobi who must be in his early sixties. He was a successful research chemist in the United States for many years and I'm told by two of my MSc students that his wife keeps him firmly under her thumb, which is a relief to me. He's obviously very busy but clearly, a thoughtful man who appreciates there are fewer and fewer expats from the old colonial days working at the university.

Perhaps, he wants to make sure I'm being treated properly, and he's well aware of the reputation of my head of department, Dr Kinama, so I expect he keeps a watchful eye on him too. Last time we met, I reassured him that after a couple of stern conversations with Richard over the past year, I'm not expecting any trouble; particularly as he was dating a stunningly beautiful English literature lecturer from the west of Kenya. Despite this rebuff, Richard continues to sing my praises. Maybe that's why the vice chancellor is keen for me to wait around because Richard handed me a copy of our first peer-reviewed paper together describing results from a trial of a new strain of wheat seeds he has developed from my derivative enzyme glucose work of last summer.

According to my postgrad students, it's causing quite a stir in the university's senior common room as it's the first example of an enzymic boost to glucose levels and growth rates for a new seed strain ready to be planted by Kenyan farmers. The seeds are being sent to villages across a large section of eastern

Kenya over the next few months. Suddenly, there's a rattle of china and Almasi returns with a tea tray displaying a few sweet biscuits. I start to relax. There's rarely any time to dwell on the past nowadays but for some reason on this rainy afternoon, I let my mind wander along with a teacup in my hand.

Teaching, research, and a growing attachment to Nairobi and its charming people keep me busy and mostly happy. Nairobi really feels like home now, although, in truth, I still get lonely at times. Even after all this time, once or twice every few months, thoughts of what might have been in Cambridge flood back with some complicated feelings about Paul. Mila is such a good listener and senses when my mood is low. She even takes me off into the old part of the city for a comforting meal at one of her favourite family-run restaurants until late into the evening. Apart from Mila, there are several good friends from the institute who try and teach me how to cook the local dishes and help me make up the beautiful colourful dresses that women wear around the house.

But some things from Cambridge have stayed with me. I couldn't resist starting up a country line dancing group; Paul would be proud of me. Half a dozen young lady technicians and a few brave men who work on field trials join me every Monday evening. It's a joy to watch how they adapt their innate sense of rhythm to the old 50s and 60s American music; they put my own efforts to shame. What's so nice is that when I invite the girls and boys around to my bungalow, we take turns preparing a local dish and talk late into the evening about music and politics. They're curious about my way of life in Britain and tell me they'd like to travel there one day.

Such enthusiasm for life is addictive and I close my eyes for a while to daydream a bit longer just when a laughing vice chancellor's booming voice suddenly makes an appearance.

'Sorry to keep you waiting, Dr Levine. Shall we have our chat now?'

Startled and a little embarrassed, I open my eyes just as Usha walks past smiling broadly and raising a hand to say goodbye before I can utter a word.

'Of course, Vice Chancellor, ready when you are. Just recovering from a busy afternoon,' I hasten to reply. We enter his palatial office and he escorts me to one of the huge comfortable high-backed chairs draped with a throw designed around bold Kenyan flag colours.

'Very pleased you can spare the time today as there's some news which I hope you'll find exciting. But first, I think congratulations are in order. I understand from Richard that your joint paper on a new high-glucose strain of wheat seeds is now in print. You'll realise, of course, how important these results are. More to the point, what impact do they have in some of our poorest rural districts? Very well done. You should know that your contribution is widely recognised, increasingly so I may say.'

I nod politely and not for the first time, feel a little awkward with all his praise; it doesn't sit easily. 'Oh, thank you, Vice Chancellor. Fortunately, the local wheat variety we chose proves well suited to my enzyme amplification technique. We're going to try one of your popular maize varieties next.'

'Very good to hear. As you're aware, Usha Chadha has been with me most of the afternoon discussing plans for the future of the institute, and I want to bring you up-to-date with them as soon as possible because they'll affect you directly. Usha will fill in with many more details later.'

I must have looked a bit shocked and hesitant since the vice chancellor is quick to react.

'Don't be alarmed, Doctor, I can assure you it's all good news. Perhaps, a little background to our plans is necessary. It's obvious that our country's economy is highly dependent on our agriculture. Not only for feeding our rural population but also to bring commercial success to what is still a relatively poor country. Our government encourages the introduction of new technology and research as a way of increasing food production but also to maintain its integrity and leadership across the region. We cannot move fast enough in this area so innovations like yours are key to success.

As I've mentioned before, our government is anxious to push ahead with help from foreign agencies such as UNESCO, NGOs, and some very generous sponsors and charities. Over the past year, our government has secured a significant increase in its capital infrastructure budget. To an extent, it's opening a brand-new agricultural research centre on a site just two miles from the current institute. You have noticed, I'm sure, some new building works in past months.'

I nod knowingly. 'Yes, we've seen a new building going up with lots of heavy trucks in and out of the neighbourhood, but we've heard it's for some new administrative offices.'

'Oh, it's a lot more than that, Doctor. Yes, it'll house a central administration block but it'll also expand the institute's research to include forestry and livestock. More importantly, as far as you're concerned, there's money to expand the facilities for Kinama's research into seed modification, your own derivative enzyme amplification studies, and those critical field trials. There's also cash to roll out a network of local branches attached to the ARC with their own laboratories across the country. You never know, one day there may even be laboratories across our borders into Uganda and Tanzania. Mind you, there are bound to be some major political obstacles in the way, so let's not get too ahead of ourselves.'

'Usha is planning to move your current laboratories into the new ARC building as soon as practicable, so you should take this opportunity to upgrade your facilities to a level fit for the late twentieth century and beyond. She's got a broad outline of a plan but tell her exactly what you need; there's money to do it right now, I'm sure.'

'Oh, Vice Chancellor, don't know what to say except that's such special news and a real coup for Nairobi and the university. Yes, it would be lovely to know her plans.'

'Look, nothing's set in stone as yet, so spend some time with Usha so she can budget properly.'

'Well, I'm just thinking this would be the right time to introduce a dedicated laboratory for automation of enzyme amplification and analyses.'

'Yes, good suggestions. You know best and you may also want to take the opportunity to improve the security around your facilities. It's not something we've thought about much in the past but commercial involvement and exploitation of your work is starting to become important, so be aware. Usha informs me you've negotiated a sole supply agreement for some so-called bespoke ion concentration columns from a company in Leeds. It's a company you've dealt with before while at Manchester I believe. As I say, this is impressive work that needs proper support as there'll be plenty for you to do, I'm sure. So, you're going to need more staff despite some level of automation.

'Richard has several bright students coming through, so please talk to him and where possible, get them on board with your research. We'll look to fund their PhDs or whatever. What do you say, Dr Levine, isn't that good news?'

I stare at him in amazement as I'd no idea Usha and Richard had been briefing the vice chancellor about my work in such detail. It's like a dream come true as I take a minute to look out of the large window at one end of the office to collect my thoughts. 'I'd little idea this was coming, Vice Chancellor, and I'm indebted to the faith you and your staff have shown in my research and to me personally. This is becoming my life's work and seeing its potential impact on your country's rural communities is beyond my wildest expectations. Turning what was originally tedious academic research into something meaningful and productive. Well, I won't let you down, Vice Chancellor, I won't.'

'I know you won't, Dr Levine.'

'May I just add a word about the staff at the institute? It's long overdue. They've been magnificent, not only with their enthusiasm but also their kindness in welcoming me to Kenya; this is my home now. But I must mention my best friend and colleague, Mila Omondi. She's one hell of an impressive lady, in Manchester and even more so here, and I wouldn't, no couldn't, be where I am now without her.'

'Be assured, Doctor, Usha is fully aware of Mila's talents and she's going to do something about her position quite soon. Don't worry, but that's a secret between us right now, ok?' He then raises his voice again with a flourish and beaming smile as he continues.

'Now what about you? First, may I take the liberty of calling you Kay after all this time?'

'Of course, you didn't need to ask.'

He laughs very loudly. 'Good, I'm not sure what you call me behind my back but informally, some people call me Julius. Can we work with that? Informally, of course.'

I smile and nod back.

'But coming back to your own position. More research responsibility, more staff, extra teaching and supervising; well, I'm sure the least we can do is promote you to senior lecturer, don't you?'

'This is a bit too much information to take in for one afternoon…erm, Julius, but that would be lovely. It's strange, I try not to reflect too much on the past but I did this afternoon sitting outside your office. The last two years have been demanding, the work for sure but also a real joy because of the people.' I hesitate. 'Thank you, Julius, your news this afternoon makes me even happier.'

'You did seem a little lost before our meeting. I wondered if there was something amiss. But you were simply taking stock of your life and we all need to do that at times. Usha tells me you're very involved with the social life of the institute. Cooking local dishes, inspiring others with some energetic American dance craze I believe.'

'Oh, dear, news gets around. It's country line dancing, sort of cowboy music. A friend of mine was mad about it when we worked in Cambridge and it's quite infectious.'

'Glad to hear it. Just a word of advice from an old man who worked his socks off when he was a youngster abroad. Keep having fun, life is more than work, believe me.'

'Julius, you're like my old boss, Professor Mikkelsen; he used to tell me the same.'

The vice chancellor breaks into another huge smile and wants to tell me one extra bit of news.

'I'll let you go now but first, I have an invitation for you. ARC's administration block, livestock and forestry departments are just about complete. The new agricultural block is also starting to take shape. Our government thinks it a good idea to hold an early opening ceremony to thank its international agencies and charitable sponsors this coming Saturday would you believe? Sort of cutting the ribbon type event, good publicity, I'm sure you understand. The government is apparently making every effort to impress and according to Almasi, it promises to be a grand affair. No doubt there'll be a few worthy souls attending with some notably boring speeches alongside what I hope are plenty of our local culinary delicacies. I understand a small dance band will also be on hand.'

His eyes are aimed directly at me. 'I realise this is short notice but may I ask a favour from you, Kay? My dear wife has found it necessary to travel across the country to be with our youngest daughter who's expecting her first baby. So, I wonder if you might be my guest for the evening. There's no major obligation on your time whilst there, just have fun, although I thought it might be a good chance for you to meet some of the important officials and moneymen backing your work. What do you say?'

I hesitate briefly but of course, I am always going to say yes.

'Excellent. I'll arrange for our chauffeured car to be at your disposal for the evening. It'll pick you up just after seven. Let Almasi know you're coming and she'll arrange everything. See you in the main auditorium around seven-thirty.'

'Oh, Julius, may I ask what the ladies will be wearing for the evening?'

'Of course, it's a black-tie affair.' He smiles and adds with tongue in cheek, 'So I'm expecting something special, Kay.'

'Well, I'd better make an effort and try not to look like a drowned rat as I did this afternoon. Thank you once again for everything. I'll now go and see if I can dodge those thunderstorms on my way home.'

It's been a real struggle to find one of the oldest Portuguese restaurants in Mombasa's old town. I'm confused and a little tired after setting off from OEAC's shipping office in the old port over half an hour ago. The port, transformed by the sparkling backdrop of an azure Indian Ocean, soon succumbs to the smells and hubbub of its traditional fish market, where red snappers and squid fresh from the boats this morning sit on wooden benches ready to stare out at me. This toxic mix hangs on well beyond the port area as I'm cruelly led astray by a maze of anonymous narrow streets, dominated on both sides by bare yellow and white buildings.

A further twenty minutes of wandering aimlessly in the intense heat and I'm starting to wilt. My OEAC colleagues in Dar es Salaam did warn me about Mombasa.

'It's not like Dar es Salaam you know.'

They were right; I should have avoided being out in the midday sun during March as it's the first month of Mombasa's so-called autumn. Daily temperatures of ninety degrees with seventy-five per cent humidity and heavy downpours late afternoon is a test for anyone, let alone for this Englishman increasingly lost in a city he hardly knows. It's increasingly obvious to the staff at my small hotel just outside the city centre as they launder up to three of my shirts each and every day. "Take your time, slow down", they all say but that's easier said than done. Such a shame as apart from my work, this beautiful historic city acts as a laidback seaside resort with plenty to catch my attention.

The architecture is a rich mix of Asian, Arabic, and African cultures with a crude dash of European white concrete thrown in from recent generations. New money is revitalising the old port as well as developing the western part of the city. It's where I've been looking for some modern premises to house our new assessment and evaluation laboratory. OEAC's head office needs to check hundreds of novel water pumps and other kits entering through the port before distribution to the rest of Kenya via Mombasa's narrow-gauge railway. But that will have to wait as I pass by a row of Indian-style houses with their characteristic ornate balconies that overlook a tapestry of narrow thoroughfares.

This should be the right part of town for the restaurant but the temperature is so oppressive that I grab a little shelter under a row of stunted coconut trees to catch my breath. Sweat trickles down my face and back; my eyes sting as I wonder if I should've shaved off my beard on the first day I set foot in Tanzania six months ago. Working in Mombasa has taken a lot of getting used to, and where every day in the so-called equatorial Tropics is exhausting to mind and body. My memory tilts back to my time in Saginawbay with its hot sultry days close to the shores of Lake Huron. Yes, oppressive at times but not like here. With a brief spell of shade, I repeat my usual mantra of "better get used to it".

Then from out of a nearby white-painted building, this tall, distinguished Maasai tribesman in traditional dress approaches and asks if I know where I'm going. In a surprising, cultured English, he's quick to instruct me and fifteen minutes later, I step into the much cooler shade of a small Portuguese fish restaurant on a shady street corner.

At last, I sit down at a small table near the front of the restaurant to wait for my colleague Robert Ochaya. It's a relief to have a little time to myself as I've been on the move non-stop for days. A wizened old man, in a gleaming white shirt, comes forward. I order a cold White Cap lager and start to relax. Ceiling fans turn slowly but the warm humid air hardly stirs; everything, everyone moves in slow motion. The shutters are closed and the dining area is in half-light as I savour a mouthful of lager and reflect on my first six months in East Africa and the special experience of working with Robert.

As OEAC's chairman and founder, he's my boss and undoubtedly a charismatic man, thick-set, powerful, decisive and in his early fifties. "Very hands-on" is how his staff describe him and I can only agree. His life story is dramatic and really matters to us all. He fled Uganda after a career in their civil service dealing with international charities and non-governmental organisations. Word has it that by the late 1960s, he started to speak out about Idi Amin and his rise to power; he soon realised his life and that of his young family was at risk. He criticised government officials for widespread corruption and felt their bad practices were directly responsible for an inability to take care of people's basic needs, to provide staple foods and a clean water supply.

Rumour is that he hung around Kampala until his whole family were able to secretly escape to Dar es Salaam. There he has continued his charity work to the present day. Robert has a powerful long-term vision for the OEAC, it includes helping his own and adoptive countries but that of the whole East African diaspora. There was a short spell at UNESCO in the US but soon returned to Tanzania to set up OEAC and started to deliver basic kits such as manual water pumps into the villages. Then came some vital irrigation equipment and so year by year, his organisation has grown.

I like him a lot and have huge respect for what he's trying to do in the region and the way he goes about it. He's a brilliant diplomat and negotiator, tough but likeable. Critically, he's able to pull in money from a wide mix of individual charities and marry it to the growing needs of farmer villagers. He's clever, using the government's villagisation programmes to improve water supplies with modern technology like novel electrically powered water pumps. Our success in Tanzania is now at a point where he wants me to establish a central inspection and assessment laboratory in Mombasa City and expand what we do into Kenya and beyond.

So, after a bumpy old East African flight to Nairobi and the delights of a very slow overnight steam train to Mombasa, I end up chatting with port office staff. They suggest I look at two modern buildings in the west of the city that might just be suitable for a laboratory. Hopefully, Robert agrees after his return from a few days in Nairobi meeting tame government officials and his university buddies. I'm sure he'll want to negotiate terms with one or other of the building owners before we sign up for a rental deal.

The large Smith's clock on the wall shows I've been waiting for nearly an hour and there's still no sign of Robert. I order some bread, olives, and another cold lager and try to keep cool and calm. It's a chance for me to think back to some of the good things that happened to me over recent months. And thank goodness, Robert put me out of my misery whilst having drinks on our first day in Mombasa. My six-month probationary period was up and I was quite anxious as my work was so different from anything I'd done before. But he was quick to reassure me with an offer of a generous five-year contract. Robert detailed my progress in regular reports to his OEAC Board in Dar es Salaam but it was good to hear it from him in person all the same.

Fellow directors are very laidback and accepted the fact that it'll take a while for me to settle in Dar, as they call it. There was a bit of luck at first when my friend, Pooja, from Leicester, fixed me up with a comfortable flat on the outskirts of the city. It doesn't have air-conditioning so I struggle to sleep at times, but now it's just about bearable. On the other hand, the traffic around Dar is a nightmare. I used the local Bajaji at first to get into the city centre. Then another slice of luck comes my way when I discover a mature graduate from OEAC's central laboratory is a bike enthusiast and manages to locate a very old Husqvarna. Can't believe my luck, although it needs endless maintenance and spare parts that are difficult to find.

At least, I've got the freedom to travel with plenty of thrills thrown in as I weave in and out of the chaotic city traffic. Even after several months, there's still the perpetual risk of falling off from horrendous potholes that never get repaired. It's great fun, although my ever-thoughtful staff think I'm mad to even try. Thinking about those first few months in Dar is quite something, to realise just what I knew, or didn't know, about sorting out OEAC's technical division. The staff situation when I arrived was fraught, having to ensure six young graduates from the local university and two experienced Asian technicians from a Nairobi technical college worked well together.

There was the commissioning of a new laboratory in OEAC's main headquarters in downtown Dar. And through it all, I had to make progress on finding a portable power supply for our new water pumps. It was fortunate I'd kept in touch with Miriam and James Alonso after leaving Cambridge. I'd wondered how their bio-battery research had been going whilst secretly half hoping to hear if they'd any news about Kay. Miriam said she was briefly in touch but lost contact before learning Kay moved away from Manchester. Direct as ever, Miriam said she was sad about our breakup but thought Kay overreacted to events.

Whereas, I let her know what happened largely lay at my door and how I was trying to get on with my life in Tanzania, and surely Kay was doing the same, wherever that may be. To my genuine surprise, Miriam is working with me to negotiate a contract with a small UK company to develop and manufacture a cut-down kilowatt version of their bio-battery. She's very excited at the prospect and we're lucky their holding company has a local sales office in Tanzania. Chatting with Miriam and James again does make me realise how much they were frustrated and upset by the government stalling on Pandora.

Back in Dar, the board is impressed with this spin-off technology and the early signs are that the bio-battery will have enough power to drive our portable water pumps. Now I need to get on and sort out a collaborative deal to everyone's satisfaction. To Robert's credit, he clearly sees the advantages of this technology in a country awash with wheat. He may not fully appreciate the intricacies of a cereal-fed bio-fuel cell but he's a pragmatist at heart; aware of the risks involved but trusting me enough to check out its performance and ruggedness before any prospect of use in the townships.

My train of thought is suddenly shattered by a call to prayers from the historic mosque in the heart of the city. It's well past noon and I'm about to order another White Cap when Robert suddenly walks in. His baritone voice is unmistakable.

'Get me one too, Paul.'

'Hello, Robert. Shall I order some more bread and olives or shall we get some lunch straight away?'

'Sure, I'm hungry. Get the owner over here, he knows what's best on the day.'

The owner ambles over and Robert asks what he would recommend from the sea today.

'The red snapper, gentlemen. Fresh this morning, grilled with garlic, parsley, and with a capers sauce. Portuguese style, best there is.'

'Then, that's what we'll have,' I reply. 'How did it go this morning, Robert?'

'Very well. I've agreed on a three-year rental for that smart air-conditioned unit in Kibokoni district. As you said, it's larger than we need at present but it's near the station and close enough to our shipping office. The price is fair and we got a bit of a break on the cost because of our charity status. The owner is very sympathetic to our organisation as his elderly parents live in one of the poorer districts of Nairobi and are struggling to get clean water. Good work, Paul, in finding that space. Now it's over to you to sort out local technicians and a few good graduates to set up the laboratory. You might be able to find some staff at the university in Nairobi.

Bear in mind though, that you'll need some assistance from the Kenyan planning and safety authorities; there are some government people I've got to know over the years that will be able to help with the process, I'm sure. Let me have your costs forecast for the next three years and we'll build that into our budget. Shouldn't be a problem with the money but always best to involve my government and university contacts in Nairobi with our broad plans. Don't expect any resistance from that quarter but always good to oil the wheels. They don't like surprises, so I'll make some introductions when you visit towards the end of the week.

They're genuinely keen to deal with the OEAC. Makes good sense for them politically; they can shout about how they are collaborating with local charities and the like to address the needs of their people. There are a lot of new initiatives going forward at present time in the region but always remember; their words are cheap but actions cost money.'

Raising my eyebrows, I quickly add, 'I'll remember alright, Robert. Had a bad experience of all that with another government, Pandora was its name.'

'Oh yes, of course. Well, just let me know if you need the heavy brigade to march in. Although you won't be facing any Idi Amin-type characters around here; much too polite and well-mannered, just like you Brits.' He belts out a laugh. 'By the way, don't suppose you've a tuxedo suit with you.'

'Us Brits like to call it a dinner jacket, or in certain circles, a dress suit. No, I haven't, not even in Dar.'

'Well, I didn't bring mine either but I can hire one easily enough in Nairobi tomorrow. Perhaps, you'd better get one made up here before the end of the week, you may run out of time once you're in Nairobi. It's expected, I'm sure. Don't worry, there are plenty of tailors in Mombasa that would be only too happy to make one up for you in no time, and at a reasonable price too. Ask the ladies in the shipping office. Better go for a white jacket, more in keeping with the smart set in Nairobi.' Smiling mischievously, he adds, 'They like to maintain their standards, you know; very chic.'

'Hold on, Robert, what's going on in Nairobi? I thought I was there to work.'

'It's work, Paul. Well, mostly of sorts. Believe me, you'll soon find out. Look, it was touched on at our last board meeting. We're one of several major sponsors of the Kenyan Government's latest initiative with the university in Nairobi and their agricultural research institutes. For my sins, I've been invited to the official opening ceremony of their spanking new agricultural research centre. It's a black-tie affair and I can bring a guest. You are my guest, Paul,' he says with a chuckle.

'But don't expect me to dance. It's going to be very grand I believe, and very political. My dear wife would love it, just up her street, as you might say, but she's back in Dar looking after our very demanding family. There'll be some tedious speeches, a delightful Kenyan banquet, and apparently, a dance band combo to entertain us. No expense spared, nevertheless, a real opportunity to spread our wings and make an impression with some good old-fashioned networking. A chance to get some of our new technology, some of it yours, Paul, into Kenya's backyard.'

'They're building this new complex a few miles out from the city centre, brand-new laboratories, and an administration block. Just think, you may even want to rent one of their laboratories in the future, maybe use their expertise and specialist staff. As for me, it provides an efficient route to understand which technology and kits are a priority for farmers and their families in the townships. You see, they're being very clever in creating a network of smaller laboratories and offices across the country, and possibly beyond their borders in the future, to improve their overall cereal production.'

'Of course, all this needs an efficient and good quality water supply. Worth getting to know the senior staff involved with this new venture, don't you think? They'll be aware of this too and ready to accept our money along with any other aid coming into the country; it's a good deal all around. Oh well, that's all my news. Must catch the night train back to Nairobi and make sure you have a hotel room for the end of the week. In the meantime, you've enough to sort out here. Don't forget that dinner jacket, Paul.'

'I won't, a snow-white jacket you said.' We finish our red snappers and Robert prepares to leave. He shakes my hand vigorously and slaps my shoulder. His departing words ring in my ears.

'You're going to be so busy, Paul. See you at the end of the week. Stay cool and enjoy Mombasa, exciting times ahead.'

And I believe him.

Chapter 17

It's gone seven o'clock and the smell from the heavy downpour lingers in the air outside Nairobi's new agricultural research centre. My senses are further disturbed by the racket of a myriad of cicadas chiming over the gentle murmur of Swahili and English. Languid strains from an obsequious music combo gradually coalesce as Robert and I walk through a grand, elegant, and to be truthful, slightly outrageous neo-Palladian portico entrance to the main auditorium. After a few minutes of seeking out the great and the good, Robert takes me to one side and whispers in my ear,

'Just as I thought, Paul, they're going over the top with this event. They must have money to burn, and it certainly isn't coming from the OEAC.'

He's proven right. The publicity surrounding this launch event is overblown and politically motivated. As I loosen the buttons on my pristine blindingly white dinner jacket, it's time to face a selection of Kenya's senior technocrats. An elite assembly of the smartly dressed and for many, the highlight of their social calendars. Perhaps, it's their way of demonstrating that their newly independent country stands proud inside a much-vaunted conglomeration of the East African Community. Maybe it's a chance too for the government's publicity machine to show how Kenya can sometimes go it alone, even though its institutions and organisations rely on collaboration with its close neighbours—Tanzania, Uganda, or even its old colonial power.

For one night only, this lavishly decorated auditorium, designed for lectures and the odd international meeting, has been converted into part ballroom, part banquet hall. Our small band of rhythm section, piano, saxophone and a trumpet play on a raised stage; microphones are set up for a singer to join them at some point. There's a lectern to one side ready for the formal opening and ceremonial speeches. But whatever Robert and I privately agree on their intentions, it's an opportunity to impress the powers that be. A chance for an embryonic organisation like ours to climb another rung on the ladder and introduce innovative technology beyond the confines of Tanzania.

What's more, there's a feeling of optimism in the air as guests talk energetically about their so-called centre of excellence and how it will make a difference in feeding and modernising an emerging nation. It's not long before Robert introduces me to some important officials he has got to know over the past year. One of them is the imposing figure of Julius Ntanga, vice chancellor of the university and clearly an anglophile. We soon get around to chatting about my time at Manchester University while he shares numerous entertaining stories about his time in academia in London and Boston, USA.

Annoyingly, I'm finding standing around chatting with such small talk a real struggle; it has never been my strong point at such events or perhaps it's just the oppressive humidity and temperature inside the auditorium. Or maybe it's being encased in a new dinner jacket and bow tie that makes a lengthy prospect less appealing; after all, it has been months since I last wore any form of tie let alone one that seems set on strangling me. There's a pause in the chat so I let Robert and Julius know I'm off for some fresh air. Time to make my way down a dozen steps towards the broad gravel path surrounded by tropical gardens bearing jacaranda trees and moonflowers.

It's also the first chance to take a close look around this impressive-looking building with archetypal white walls and angular modernist styling that's springing up across much of Nairobi. The central administration block lies towards the front with extensive laboratories to the rear, although yet to be fully laid out and commissioned. My composure starts to return when I hear, unsurprisingly, a wall of sound from cicadas competing against the strains of the tune *Maria* from *West Side Story*. It's surreal, of course, but reminds me of when I saw a Hollywood film in my second year at university in South Wales.

I look around; more guests appear from along the gravel drive with happy smiling faces and dressed in equally strangulating bow ties and wives bedecked in either the traditional brightly coloured African-style evening dress or the latest trend-setting trouser suits. They make their way up the steps through the Colonnade, and all the while in the distance a string of taxis with dazzling car headlights head towards the entrance. There's still rain in the air and it's getting noticeably cooler; making me grateful that Nairobi's altitude at least allows its sub-tropical wet season to be tolerable compared to the suffocating evenings of Mombasa or Dar.

My improving spirits are mirrored by a sea of faces climbing the steps as I quickly glance at my watch. Nearly seven-thirty and suddenly, there's the gentle sound of a tenor voice singing a rendition of *Edelweiss* from *The Sound of Music*. Why this persistent local combo like tunes from the musicals so much is a mystery to me but I succumb and make my way back to the auditorium to join Robert and Julius. I can hear Julius' booming voice inviting Robert on a tour of the building later in the evening after the speeches and banquet. Oddly enough when I join them, Julius appears anxious, even distracted, forever looking over towards the reception area as if he's waiting for someone.

All the lights are on in my bungalow as an afternoon thunderstorm dances around with threatening skies and noisy droplets falling from surrounding trees and shrubs. Mila and Usha wait patiently in my living room while I finish dressing and put on some make-up. A car's approaching and I tell myself to hurry up so as not to keep people waiting, particularly as everyone keeps reminding me that Julius is a stickler for punctuality even though he doesn't always set a good example himself. There's a knock on the bedroom door followed by Mila's raised voice.

'Hurry up, Kay, you'll be late, we'll be late. The vice chancellor's car is just outside. What's keeping you?'

'So sorry, Mila, won't be a minute, just finishing off my make-up. It's been a long time since I've dressed up so much; I'm wearing my mum's emerald green ball gown and I've forgotten how much effort it takes to get ready.'

That's only part of my excuse as I've been distracted by the memory of the last time I wore the gown in Cambridge at the Grad Pads' Christmas Ball. It seems an eternity ago but the memories keep coming back and for whatever reason, my emotions are all over the place this evening. *So silly,* I tell myself, quickly finishing off with some lipstick and straightening the dress with a quick look in the mirror. To my amazement, the dress still fits perfectly. Thank goodness Usha and Mila are coming with me in the car as I need some moral support.

This is such an important event and I barely know Julius Ntanga. He's such an imposing figure and I'm his guest of honour to boot. But tonight, my thoughts are with Mila as it's the first chance to congratulate her on the promotion. Julius and Usha were true to their word as it was let slip this afternoon that she is now head of the department for Field Trials and Analyses in the new ARC. She'll oversee two activities vital to the success of our research and she's got plenty of help too from some of our best young scientists and technicians. It must mean a lot to her and even more so to her very proud family. At last, I walk through to the living room and Usha and Mila stare at me.

'What's wrong?' I ask.

'Nothing's wrong,' says Mila. 'You look so beautiful. We've never seen you so dressed up before and that dress, it's simply out of this world. It makes you look, well stunning; like a film star, as if from a page of a fashion magazine.'

'Oh nonsense, ladies. It's just because it's a rather traditional classic look from the 50s which I rather like I must say. A bit old-fashioned compared to nowadays but my mum always knows what suits me best and she makes it fit so well. Such a wonderful seamstress.' Quickly changing the subject, I go to Mila and give her a hug and a kiss on both cheeks. 'I'm so very happy for you, Mila, you so much deserve the promotion.'

Mila beams with delight while Usha looks at her watch and interrupts us.

'Let's get going otherwise we'll be late; Julius is bound to be waiting by now. Oh, hold on, just one minute, I almost forgot.' She delves into her handbag, pulls out a long thin jewellery case and hands it to me.

'What's this?' I ask.

Usha smiles. 'Open it and you'll find out, it's just for tonight. Mila told me you're wearing emerald green so I thought it would go well.'

I open the box and inside is this beautiful thin gold chain choker holding seven delicate emeralds set in fine gold pearl clasps. It's a struggle to know what to say except "It's so beautiful" as I give Usha a kiss on the cheek. 'But I can't wear this, it's too valuable, Usha.'

'Nonsense, of course, you can, if you like it. It was my late mother who passed it on to me. Never seem to find the right outfit or moment to wear it. But it's perfect with your dress. Please, wear it.' Usha quickly secures the choker around my neck and with a slight irritation in her voice, maintains, 'Right, let's get moving as it's time we all went to the ball, ladies.'

We carry on chatting and laughing as we climb as elegantly as we can into the back of the vice chancellor's impressive limousine.

'How very grand,' I mutter to myself. Mum would indeed be most proud.

During the short ride, I try to contain my emotions. My senses are heightened and I feel so alive, more than at any time since I've arrived in Kenya. So powerful are they that nervous energy trickles through my whole body. I wish I knew what's got into me today as I feel my face reddening; thank goodness it's dark in the back of this car. Maybe wearing mum's dress and all the memories it brings back has something to do with it. Although it must be more than that, surely. Such excitement is unrelenting and for the first time in ages, I suddenly feel admired, even cherished, not as a scientist but as a woman. Perhaps, it's the feeling of being special to others and, yes, to myself.

Not for the first time, this evening my thoughts hail back to Paul and how he used to make me feel; it's palpable. Oh, I remember with a smile how early on Richard Kinama tried to flatter me with his fanciful comments and praise but I never took any notice of them; they seemed so trivial and silly. There's been a fair share of praise coming my way for my work over the past two years; it makes a big difference of course and there's a sense of pride though friends' comments are exaggerated at times. Whatever the reason, my whole being is alive tonight; happy, yes, but also bright, warm, and somehow more feminine.

They're wonderful feelings and I wonder why I've been suppressing them for so long and how can I ever keep them. My daydream continues until our car rolls up on a noisy wide gravel path to stop near the front of the stately entrance. Mila and Usha carefully help with my gown as I mount the steps under the Colonnade and slowly head towards the reception area. I hear the familiar strains of *My Fair Lady* drifting over a sea of heads and animated chatter from the assembled dignitaries. A young girl in a long scarlet dress from ARC's administration fiddles with the microphone behind the lectern, adjusting the sound level above many excitable noisy guests. Most of the dignitaries are collecting around the stage area with a drink in hand engrossed in earnest conversation. Robert, Julius, and I are doing the same, spending some time discussing what a potential ARC and OEAC collaboration would look like. Robert even raises the possibility of OEAC using ARC's proposed network of local laboratories for our charitable technology outreach scheme.

Julius seems keen enough but still appears distracted and we start to wonder what's going on when he asks how a scheme may work in practice but breaks off mid-sentence to look towards the reception area and then back to us.

'Robert, Paul, please excuse me for a minute,' implores Julius as he walks purposefully towards the reception area.

Robert and I look at each other in amazement. There's a rustle of dresses amongst a collection of raised voices. Robert raises an eyebrow and shares a broad grin. Julius is politely kissing a group of ladies entering the auditorium. From the corner of my eye, I spot what appears to be the silky bodice of an emerald green ball gown. I look again, the shape and form of that dress are engrained in my memory. Above the bodice is a ring of brilliant green droplets that glisten in the spotlight casting its light across the wooden dance floor. My gaze is drawn to a body of beautiful shiny black hair cut in a tight bob.

I blink and blink again, to secure my gaze once and for all. *Am I dreaming?* I ask myself deliberately closing my eyes and ever so slowly opening them again. There's a tingling sensation around the nape of my neck through my shoulders and down my back. My breathing seems to stop working for an instant; my shoulders tighten and I'm lost in a maze of unresolved thoughts, memories, and expectations. *Is this happening, can it be right?* I question myself while trying to absorb Julius' and his guest's conversation gently echoing around the room.

'Dr Levine, Kay, you've surpassed yourself. Absolutely stunning, my dear.'

Usha smiles broadly and says how she and Mila thoroughly agree with the vice chancellor's bold assessment.

Julius quickly sorts out some drinks for the ladies, as he calls them, and continues. 'Let me make some introductions before all the ceremonials start. There're some people I would like you to meet.'

He moves down one side of the dancefloor and introduces them to one of the junior government ministers resplendent in a dark blue velvet tuxedo and very large matching bow tie. Eventually, he escorts his party around to us standing by the stage. Robert quickly went to grab some drinks from a small bar at the rear of the room. He offers me and Julius a glass of wine. A beaming Julius is quick to sample before turning to face the ladies.

'Robert, Paul, may I introduce my special guest for the evening, Dr Levine from the university's Department of Plant Science and Crop Protection. Kay is one of our lead researchers and lecturer. She's busy finding new ways of accelerating cereal crop yields with some very clever, you might even say revolutionary, bio-engineering techniques she calls derivative enzyme exchange.'

My eyes fix on Kay. My mind's racing ahead but still not knowing what to think. I place my glass on a nearby table, but before I can utter a word, Robert is shaking her hand and speaking.

'Dr Levine, such a pleasure to meet you. Let me introduce Paul Wright, he's our director of Technology and Innovation at our Organisation of East African Charities based in Dar es Salaam. He oversees the introduction of all exciting new technologies across the region. I'm sure you'll have plenty to talk about.'

Robert, ever the charmer, makes light of his own role in OEAC as he starts to chat with the other two ladies.

With some difficulty, I try to smile. Happily, Kay smiles back. Julius is clearly put out by a lack of formality and immediately steps forward to complete the introduction of Usha and Mila. Kay raises her eyes towards me as I shake Mila's hand. Time continues to stand still while I'm loss for words, unsure what to do or say. In the end, without giving it any more thought, I take a deep breath, step closer to Kay, and gently cup her bare shoulders in my hands and kiss her lightly on both cheeks. As I step back, she appears as shocked as I am with the events before us. Her face and neck colour slightly and I pretend not to notice.

'Lovely to see you, Kay,' I add quietly. 'You look lovelier than ever. The Tropics clearly suit you, and it's been a long time.'

'It has, Paul,' she hesitates before replying further, stuttering slightly. 'Ahh…what are you doing here?' Before I can say another word, Julius interrupts.

'Do you know each other, Paul?'

'Yes, yes, we do. We did research at Manchester, separate departments of course, then worked on the government's Pandora project.' As I turn to face Julius, my words proceed in a sort of slow motion. 'This is quite a shock for both of us, meeting like this I mean.'

Julius is clearly taken aback but quickly replies, 'Oh yes, Manchester, I should have realised. What a coincidence. Quite a shock, I'm sure, Kay.'

Kay nods vigorously. Julius and Robert look at each other, both carry deep frowns and are clearly bemused. But before another word is uttered, the government official announces the opening ceremony is about to begin and asks everyone take to their seats. Julius is keen to react and escorts Kay to one of the VIP seats near the front of the podium whilst assuring her that there'll be plenty of time to catch up with her old friend later. Kay looks in my direction, tilts her head slightly, and sits next to Julius while Robert and I find our own places.

It's not long to wait before a ponderous government minister makes a long, predictable, and eminently worthy speech about the importance of the ARC, the generosity of the government's strategic investment, and how he knows the university and its sponsors, including the OEAC, will contribute to its success. The official has carefully rehearsed his brief and continues to describe this venture with a flurry of rather mixed metaphors; 'It's a key plank of the role of science and technology in our independent and enterprising Kenya.' Polite applause follows this motherhood and apple pie sentiment as I'm immediately transported back to the equally worthy speeches rolled out by our own government minister during the early stages of Pandora.

Turning to Robert, I cannot stop myself from quietly commenting, 'Just hope such ambitions somehow evade the whims and manipulations of the politicians.'

For so many reasons, I want to believe that's possible, hoping for Kay's sake that she thinks and believes the same. Sadly, for the minister, I only register about a tenth of his speech. The rest is lost to my confusion, heightened emotion, and an overwhelming sense of excitement. My thoughts escalate to wondering how Kay is feeling as we move to sit at opposite ends of a surprisingly long and highly decorated top table heavily laden with food. Julius is in his element during the meal. His manners are excessively polite, almost Edwardian at times; he hasn't quite come to terms with the Swinging Sixties and many of the changes in our so-called youth culture. As I look around, many of the men are wearing bell-bottom trousers and strut around with wide lapels on their jackets and outrageous lurid bow ties. Whilst the women, especially the older ones, stun us in their brilliantly colourful dresses and gowns. Maybe because I'm wearing an old-style 1950s gown that Julius thinks deserves an exhibition of some good old-fashioned manners.

Who knows, but he's a courteous man by nature, so sitting opposite him is a delight as we're served with an array of dishes that I struggle to recognise or have come across in Nairobi's street markets. There are stuffed baked oysters from Mombasa, local artichokes and avocados, fresh trout, and even a dish called boozy goose. Julius is lovely as he includes me in all his conversations with officials and university colleagues, easing my way into every kind of topic. I'm flattered, of course, who wouldn't be, but I just wonder what his wife might think if she was here.

Several guests close by seem genuinely interested in my work, albeit a little curious about my life back in the UK. Their questions suggest they think it quite glamorous, even though I go out of my way to explain that most of my time is spent in an oversized white coat down to my ankles running tedious experiments with cereal crops, ion-exchange columns, and the odd test tube. Thankfully, the time passes quickly enough as my emotions are still in free fall from the shock of seeing Paul, feelings that I don't fully understand or even manage to control at times. Then there was his kiss. It may seem like nothing to those standing nearby but it sent tremors throughout my body.

Oh, the memories; just what is happening to me. I don't understand how he's come to work in East Africa let alone turn up out of the blue in our new research centre. None of my close friends from Cambridge or Manchester know about my move to Nairobi. Being so angry, I went out of my way to stop Paul knowing my whereabouts; but of course, there's Andreas, he knew. Now what? Paul's this director of a charitable organisation doing what I assume is important work across this corner of East Africa. It's hard to believe but yet again, Paul always manages to surprise me. He did in Cambridge and now here.

When I sneak a look at Paul at the far end of the table, I can only come to admire and respect him for making such a bold move, and a million miles from his past existence. Now he looks so mature, so tanned, and, well, handsome with his dark beard, although I don't understand why anyone would want to hang on to a full beard in this climate, but that's Paul I suppose. As for his white dinner jacket, for heaven's sake, such a contrast to his rented DJ from Moss Bros in Cambridge. Now I must know more, indeed everything, about this new Paul. Turning to Julius, I carefully question him about the OEAC. He's very straightforward with me.

'Kay, you can tell Robert is enormously impressed with Paul, his abilities and skills. Apparently, he's new to Africa and its ways, but in six months, he has brought together a team of bright young graduates and technicians at OEAC's technical centre in Dar es Salaam. Robert is confident he'll do the same in Mombasa and Nairobi. He clearly recognises a rare gift of quickly understanding people's nature and directing their energies to work with a single purpose. From my experience, Kay, that's a rare skill indeed amongst many of my scientific colleagues, and particularly in one who's still relatively young.'

Julius goes on to describe what the OEAC is planning over the months ahead and the possibility of our serious collaboration. I listen intently amongst a hiatus of pleasant, subdued chatter whilst guests wait for coffee and liqueurs and the band starts up again. My wine glass is regularly topped up as I sit back and reflect on what I've just heard. More and more in recent years, I've driven my research to do some genuine good in the world and it sounds as if Paul thinks the same way; how amazing. Perhaps, I'm being unfair. Maybe he has always had that ambition but was too self-absorbed to recognise it for what it was.

He would often say, "I just bob along on a tide of serendipity". Well, in reality, maybe we all go through that stage in our lives sometimes. Who knows, I certainly don't. Oh my god, why do I always underestimate him? Not only underestimate but misunderstand him, taking him so much for granted. A man like Paul, with such energy, will always throw himself into any role so passionately, often to the detriment of his own ambitions. He was so embroiled in achieving Pandora's goals that he assumed everyone around him had the same level of good intentions and drive. People probably think of him as naive but to my eyes, it's a good trait to have.

Thinking back to my time at Heddington, I blush at what I took for granted. All his effort ensuring the project got delivered, how it must have affected his own self-esteem, confidence, and personal wishes, and how it destroyed our relationship. How selfless. Will he ever forgive me? My dear Paul, you wrote all about all this in your letter and I should've faced up to what you were saying and believed in him. My heart races. My only desire is to tell him how I feel; and why I reacted the way I did, partly through disappointment and sadly through ignorance.

My head is in a tailspin, and it's not the wine. I take a few more sips and wonder how and when I can speak with him alone. At the far end of the table, Paul is engrossed in some animated conversation with Robert, Mila, and Usha. They are so at ease with each other, they're laughing at some remark of Paul's, which curiously makes me feel more relaxed. His easy charm is already having an effect. I feel desperately left out and want to join them. Then, as if by some yet indescribable attraction, Paul looks my way, smiles broadly, and gently moves his head to one side in such a way that shouts in neon lights, "Let's meet soon". I don't know why I think that, maybe it's just the look in his eyes.

My senses spring alive. As if we're in a punt drifting down the River Cam or chatting in my digs after a Chabrol film, or even, I dare say, listening to his cool sensuous jazz. I slowly nod back; his smile grows broader before he returns to his conversation. On cue, coffees and liqueurs arrive. Julius leans forward and speaks softly, 'Kay, it's been a pleasure to have you as my guest this evening. Can't thank you enough. You've set all these young chaps talking. I'll let you go now so you can enjoy the rest of the evening with your colleagues from the institute and your friend, Paul.'

'Time is pressing and I need to show Robert and some other dignitaries around the new building and talk about the future. Duty calls, so off you go, Kay, and enjoy yourself. It's time for you to relax; the night and you are still young.' He grins and even gives me a wink as he leaves, adding, 'It's been a delightful evening, my dear. I know you like your dancing and the music is about to start again.' Somehow, I know not how, I find myself alone with Kay in the new science library across from the entrance to the auditorium, surrounded by shelves of books and scientific periodicals. We talk quickly, earnestly, and naturally for what seems an eternity, neither of us daring to sit down. Kay leaves the library door ajar. Our curious band continues to play a selection of popular dance tunes from the musicals as our nervous energy unties memories from past years, we can hardly catch our breath. I tell Kay everything: about my time in Leicester, the frustration with my colleagues, and government officials, even the research and the growing feeling of just treading water.

Also, how my wonderful friends from Tanzania are instrumental in steering me towards the OEAC. This isn't the time to talk science even when I insist there's a real possibility that Miriam's bio-battery may eventually be used to power water pumps in Kenya and beyond. Letting myself go, both impulsive and brave, I tell her how beautiful she is, how she hasn't changed, and how I missed her beyond my imagination, that I understand why she didn't want to see me again and how I hoped my letter, in part at least, tried to put the record straight. Throughout this diatribe, Kay's dark eyes never leave me but only outshone by the emerald pearls resting around her neck. My thoughts are in free fall as I try to explain how I feel, about her and her passion for who she is.

'Honestly, Kay, I didn't appreciate how driven you are; how you always want your research to make a difference, wherever that may take you. You're so strong and a torchbearer for many, I'm sure. I'll never match that but maybe take some strength from you with my work for the OEAC. Do you think there's a chance we can ever work together again? Would you ever want to?'

Kay sighs deeply with her shoulders rising to a pinnacle before replying.

'I'd love to, Paul, we should try. Let's see how well our two bosses get on tonight, there must be a good chance. But we best be cautious, it's difficult to predict such things. We seem to be going in the same direction; combining our efforts to improve cereal crop production in the poorest of neighbourhoods across the region. If all goes well, then not only will the villages need drinking water but also the best technology in power generation to help cultivate and deliver their crops. Experience tells me that progress in this young vibrant country can happen quickly. Surprisingly, there's a real self-belief in the goodness of science here.'

While trying to stifle a laugh, I reply, 'Well, yes, that's true I'm sure and if we get the chance, let's hope it turns out better than Pandora, good intentions and all that.'

Kay hesitates and takes several deep breaths. Her eyes cast to the floor and I wonder if I've said the wrong thing but quickly realise there's something much more personal she wants to say.

'It's ok, Paul. You're right to be critical, of course you are, I understand. We can't forecast the future or even control it to any great extent. We'll have to wait and see and work our hardest. No, it's not that, there's something else on my mind which you ought to know about as it goes back to your amazing letter. I've had some mixed news from my family. As suggested, mum has kept in touch with dad's old army friends from New Zealand. She's hearing how they're lobbying their government, and ours too, to come clean over the cause of their mates' radiation sickness.

It seems such a long time ago now but mum is absolutely adamant that one day, the world will know the truth. It won't bring Daddy back of course, but it may draw some sort of line for the families affected, including mum.'

Kay's face suddenly lights up when she tells me she's going back to Leek next summer to attend her mum's marriage to Eric Smithson. She laughs as she recalls how her mum wrote to her saying how, "It's never too late for romance". Kay quickly fixes on me and adds, 'Please, don't say a word, Paul. Mums always like to give their daughters a kick up the pants when it comes to boyfriends. It's the cross we bear, you know.' There's a long silence before she continues.

'But I want to say something else you deserve to hear. No, that's wrong, you must hear. Your letter, I've kept it and I must admit that I've shared a little of its contents with my dear friend, Mila. You know, about what happened between us. I saw you were having a nice chat with her earlier. Look, she's a lovely lady and I think the world of her…'

I interrupt. 'Look, there's no need to explain, it's fine.' Then suddenly, she reaches out and takes my hand, squeezing it ever so gently.

'No, it's not fine, my dear. I need to try and explain my feelings too. This is not easy for me as I'm not the best at it. Our time together in Cambridge felt like a beautiful dream that suddenly became a nightmare. My mind was all over the place. I didn't know what to think about you or even about the work we were doing. Ending up questioning myself and whether I could ever trust you again. That's why I left so abruptly. But now I realise that I should've followed my instincts more, knowing you as I did. That you're a good man, not perfect, mind you, but who is.' She laughs and squeezes my hand even tighter.

'We can all agree on that,' I reply before she continues.

'But I should've trusted you more and not assumed I knew all the politics surrounding Pandora on that awful day at the press conference. It was naïve of me but I felt so bitter and let down by the one person who had made such a difference to my life. It's obvious now how much you invested in building up the rapport and trust within our team to deliver that project. How shattered you must have felt when suddenly it came crashing down, and me with it. Robert told Julius you have a rare skill and have already made a huge difference in Dar es Salaam, and how you'll do the same in Kenya. He's right; you are special, I know that.'

I'm taken aback. 'Christ, he said that?'

'Yes, you do have a special way with people. They pick up on it and I've changed as a result too, hopefully for the better. You've made me think differently about things, about how blinkered I was in Manchester. Andreas knew this too and tried to tell me in his own way. You know me well enough. How I can be overbearing, too overbearing at times, wanting to do good with my research. I really believe it will happen here, but I need to try and see work more broadly and, yes, more realistically. Oh, who knows? I just needed to say this.'

'Don't be too harsh on yourself. The prospects for collaboration look pretty good to me. Old Julius clearly thinks very highly of you, why wouldn't he?' Smiling, she modestly shakes her head.

'He's a sweetie really.' Kay giggles. She goes on to say that after Pandora, she knew she had to travel and experience a different way of life, a bit like I had. Taking a risk in the big wide world, made her gain a new enthusiasm for work and life in general. All the while, Kay gently runs her hand along my forearm towards my shoulder as if trying to comfort me. Her words soften and take on an even greater reflective nature.

'I've often thought about you, Paul, over the past years. Sometimes it made me homesick and sad. Other times, it gave me strength because I remembered how I was able to open up to you about everything, even that painful time when I was a young girl. You're understanding and love helped me come to terms with difficult emotions and memories. That strength is still important to me; maybe it's needed even more now.'

A torrent of words continues to wash over us as we take these fragile minutes to understand ourselves and what is happening to us. Then, as is the way, we hear the band play the opening bars to *Moon River*. We look at each other, instinctively hug, and with my hands tight around her waist, I whisper words that flow from a distant time.

'Well, my love, it's time to dance.' It seems *Moon River* is destined to bind us together. A dreamy tenor voice sweeps over the auditorium as Paul guides me around the dance floor with his usual grace and elegance. Mum would love to see us now. He holds me in his arms so gently as if I'm hardly moving or breathing. Every step falls naturally in unison, every movement of his body etched against mine. We share a few words but there's no need for more. My thoughts flicker back to dancing with Aden to the same song all those years ago at the Station. Little did I realise then, how much it would come to mean to me.

Then, there was our first so-called date at the Cambridge Grad Pad and how he swept me away by dance, as natural as breathing. Thank heavens, he's not just interested in country line dancing. But Paul has always had a way of surprising me, maybe that's why I love him.

'Did you ever tell me where you learnt to dance the waltz? It wasn't as a boy in Boston, surely not?'

Paul smiles, gently kisses my neck, and whispers, 'No, it wasn't. Not surprisingly, my parents didn't see me as a dancer. I remember dad telling my teenage sisters to never trust a single man over forty who can dance. Not much of an endorsement, is it?'

I try not to laugh too much. 'Maybe he has a point, Paul.'

'Well, he may have a point, but I'm not yet over forty, nowhere near it in fact. To tell the truth, David and Mirabelle at Saginawbay, my line dance teachers taught me. They pulled me to one side early once in a class and forced me to learn how to dance the slow waltz. "Every man should learn the slow waltz", they said. "You never know when it will come in useful". They're right, and I hope there'll be many more times for us to waltz, darling.'

"Darling" sounds strange at first after such a long time but I'm sure I'll get used to it. Squeezing his arm, I speak softly.

'My dear, I'm sure there will be.' After my gentle kiss, I notice some of the guests, including Mila and Usha, are looking at us. It's not just our old-style ballroom dancing, although disco is everywhere in Nairobi. No, it's because of us, being together as one that's so transparent and so special, it demands no explanation. But I don't really care what people think. Everything feels right, is right, it's our destiny and we're happy to share our love in front of our friends, whoever they may be. The singer finishes the beautiful tune with a flourish but we stay in each other's arms.

'I can't quite believe what's happening, Paul.'

'I know. It's as if life has been kind and given us a second chance. And you don't get many second chances for real happiness in life, do you, Kay? We need to grab it while we can. Where can we go to be alone?'

My mind is clear and I'm direct with my words. 'Meet me on the steps under the Palladian arch. I won't be long, give me five minutes. I'll speak with Mila.'

He squeezes my hand and leaves the dance floor heading for the reception area. My face starts to redden as I walk slowly towards Mila. She hasn't stopped smiling all this time. She grabs my arm.

'It's so lovely to see you together, Kay. You look very happy, my dear.'

'I am, I am. Still can't quite believe what's happening. Mila, please would you do something for me? Will you go and ask the chauffeur to come around to the front entrance in front of the Colonnade? We're going to sneak off. Please make sure he knows to come and pick you and Usha up when you're ready to leave. Will you do that?'

'Of course, I'll go straight away. Where are you going, Kay?'

'Home, we're going to my home.'

'Good for you, girl. Maybe I'll see you sometime over the weekend.'

With an embarrassing smile, my face reddens as I grasp both her hands. 'I do hope so. Not sure what's happening but I'll call you, really want you to get to know my Paul.'

As I reach the front entrance, Paul is looking beyond the tropical gardens towards the horizon. Storm clouds gather as distant flashes from an electric storm decorate the night sky over west Nairobi. The evening is still humid but the cacophony of sound from cicadas is quenched in anticipation of further rain. A distinctive honey smell from blue jacaranda trees takes centre stage as I join Paul and put my arm around him. He leans over and kisses my neck. My body tingles as we look at each other and I whisper, 'What are you thinking, Paul?'

'Oh, how quickly things can change. How different it is living abroad, even more so in this part of the world. It's a magical continent, an unknown world in many ways which will always surprise me. I'm forever taken aback by how it makes me feel, that sense of freedom that I never really knew back home. Not sure why it should be so, but it is, and there were similar sorts of feelings while in Saginawbay. Guess it's about being true to yourself. Does that make any sense? Do you feel the same, Kay?'

'Oh, yes, I do. I've found my place, my home, my real life is here. It's that certain feeling, about being alive and not hemmed in by convention or what's expected of you. It surprises me too but it means I can choose the life I want to lead much more easily. Of course, I miss my family and one or two other things, but here I'm in charge and can explore a whole manner of different things.' But then I think of what lies ahead and take a deep breath, almost starting to giggle. 'Well, perhaps not in total control all of the time,' I add as I grab his hand.

'Don't you think it odd how the love of our research has somehow brought us together? Do you know what I mean, Paul? You, with all those wonderful ions flowing around, make a super battery. Then me, exchanging ions in a column to make things grow better.'

He steps back for an instant and shakes his head.

'Well, that's a showstopper, Kay, never quite thought of it that way. Did I ever tell you about one of my old chemistry lecturers who got me started in research? He once said that life is full of ions, you know anions and cations, and how they drive things forward. How cations flow around releasing electricity everywhere, whereas anions grab that electricity to make things happen. Maybe he thought people's lives follow that sort of chemistry. Mind you, I think the guy was getting a bit whimsical in his old age.'

'Sounds like it,' I say bursting into laughter. 'So, am I the cation, Paul, and you the anion? Um…not sure about his theory, although they do form a big part of what we do. But we all know life is so much more about how serendipity falls, nothing much to do with those ions of yours.'

Paul curls his arm around my waist. 'Yes, I know. You're right, of course, it's mostly serendipity. But serendipity can be driven along by some real purpose. You've always had that, Kay, and now we both have that right in front of us. You've made me realise that. Even so, I still quite like the thought of what shall we say…a love of ions.'

He looks up and there's another flash of lightning silhouetting Nairobi against the night sky before he continues.

'Dwell and your time has gone; do and your life grows.'

'Goodness, Paul, who wrote that? Sounds quite profound.'

'Paul Wright, 1976.' He smiles.

'I didn't know you were a poet.'

'Clearly, I'm not, but you do inspire me, Kay.'

'You're always surprising me. So, as you say, let it be…Carpe Diem.'

Paul pulls a face. 'Never any good at Latin but I know what it means. I think we've both put our work and careers well ahead of our feelings at times, perhaps for far too long. We did it in Cambridge. Maybe we need to remind ourselves that we're not on this planet for long. Let's not waste time thinking of what might or might not be.'

We hold ourselves tighter and tighter together as we drink in the sights and sounds of the night. Hairs on the back of my neck tingle as his powerful arms secure and protect me as never before. I can sense him trembling as my thoughts race ahead of me like the lighting flashing across the sky. Silly thoughts, profound thoughts but true ones nonetheless. When you give your love to someone, don't ask for anything in return; it's your gift of love. When you receive love, don't stop them, accept it as their gift of love too. Without warning, a trickle of tears flows down my burning cheeks.

'You're crying, Kay. What have I done?'

'Forgive me, I'm being silly. It's the thought that I'd lost you forever. They're tears of happiness, Paul, tears of joy.'

A deep rumble rings out as the vice chancellor's limousine appears from around the back of the administration building. The chauffeur steps out to open one of the passenger doors.

'Where are we going, Kay?'

I kiss Paul passionately as never before and walk towards the car. 'To my home. Our home for now at least, where we belong.'

Paul follows. 'Do you think the others will miss us?'

We look at each other, shrug our shoulders in unison, smile and climb into the back of the car. There's a sweet silence between us before Paul holds my hand and whispers, 'Are you sure, Kay?'

'My dear, I couldn't be more certain. We've waited long enough to grab life. Our science will find its place in our lives. Our happiness is what matters and it's time to take hold of that life, together. Right now, my feelings, my life is with you, Paul.'

The limousine edges slowly forward. Through the rear window, I briefly catch sight of Mila looking in our direction. She's standing next to Julius and Robert in the reception area just beyond the Palladian arch. We fall back into our seats. A passionate overwhelming silence falls between us as we pass by the tropical gardens shimmering with rain from the intoxicating black sky.

'Is that Kay and Paul in the back of my car, Miss Omondi? Where are they off to?'

Mila turns to face Julius. 'Yes, they're going home, Vice Chancellor, or what counts for their home just now.'

'Seems that they've known each other for some time,' adds Robert.

Mila nods knowingly and smiles.

Julius raises an eyebrow and stares into the distance. He glances over to Robert and with a deep sigh, adds, 'They're quite close, I think. It surprises me as I sort of assumed they were both unattached.'

The sound of the band permeates the air once again. Julius turns towards the auditorium but then suddenly, turns back to declare, 'It's from *Guys and Dolls* you know. Saw it on Broadway years ago. Do you recognise the song? It's a famous love song.'

Mila and Robert look blankly at Julius.

'Kay would know. Ah…that's it; *those eyes are the eyes of a woman in love.* You know, Robert, sometimes the obvious can become so clouded in uncertainty, even mystery, especially if it's to do with affairs of the heart. I'm only a simple chemist but I thought they were both sort of free radicals in the way they live their lives. Looks like I'm wrong. What do you think, Miss Omondi?'

Mila follows the limousine's glowing rear red lights as they fade gently into the distance. She takes in a deep breath of perfumed air and declares with calm confident satisfaction.

'No one is ever a completely free radical, Vice Chancellor. Paul and Kay are not. What they have is a powerful attraction, a strong enduring love, and perhaps as you're a chemist, Vice Chancellor, an enduring love of ions.'

THE END
(or just the start)